SECRETS OF THE DEEP

RED SAILS
BOOK ONE

ANDRE JONES

ALIEN
PRESS

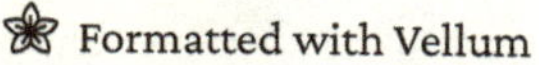 Formatted with Vellum

CONTENTS

Foreword   v

Secrets of the Deep   vii

PART ONE

Chapter 1   3
A Surprise Visitor

Chapter 2   15
Bad News

Chapter 3   27
Encounter

Chapter 4   42
Council Meeting

Chapter 5   58
A New Ruler

Chapter 6   67
Dawn Attack

Chapter 7   83
Betrayal

Chapter 8   98
The House of Secrets

Chapter 9   115
A New Port

Chapter 10   126
Hairpins and How to Use Them Effectively

Chapter 11   140
An Opportunity

Chapter 12   150
The Banquet

Chapter 13   157
Healing

Chapter 14   168
A Bloody Escape

Chapter 15   182
To The Docks

Chapter 16   194
Revelations

Chapter 17   204
Southbound

Chapter 18   218
The Return

Chapter 19   228
Important Visitors

Chapter 20   241
Full House

Chapter 21   253
Tragic News

Chapter 22   264
Strange Customs

Chapter 23   277
The Test

Chapter 24   288
A Coward and a Bastard

PART TWO

Chapter 25   299
Towards the South

Chapter 26   318
Exploring The Crags

Chapter 27   339
Serious Discussions

Chapter 28   352
New Developments

Chapter 29   370
We Warned you

Chapter 30   383
Plan Ahead

Loose Ends   389

Acknowledgments   393
About the Author   395
Also by Andre Jones   397

FOREWORD

Reality can be stranger than fiction ...

After watching Black Sails, I had wondered whether there were female pirates in history. Needless to say, in researching this novel, I found quite a few entries of women who had, for one reason or another, taken to piracy.

Generally, it was for revenge for one atrocity or another, and of course, for betrayal. Sounds familiar ...

If I may suggest, do a websearch for yourselves. You'll be surprised at what you'll discover!

SECRETS OF THE DEEP

BOOK 1 OF THE RED SAILS SERIES

by Andre Jones

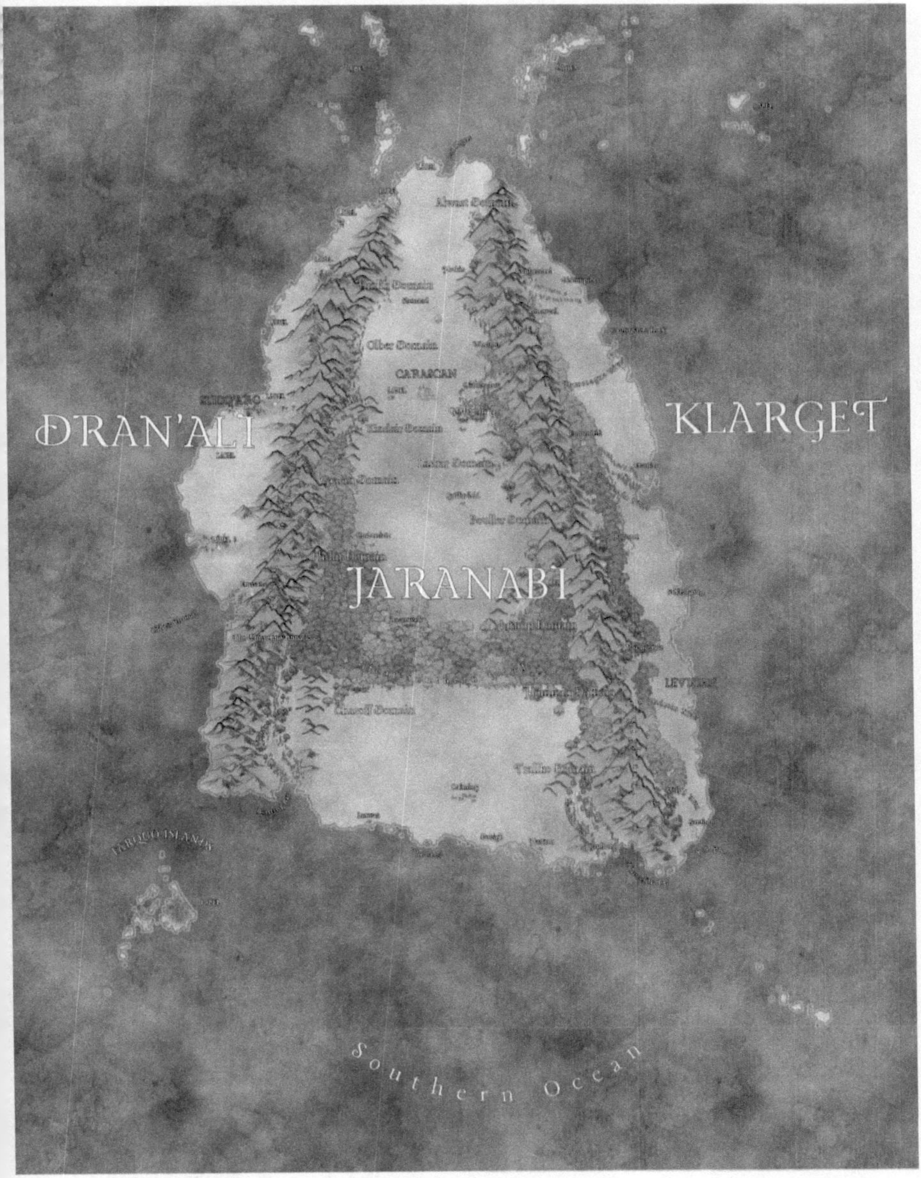

DRAN'ALI
KLARGET
JARANABI
CARASCAN
Southern Ocean

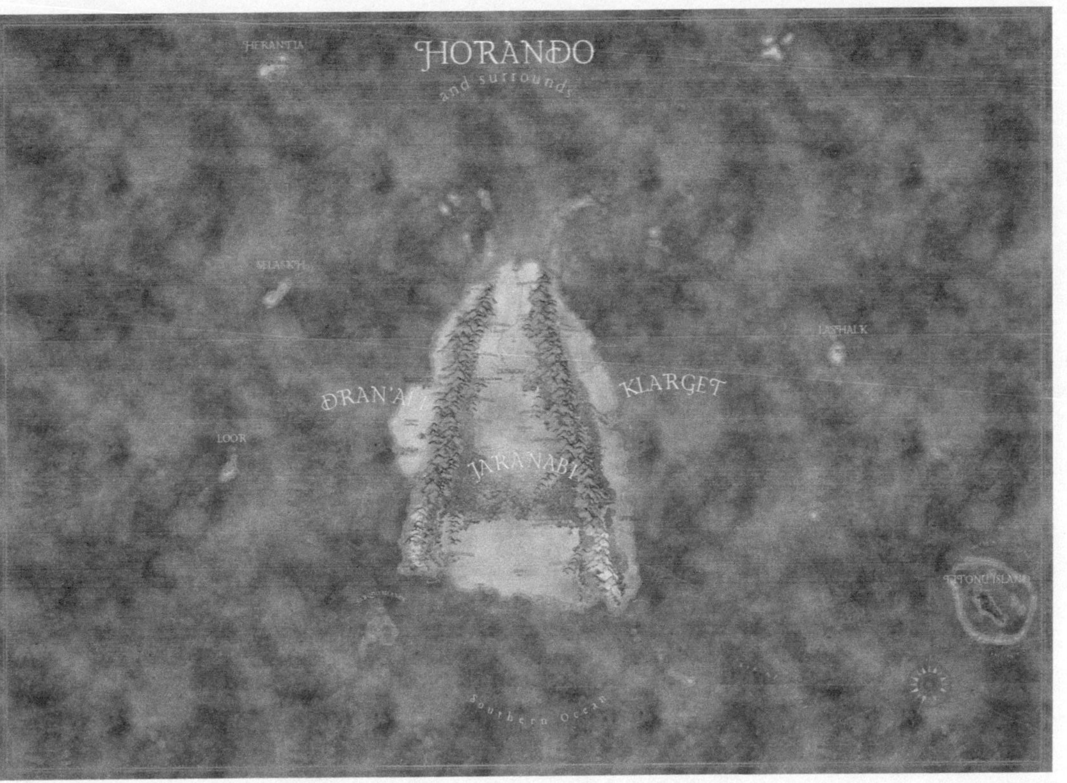

HORANDO
and surrounds
HERANTIA
SELARKH
DRAN'ALI
KLARGET
LASHALK
LOOR
JARANABI
TITONU ISLAND
Southern Ocean

PART ONE

CHAPTER

ONE

A SURPRISE VISITOR

Marra was in the summer courtyard garden of the High Lord's domain when she heard horses arrive. This could mean only one thing: *Another trade talk.*

A quick shinny up the ancient oak and scramble across one of the limbs put her slightly above the rear terrace. She carefully lowered herself, hanging from one of the branches. It cracked alarmingly.

Shite. I'm getting too big for this! Deftly swinging her legs for momentum, she let go and landed on the tiled floor of the terrace that overlooked the courtyard. Marra paused in case her landing had been heard.

"Good. No one's in the study yet." Her sandals were fine for strolling in the garden, not the most appropriate footwear for sneaking or climbing, but these visitors had caught her by surprise.

As Marra waited hidden behind the shutters, she slowed her breathing, annoyed that her lack of exercise meant she wasn't as fit as she had been. Her eyes strayed around the inte-

3

rior of the study—her favourite room—taking in the many pictures, wood-panelling, and exotic carpets. She started to think she'd been mistaken about the meeting. It had been many minutes, and no one had turned up. Deciding she had misjudged the meeting location, she made to step out from behind her cover.

She quickly ducked back as the door opened and her father strolled in, making his way to the large, ornate table that had been in the family for several hundred years. He sat down, sighed deeply, then shuffled through the small pile of parchments laid out before him.

Shortly after, there was a knock at the door.

"Enter," High Lord Pertram Olber called. He stopped shuffling the papers when her Uncle Blarik and two strangers walked in. Her uncle was in his riding gear, scruffy boots, black leggings, and a loose cream shirt that couldn't hide his obesity.

If anything, the two traders were overdressed, their silk finery powdered with dust from the hour-long journey from Carascan, the capital. The taller trader wore several rings.

Marra had not seen these two before, but after the introductions, she recognised their names, Fositt Heama and Greal Shioxin, from other times she'd eavesdropped on her father's discussions, as successful traders. They gave the expected courtesy of bowing to their lord, but her uncle merely poured himself a drink. It annoyed her. In times past, the High Lord had mentioned to him that, regardless of family ties, Blarik should acknowledge him in front of others.

And he only poured a drink for himself!

Despite the rudeness of this oversight, her uncle stayed quietly in the background while the two merchants spoke rather heatedly.

"Gentlemen, you're trying my patience with this paltry problem," Lord Olber declared after several minutes of bickering. "There's an increase in pirate raids. I have treaties with several island nations to contend with, and now you pester me with this? Did either of you think to bring any documentation to corroborate your claims? You certainly didn't think to make an appointment."

The merchants erupted with a myriad of details, including the type of goods and their origin, each hoping to somehow prove ownership simply by description and by being louder than the other.

"Silence," Lord Olber ordered as he stood, scraping his chair back.

Both men shut up and, after glancing in her uncle's direction, looked sheepishly at the floor, murmuring something Marra couldn't hear.

"So, I'm to take one's word over the other? Considering your reputations, I'm deeply disappointed in both of you." Olber moved around his desk to the wine cabinet and poured himself a drink.

Marra didn't hear what was said between her father and uncle, but she was sure Blarik would have muttered something snarky.

As the High Lord strolled back to his desk, he said, "Blarik. What say you to this predicament? You are, after all, the Minister of the Interior and Trade. This would be within your purview."

"Ah, yes, my Lord..." Her uncle paused his drinking, looking annoyed at being put on the spot. "How about an even split? Fifty-fifty each?"

"Perhaps." Her father paced as the two merchants wisely remained silent. "Gentlemen. I have a solution, but you won't like it...unless you pair of *professionals* can come to an amicable agreement now." He paused and paced while he let that sink in, sipping his wine. "No? Very well. My decision is...we won't divide the wares half and half... instead they'll be divided into *three* portions: thirty per cent to each of you and the remainder to the Jaranabi General fund—"

Their protests cut him off, but he continued as he returned to his desk.

"I'll send a contingent of guards with you to ensure my order is carried out. Maybe this will be a lesson to you—and I'm sure for every merchant house once word gets out: come to me unannounced, waste my time with paltry complaints, and it will result in unpleasantness."

He rapped a gavel on his desk. The doors swung open immediately.

"Trinol. Have a contingent of guards escort these two back to their warehouses in Carascan." Olber wrote quickly onto a sheaf of parchment, folded it, and held it out for his guardsman to collect.

Marra had rarely seen her father get angry. She looked to her uncle and swore under her breath; he was chuckling to himself, but when Lord Olber looked up, he seemed as mild as could be.

The bastard is enjoying this. She seethed quietly.

She watched Trinol take the note and escort the two merchants out the door. As he turned to close it, she could have sworn he winked in her direction.

At their departure, her uncle wandered over to one of the recently vacated plush chairs, brushed at it briefly, and sat.

"And you just happened to be passing this way, and these two coincidentally turned up as well?" Lord Olber asked, shuffling through his paperwork.

"Pure chance, Pertram. Unfortunate timing, I can assure you."

"I would have thought you'd have a handle on this.

Instead, I'm having to deal with these trifling squabbles. Is anyone manning your office in Carascan?"

"Of course there is. Though I will admit to being distracted of late."

"Really? By what? Anything I should know about?"

"Oh…nothing unusual. Same old stuff, but now it seems all at once: Urgad has his minions searching for his next bride, and rumour is he's looking across the borders; constant reports on the low crop yield due to the drought, lumber stocks down, petitions to build more ships are on the increase, and then there's reports of an increasing military presence in Klarget's northern provinces."

"They're always doing that. A bit of sabre rattling, then it all dies down. Unless there's more now than in previous years?"

"Not overly, no."

"And Urgad… What's this news about a wife? Hasn't he already got several?"

"You know these Dran'ali: they're not all that much better than the wild animals they ride."

"I have to admit, their horses are remarkable, but as I said, some things don't change." Lord Olber strolled over to the drink cabinet to refill his wine, pleased that this vintage was fruitier than the previous years. "So, what brings you all the way from your comfortable estate?"

"Partly the request to build more ships. As you noted, there's been an increase in reports of pirate activity. More ships mean more funds are required from the Treasury."

"Surely your office budget covers that?"

"My Lord, but since the coffers are still diminished after last year's drought, I thought it best to see you in person to request an increase, or I'll have to cut funding elsewhere."

"And our fleet?" Pertram sipped. "In light of these attacks,

I'll schedule an update with our Defence Ministers. That reminds me, it's time to renew the Privateer commission for the Red Sails Fleet."

"Those witches? The Crags and those dregs of society should be wiped off the map!"

"Harsh words for women abused by men…but then, *you'd* know more about that than most, I guess."

"Ha!" Blarik scoffed. "Not one alleged assault has been proven. And it could be embarrassing for you if I were ousted under those accusations."

"Perhaps." Olber swirled his wine. "But you *are* the brother of my wife, so if you assure me that you'll modify your behaviour…"

"My Lord. I give my word. I'm even taking meditation training from my head eunuch."

"Ont'eba? Splendid." Her father finished the remainder of his wine. "A good man that."

"Indeed," Blarik agreed. "My Lord, given our dire fleet issues, perhaps an order to commandeer these Red Sails would be appropriate?" he pursued his idea. "We could put them to far better use."

"These *women* are doing a damn fine job where they are. I'm hearing a lot less about pirate raids down south. Have you heard differently?"

Blarik shook his head.

"Good. You'd be failing me in your duties if you had and not told me." Pertram placed his glass down. "So, there's nothing serious enough to prevent my little excursion?"

"No, my Lord. Nothing unusual, and what there is can be dealt with accordingly. And I can always send a falcon."

Pertram nodded. "I was thinking of the Black Hills district. I haven't been there for a while."

"May I humbly suggest your hunting party go to Grillon

Woods instead? There have been rumours of several large boars in the area. They're playing havoc with the local farmers and their already-reduced crop yield."

Pertram shrugged. "Certainly. My foray into the Black Hills was a whim only, and to take the opportunity to call in on the Kindairs. Grillon Woods it is, then. And in the meantime, I'll consider extending the budget for the interim."

"Splendid.« Her uncle grunted as he stood. "I'll gather the documentation for you to go over before you sign. And, of course, since the woods are just to the north of my estate, you and your party would honour me with your presence, and I'll have the documents ready for you. We could then roast the boars I'm sure you'll find, and we can have a feast."

"I haven't been to your estate for a while...not since..." Pertram paused, his thoughts darkening as he once again looked at the family portrait. The last time he'd ventured to Blarik's estate was when Larina was still alive. Realising the prolonged silence, he cleared his throat and continued. "You will, of course, keep me apprised if the northern situation changes."

"Of course, my Lord. You have my word." Blarik bowed and left after downing his drink.

"You can come out now, Marra." Lord Olber moved back behind his desk with a grin.

Blushing and annoyed at herself, Marra stepped out from behind the shutters.

"How did you know?"

"You're missing your hair ribbon." He inclined his head.

"I'm no good as a spy," she huffed, following his gaze and seeing the miscreant ribbon fluttering in the branches. "Maybe I need expert training?"

"Spying? I didn't realise it was something you were interested in, though you do tend to sneak around a lot to overhear sensitive matters of state. But, if you insist, Ont'eba is the man to do it. You probably met him a few years back. Shall I send a falcon to expect a new recruit? It will be hard work and training. No more pastries."

"Can I take Sleena?"

Pertram shook his head in doubt. "I don't think an expert spy trying to remain secretive should be riding such a fine mare, especially one with the Olber branding. You could get hung for horse stealing."

She looked glum. "So, I'm stuck with a life of horse riding, crochet, and gardening?"

"It's the way of the world. Your current life is far better than most. Maybe, one day, a far better man than me will make the change, but it's far off."

"Why is it like it is?"

"It wasn't always," her father sighed. "I should get Froshingha to get you to study the histories more. Over a thousand years ago, we were all in dark, chaotic times. It's only in these last few centuries that we've regained a semblance of civilisation. With the wars we had, much of the knowledge was lost, but scholars from far and wide have been putting it back together with snippets of information here and there. We don't know where or exactly when we came here, but it seems we're not native to these lands."

"To Jaranabi?"

"No, to all Murrela."

"The whole world?" Marra looked confused and started to bite her lower lip. She stopped quickly, thinking of how her mother used to tease her when she did that.

"Anyway, nothing to be done about it until we know for sure. I suspect many of these *scholars* are simply out to make more coin for themselves. But at least you'll know why things are the way they are, and then you'll truly understand why you're far better off than many."

"Now you're making me feel like a spoiled brat."

"Not at all, but you are leading a life of privilege. Yes, in many ways it's easier than some, but we also deal with many things the population has little mind or stomach for."

"Why is it only a man can make any changes?"

"Several reasons come to mind—remember the histories I mentioned? But I try to believe it's because women are far too precious. They can nurture and bring life to an otherwise dangerous and gloomy world—"

"Maybe, if a woman were in charge and making the decisions, it wouldn't be so..."

"Ah. My sweet, young dreamer. There are many lands, all with differing beliefs and cultures, but in all that I know, women are to be protected and loved."

"It's not like that in Dran'ali, I hear."

"Dran'ali is an exception, to be sure." He saw the disgruntled look on his daughter's face. "But, perhaps, one day your dream will come true. It would be good to see that day, but I doubt it will be in my lifetime."

"I was watching Uncle Blarik. The way he looked when you weren't watching. He's up to something."

Her father nodded. "He's had a troubled life. His whole family did, so I've been told."

It was just like her father to see people in a positive light. "Is that why you married Mother?"

"Not at all. I loved your mother dearly. Her family troubles had nothing to do with it."

"I wish I'd known her better." Tears brimmed. She wiped them irritably. "I don't know why that came up. Sorry, Father."

Pertram reached out to hug her. "You never have to be

sorry to talk about your mother. She was a fine, strong lady, as I have no doubt you will be."

Marra breathed deeply and pulled away, wiping her face.

"I can call off this hunting trip," her father offered. "Plenty of things I could—should—be doing."

"No, no. Please. You rarely take time off for yourself. Time away from your duties will be good for you..."

"But you're still worried? I'll have several armed guards with me, and not forgetting Havlyn, one of the best mancers in all Jaranabi."

"As long as he doesn't go too crazy," Marra joked.

"True." Her father chuckled.

She smiled, not having heard him laugh much lately.

"Playing with the elements is fraught with its own dangers." His tone grew more serious. "That's why we do the Testing for anyone who shows the slightest inkling of Talent. Untrained elementalists would be a danger to all of society."

"We're all safe then. I've been tested."

"You have? I assume Havelyn has had a good reason not to tell me. Your mother had Talent."

"She did?" Marra asked, completely surprised by this news.

"Most certainly, though we had to keep it a secret."

"Why?"

"Political reasons. It is a sad indictment of our society that we choose to think unkindly of those who are different."

Mara grew quiet for a moment, wondering what it would have been like to be an elementalist... *A childish whim.*

"Oh well...I'm sure a full belly from the roasted boar *after* your successful hunt will keep Havelyn sane," she said, noting her father's stray to his desk and the day-to-day reports awaiting his attention.

"All for the good of the local people, of course." He turned to smile back at her.

"Of course. For the people." Feeling more positive, Marra kissed him on the cheek and left. She needed to take a ride on Sleena to cheer herself up, and walked to the stables, noting the two traders' horses quietly standing in the shaded court-yard. *They should have left by now.*

She nodded to Graff, the stable hand, as he led Polla, her uncle's mare, out to the courtyard. *Good, he's leaving.*

Inside, she heard some fierce whispering coming from one of the back stalls. It sounded a lot like her uncle, but she couldn't be sure. *Time for more spying.*

Crouching and stepping lightly onto the soft patches of fresh straw spread out on the stable's floor, she snuck into the adjoining stall. The wooden palisades were old, with signs of wear and tear, but they were solid. It took her several minutes to find a crack between the planks to see anything. A broad back obscured most of her view. There were three figures. She recognised the scuffed riding boots of her uncle and assumed the two traders were still with him.

She heard a clinking of coins. A pouch dropped to the floor, and while she didn't see a face, the fingers that retrieved it wore several rings, one with a black stone.

"You oaf," she heard her uncle berate his companion.

To her way of thinking, money exchanges often signalled the final moments of meetings. Marra quietly retreated several stalls to where Sleena was kept. Closing the door, she busied herself with checking her hooves. Several footsteps came and went. If they noticed her, they didn't say anything. After rubbing Sleena down, Marra saddled her and led her into the now-empty courtyard before mounting.

Clear of the yard, she saw the two merchants in the distance heading east towards the capital. *They seem quite chummy now.*

Her uncle had veered off to the north-east, back to his estates.

What was her uncle up to, and why was he doing deals with traders in secret?

These thoughts darkened her mood. Her father was too kind, and she hated seeing his good nature being exploited.

Eager to run, Sleena snorted impatiently.

Marra turned towards the open fields to the south and headed for the river and loosened her grip on the reins. Sleena's trot became a gallop in a few strides.

With the breeze flowing through her long black hair, Marra laughed, and her dark thoughts disappeared.

CHAPTER

TWO

BAD NEWS

The loud, irregular hoofbeats echoing from the gravelled courtyard woke her. Slipping out from under silk sheets, Marra went to the window overlooking the area below. In the dimness of pre-dawn, she saw her father's horse, Duyma, stumble in, lathered with sweat. Its movement was erratic, and it stepped sideways several times. The animal snorted and whinnied like she'd never heard before.

Part of her mind fretted for the horse's condition. *But where was her father, and why would Duyma be so badly injured?* As she was about to head downstairs, she saw the stable hand stagger out, half asleep from his bunk above the stalls, and immediately began to tend to the stricken horse.

By the time she arrived, half the house guards were milling in the yard. At her approach, they fell silent and bowed. Surprised and unsure of a response, she clutched her nightdress closely and walked past them quickly towards the stable.

Duyma was now settled in his stall. Graff was applying liniment to the wounds on his flanks.

"What happened? Where's father?" What she had thought to be just lather and sweat was also blood.

It had been two days since her father had set out with his mancer, as well as the hunt master and guards, to hunt wild boars. Six armed men in total.

"M'lady." Graff stumbled back, nervous. "Duyma 'as terrible cuts down 'is flanks."

"I see. And Father? Where is he?" she repeated, though she realised Graff would have no more knowledge of his where-abouts than herself.

"I—"

"Missing, my lady," said a voice behind her.

Marra turned. Trinol, the Olber Domain head guard, walked through the entrance.

"I don't understand. How could he be missing? What about his retinue?"

Trinol shook his head. "Lady Olber, I've already sent men out to search, but from Duyma injuries, it looks like there may have been an attack by rockions."

"Rockions? Father was nowhere near the Black Hills. He was supposed to be hunting further north and east in Grillon Woods."

"True, and he was, but the rockions could have migrated, or at least widened their hunting area with the drought. Forgive me, I'm not that knowledgeable of these large feline creatures." He stepped closer and examined the lacerations. The three foot-long cuts still oozed blood. "From what I've heard, these lacerations resemble the claw marks of a rockion."

Worried and at a loss for words, she stared first at the guard, then Graff, who suddenly looked worried at the attention.

He dropped his head at her stern look, the pot of liniment hanging in his hands. "I—I d-did what I thought best, m'lady."

"You did well, Graff. And did it quickly." She changed her tone for the poor boy. "Please continue your good work with my thanks. I'll see to it you get extra bacon for breakfast."

Graff nodded in relief and turned to continue tending to Duyma's wounds.

Marra quickly walked to her own horse, Sleena, and gave her neck a calming rub before leaving the stable, silent, deep in thought.

Trinol, following several paces behind, was joined by three more guards.

As she approached the stairs leading into the manor house, Marra became aware of the footfalls echoing off the courtyard walls. She paused and turned to look, noting the extra guards.

"Trinol? What is it?"

"My lady. Extra security. If your father is—"

"Is what? Missing? Dead? He's a master horseman and experienced hunter..." *And yet, Duyma returned alone and injured.*

"It would be wise to ensure your safety until we know for certain what has happened."

Marra took a few more steps before stopping and turning again. "We should inform Uncle Blarik—"

Trinol anticipated her words. "The moment I saw Duyma return alone, I organised a rider to go and inform him, my lady."

"Well done." Marra resumed climbing the stairs. At the top, she felt a warmth on her bare neck and through her thin night-wear. She glanced behind her; the horizon glowed with the dawn. Glancing down to the bottom of the staircase, she saw the extra guards assigned to her.

Do I need protection in my own house?

"I'll take care of it, my lady," Trinol said, noticing her uncertainty.

Shrugging off her yawns, Marra headed for the kitchens where Thelum would be baking fresh bread and other treats. She wasn't hungry, though she usually ate a hearty breakfast; it was more out of habit than anything else.

Routine. She nodded at Thelum, busy by the oven as always, and lifted two hot pastries from the tray.

"Are you sure Father went to Grillon Woods?" she asked Trinol as she continued out the back door into the garden. He kept pace by her side.

"He did, my lady. A patrol saw his retinue heading that way," Trinol replied. "We should have some news by nightfall, when our scouts return. In the meantime, I've also taken the liberty of doubling the patrols around the domain."

Marra paused her chewing. "You think there's a threat?"

"I always think there's a threat. It's my job. The possibility has recently increased significantly."

"Until Father returns."

"Yes, of course." The guard nodded.

"You don't sound so sure."

"My Lady. It pains me to be blunt, but half a dozen well-armed and experienced hunters went out...and only one horse has returned bearing the injuries inflicted by the largest and most cunning of beasts in all of Jaranabi."

Before Marra could offer a reply, a commotion came from the courtyard. More horses and voices.

"See? They have returned." The last pastry forgotten, she leapt to her feet and ran around the garden to enter the courtyard from behind the stables. To her utter dismay, her uncle was dismounting with several of his household guards as part of his retinue.

"Uncle Refin—"

"Dear Marra. I only just heard." Sir Refin Blarik was middle-aged, several years older than her father, overweight, and balding with a full beard. Dressed in his riding gear of an open shirt, cape, and black leather leggings, her uncle struggled to get his portly frame out of the saddle. After several curses at his guards for their sluggishness, he managed the climb without losing his footing. He threw the reins at one of his men and walked briskly to Marra, where he reached out to hug her in mourning.

"You got here quickly." She pulled away from his embrace, which to her mind was being far too familiar than what was proper, or what she would have liked. "A messenger was sent out only a short time ago."

"I was already on my way with other alarming news when we intercepted the rider. Tragic news to be sure."

"Surely they're just missing?" At first, the way her uncle was looking at her, she thought her uncle's vision was fading. A cool breeze picked up, chilling her and making her realise she was still only wearing her flimsy nightdress. Now conspicuous of her looks, she blushed at the old man's ogling.

"Not if rockions were involved, Marra. They are—"

"Yes, the most fearsome beasts in all of Jaranabi. I've heard." She looked crestfallen at his confirmation.

"Well, it's true, nevertheless. I can assure you."

"I—thank you, uncle," she said as he turned towards the house. "Oh, you're staying? I should show you to your rooms."

"Another time, perhaps. You do what you need to do here. I've been here plenty and know my way like it was my own."

Marra nodded in relief and searched for the house staff to arrange refreshing drinks to be sent to him and his men. She then turned and noticed her head guardsman standing by a column in the hallway to the entrance.

"Lady Olber, may I have a *quiet* word?" At her nod, he sent the three other guards to carry out their duties.

She crossed the foyer, walked through the hall, and moved

back out into the chateau's gardens. A flock of pigeons, in a pecking frenzy at the earlier discarded pastry, erupted at their approach.

"Is this quiet enough?" she asked. "What is it?"

"Pardon my overhearing the conversation with Sir Blarik." He continued after her nod. "I don't wish to cast any suspicions on anyone, but when I sent out my messenger earlier, he knew nothing of any rockion attack. I simply sent him the news of High Lord Pertram's horse returning alone."

"That is...interesting. I will think on it." *That's what father said when he didn't have another response.* "You'd better go and see to your men."

"Yes, my lady, after I escort you to your rooms, assuming that's where you're going."

She smiled, more at herself. "Yes. I am."

Entering the large house, she went back through the foyer and continued up the main stairs. Her suite was halfway along the floor.

She turned to her guard. "All safe now."

"Very good, my lady." Trinol bowed and pivoted towards the door.

"Trinol?"

"Yes, my lady?" He stopped, pivoting on the carpet.

"I do thank you and appreciate your work and that of the other guards."

"We are proud to serve and carry out our duties, my lady." Trinol bowed again, closing the door behind him.

It was still early, but going back to bed was out of the question. As she changed into more appropriate clothing for the day, she wondered at how Refin knew of the rockions. "Well, he does work with the spymaster, after all," she muttered. "That must be how."

For the remainder of the day, she tried to keep busy with menial tasks while awaiting news of her father and the hunting party. As the day continued, what she had hoped to be a mere accident was becoming less likely.

Dinner was a quiet affair, though her uncle tried several times to have a conversation. In the ensuing silence, he kept eating and drinking. Two of the staff came through; one gathered the used plates while the other laid the next course.

Refin was seated across the table. Without being obvious, she watched him. Her recent conversation and Trinol's observations still on her mind. Now and then, she saw her uncle look her way, then drink more of the wine.

Weary and depressed, with little appetite, she bid her uncle goodnight and headed for her rooms. She quickly bathed and changed before climbing into bed.

As she was about to drop off, Marra heard fumbling at her door. It had never occurred to her to lock it in her own house. She sat up when her uncle stumbled through and closed the door behind him, a wine bottle in his pudgy hand.

"Uncle Refin? Are you lost?"

"Noth ath all, my dear." As he stumbled over, it was clear from both his movements and his speech that he was already drunk. "Before you were born, thiss used to be my ssuite when I visited."

"Yes. Mother told me."

He stood by her bed, swaying, looking at her. "Ah, yes. My dear sisster...your mother..."

"What is it?" She pulled her nightgown around her, feeling uncomfortable with his gaze. "Have you news of Father?"

"Your father? Oh...yess. My agents tell me of ssad tidings, I'm afraid." He took a swig from the bottle and wiped his dripping beard with his sleeve. "They visited the area in Grillon Woods and found the remains of several men and their horses, all horribly gored and mutated, umm...mutilated."

Marra went cold at the gross, callous description.

Refin moved around the bed. She thought he was offering a condolence hug, but after he put the bottle on the bedside table, he climbed onto the bed, grabbing her and pulling her closer. *Too close. Too firm.*

"Stop it! Uncle—" She pulled an arm free and slapped him, made awkward and ineffective by the closeness. "You're drunk."

"What of it, vixen?" He moved forward to kiss her. "You sound just like your mother."

His foetid breath nauseated her. She turned her head and grimaced in disgust. Shocked and stunned by his words and actions, she found the strength to push him away, enough to break free and shuffle back. Tangled in the sheets, she was at a disadvantage.

"Guards!" Marra extricated herself from the linen and managed to crab backwards as he reached for her again. She fell onto the floor, hitting her head. Luckily, the thick rug prevented anything more serious than a bump.

Refin moved awkwardly to the side of the bed.

Marra aimed to kick him in the groin, but his obesity prevented a solid contact.

He doubled over, winded, cursing. Losing his balance, he slipped off the silk sheets and toppled to the floor.

"Guards!" she yelled again, scrambling back to avoid his falling body.

"Cry all you like," he grunted as he rolled over and grabbed her by the ankle. "My men will prevent anyone from entering."

He may have been old and fat, but fortified by his wine and

lust, he was stronger. Blarik grabbed her ankles and began to pull her closer.

Marra writhed wildly, breaking his grip and kicking at him, but only landing a glancing blow to his jaw. Before she could move far, he angrily held her down and started to crawl onto her struggling body. She brought her leg up and managed to knee him in the stomach, which served only as a temporary hindrance.

Fuelled by his drunken state, he grabbed her hair and slammed her head onto the tiles.

Marra blacked out momentarily. As she recovered from her daze, she realised he had ripped open her nightdress and was running his hands over her breasts like an eager child with a new toy. An incoherent scream ripped from her throat as she scratched at his face, digging her nails in deeply.

He cried out in pain.

Quickly, her hands were slick with his blood. The floor started shaking. Distantly, Marra could hear horses whinnying nervously from the stable and the staff raising their voices in fear and alarm.

Over this came the sound of metal ringing on metal. When the door burst open, Trinol barged in with more of the house guards, swords drawn and bloodied. On the corridor floor, two of Refin's men lay unmoving.

"Get out!" Refin yelled. Blood trickled down his cheeks into his beard.

Marra took the opportunity of the distraction and hit him in the nose with the palm of her hand. She heard and felt the satisfying crunch.

The old man shrieked, clutching his nose. Blood trickled out freely. "Little shrew. You broke it!" His voice now had a nasally twang. "You'll pay—"

Trinol raced over and pushed the drunk lord away roughly with his boot, sending him to sprawl back onto the floor.

Marra stumbled to her feet, attempting to pull her ripped blouse closed.

"Escort Sir Blarik to his room!" Trinol ordered as he grabbed a sheet and stepped over to wrap it around Marra's bare shoulders.

She pulled it tighter, looking embarrassed, relieved and thankful.

"You little pup," Refin raged from the floor. "You don't order me around!"

"Minister or not, in this household, where you are a guest, he does!" Marra retorted.

"Agril, Robern, take Sir Blarik to his rooms now!" Trinol ordered again.

The two guards moved to pull the old man to his feet.

Refin shrugged them off. "You're mistaken. I am *High Lord* Blarik now, and I'll do as I please, where I please, with whom I please."

Marra shook her head. "You? High Lord? You're just an old lecherous drunk. My father—"

"Is dead, and as the Minister for the Interior, I gained the title the moment his heart stopped beating." Refin stumbled to his feet, swaying slightly.

"In the absence of Lord Olber, the head of this house is Lady Marra Olber. I will obey her orders and no one else's." Trinol reached over and shoved the old man towards the door.

"You're making a grave mistake, young Trinol."

"My mistake was letting you through the gate. Men, please use force if he resists. There will be an accounting for this behaviour tomorrow."

"Tomorrow you'll realise I'm the legitimate high lord. Then

I can assure you all, there will definitely be an accounting of your treatment."

Trinol looked sternly at his men. "Why's he still here?"

The two guards turned quickly and pushed Refin out the door, almost causing him to trip over the bloodied bodies of his protectors.

"Who killed my men? Unhand me, you insubordinate oafs!" His curses and threats continued for several minutes.

In the uncomfortable aftermath, Marra looked at the shambles of her bed. She shuddered and pulled her sheet tighter.

"Lady Olber..." Trinol stood, head down. "You have my humblest apologies for this neglect. I—"

"You will ensure Refin stays locked in his room and set guards. None of Refin's men is to set foot within the grounds."

"Of course, my lady." Trinol nodded. "Shall I call for the healer? Are you injured?... Did he..."

"No! No healer is necessary. I'm bruised and shaken only." Marra looked up as her maid ran in, woken quickly from her sleep.

"Oh. My lady!" The maid glanced at her, seeing the sheet covering her, the state of the bed, and the drops of blood on the floor. Nervously, she started tidying up the room.

"Cinnam. Leave that. Stop fussing. Please go and fetch Froshingha." Marra reached for the wine bottle and took a quick sip while looking around the chamber. "Tell him to meet me in the library at his earliest convenience. I need his counsel more than anything else right now."

"Very good, my lady." Cinnam curtsied, looking relieved to be somewhere else and left quickly.

"You think he will know of what Refin claimed?" Trinol asked.

Marra shrugged, taking another sip. "If there's anything to know of the obscurities of lore, Froshingha will know it."

The head guard nodded. "I'll warn my men of the potential threat. On my life, none of Refin's men will get in. No doubt that tremor and sudden storm alarmed them as well."

"Tremor?"

"Yes. Did you not feel the ground shake? It was only for a moment...and a sudden gust of wind."

"I had no idea." She shook her head. "Thank you, again, Trinol."

The moment the door clicked closed, she dropped into the nearest chair and sobbed into her hands.

CHAPTER

THREE

ENCOUNTER

"Ship to port!" The lookout's sharp cry pierced the salty air. Ripples of anticipation ebbed through the crew of the *Revenge*. Perched high in the crow's nest, the lookout pointed toward the distant speck on the horizon. Below, the bustling deck of the ship stilled as heads turned toward their captain.

Corra Sienna stepped up to the gunwale with the grace of someone who had spent years mastering unpredictable seas. From a sheath crafted from the skin of the elusive *barbon* fish, she drew her long-eye, a finely crafted spyglass. Hooking her arm through the shrouds to steady herself, she peered at the ship in question.

Most of the crew continued with their tasks, though they remained wary and upbeat, expecting a change in orders at any moment.

"Are they pirates?" asked Olinda, one of the younger newlings, her wide-eyed eagerness betraying her inexperience. Leaning on the gunwale, she squinted at the horizon.

Corra lowered the long-eye and fixed Olinda with a

measured look. "Possibly. Too far to say. Olinda, isn't it? You're too keen by half. Pirate hunting sounds noble enough, but it's more dangerous than you realise. It's not something to sail into unwittingly."

Satisfied her caution had been heard, Corra turned her gaze back to the horizon. "Let's catch up with them," she ordered, her voice calm yet commanding. "See what they do."

"Aye, Cap'n!" Tully, the first mate, relayed the order with a bark, setting the crew into motion. With the sails adjusted, the helm spun to port. The *Revenge* surged forward, slicing through the oncoming waves. It was choppy at first, but then the ship found its rhythm and soon its movement was a steady and graceful rising and falling motion.

Olinda, still curious, tilted her head. "What's that noise?" she asked, as the sound caught her attention.

"That's water rippling along the hull. You'll get used to it," Corra replied with a faint smile. "Or not...»

AFTER A COUPLE OF HOURS, the *Revenge* was steadily closing the gap between itself and the unknown ship. As they drew near, Tully called out, her telescope trained on the vessel's stern. "It's the *Dimantin*, Cap'n. A trader out of Erranier. Last I heard, Erdun Walsch was in command."

Captain Sienna nodded. "Flag our request to parley." She handed the sheathed long-eye to Tully.

A pennant was sent up *Revenge*'s mainmast; a fluttering signal of peaceful intent. Minutes later, a reply came from the *Dimantin*, its own pennant rising in acknowledgment. The trader slowed as sails were pulled in.

As the two ships drew alongside, Corra maintained her ritual. Stepping to the gunwale, she gave a brief salute toward the *Dimantin's* ensign. Olinda, observing from the sidelines, turned to a crewmate. "Why'd she do that?"

"Mark o'respect," one of the crew replied as they readied the gangplank. "Our cap'n always salutes, no matter who's on the other side."

"Even pirates?" Olinda failed to recall the name of the crewmember, but hoped she'd get to learn the names of the thirty-women crew in time.

"If they be showin' the flag to parley, assumin' we're not already fightin', or they're not runnin' in panic. The ship ain't the problem. Wanna lend a hand 'stead of gawpin'?"

Blushing at the mild rebuke, Olinda rushed closer to help.

"Reduce sail," Corra called out. "Slow speed. Helm, bring us alongside. Steady, still a bit choppy."

Tully repeated the order before turning to her captain. "Want a Calmin'?"

The captain judged the swell between the two hulls separated by the length of the gangplank—about ten feet. "Sure. I don't feel like swimming at the moment."

Tully gave the command, and *Revenge* eased into position beside the larger vessel.

Four crew members—hydrons—elementalists trained in water magyk, spaced themselves along the port side. They raised their arms in unison, murmuring incantations that dampened the waves around the two ships. The sea's natural rhythm was subdued, creating a still, mirror-like surface between the vessels.

Olinda gawked. "How are they doing that?" she whispered to herself, her astonishment growing as she climbed into the shrouds to get a better view. Beyond the immediate calm, the open sea swelled as usual. The contrast was mesmerising; it was as if there were a hidden wall surrounding them.

Sienna strode across the gangplank, her balance as

unerring as her reputation. She eyed the trader ship and its crew warily. Just because they complied didn't mean they were not going to give any trouble. Many men were standing and watching with interest at both the metal-hulled ship and the all-female crew. She doubted they'd seen a woman crew before, and after a few whistles and catcalls, it definitely confirmed they had never encountered the Red Sails. As expected, her girls ignored them completely.

As she came to the end of the narrow walkway, she was met by two burly men, their long, curly black hair tied back. Their shirts were half undone, revealing broad chests. Bulging muscle evident with the short sleeves.

"Permission to come aboard?" she asked the two men approaching.

"For you, lovely, anytime." One's grin showed surprisingly white teeth. He raised his hand to assist her down.

She ignored it and dropped like a cat to the deck. "Captain Walsch about?" She was thinking this man was too young to be a ship captain, then again, he wasn't much older than herself.

"He'll be along shortly. In the meantime, been at sea for a while. Why don't we get acquainted first? The lads here would be keen to meet yer girls too."

If it had been quiet before, it was deathly still now.

Corra breathed calmly. "You're either new to the sea, or a canvas short of full sail?" Her voice, heard over the unusually becalmed waters and wind, was crisp but not unfriendly.

Any crew that heard—men and women—chuckled.

"Nah. Plenty of experience, and in other things too." He winked.

"Right. So, you've not heard of the Red Sails?"

"I've heard *stories* in taverns and the like." He smirked to his companion. "But many tall tales are told in taverns. Can't believe everythin' some drunk says."

"What do these tall tales say?"

"Women chasin' pirates and stuff and cuttin' their balls off." He chuckled. "I know women, an' I seen pirates. I reckon I know who'd come off best."

"I see. And where have you seen these pirates?"

"Zaran town square. The gallows jus' afore they was hanged." He shrugged. "Didn't look like much."

"Most aren't. Then again, many men are like that, I find." Corra was disappointed, though not overly surprised at the way this encounter was going. Too much to expect any respect from a man to a female captain. "I'd appreciate it if you'd go and fetch your captain. This conversation is getting tedious."

"Off ya git." He nudged his companion. "Don't worry. I'll save yer some."

Once he left, Muscles turned his full attention back to the long-legged beauty in front of him. "Wot's yer name, girl?" He raised his hand, reaching out to her.

She didn't flinch and showed no interest. "I wouldn't advise it." Corra casually raised her arm.

"Why not?" The smile wavered. The hand paused.

She clicked her fingers. Seconds later, three arrows with red fletching thudded into the deck by his scuffed and worn-out boots.

Muscles jumped back in surprise and alarm. Some of the men cursed in anger, looking to see the archers high in the rigging. Their arrows already drawn for the next volley. An equal number of his fellow crewmen chuckled at his discomfort.

"As to why not?" Unphased, Corra cocked her head to the side with a sly grin at his sudden change of stance. "Because I didn't ask, and we're not in a playful mood."

Having backed away, Muscles covered his embarrassment with false bravado. "You dare attack me on my ship?"

"*Your* ship, is it? And yes. I dare. The next arrow will be painfully closer if you make any attempt to touch me again." She raised her voice for the benefit of the others. "This goes to any man who tries. My girls haven't drunk blood all week and are getting thirsty."

Muscle's tanned face quickly lost a few shades.

"What's goin' on 'ere?" An older man bellowed as he strode across the deck from his cabin. "Klort. Ye bein' disrespectful again? Be off with ye, lout!" He turned to another senior man. "Veral, get these laggards workin'!"

"Aye, Cap'n." Orders were yelled, and the onlookers quickly went back to their tasks.

With a vengeful backwards glance, Muscles sauntered aft, the first mate berating him as he walked.

"Captain Walsch, I take it? Captain Sienna of the *Revenge*," she addressed the older, grey-haired and bearded man.

"I am." The captain stepped closer. "Glad tidin's to ye, Cap'n Sienna. Welcome to the *Diamantin*. My apologies for Klort, and not greetin' yus," Walsch replied, his own tone tinged with uncertainty, seeing the arrows in the deck. "If yer find yerself in Samanko, stay away from their eel dishes. Goes right throu yer, it does."

"I'll keep that in mind."

Walsch nodded as he continued. "Klort's a cad. I blame meself for not bein' there for 'im more."

"He was of little concern, so don't fret." Corra nodded, then changed the subject. "Thanks for not putting up more sail and avoiding us."

"'eard of the Red Sails, I 'ave. 'ear's ye'd catch us if ye wanted." Walsch's eyes flicked to the elementalists maintaining the calm waters and the all-woman crew, curiosity clear in his expression. "No point pissin' yer off."

"True enough," Corra admitted, a slight smirk playing on her lips. "I've a good crew."

"An' a good ship too, so I 'ears. Be that a metal 'ull?" He stepped closer to the side and looked along the neighbouring ship's length. "Ain't never seen a metal one a'fore."

"*Revenge* is a very unique and capable ship. One of three." She waited for him to face her again and handed him a rolled document. "Just to allay any doubts or fears that we're no threat to you and other merchants. The Red Sails are Privateers, commissioned by Pertram Olber, High Lord of Jaranabi, and countersigned by Logar Glerin, the ruler of Klarget." Corra waited for him to read over the document.

"As I says. I've 'eard of ye. Tis why we're headin' sou'west now, it be safer waters, thanks to yous. What can I do for ye?" The tension in his voice faded quickly now that he was assured they meant no harm. He rolled the parchment up and handed it back.

Corra slid it back into its leather holder as she spoke. "We've had reports of raiders in these waters. It's a large area. I'm asking merchants if they've seen anything to narrow it down?"

Walsch frowned, his expression darkening. "Not seen 'em myself, but word is the *Gon Falmo* was 'it four nights past, north of 'ere. Damned pirate scum's gettin' bolder." Walsch turned to his runner. "Get me charts, boy."

Corra's expression grew grave at the news. "How did the *Gon Falmo* fare?"

"Not well. Took 'eavy damage but was continuin' on to Lashalk. These attacks are worse with every report." He motioned for her to follow to where a chart was hastily laid out on a weather-worn bench. Several large, smooth pebbles were placed to prevent the parchment edges from curling up.

His runner ducked away, but his wide eyes watched the tall woman from behind a barrel.

Walsch pointed to a location north of the Shevron Reef. "They seem ta be stickin' to this region for now."

"No doubt because of the kraken season in other waters further south," Corra surmised. "The reef will give traders limited movement. Easier pickings."

"No doubt, and also why we're 'uggin' close to the reef to avoid the kraken. No sane captain will risk a kraken—even if it ain't the season. We're runnin' light, so takin' advantage of the shallower waters."

"And your destination?"

"Port Angrom over in Dran'ali. We got mostly cotton and oils for 'em."

Corra nodded, looking over his chart. "Next time you venture to Herantia, go and see Farand Daral Shis. She's one of the best cartographers to date. Price is high, but better than ripping your keel in uncharted waters. May I?" She plucked a charcoal stick from an engraved pewter mug nearby.

At his dubious nod, Corra made a few minor additions.

"There are spurs to the reef, here...and here."

When the captain of the *Revenge* was finished, Walsch studied the annotation to his chart and was well-pleased, remarking, "Many thanks to ye, Cap'n. I'll heed yer warnin' and keep 'n eye out and give those shoals a wide berth."

The parley concluded with mutual respect, and the *Revenge* set a course for Titonu Island to investigate the raid. The journey would take them through a treacherous channel, a shortcut known for its narrow and shallow waters. It was a risk, but one worth taking if they hoped to gain the advantage over the elusive raiders.

"If we're lucky, we'll be at the reef before sunset." Tully judged the angle of the lowering sun.

As *Revenge* turned toward its new heading, Captain Sienna addressed her crew. "Prepare for a reef crossing. Most of us have done it before. Keep alert. We'll need every ounce of skill and a bit of magyk to see us through."

The crew cheered, bolstered by their captain's confidence and the possibility of action. Olinda, watching from the rigging, felt a spark of pride, excitement, and a bit of nervousness. She was part of something extraordinary, aboard a ship where courage and cunning charted their course.

And somewhere ahead, danger waited.

~

"Reef starboard bow," came the call from above.

A short time later, the troubled waters of the reef became evident to all those on the deck.

"Helm, keep it on the horizon until we get to Keelhaul Channel," Corra ordered, then turned to Tully. "Looks like the tide isn't full yet. We'll need more water beneath us, and speed. Dusk will be upon us shortly. Assemble our mancers. I'm heading up to the bowsprit. Send a runner."

Tully pulled out her whistle and gave a series of short, high-pitched blasts.

Overhearing the conversation and taking the initiative, Olinda took on the job as runner. She was a few steps behind her commander.

Captain Sienna walked briskly to the fo'c'sle, mounted the bowsprit and shinnied along the smooth metal spar until the lines for the jib boom were in reach. Pulling herself up, she slipped her boots into a loop of rope to secure her footing, curled her arm around a jib line, and surveyed the reef with her long-eye.

The search for a slightly smoother and darker section of water—the telltale sign of the deeper channel—was hampered now by the lowering sun. Every minute, the light was waning.

"Keelhaul Channel sited, Cap'n," the spotter in the crow's nest called out, her voice easily being carried forward by the wind.

"Just in time." Raising her right arm, Sienna kept it there as the *Revenge* changed direction. The angle of the deck increased with the turn. Olly had to use both hands to hang on until the captain dropped her arm.

The bow of *Revenge* rose up the face of a wave.

Olinda lost sight of the sea for a frightening moment, then, as the bow dropped, there were some loud bangs and the ship shuddered when the hull hit the water. Spray cascaded over the deck, sending a brief shiver down her spine as the cold water soaked her clothes. Gradually, the deck levelled as the ship straightened out of the turn.

"Keelhaul Channel dead ahead, Cap'n."

Corra studied the channel to make sure their line was true. When she pulled her gaze away, she saw the young newling, white faced and gripping the railing, standing behind her.

"Tell Tully we need more speed and at least a fathom of swell."

Olinda looked puzzled at the wording, but ran, dodging coils of rope, back to the first mate and repeated what she hoped was the correct order.

Tully nodded. "Olly, never run. Walk briskly and always try ta maintain hand contact; otherwise, the slightest roll will send ya a'fallin'." The first mate then addressed the two groups of elementalists forming up nearby. "We need 'bout six feet under the keel and get 'er to flyin' speed." She turned back to Olinda, who was watching the new activity with interest. "You're about ta see somethin' no other ship can do, 'cept our Red Sails. Now, back to the bow ya go. Walkin', mind."

There were now six water elementalists—hydrons. Olinda followed them as they moved forward. They spoke briefly to one another before they lined up in a wedge shape and began their concentration. In slow rhythm, they made circling motions with their hands like they were balling up yarn or fishing line.

The six air elementalists had moved to the stern. Like those at the bow, there was no need for chanting; it was simply a matter of concentration, a power of will, to summon a steady flow of air to fill the sails.

At the same time, there was a flurry of activity as the remainder of the crew began raising every yard of red canvas they could find. All bar two strong women, Dara and Barb. While the others moved swiftly and precisely to do their tasks, this pair were facing each other, their hands on a wheel drum with eight short, thick handles on each end.

The sails began to fill as the wind picked up. As the ship gained speed, an order from the first mate got them turning the wheel drum steadily.

Olinda grabbed hold of the nearest line as she was buffeted by the increasing gusts.

Corra also firmed her grip as she concentrated on the reef ahead. Every so often, she would put one of her arms out to indicate an adjustment to port or starboard.

It dawned on the young girl that something unusual was happening. She had grown up around fishing boats—nothing as grand as the *Revenge*—and she knew there should have been far more movement of the ship, yawing port and starboard, and rising and falling as it pushed through each wave. This time, though, the bow rose slightly and stayed level. It was the smoothest ride she'd ever felt on the ocean. There was also an unusual noise. At first, she thought it might have something to do with the volume of air the aeyrons were controlling, but she soon realised it was coming from below. Since the deck was much steadier now, Olinda moved to the gunwale and looked over the side.

She didn't know—or believe—what she was looking at. About a third of the way from the bow, strange metal struts came out of the hull and disappeared into the water. As she watched in awe, she spied a long, thin shape below the surface stretching out of sight underneath the vessel. The keel was completely out of the water, with the struts and rudder the only parts of the ship still in contact. Moving quickly to the other side, she saw the same thing.

"We call 'em waterwings."

So enthralled at the sight, Olly jumped at the voice beside her. One of the strong women, Dara, who had lowered the strange device, was also looking over the side, examining her work.

"We're in the channel! Olly, tell the helm to watch for my signal. Everyone, brace yourselves." Corra, still on the bowsprit, slid the long-eye into its sheath and wrapped an arm tightly around the nearest line, but her concentration never wavered from keeping careful watch on the reef mere feet below the waterwing.

Olinda raced back to the helm and repeated the order.

"Brace. Brace," Tully called out. "Olly, stay 'ere for the moment, lass, and 'ang on."

"Here." Dara guided Olinda to the centre of the ship, where loops of rope had been tied around the mast in case of rough seas. "This shouldn't take long. We'll be fine," she reassured her.

With only the waterwing and a few feet of rudder in the water, *Revenge* skimmed across the shallow channel, splitting the reef.

Several tense minutes passed with only the sound of the wind reaching their ears.

Sienna suddenly flung her arm up to port. At the helm, the wheel was spun rapidly. The deck angled sharply. The ship turned. Wide-eyed and hanging on tightly, Olinda looked for reassurance from Dara; she looked relaxed and gave her a confident smile.

And then, they were clear.

With one final look at the water, the captain climbed down to the deck and stopped in front of the water elementalists.

"Relax now, ladies. Good job. Rest up. We'll probably need you if we cross any raiders."

The six women lowered their arms and took deep breaths, clapping each other on the shoulders and backs in congratulations and relief as they found a place to sit and let the setting sun and warm breeze dry their clothes and hair.

"Olly. Go and get dried before you catch a chill," Corra suggested as she strolled past to check the aeyrons.

As the hydrons did, the young newling basked in the waning sunlight as the rough waters of the reef dwindled in the distance. When dry enough, she headed to the crew quarters, passing a couple of other newlings as they brought out covered lanterns under the guidance of a senior. She paused to see what they were going to do.

The vents on the lantern directed the light down towards the deck, allowing safe passage during the night. The cowling on each lantern prevented the flame from blowing out or getting wet. The lanterns were also kept low so they couldn't be seen by other ships.

There was a change of watch, and a number of other crew went topside after having a meal. Several minutes later, the day crew came downstairs to clean up and eat.

Dara and Barb were already lined up for their dinner. "Isn't sailing at night dangerous?" Olinda asked them.

"Need to keep movin' to keep the ship stable. A ship not under sail will bob and bounce all night."

"An' no one wants dinner to reappear ag'in," Barb quipped. "Goin' down once is bad enough."

"Hey. I 'eard that!" Floria barked good-naturedly. "Jus' for that, youse get extra. Make sure you finish it all, mind! I be watchin'."

Olinda smiled at the joking, but wanted to slap herself for her silly question. She should have known from her fishing experiences that a rocking boat can cause great discomfort to many. "Um...I mean, can they see, or do they know these waters that well?" She tried to cover her mistake.

"Seas at night look much the same, lass." The two women chuckled. "But the night shift can touch a bit of spirit."

"Spirit?"

"Spirit, as in the element. Some spirons may not be strong with it outwardly, like our other sisters with air and water, but internally, several of us can see pretty good in the dark, hence why they have the night-watch."

Olinda realised she must have looked ridiculous with her mouth open and wasn't sure if she was being teased. After her duties and her meal, she decided to slip up top and see for herself.

She made sure she kept out of everyone's way by standing between some canvas-covered crates. She loved watching the night sky. Tonight was especially good as there were no moons, and the sky was crystal clear with thousands of stars twinkling down at her.

The newling watched the crew too, and it was true. While her eyes adjusted somewhat to the dark, the night shift was doing minor tasks, but as quickly and efficiently as any dayshift crew had been. Satisfied she hadn't been the butt of a joke, she resumed staring at the stars for a bit longer before heading to her bunk.

CHAPTER

FOUR

COUNCIL MEETING

"It's an ancient lore, dating back several centuries." Froshingha looked over his glasses at Marra like she was a student in class. "It was a vastly different society then. No one has used it in all that time…a very strange lore indeed. And very strange times….»

"But what is it exactly?" she asked.

They were in her father's office. Marra sat in his chair while Trinol leant against the wall by the closed doors after detailing the two guards outside. Froshingha, holding an old manuscript, stood to the side of the table near one of the bookshelves. With the abrupt late-night summons, he had thrown a dressing gown over his nightrobe.

Normally dressed with great care and decorum, Marra's aged mentor had never appeared before her so out of character.

"This automatic gaining of the role of any minister is pure bunkum. With his position, though, he could claim a temporary role if the country is facing war or unrest." Her mentor's long, elegant fingers ran down the vellum page.

"War? Unrest? My father is missing, perhaps dead, but surely this is not sufficient grounds to do this?"

Trinol cleared his throat. "You may be aware there have been recent reports of trouble to the north, my lady."

Marra rolled her eyes. "Klarget is always skirmishing at our northern borders. This is nothing new. Surely, Refin was rambling in his drunken stupor." She suppressed a grim smile when she realised she was mimicking her father's words. She also recalled her uncle mentioned the Klarget trouble as minor...*and* he *suggested the visit to Grillon Woods—*

"Perhaps, but being Interior Minister, he may be privy to information no one else knows."

"Blarik fobbed off any serious threat. And father would never go off hunting knowing there was an imminent threat on the borders.' She hesitated. "Is withholding vital information from his liege not an offence of some description?"

"If we could prove he knew of it, but did not tell your father...there could be a case."

"What about sexual assault?" Marra asked.

"Umm. Sexual assault? It's been tried. We'd need the victim and undisputed proof, otherwise it would merely be another 'she said; he said' scenario."

"I'm the victim and have three witnesses."

"Ah. Your injuries... I didn't want to speculate." Froshingha slumped in a plush chair, the vellum scrolls loose in his lap. "I'm so sorry this has happened to you. It's a truly despicable act." The senior advisor sighed, thinking. "But I see a quandary."

"How so?"

"You alleging this assault—"

"I'm not *alleging* at all. I'm telling you it happened. Trinol and his guards witnessed it! They had to kill two of Refin's men to get into my room."

"And there's the nub of the matter, my lady. This contestation of being the head of state is between yourself and him. It could be seen that your accusation is merely to discredit him further in the face of the councillors. It would appear your witnesses will be beholden to you and your house, and it might be presumed they are simply following your orders."

"But it *did* happen! Doesn't swearing an oath mean anything to these people?"

"Please believe me. I have no doubt. There have been many accusations made against Refin, all unproven."

Marra wiped her tears of frustration. "What chances have I got, then?"

"Limited." The advisor shrugged. "And slim at best."

"So, Refin gets away with it—again—and is now possibly to be the next ruler of all Jaranabi? This has to be wrong. Surely, as an in-law, he isn't in the line of succession."

"I will need to look into it further, but I believe your great-grandfather was in a similar position. At one of the first major incidents with Dran'ali. There was no clear line of succession, but Patraig Olber came up with a strategy. The Houses back then were far less organised, so in an emergency session with borders being overrun, they voted him in." Froshingha paused. "We won't mention that unless asked. Within two months, the borders were secure. There's been an Olber in charge ever since."

"Until now." Marra looked glum. She sighed, turned to the family advisor and spoke softly in a steely voice. "Froshingha, now you can tell me what you know about these other allegations of sexual assault. I want to hear everything, every sordid detail."

~

Graff stared at all the activity in the courtyard, not having seen so many people in one place at one time.

"Boy. Git to workin'. These horses need tendin' to and won't be doin' it themselves."

Jolted into motion by the head ostler's vexation, Graff grabbed the reins of the two closest horses and encouraged them into the stalls and out of the sun. Duyma, Sleena and Polla, the only other horses in the manor stables, whinnied at the new arrivals.

In the courtyard, nobles from far and wide, crotchety with the rapid travel in the heat of the day, trudged towards the manor house.

Just outside the walls, the lush fields surrounding the manor were pockmarked with the formation of encampments of their retinue and armed escorts. Each was setting up a discreet distance from the camps of the other houses, their house colours flapping in the breeze and stating their presence.

Marra and the household staff had been busy since the moment they saw the standard of an allied house come up the road, realising a High Council had been arranged. She had to quickly get the staff to prepare the suites for visitors. Now, on the balcony overlooking the courtyard and the front of the estate, she stared at the kafuffle below and beyond the domain walls. "But how could they get here so quickly, and why here and not where they normally meet, in the Great Hall in Carascan?"

"They couldn't, my lady." Trinol moved closer to the parapet and pointed. "See there, the colours of Alwart House? And to the left, Hommin House? They are at least three days' travel by horse, maybe four by carriage if pushed."

"Refin must have planned this in advance."

"It would appear so," Froshingha agreed.

"The scheming pervert. That was why he arrived yesterday.

He must know something more about the threat posed before Father left. He kept the information to himself and... This is a coup! That's why he wanted the meeting here. Much easier than in the middle of the capital—too many eyes and ears."

"And protocol decrees the mancer bodyguards of each house do not attend formal meetings. I'm sure they're indulging in the delights of Carascan at the realm's expense while waiting their summons to return."

"Father wouldn't have left if he had known of any impending threat," Marra insisted.

"I believe you, but it's not me you need to convince. Would the councillors believe you? May I be bold, my lady?"

"Of course. You can always speak plainly with me, Froshingha."

He bowed his head briefly in acknowledgement. "With the greatest respect, your father was not the most perceptive or dynamic leader. This is the gossip among the local villages. Yes, we all loved, adored, and respected him, but for those very same reasons, he was more of a chummy noble than a force to be reckoned with. However, thanks to your great-grandfather's forethought, Jaranabi has not had more than minor border skirmishes for well over a century. No one here has actually experienced a real war. Peace makes society complacent...and vulnerable to attack...from within as well as beyond its borders."

Marra's face paled at these words, though deep down, she knew the truth of it.

"The point is, though: how does the council perceive our High Lord?" her advisor continued. "I've little doubt that Refin made out the problem to the north is no more than a minor dispute, and nothing to worry about. That would make it far more plausible for your father to go hunting. And, possibly, to look negligent or uncaring in the eyes of others."

Trinol spoke after the advisor. "Or to put it another way: how does the council perceive Sir Blarik? We've all heard the stories. Like him or loathe him, he is cunning and ruthless. Is he someone they want to make an enemy?"

Marra paced, as she had witnessed her father do many times.

"This is not going to end well for any of us. Let me think on it, and thank you both for your words."

Each with a polite bow to her, the two men left. Marra remained on the balcony, hoping the fresh air would somehow ease her tension. "I have to do something..." She leant on the railing and mulled over her limited options, but still unsure of her actions, she eventually returned to her bed for a fitful night's sleep, thankful that Cinnam had tidied the room.

Marra woke, listless, but put on a brave face for the household staff. She thought that her apprehension was the aftermath of the assault and restless sleep, but as the day progressed, the bad feeling in her gut only worsened.

She approved a wagon to fetch extra supplies from Carascan, then tried to bury her foreboding and busy herself with reacquainting herself with the leaders of the various Houses. While she knew some of them well, she was almost a stranger to those domains further afield.

For all such meetings, only the senior nobles were expected to attend, and she was pleased to see her father's friends—strong allies of the High Lord. However, there were always those who opposed every decision her father made.

Marra would have to watch her tongue when speaking with the Droliks, Charrofs, and Alwarts.

That left three other noble houses to consider. She saw

the standards of Houses Laskar, Bouller, and Nurnup flapping in the breeze. They were barely known to her as they rarely raised a quibble. She thought wryly that those who caused the nuisance seemed to be most prominent in her father's life.

And now in my thoughts!

As expected, they had all received the message for the High Council the day before her father had gone on his hunting trip, and many of the lords and ladies were aggrieved with Sir Blarik for the impromptu appointment.

"And where is he now?" Lord Hommin asked, looking around as if he expected to see Blarik waltz in from the rear courtyard. His hat, too large for his bald head, nearly slipped off.

"Umm, currently indisposed with matters of state, Infar." Marra didn't feel it was appropriate to reveal her uncle was under house arrest. "I'm sure he'll be at the council meeting."

"He had better be! I didn't come all this way for nothing. Oh, though it is a pleasure to see you again, Marra," Infar finished.

With a wink, Lady Hommin ushered her husband away before he embarrassed himself further.

PRIOR TO SITTING FOR DINNER, Marra summoned her head guardsman. Even with an herbal remedy from the house apothecarist, this feeling of imminent catastrophe had only grown worse. Several times during the afternoon she had almost blacked out. Even the weather had made a drastic turn, and now ominous clouds gathered, darkening her mood even more.

"Trinol, after escorting Blarik to the meeting, you and your men must leave. You aren't safe here! I can't explain it, but I feel it in my bones. I *know* something bad is going to happen."

"My lady. We will not abandon you with this miscreant."

"Dear Trin, be realistic." She gazed up into his hazel eyes. "You heard what he said last night in my chambers: '*I can do what I want, where I want and with whoever I want.*' I don't know about your men, but you have a family. You must think of them first." She put a hand on his arm, feeling the heat of his skin. "I'll not hold it against you."

Trinol opened his mouth, but couldn't bring himself to deny it. He hung his head in shame.

Marra continued, "Blarik isn't stupid. He has some plan, of that I'm certain. Very soon, what he says will be indisputable. I fear that with our recent treatment of him, it will not go well for either of us."

"But you—"

"Will be fine. There will be at least one successful outcome in this fiasco; it's that every noble house in Jaranabi will know of what has gone on between Refin and myself. With all the major noble houses as witnesses, I doubt even *he* can do anything to hurt me. But he'll have absolutely no qualms in doing harm to you, your family, or your men. The best thing he could do is conscript you."

"You think that's *good*?"

"Not at all, but I'm sure there are far worse things he could do."

Trinol took a deep breath. "I swore an oath to your father, as did my men, to defend this family and this house."

"Then I formally rescind you and your men from the oath. You are free to go to your family and get as far away from here as you can. Take any married men with you. If anyone asks, tell them you're retrieving the remains of the hunting party. Once you're clear of the domain, scatter. Go to your loved ones and get away. There are at least five noble houses that would take you in."

"I could not possibly—"

"You can and you will! When you took the hand of your loved one in marriage, did you not swear to provide for her, to defend her?"

"I did, but—"

"But nothing. You can't do that if you're dead. Go to them. *They* are now your priority. They should have been from the start. What do you think will happen to them when you're not there? Maybe not by Refin's hands, but his thugs are no doubt just as violent and dishonourable as he is. It's probably in their job description."

Trinol looked at her pleadingly. "You must come with us! Hide in a wagon until it's safe."

She saw the anguish in his eyes. Her mind cast her back fleetingly over the years he had been there. Like all spoiled brats, she had been childish and teasing—a noble girl having a strong, handsome man watching over her—but he was steadfast and true. He'd laugh at her jokes, acted surprised when she tried to scare him... *And now I'm sending him away.*

"My lady? Marra?"

The use of her name on his lips broke her reverie. "Dear Trin...I'm Lady Olber of House Olber, daughter to the High Lord. I can't leave. There's a banquet shortly and I need to be here to allay any suspicion. House guards going out to retrieve their Lord's remains is quite plausible."

She walked along the path a few more steps. "There's a drawback, though. A handful of guards must remain, patrolling the grounds as per normal."

"I will ask for volunteers."

"Single men." Marra nodded. "Go and tell your men. Head south. Most of House Olber's allies are down that way, and it's further away from whatever he has planned in the north."

"We are not afraid of fighting!"

"Of course you aren't, but this is Blarik being a tyrant. There's no pride or glory in playing his game, even less being a victim. Be well." She grasped his hand briefly as the dinner bell rang out across the garden. She turned before he saw the welling of tears and strode into the palace, wiping her face.

AFTER DINNER, four Olber house guards escorted the guests to the ballroom, where the intrepid Madam Krishly had managed to get the staff to set the room up in time for the meeting. She was ushering her staff down a side passage when the dignitaries came up the main stairs from the dining hall.

The seneschal waited, curtsying at their arrival.

"You have my undying thanks," Marra whispered to her as she passed, noting the beads of perspiration on the stout woman's brow.

Once everyone had filed into the large room, her guards closed the double doors and took up their positions in the hallway.

Inside the ballroom, several tables had been arranged into a rectangle large enough to comfortably fit the dozen councillors, with a couple of chairs placed behind for the wives and retainers if the various lords had brought them.

As hostess and last Olber Domain representative, Marra was to the left and slightly behind the Chair.

Rubbing his red wrists and scowling, Refin Blarik strode in, glancing around at the gathering. His eyes paused, seeing her, then moved towards an empty chair at the large table. Not being a member of the council, though, he was ushered to the side to a plush chair by a smaller desk. The High Lord's chair remained conspicuously empty at the head of the room, as did one of the chairs behind the High Lord's.

"Lady Marra, any idea where the Royal Advisor is?" the Chairman asked her.

Marra looked to the vacant chair beside hers. She shook her head. "I'm as surprised as you, Lord Trallko."

The tall man tsked and sighed before lightly tapping the gavel until everyone was seated and silent. "As designated chairman, I officially open the High Council, and on behalf of our hostess, Lady Marra Olber, I welcome you all to this impromptu gathering."

"Blarik, what's the meaning of this?" A thin, balding man spoke up from the far end of the room. "Why have we all been summoned at such short notice?"

The aging woman sitting behind him nudged his back.

"And why here?" he added after the prompt.

"Lord Phillit," Harrod Trallko spoke up. "All in good time." He turned to the ashen face of Marra. "Lady Olber, it would be remiss if I, as Chair, did not commiserate formally to you on behalf of the full Council the sadness we all feel to hear the tragic news of High Lord Olber. It has come as a shock to all of us. He will be sorely missed. Would you care to say a few words before we begin? I can understand if not..."

Marra had sat in on a couple of these meetings in the past and had a fair idea of what to expect. Her father generally made a few pleasantries before the real discussion began.

"Thank you, Lord Trallko." Marra nodded, stood, and moved closer to the table to address the assembled dignitaries. "And thank you all for your kind consideration. Once High Lord Olber's remains, and those of his colleagues, are returned, we will arrange for a formal burial service." Her voice broke slightly, and she paused for a sip of water before continuing.

Those seated around the table waited graciously for her to resume.

She looked out over the lords of the major domains around the table, their ladies sitting behind them. There were a few she had known all her life, and others only from passing conversations, or from when she had snuck in on meetings. Marra knew who her father's friends and allies were, and had a good idea of those who weren't. This wasn't the time or place to pick sides, though. All were equal at the High Council.

Marra cleared her throat and took a deep breath to steady her nerves. "As you would have known from our discussions earlier today, I too was caught unaware of this unannounced council meeting until the first carriage showed up. An inconvenient oversight by Sir Blarik.

"I can only hope that after your days of travel, the suites are acceptable. Regardless of the reasons or the sad tidings, I'm so glad you have all made the journey. Some of you I know well, and others I've not yet had the pleasure. I'm looking forward to getting to know you all. Thank you again." She nodded and resumed her seat.

Nods all around and a soft tapping of glasses indicated their appreciation of her words.

Harrod stood. "Now, to business. The Chair recognises Sir Refin Blarik, Minister of the Interior and Trade. Please address the council, Sir Blarik."

With an impatient huff, Blarik pushed his large frame out of the plush chair and approached the table. "So sorry for any discomfort or stress my actions have caused you fine people, but it was imperative we all met to discuss the situation to the north—"

"Blarik, what situation is this?" Harrod asked.

"We're a few steps away from war with Klarget," Blarik declared.

The gathering erupted with alarm and surprise.

The Chairman let it go for a moment before restoring order with a rap of his gavel.

"War? Surely you jest in bad taste! We've heard of no such thing."

"I regret to say, it's a surprise to me also. In fact, it's serious enough that I've replaced our spymaster for the lack of warning. Ont'eba is now in charge, but that's a side issue. If we are to meet the challenge—"

"Sorry, I'm late." Froshingha burst through the doors, panting. "Point of order!" He had to speak loudly over the Interior Minister and the shocked mutterings around the table. Carrying several scrolls tucked under his arms, he quickly strode to his chair. "Point of order," he repeated louder.

The Chair stood quickly, banging his gavel again for silence. "Froshingha? This is unheard of. You're already tardy, and now you want to disrupt this meeting even further? If what the Interior Minister says is true—"

Blarik went red in the face at the accusation. "Of course it's true, man! I don't—"

"My abject apologies for being late." Froshingha dropped the scrolls on the table and wiped his brow and face with his silk kerchief. "In fact, Lord Trallko, it is precisely the reason why I make this point of order here and now," the aged advisor continued over Blarik's outburst. "I must be heard before we continue!"

With a great sigh, the Chair laid down his gavel and sat, waving for him to come forward. "The council recognises Master Druon Froshingha, Royal Advisor. I'm sure we would be pleased to hear it."

"This is preposterous!" Blarik raged. "I have every—"

"Sir Blarik, kindly desist and return to your seat. We're tired, with frayed tempers as it is. It is unusual—like everything about this meeting—and out of character, but we will hear the High Lord's advisor. As you know, he's renowned throughout all Jaranabi for his cool head and wise counsel. If he feels there's a point of order to be made, then it's his right and duty as Royal Advisor to make it as much as it is mine as Chair to accede to it." Lord Trallko stared at Blarik until the rotund individual stomped back to his seat, cursing under his breath. "Master Froshingha, if you please, continue, but please make it brief."

"Thank you. My lords and ladies, my point of order is simply that the full council has not yet convened," Froshingha stated.

The seated nobles looked around in confusion, still getting over the shock of the stunning news of war.

"What do you mean?" Lady Laskar questioned, glancing around. "We're all the nobles on the council."

Now that he had cooled and settled, Froshingha was back to his orderly self. As he spoke, he carefully folded his kerchief and slipped it back into his breast pocket. "With our recent tragic loss, and the weariness of your travels, it's understandable no one has mentioned there's still one position yet to be taken."

Others muttered quietly behind handkerchiefs. Lord Phillit leant back in his chair to whisper to Lady Phillit. "Poor man has gone mad in his grief."

Harrod tapped the gavel for order. "Froshingha, I've no doubt you're extremely good at what you do, but I'm afraid High Lord Olber is no longer with us, so his seat will remain vacant until another noble takes it."

"Finally!" Blarik jumped up. "Send the dithering fool—"

"There *is* one other noble..." Froshingha said loudly, looking pointedly at Marra.

She spat out her wine. "*Me?*"

"Lady Olber," Froshingha continued over the stunned silence of the room, "though a female, you are the next-in-line as head of House Olber. Therefore, unusual as it may be, you're also next in line to take your father's council seat. There's an obscure entry: Bylaw 73, paragraph 6: 'In the event of death, the oldest legitimate offspring is permitted to carry out the duties of their predecessor if agreed to by the High Council.' Lady Olber, I believe the last seat on the council is yours if the remainder of the High Council agrees."

Marra's face paled as she glanced around the table and at the nodding heads.

Refin knocked his chair over as he jumped up in protest. "This is preposterous! I've never heard such shite! You can't seriously be thinking this *child*—this *girl*—can take the place of an adult male?"

"While there could be an argument put forward if the next in line was a juvenile, in this case, Lady Olber is the requisite age," the advisor replied.

"I'll take the seat, then," Refin offered. "I'm a senior Minister! Pertram was my brother-in-law. I'm—"

"Refin, you're not directly related to Pertram, and if I'm correct, you aren't, in fact, noble," Froshingha said.

"What? I am a Sir—"

Lord Trallko intervened. "Refin, how can I say this politely? I believe the term is *honorary*. High Lord Olber granted it to you after he married your sister, Larina. By his generosity, he also allowed the title to stand after her tragic passing." Harrod looked to the advisor. "Do the bylaws mention anything about having *honorary* nobles on the council?"

"They do not, my Lord," Froshingha answered.

"Ah. Furthermore, is there any mention that a female cannot take the seat?"

"There is not," the scholar replied smugly. "I should also

point out, under the extenuating circumstances Sir Blarik has just told us, *especially in times of war*, it is paramount to have a full council of nobles."

"Very good, Master Froshingha." Harrod shrugged, turning back to Blarik. "Well, there you have it, Refin. Let the records show Marra is clearly entitled to the seat, and you are not. What say the Council? All those in favour of Lady Marra Olber taking a seat at the Council table?" The Chair turned to the others. Out of all the nobles gathered, only one declined to raise a hand.

"We have a majority in favour of the change." He turned to Marra. "As the oldest—and only—legitimate offspring of Lord and Lady Olber, do you, Lady Marra Olber, consent to continue the duties of your father, High Lord Olber, on this council?"

Marra went from pale-faced in shock to the red face of someone now under the scrutiny of the most powerful houses in all of Jaranabi. "I–I do so consent to take up the duties in High Lord Olber's absence."

"Preposterous!" Refin repeated, but his complaining was drowned out by the clapping and foot-stomping of the others gathered around the table. For at least a few moments, they could forget the terrible impending news.

"Due to the unusual circumstances of our newest member joining us, we shall take a short break and reconvene in thirty minutes." Lord Trallko banged the gavel.

Refin scraped his chair back as he stood and stormed out of the room under escort. Some of the nobles began softly chattering among themselves at Refin's sudden departure and stealing glances at Marra. Several women rose and approached the blushing girl to officially congratulate her.

CHAPTER

FIVE

A NEW RULER

Once the council reconvened, Blarik was called again to address the nobles. He calmly placed his wine glass down, stood, and approached the table to the designated position for supplicants. His manner now was completely opposite to the bluster and cursing a short time earlier.

Lady Marra was suspicious of the sudden change in her uncle's demeanour. *He's definitely up to something.* The ill-feeling still caused the occasional spasm in her gut.

"Lords and ladies, apologies and all that for the short notice of this meeting here and not the usual hall in Carascan. Under normal circumstances, there would have been more time, but I deemed the requirement for the impromptu summons appropriate with the imminent breach of our northern borders that will lead to all-out war."

"*You* deemed? Has that fracas with Klarget erupted again? This happens so regularly," Lord Trallko said.

"This one is different—or looks to be."

"So, you're saying it *isn't*? Make up your mind, man! What happened to the prospect of war your message purported?"

"The information from our network of agents indicates a larger buildup of troops than in previous years. Where possible, I have also increased what troops I could—"

"Did High Lord Olber grant you that authority?" Lord Phillit interrupted. "Or did you do it on your own?"

Without hesitation, Sir Blarik replied, "High Lord Olber did suggest I could if I deemed it necessary."

"With no oversight? He allowed you to command our troops?" Harrod frowned.

"He did. Yes." Blarik nodded.

"He did no such thing!" Marra spoke up, aware that all eyes suddenly turned to her. Trying to keep her voice from quavering, she turned to the Chair. "Unknown to Uncl—Sir Blarik—I overheard several conversations; one was in High Lord Olber's office several days ago, the other when I was seeing to my horse Sleena in the stables the night before Father went hunting.

"When my uncle suggested increasing the troops in the north, the High Lord absolutely refused. He wanted more precise information before he committed to anything, stating that *our* increased troop presence could be seen as a threat to Klarget. Sir Blarik is lying." She turned defiantly to her uncle. "He even went as far as to suggest my father's hunting trip could continue, as the *apparent threat* wasn't so dire. If he increased the troops to the north, he may have triggered Klarget all without High Lord Olber's approval. In fact, he disobeyed him!"

"Careful of what you accuse me of, Marra," Refin replied in his nasally voice.

"Sir Blarik, although she is your niece, you *will* address

council members by their honorific. In this case 'Lady' would be appropriate, especially on formal occasions."

"You know it's the truth, uncle," Marra continued. "It isn't as if I've accused you of attempted rape or anything, though I'm curious who scratched your face and broke your nose. We know how that goes from the many other accusations." She made a point of touching her bruised cheek as she spoke. "Isn't that right, Lady Laskar?"

"Nothing was ever proven!" Refin's face reddened with rage.

Lady Lowis Laskar, a striking woman in blue at the far end of the table, blanched at the mention of her name. Her eyes darted from Refin, then to Marra, and back to Refin. "My dear... I'm at a loss as to what to say," Lowis muttered meekly.

"I understand all too well. It's probably best to forget about it. I'm sure Gracin and her daughter agree with you." Marra looked pointedly at Lady Kindair, two seats away to her left.

"This is preposterous." Her uncle slammed his fist down on the table, making everyone jump. "If you have something to accuse me of, say it plainly."

"I just did. You blatantly disobeyed your High Lord. My father advises me on every nuance of the nation. If there was imminent war with anyone, it wasn't disclosed." Marra turned to address the Chair. "Further, if my uncle knew of this when he arrived here yesterday—before he indulged in our wine cellar—he failed in his duties to inform his superior of pertinent security information."

"That's enough!" Refin jumped up, enraged.

"Or what? Going to grope my breasts again?" she fumed. "Let's see what I can break the next time, but be careful, there are more witnesses now. Or, let me guess: you'll threaten them?"

"Guards!" Refin shouted.

"You forget my men ousted your guards after you broke into my chambers. This is *my* house, what *I* say goes." She knew this was sounding childish, but she was angry her uncle was casting her father in such a bad light, just as Froshingha suggested might happen. "It's interesting that you knew it was rockions that killed my father *before* anyone else did. What say you to that?"

"Our agents—"

"Cannot predict the future. You apparently knew it was a rockion attack when you arrived here on the morning of his disappearance."

Refin took a deep breath to control his anger. "Lady Olber is obviously distraught. It's a great shame High Lord Olber isn't here to preside over this council and guide us with his vast wisdom, or any *man*, for that matter."

"*You* contrived for his hunting party to go to the Grillon Woods. *You* planned this. Did you arrange to assassinate High Lord Olber?"

"Preposterous!"

"Enough!" The crack of a gavel hitting the sound block resonated loudly. Lord Trallko stood up in exasperation. "I'm sure I speak for all of my fellow councillors when I say that after the unexpected summons and several days on the road, none of us are in the mood to listen to family squabbles.

"Lady Olber, the passing of your father is truly a devastating blow to all of Jaranabi. I am certain the news of his death will sadden every citizen throughout the land. But you also raise some interesting points, as well as serious accusations."

"All unfounded—" Blarik spluttered.

"I was talking about the rockions." Lord Trallko shook his head with a wry grin, turning to the First Minister. "However, apart from forgetting your place, you also forget whom you are addressing. We know all too well the many, many accusations of your improprieties."

"Harrod, then you also know very well I was acquitted of all charges!" Refin argued.

"*We* are the High Council, Refin. You aren't, but I'm sure even as Minister to the Interior, you'd be aware we are privy to much of the information the rest of our citizens are not. Your acquittals have nothing to do with your supposed innocence, and have more to do with the lack of spines of our judiciary. But, enough of that. I'm simply saying you are wasting your breath trying to convince any of us you haven't assaulted dozens of women across the land. We know the truth." He looked around at the nodding heads of the women present. "Lady Olber, you have our deepest sympathies for the double trauma you have recently experienced."

"I, too, would like to know how Refin knew the manner of Pertram's passing before anyone else," Esbeth spoke up.

"I want to hear more about the broken nose. Looks painful." Lady Gracin winked as she caught Marra's eye.

"All in good time. What we need to do now, as a priority, is to determine our actions if there is, in fact, a threat to our north," the Chair stated.

Froshingha rose from his chair and waited.

With a sigh, Lord Trallko looked his way. He didn't bother standing. "You have another point of order, Master Froshingha?"

"No, my Lord." He put down the vellum roll he was reading. "But for the record, so we are all clear on the finer nuances and legalities—"

Harrod cleared his throat.

"A question then, for Sir Blarik. Are we, or are we not, at war?"

All eyes at the table turned to the First Minister.

"I said as much a moment ago! We haven't drawn swords as such, but there's a definite air of unrest and turmoil—"

"Point of order, My Lords and Ladies," Froshingha declared.

"Froshingha! I swear, man, you'll be the death of me! I just asked you if you had a point of order."

"At that time, my Lord, I did not. However, upon seeking clarification from our Minister of the Interior on the real threat of war, I now have one."

All the members of the council sighed and muttered their displeasure.

"Get on with it, man." The Chair's patience had visibly dwindled.

Froshingha collected his vellum scroll and located the passage he was after.

"In matters of civil unrest, major catastrophe or *war*—" He pointedly looked over his glasses at Refin—"the Ruler will have full and immediate discretion on all military matters."

"Duon, have you been at the whiskey again? We do not have a current ruler."

"Then, my Lord, who is in charge of our military?" the advisor asked.

"Ahem... Our First General, Sir Onwahld, is the military leader of our army."

"In peace time or minor emergencies, true." Froshingha nodded. "But that's where his authority ends."

"As Minister for the Interior and First Minister, this burden falls to me." Refin stood up, looking smugly at the Royal Advisor. "I'm the senior government official, so in the case of no ruler as such, I—"

"Yes, yes, Refin. You want the job. However, as heir to the High Lord, Lady Olber is a strong contender too."

"She's a young, inexperienced *girl*. What would *she* know about military matters?"

Fighting down her nerves, Marra calmly replied, "I believe, from what we all know of your pastimes, I know as much as you, Uncle. Your *battle* experience is limited to the bed chamber."

Her uncle glared at her. "With the intelligence *I* gather from our network and the advice from our military leaders, *I* will be in a substantial position to make decisions."

"Funny, I was going to say the same thing," Marra responded.

"It has always been so," Froshingha remarked. "Our leader follows the advice of our experienced military leaders. Despite her young age, her noble birthright and education would put her in a favourable position."

"Bah!" Refin spat. "I cannot believe anyone—even this council—would put a mere girl over a grown man!"

"A *noble* girl of high esteem," Lord Trallko stated, steel coming back to his voice. "May I remind you, Refin, you are not of noble birth. You are *not* of high esteem... But, personal feelings aside, this is a matter for a High Council vote."

"My Lords," Froshingha added, "just to be clear, while under normal circumstances an assembly of all the nobles, major and minor, would be required, but with the apparent *'imminent* threat of war', we have grounds to put it to the vote, here and now."

The Chair nodded to the Royal Advisor. "Understood. And is there any precedent of having a High Lady?"

"In ancient times, my Lord, before the lands of Harando were divided into the nations we have today, women had much greater influence in societal matters, taking many leadership roles and serving in the armed forces as officers as well as soldiers. There's a record of a female Commander in Chief, and even mention of a queen—"

"Enough." Without preamble, Lord Trallko continued. "All those in favour of Sir Refin Blarik—a commoner of ill repute—taking the seat of High Lord..."

Many eyes looked without surprise at those who raised their hands.

"Typical of Domains Charoff and Drolik to take his side," Lord Hommin muttered.

Speaking over the murmurs of disapproval, Harrod continued. "All those in favour of Lady Marra Olber taking the seat of High Lady in place of her recently deceased and beloved father, raise your hand."

Again, the earnest counting. Heads bent together to converse.

"With eight to two, and two abstaining, in favour of the incumbent. It seems we have a new ruler. Congratulations, High Lady Olber."

Master Froshingha approached the table, applauding, and waited to be recognised.

"Froshingha, your counsel, *if* you must," Harrod sighed.

"In the matter of a new ruler, there should be an official swearing-in ceremony."

Lord Trallko stood. "Excellent. We shall resume this council tomorrow morning with our scribes. We will then formally accept and acknowledge Lady Marra Olber as the new legitimate ruler of Jaranabi. This council meeting is over." He ended the session with the strike of his gavel. "I'm sure—"

"You utter cretins!" Blarik jumped up. "None of you have any idea what's going on," he shouted at the nobles.

Marra buckled over. The pangs of foreboding—troubling her all day—worsened suddenly.

"Guards!" Lord Trallko called. "Take Sir Blarik to his rooms under house arrest. We'll deal with his nonsense tomorrow."

Refin backed away from the approaching guards. "Foolishly, I tried it your way. Now it's my turn." With an evil grin, Sir Blarik motioned to Lord Drolik.

From his pocket, the thin, quiet man calmly retrieved an unusual-looking device resembling a whistle. He placed it to his lips and blew.

CHAPTER

SIX

DAWN ATTACK

It was still dark when everyone was woken by one of the night crew. Only a small lantern swinging from a hook shed a dim glow in the suddenly crowded quarters.

"Dawn comin'. We spotted a ship a few hours ago and been shadowin' it. Everyone bett'r git ready or miss the fun," the speaker said.

It hadn't taken long for *Revenge* and her sister ships, *Vengeance* and *Emancipator*, to become a sight feared across the seas to any raiders or men with ill intent. The crimson sails were more than a beacon; they were a warning.

The women aboard, fleeing abusive pasts, had all made their way to The Crags to find refuge amongst a supportive community of women escaping similar situations. Many also found a renewed purpose and eagerly signed on to join the crews of the three magnificent vessels. With vigorous fitness and weapons training, the women learned to fight with unmatched ferocity.

But the crimson sails were more than a beacon to women;

they were a warning to men, and the *Revenge* and her sister ships, *Vengeance* and *Emancipator*, had become a sight feared across the seas to any raiders or men with ill intent. Pirates were hearing of their fates...

Captain Sienna stepped onto a crate as the crew emerged. The experienced women moved off to carry out their tasks while the newlings were ushered aside and positioned around their leader.

"You've all done very well so far with adapting to life at sea. I make no apologies for pushing you hard. You'll soon see why."

Young faces glanced at the glowing horizon.

"Who can tell me what happens to pirates?" the captain asked.

"You kill their captain," Olly said after a brief hesitation.

"One hopes. And what happens to their crew?"

"They're branded," Ilya stated.

"And if they are already branded? What then?"

The young girls fell silent.

Corra turned to the first mate who had stepped lightly to her side. "Show them, Tulls,"

Tully held up a string of sad-looking tomatoes and made a quick slicing motion with her dagger. The tomatoes dropped to the deck with a splat. A couple of newlings stepped back.

"It makes a good deterrent," the captain added.

Every woman was wide awake now as the sun crested the horizon, and each with their own tasks. While they could all fight and defend themselves, the ship couldn't function without someone attending to the sails and lines. The newlings were certainly not allowed to get into the fray, but they were given jobs, one being to take the lanterns back below decks. A handful of the veteran crew would remain behind in case—unlikely as it may be—any pirate managed to get onboard.

"Sorry, you have to stay back to nurse us," Ilya said as she grabbed a couple of lanterns.

"'Tis nothin', child. We can't all 'ave too much o' the fun, n' I've had fun a'plenty." Barb was the short, stocky woman who'd paired with Dara to work the waterwing. Her close-cropped hair made her look younger, but she was the oldest crew member and almost a decade older than Sienna.

"Does the captain stay back?" Olinda asked.

"Nay, lass. She dun everythin' yous or I dun. She weren't born to bein' cap'n. She worked hard for it. For all yous know, yous could be a cap'n one day. Now, sit back there out o' the way. Watch'n'learn."

On the horizon, they could clearly see the ship in question, three masts and every sail billowing.

"Is it the pirates?" one young girl squinted into the bright light. "How'd you know?"

"'Cos they be runnin'. You saw yest'day, 'onest traders rarely run," Dara explained. She and her partner were now at their post by the waterwing device.

"Pirates be cowards. Soon as dey spots us, dey put on sail an' turn," Barb said. "Gooders don't do dat, only badders run."

"I heard they had a black flag with skulls on it."

"Dey do, but while dey be cowards, dey ain't dumb an' p'raps fly a flag of de country dey be near, to allay any suspicions like."

"An' sometimes they be tricksters, pretendin' damage. When the traders get closer, they're set upon," Dara finished.

"Shut it now. Git those lanterns stowed. Then watch'n'learn," Tully said as she passed. "Yous'll be doin' this one day."

Captain Sienna was aft speaking to Shilo at the helm before she turned to Tully.

"It's the *Tormentor*, a'right," the first mate confirmed as she walked up. "Granna Forjin's the captain."

"Shark Bait's still around?" Shilo asked.

"Not for much longer." Sienna grimly watched the ship as they closed in.

Nodding, the first mate blew the whistle, the summons for the elementalists—not that she needed to, as they were already assembled.

"Wind ain't good 'nuf. We'll need a boost," Barb explained to the newlings nearby.

"And the hydrons? Are we in shallow water?" Olinda dared not get too close to the gunwale to check.

"Deys can do plenty more. Jus' watch—"

"And learn," Olinda finished the phrase.

With all the canvas raised to maximise their speed, *Revenge* surged forward with a steady wind summoned by its air elementalists.

Corra addressed her crew after the waterwing was lowered. "Let's show them what real speed looks like."

The ship's unique design came alive as they lowered the waterwing, lifting the vessel above the waves. With the drag reduced, *Revenge* surged forward, closing the gap between itself and its target with astonishing speed. Even the most brutal pirate captains, hardened by a life of blood and plunder, knew better than to willingly face them. When they saw red sails on the horizon, they turned and fled, though in the end, resistance proved futile.

Within the hour, the *Revenge* was almost upon them,

despite the *Tormentor* manoeuvring evasively, but Sienna ordered a speed reduction.

"Why are we slowing? And what happens when we catch up?" Olinda wondered aloud, but no one answered, too engrossed in current events. She soon found out when a pre-emptive shot from a ballista grazed across their bow, slightly damaging the gunwale. Another bolt from a ballista bounced off the metal hull.

Corra signalled the aeyrons. "Not too close. We don't want to risk a broadside, not with those ports open." She then turned to the assembled hydrons. "Let's do something about that, shall we? Extra rum if you can toss some of them overboard. Go play."

The hydrons began their concentration. Soon, the water around the *Tormentor* began to become choppy. Before, they had all worked in unison to create deeper water under their keel; this time, they worked as individuals but still with a common goal. Moving their hands rapidly and randomly, they directed the rolling foaming waves to crash into the hull, splashing in through the open ports, removing any chance of getting hit again by their ballistae. The pirate ship began to sway, slowly at first, then more precariously as the mounting waves smashed into it in rapid succession.

With further attacks by the aeyrons, hitting the top sails with fierce bursts of air, the ship rocked back and forth wildly. The men on board were sent clutching for handholds, and several were sent tumbling and sliding across the heaving deck, striking masts, crates and other cargo. From the sounds of the cries of anguish and pain, it was obvious some injuries had already been inflicted.

The elementalists continued this until they started getting weary, but as it turned out, several pirates were so weakened by the onslaught of weather, they slipped and were washed over the side. Floundering briefly, they soon disappeared into the murky depths.

"Calm now, and bring us in." Captain Sienna was not only watching for any attacks from the pirates, but also targeting the captain...if she could spot him. The *Revenge* steadily closed the distance between them.

"'Ere we go, bitches," Tully called out, then turned to her captain. "They say Shark Bait's lousy with a sword. If yous see a dagger, that be what 'e'll use."

It was a mere breath of wind to close in on the pirates' ship, and they passed a few feet from its side, close enough for the *Revenge* crew to jump the gap and start laying into the unsteady men with their weapons of choice. Five of the best archers had climbed into the shrouds, ready to shoot any pirates posing the greatest threat.

With the intense training back at The Crags, most of the crew were skilled fighters, good enough to pull a killing stroke and only wound or knock out at whim—especially when their opponents were too weak and unsteady to put up a reasonable defence. It was a fact that many pirates were not good fighters, preferring to use cowardly tactics and deceit rather than risk full-on confrontations.

Despite the rumours—and the expected yearning for payback—the Red Sails crew weren't out to kill every pirate they crossed. They were prepared to, if need be, but better to let them survive and pass on the message.

With full quivers, the remaining archers climbed the shrouds to strategic positions. Their job was to protect the backs of fellow crew. They secured themselves in place by entwining a leg around the ropes; this left their hands free to reign arrows on any pirates cowardly enough to attack a woman from behind.

Shortly after the women boarded, the deck of the *Tormentor* became a scene of chaos, of men and women shouting, of people pummelling each other with fists or batons, of clashing swords, men sprawling across the deck or running from the pursuing women.

It wasn't all bloody work. The young and less experienced pirates were subdued quickly, taken out of the fray, bound, and kept under watch, but those in slightly better condition put up more of a fight—as the desperate often do.

Corra made her way towards the stern, where she at last saw Granna lurking in the shadows. He shouted orders, and several pirates came at her. Two were taken out almost immediately by the archers, leaving Sienna with just the one.

It was clear from his first amateurish thrust that he either had minimal experience or doubted a woman could fight. When he lunged, she sidestepped and clubbed him on the back of the head. He dropped to the deck, unmoving.

The pirate captain, Granna 'Shark Bait' Forjin, however, was a different story. He'd known his fate the moment he saw the Red Sails bearing down on him, and he backed away at her approach, a cutlass in one hand and a dagger in the other.

Sienna was captain of the *Revenge* for many reasons, the main ones being her seafaring skills, her leadership, and her ability with swords. One of her weapons was a normal short-sword with a keen edge; the other was one of the finest-looking cutlasses to be found across the many seas. Corra drew her shorter blade and moved in, Tully's warning in mind.

Granna fought desperately from the beginning, hacking and slashing with his cutlass, swearing and cursing at his opponent's relentless pursuit. After one wild swing, he thrust with his dagger, only to be blocked and disarmed. The dagger skittled across the deck, stopping against a coil of rope.

The mediocre swordplay by Granna was no match to Sienna's skills. She knew her task well, and if she showed any leniency, the survivors could spread rumours that the Red Sail bitches had gone soft, thereby emboldening pirates to continue their bloodletting, raping, and pillaging.

Granna moved back, each step bringing him closer to the side of the ship. He dived to the left, only to be sent scurrying when forced back by a blast of wind from one of the aeyrons.

"I yield. Mercy!" he pleaded in desperation, hard up against the gunwale.

"You know that's not going to happen. How many of your victims begged for the same thing?" Using her off-hand, Corra swept her shortsword in the *swinging boom* manoeuvre. It was a feint, but still would have taken his head off if he hadn't ducked. Anticipating his attempt to dodge, she lowered her cutlass to pierce his guts. He screamed and sprawled to the deck.

Sienna showed no reprieve. She couldn't afford to. Detesting torture, she slashed his throat immediately to end his agonised screaming. Breathing heavily, she looked around to see how her crew was faring while she wiped her blades on his tunic.

"Cap'n!" a voice towards the stern called out.

Sensing bad news, Corra moved aft where several of the crew gathered around a prone figure. When she was a couple of strides away, she recognised Jinan, one of the newer members.

The woman lay unmoving in a slowly spreading pool of blood that glistened on the deck. Already, Lida, one of the spirons, had begun tending to the bloody injury. She looked up at her captain, giving her a grim look.

Corra took a deep breath and kneeled beside them. She reached for Jinan's hand.

"Hey there, Jin," she said softly. "I see you took out two savages all by yourself."

Jinan took a few moments to answer. She opened her eyes and saw her commander beside her. "We gave 'em hell, didn't we, Cap'n?"

"We certainly did." Corra nodded. "*You* did."

Jinan's hand felt cold and clammy. Her chest rose marginally, indicating shallow breathing. She remained silent for a while.

"I don't reckon...I'll be doin' much fightin'...again," she said eventually.

Corra shook her head. "Our best healers are here to get you fixed. Get through this fight first. You'll be doing plenty soon enough."

"Cap'n. I love ya...We *all* love ya, but ya full of shite. I seen enough stabbin's...to know I ain't comin' back fr—"

Jinan didn't finish her sentence. Her chest stopped rising.

With tears streaking her face, the healer felt for a pulse before laying the woman's hand across her breast.

Corra placed the other hand on top but remained by her side. Silent.

Tully gently tapped her shoulder. "Cap'n, we'll look after 'er," she said softly.

Captain Sienna wiped her face and nodded.

The first mate helped her to her feet. "Losin' one ain't ever easy."

"I sometimes wonder if it's worth it..."

"It's a 'efty price we pay, clearin' the seas of this trash. But Cap'n, believe me when I says not one of us'll stop, even knowin' the risks."

Corra looked around, realising the bulk of her crew were standing, watching, waiting. Some were bleeding and clutching their wounds. This was not the time to shirk her duties, regardless of the kick in the gut she felt when she lost any crew. She took a deep breath.

"Tulls, let's get this done," she said in a steely voice.

"You 'eard the Cap'n." Tully's voice relayed the captain's orders.

Despite their injuries, the crew jumped to obey. Those too wounded were directed back to the *Revenge*, to await healing.

Corra saw the newlings huddled on the *Revenge*. She waved for them to cross over.

They carefully walked the gangplanks and jumped down to the deck, slippery with water mingled with blood. It was a mess; ropes were strewn everywhere, barrels had rolled and smashed, spilled contents mixed with the water and sloshed against the bodies scattered around the deck. One group of women had the gruesome task of throwing the dead overboard. A glance over the side showed a red foaming disturbance.

"Sharks," Dara informed them. "Such a fittin' end for 'im."

"So soon?" Olinda asked.

"We're close ta the reef." Dara pointed to the rough water.

"Those critters can smell blood for miles, and can move damned fast too," one of the other women said, looking over the edge.

The newlings, uncertain, moved to where their captain stood next to the body of Jinan.

She turned to address the newlings now gathering around her, noting some looked pale from the violence and bloodshed.

"I want you all to look closely. We're in a ruthless and bloody business. There's no shame in feeling sick or disgusted with what just happened, and what will happen next. This is what we do. If you're going to be part of the Red Sails crew, you'll learn to do this, too. I threw up on my first trip. I was about your age, but coming from a violent background, I learned this was a possible way to end it all. It's slow, and sometimes we too get injured, which is why we push you hard with your training.

"This is a harsh reality. We rarely lose anyone...but it does happen." Corra looked down at her fallen crewmember. "It's a difficult sight, but I want you to remember. We can die far too easily!"

Captain Sienna watched the younger girls for a few moments. She didn't regret for one second the tears, the looks of shock and horror she saw on their faces. *If it saves a life, it's worth it.*

"You heard Tulls earlier; it's the price we pay to make the seas safer. If you find this isn't for you, we've many other equally important tasks back in The Crags. As a community—as well as on the ships—we all do our part." Corra let it sink in for a minute, watching their expectant, upturned faces. "Questions?"

At first, they were reluctant to speak.

"Our elementalists are amazing. Could we not have capsized the ship to avoid the fighting?" Olinda asked.

"Good. Yes, we could have, and we've done so in the past, but there's the cargo to consider—which is worth a lot—and sometimes they have slaves or hostages. Several years ago, the *Emancipator* did just that. They took on some heavy fire from the ship they were pursuing. Our mancers pushed it over on its side. Luckily, it was shallow water. Half the complement survived, but six slaves drowned. These were innocents—" Corra saw the first mate approaching, so she finished by saying, "Our mission is not only to fight off and deter sea raiders of any sort, but—where possible—save lives and retrieve the stolen property."

"What'll happen to..." Ilya was staring at the body.

"We'll sail away from here, away from the other dead,

away from the reef and sharks to deeper waters. Then we'll do a burial at sea."

Tully nodded. "All set, Cap'n."

"Move forward and see how first-timers are treated."

THE PIRATES, now tied and sullen at being defeated by women, were forced to kneel in the blood of their comrades mixed water. Unarmed and sporting injuries of various degrees of severity, they all knew the outcome of this encounter. The first-timers would be branded, and those already bearing a brand faced castration.

"Witches, the lotta ya," one bleeding pirate spat. He had a brand discernible on his left cheek despite his many tattoos.

"Too late for flattery." Tully pushed him to the deck with her boot. "Okay, bitches. Ya know the drill, branding fo'ward, the others aft."

Some men were dragged as they were either too injured or simply refused to move; a few retaliated and fought the women, but were quickly smacked down with cudgels or the hilts of swords and then dragged. A few meekly stumbled after their comrades.

GATHERED AT THE BOW, a fire in a cauldron fuelled by anything dry enough to burn, was heating the branding iron. All the sailors without markings were huddled together; most were young, but a couple were older, fallen on hard times. In all encounters, the first-timers were told to seek employment elsewhere and give up the pirating trade.

Some pleaded. Some cried. All looked demoralised.

"Listen up, ya sorry lot." Tully smacked a few young pirates moaning about how unfairly they were being treated. "I'm gonna assume yer all too slow-witted to know or believe what we do to scum o'the sea, so, I'm gonna tell ya."

As the pirates started jabbering, a couple of the crew came in and knocked heads until there was silence.

"When we capture pirates, four things 'appen; yer cap'n dies, first-timers get branded, the rest castrated—no exceptions—then we take ya to the nearest port and 'and ya to the authorities."

The pirates again set up a clamour and were once again knocked about until they were silent.

"You bitches enjoy this!" one spat, blood flying in droplets from his mouth.

"Ya bet. Prolly some of us more'n' others, but we'd not be here if men were decent folk and kept their dicks in their pantaloons. But they ain't. What ya sees 'ere is the result of yar raidin', and as much because of the way men treat womenfolk. Every one of us, somewhere, sometime, 'as been mistreated, most sufferin' abuse, and some raped. We definitely didn' enjoy that. This 'ere brandin' will 'urt, now'ere near as much as the pain yous done to women."

Sienna strode up. Most of the pirates had seen how she'd dealt with their captain. The ruckus stopped immediately. "For whatever reason, you chose to be pirates. And those choices have consequences. Man up and face them. The branding is your wake-up call. Time to change your ways. Get another job, or the next time we cross you, we'll cut off your balls and feed them to the sharks, like the ones that just took your cap'n and fellow crew."

As she spoke, there was screaming heard aft. If the pirates were sullen before, they physically cowered now, shifting uncomfortably in their sodden clothes.

"Tulls, get this done, then we set up the tow to Savarik." As she was about to go aft, she spotted a young boy among the pirates. "Why are you in this mess, lad?"

"Me da put us 'ere to pay a det to the cap'n."

"A debt?" Sienna swore. "Where's your da?"

"He ony got one arm." The boy shrugged, looking sullen and lost.

"What's your name?"

"Jag."

"We'll let Jag go when we get to port, but he should watch. That'll be his lesson," Sienna said to Tully as she tussled Jag's unruly hair. She looked down at him, seeing his dark eyes and a face that hadn't smiled for far too long. "Captain's dead. No more debt. Once we get back to port, you're free to go. You know what'll happen next time." She turned and strode aft.

The branding was quick and simple. The first pirate was hauled forward, and the hot iron was brought to his left cheek.

"Quit yer squirmin' or else, I'll prolly poke your eye out."

The young man remained motionless, but his head was still held firmly because he would flinch instinctively at the burning of his flesh. There was no scream, only a deep groan and gritted teeth. Once released, he crawled to the side, and the next first-timer was brought forward, whimpering. This continued, and the newlings watched, white-faced, until the last man was marked.

Olinda was trying not to stare, but she had difficulty in making out what the actual brand was. "Is that a...three...on its side? Or are they..."

"Tits? Ya. Nice 'n' simple." The woman chuckled. "No man's goin' ta burn a pair o'boobs on 'is face."

Once the branding was done, the newlings were ushered aft to see the remaining castrations to drive the message home. It was as gruesome and bloody as anything they'd seen before.

One at a time, the captives, now prone and weirdly

motionless and silent, had their pantaloons pulled down to their ankles. A woman was kneeling by a captive's head. Opposite her, another pulled down his pantaloons, and another, without preamble, reached in and sliced his ball sack with a razor-sharp blade. Her dexterity was uncanny. In a few moments, she tossed the excised sack and testicles over the side, and the team moved on to the next pirate.

"Next time I see ya out here I'll cut off ya sausage and have it fer me breakfast," the woman called back.

The young girls could barely speak at the bloody mess.

"That's Minka. She were a fishmonger's wife...until she diced 'im up. She be an expert with a blade an' takes pride in her work, even on this scum. And she can fillet a fish in the dark, or shuck an oyster quicker you can blink."

"Why are the others so still?" Olinda asked eventually.

"Spirons quiet them. Makes it much easier when they're not kickin', fussin', and cryin'. But tis on'y 'alf the fun."

Olly wasn't sure if she was joking. "We heard the screaming before."

"Ya. Some bastards are 'ard to spirit. 'Ad to use the cudgel on the stubborn bastard." She looked to an unconscious form against a crate.

"We aren't half as cruel or ruthless as men." Sienna came over to them. "Most of us aren't man-haters, but we deal harshly with those that treat us poorly. We even heal them to reduce the chance of infection."

"Treat 'em betta than they treat us womenfolk."

"Proving we're not like them. We're better," their captain explained. "This is partly revenge, no doubt in that, but it's one proven method to quell the violence. In the years we've been at sea, not one castrated man has been found out here again."

"And it serves as warnin' t'others," Tully finished.

"What happens next?" Olly wondered.

"We search the ship thoroughly for stolen goods and slaves, or prisoners. Then we secure this scum and take them to the nearest port authorities to be dealt with," Corra answered. "Some of them may be strung up as an example, but many will be imprisoned and given hard labour."

"I thought pirates were hung?" Ilya asked.

"Dependin' on whe'er the port were directly affected by this lot or not—bein' rendered a eunuch might jus' stave off the gallows."

CHAPTER
SEVEN

BETRAYAL

Marra winced at the unexpected pain in her ears, though nothing could be heard from the strange whistle. Moments later, the balcony doors burst open, and three robed men entered the council chamber. Outside, the clouds that had been gathering all afternoon swirled and darkened, threatening to become a massive storm. Thunder rolled distantly.

Some of the nobles jumped from their chairs in shock at the sudden intrusion. The pair of guards about to arrest Blarik angled to confront the imminent threat to the nobles.

"What's this now?" Harrod spluttered in disbelief, his eyes darting from the grinning Minister of the Interior to the trio of elementalists.

Marra slumped in her chair, sullen and hunched over, fighting back the nausea that suddenly rose like a black tide.

Blarik spoke loudly over the tumult. "This farce is coming to an end. I'd like you to meet my mancers."

Before the guards could move more than a few paces, his mancers, a mixture of earth and fire elementalists, from their coloured robes, were already preparing to defend their leader. The guards were wrenched off the floor to smash into the ceiling. Their bodies dropped unmoving to the carpeted floor.

Outside came the sound of many horses and the ring of steel against steel.

Blarik looked around with a smug face. "With an eight-to-two vote—you abstainers need to find your backbone," he sneered. "It seems many of you other nobles haven't learnt your lessons." He turned to Master Froshingha. "You, sir, are no doubt loyal to the core to the Olber House. You also have a brain in your head and if you had access to an array of agents and elementalists like I do, you could be my equal. We can't have that." He turned to his elementalists. "Groca. End him. Now."

With a hand gesture by the lead mancer, the Royal Advisor rose off the floor and was hurled into the wall. There was a snapping sound as his neck twisted sharply.

Gasps, cries, and moans of disbelief echoed around the large room.

The floor and walls began shaking with another ground tremor. The ballroom erupted with yells and screams as the nobles panicked. Doubled over in pain, Marra stumbled around the table to the body of her advisor, but clearly his neck was broken.

"Will you be still!" Blarik yelled at the cowering nobles. "This comes down to you dismal lot. How easy it seems for you all to forget who really pulls the strings around here. I don't need to be noble-born to be in charge; I just need to do what you are all unprepared to do." He surveyed the horrified group in front of him. "You want to make rules, yet you can't stomach seeing a corpse or two. Is this what we've become? How pathetic.

"There *will* be war. Someone needs to put a stop to Klarget hounding our borders.. Pertram wouldn't listen, so now he's out of the way, and things will change. To aid in the war effort, your Domain taxes will increase by fifteen percent, and I'll expect a third of your guards to be reassigned to help fight for our nation. You have two weeks to comply, otherwise, my elementalists will be paying a visit. There are plenty more where they came from."

The head mancer cleared his throat and tugged at his master's coat.

"Ah, yes, Groca." Blarik slapped his hand away. "This localised ground shake and sudden storm confirms my suspicions. There's another elementalist around here. Who is it? He can be of great benefit to all of Jaranabi. Or he can die."

The white-faced councillors stared at him, confusion etched on their faces.

"Tell me now! He can't hide forever, and if my men have to search every tent and carriage to find him, we will..."

"N-none of us has a mancer here," Lord Trallko stated, still shaken at the brutal death of the advisor. His friend. "You know it's forbid—"

"*Pah!* to your pathetic rules. I'll ask one more time: where is this terron?" As he said this, two more House Olber guards rushed through the double doors to the hall to investigate the noise and screams.

No sooner had they entered than several of Lord Drolik's men raced in behind them. The house guards turned. With weapons drawn, they didn't hesitate to defend the council members, but being outnumbered, the sword fight was quick and bloody.

Some of the blood spray reached Marra, spattering across her hair and shoulders. She recognised the face of one of her guards as he dropped to the floor and died in front of her. His sword clattered to the floor a couple of feet away. Feebly, she reached for it.

I should have sent them all away!

Moving back from the melee, Blarik continued to address the nobles. "This will not go well for any of you. When I find out who is hiding this rogue elementalist, I will confiscate your holdings and put you out on the street! I'm sure to find some use for your brats, too, if they are suitable for my needs." He glared at them for another moment before addressing the mancers. "Grab her." Blarik pointed to Marra kneeling by the bodies of the soldier and the head advisor. "Bind her tightly. She's coming with us. I believe I have an even better use for her. One that will be of great benefit." Blarik stormed out, not waiting for their response.

The mage behind the leader stepped forward promptly. With a chant and a hand-twisting gesture, Marra found herself constricted of movement; bound but without rope, the sword ripped from her hand. He loomed over her, checking she was unable to move, a manic gleam in his eye as though he were looking through her.

Unseen forces lifted her off the floor. The nobles gasped as she was then directed towards the balcony.

"Get yer filthy heads down," Groca barked at them as he passed, making his way outside.

A few of the nobles wept, some lowered their gaze. Ladies Gracin and Hommin continued to stare defiantly, but each was doubled over by a punch to the stomach from the head mage's underlings.

Out in the cooler night air, Marra floated over the railings to the courtyard and from there toward the back of a wagon. Evidently, Blarik's men had quietly taken control of the grounds over dinner and the council meeting. The few guards of House Olber who'd remained behind were on their knees against a wall, Blarik's men standing over them. She saw more House Drolik and Charoff soldiers around the yard, too. *Damn traitors.*

She then recalled the two votes in favour of Blarik's bid for High Lord.

Trinol was nowhere to be seen, and Marra was relieved he had taken her advice and left with his other men. If they had stayed, these mancers would have captured them too.

She saw Groca emerge from the house and head towards her as she was dumped unceremoniously into the wagon.

"Tie this one up, secure, mind. She feels...slippery." Groca cast his crazy eyes over her as she was lifted into the back. "Make sure it's tight," he ordered the young guard. "There's something suspicious about her. I'll come back and check, and if I'm not satisfied, I'll chew your fingers off one joint at a time."

"Y-yes yes, m'l ord." The guard cowered, staring at his feet.

"Pah. I'm not a *lord.*" The mancer smacked the guard across the side of his head. "Do I look noble to you?"

"No, my..." The young guard shook his head vehemently. With shaking hands, they proceeded to wrap a length of rope around her body and her arms, then her ankles. The harsh cord abraded her skin, making her grimace.

When she saw the mancer's sly grin at her pain, she forced herself to push through it, even managing a smile. "All you oh-so-powerful mancers, scared of a girl. How brave and manly you must think you are."

"Pah!" he spat. "If only you knew the power I wield."

"I'm not convinced," Marra smirked. "All I'm hearing is a madman gloating, vainly trying to impress. You're even scared of a fat old drunk."

"I'll show *you* fear." A dark look replaced the smile. His

hand rose, and it looked like he was about to chant, but then one of his colleagues called for him.

"Perhaps another time." He whirled around and stomped away.

"Maybe after you find your balls," she muttered to his back.

Finished with the task, the young guard was about to leave her.

"At least he didn't bite off your fingers."

Marra tried to sound meek and humble to take any advantage she could get, and she said: "Could you at least have the courtesy to sit a young girl up?"

He wasn't much older than her, but after a slight hesitation, he grabbed her shoulders and turned her so she was facing the rear.

"Thank you." She tried to ignore the rope as it cut into her skin.

The guard nodded shyly, then jumped off the wagon. "You're very brave," he mumbled and left before she replied.

"Not brave enough, it would seem," she muttered to herself. "Just angry and stupid." *Very stupid.*

To the side of the courtyard, she saw the mancers climb into another wagon with heavy metal bars, similar to the ones she'd seen prisoners in. She'd heard these elementalists were insane, and judging from what she had seen, these were at least heading that way. The stronger they were, the crazier they became, they said, had something to do with controlling the elements through mere flesh and blood: it just wasn't supposed to happen.

She'd heard rumours of female elementalists—down at The Crags—, but she'd never seen one. These women— witches—were rare and could work through the water and air elements, whereas men used earth and fire. The fact that some of these male elementalist could control air—even a bit—was unusual. The story went on that men were far stronger elementalists despite the drawback of inevitable insanity, simply because of the sheer power they controlled and the massive damage they could inflict. A powerful elementalist could turn the outcome of a war if he didn't lose his mind first.

And Blarik had at least three for himself...and plenty more now the Drolik and Charoff Domains had joined him. She guessed several other men not dressed as guards were mancers from the traitorous nobles who had aligned themselves with him. She put their names to the back of her mind for later.

One of many stray thoughts entering her mind lingered. *The craziest mancers were always male.* Perhaps this was why some men were so ill-tempered, that even with minimal talent, they all had some unnatural connection to the elements and were therefore more prone to acts of violence and madness.

Marra didn't really believe that nonsense. All people could be violent, given the right prompting or stimulus. Had no one seen a female cat or dog defend their young? She'd even seen a sheep confront a wolf in an attempt—admittedly futile—to defend her lamb.

Had she, a mere slip of a girl, not raked her nails down her uncle's face and broken his nose? These thoughts drifted through her hazed mind. She noticed the sound of thunder had diminished, the tremor in the ground had dissipated, and wondered if this meant the rogue mancer had been caught. It also dawned on her that Refin's nose had been in far better shape than it should be. One of his mancers must be a healer, able to channel spirit.

Just before the wagons pulled out, her uncle came past with a rotund woman and another burly guard.

"Dose her," he ordered. "Make it strong. She deserves it."

"But she's already bound—"

"Do it!" he bellowed. He slapped the woman and stormed

off to deal with his mancers, who seemed to be causing a ruckus inside their cage.

The guard cruelly pinched Marra's jaw, forcing it open, and the woman, tears down her face from the beating, poured some vile concoction down her throat. Marra spat it out and got a stinging slap from the woman.

"You like giving it as well as receiving it, apparently," Marra vented.

Several more beatings were required before a sufficient amount of the foul brew took effect.

As the world around her grew foggy, she heard, more than saw, Duyma and Sleena, along with the other horses, being led out of the stables and tethered to other wagons.

At least they won't be left and forgotten.

There was a jolt, then her wagon moved off over the cobblestones. By the time it went through the main gate, her head had dropped.

Marra awoke to soft music and the sound of trickling water overlaying indistinct chatter. When she opened her eyes, everything was hazy, and her head had a dull ache. Then the nausea hit her, and she barely had time to roll over and vomit on the tiles. *Marble?* As if from a long way away came the sound of rapidly approaching footsteps.

She was in a bed. It was very comfortable, as good a quality as those back home. Once her eyes focused, she saw the room she was in was a reasonable size, though sparsely furnished.

So, whose bedroom is this? Where am I?

The owner of the scurrying, sandalled footsteps came into view. A woman about twice her age knelt with several cloths and a bowl of water to wipe up the bile on the floor.

"Oh. Sorry. I'll do that," Marra croaked, reaching forward.

"Not at all, m'lady. If the lord heard or saw you gettin' sullied over menial duties, he'd have my tongue."

"Where am I? Who is this lord?"

"High Lord Blarik, m'lady. This is his Domain, and you're in his harem."

"High Lord? Harem?" She went cold, despite the warmth. "Not bloody likely. I'm not going to be his concubine!"

"Oh, m'lady, no." The woman tittered. "'Tis nothin' like that, I can assure you."

"Then why have me here at all?" Marra sat up to take in the place fully. "This is some mistake."

"Be gone, Zelni. We will take it from here."

Marra looked up at the owner of the new voice. Three young women—the source of the chatter—now filled her doorway.

"Yes, of course, M'Lady Shayr." Zelni bobbed her head, grabbed her bowl and cloths, and backed away quickly. The girls moved in and to the side to allow Zelni to depart, the soft thud of her footsteps on rugs alternating with the click-clack of her shoes on marble tiles and back.

Sounds like the other room is larger.

"I see you're alive. It looked pretty unclear whether you'd make it when you arrived earlier this morning. We were wondering whether we'd have to call in the grave diggers. I'm Shayr, and this is Leesa. And that's Florin," she added as an afterthought.

"Marra," she introduced herself, looking at them. She had rarely seen such elegance and beauty before. While the garments they wore were similar in make, each was slightly different in colour and pattern. All were lacey, see-through, and looked to be of the finest Jabanari quality. They clung to accentuate every curve.

Surely, only a man would come up with this?

These women were about her height, but Shayr was a tad taller with brown hair and eyes, and a light tan to her perfect skin. Now that her mind was clearer, Marra did notice a difference in Shayr's nightgown compared to the others: as if sheer wasn't enough, Shayr's had a much lower cut, revealing a lot more of her ample cleavage.

She definitely loves to flaunt it. Marra looked down at her own attire in surprise. It was similar to that of the other girls, and just as see-through. She had to admit, it felt like being enveloped by a cool spring evening.

"You looked like death warmed up on your arrival," Shayr continued. "We had to wash you. Your clothes were covered in blood, but it was not yours, it seems." She sounded disappointed.

"And a healer came in to make certain you were not injured in any way." Florin was looking at the bruising on Marra's cheek.

"Oh, but the healer only saw to you after she saw to Lord High Blarik. He was injured in some melee at the council." Leesa looked surprised at Marra's deep laugh.

"Utter crap. I did that when he tried to...when he was drunk." She used her elbows to crawl back into a sitting position. "Refin is not a fighter, by any measure, if I can break his fat nose."

"You should not be so forward in using his name," Leesa admonished. "It's not right."

"He's a drunk, a lecherous bully, and my uncle. I'll call him what I like."

The three girls looked shocked at her outburst.

"You're his *niece*?" Shayr asked. "That explains it!"

"Explains what?" Marra asked.

"Um… Explains why you talk about him that way, because he's family and you know him."

Seems I don't really know him at all. Marra shrugged, looking glum, the trauma of the last couple of nights returning: *Froshingha dead, her guards killed, her assault, and now her imprisonment.* "Was there anything else you heard about last night?"

"I overheard some of the guards talking…saying High Lord Blarik had to deal harshly with the council and that House Olber was no…more." Florin seemed to be slow to realise who she was talking to.

"What?" Marra cried out.

"With High Lord Olber dead and no one to take his place, the Council chose Blarik as the new High Lord," Florin continued.

"They did no such thing!" Marra fumed. "Even our councillors aren't *that* stupid."

The three women backed away from her as she sat up abruptly.

Marra's head spun, and she paused until the surroundings became stationary. "*I* was next in line for the high seat. Blarik threatened them, usurped the High Seat, and now he's imprisoned me here for what? To be another conquest for his depraved debauchery? Unlike some, I will not be so compliant." Marra attempted to stand up, but promptly fell back onto the bed.

Shayr snorted, barely trying to hide it.

Bitch. "I need to get out of here." Marra tried to stand again and had to reach for the bedhead before she lost her balance. When the floor stabilised, she walked slowly through her door and into the larger room. The three girls moved back, out of her way.

As she had expected, it was a larger area of white tiles scattered with rugs and furnished with plush lounges of various shapes and sizes. Near the fountain in the centre of the room was a glass-topped table laden with fresh fruit, pastries, and slices of cheese. One wall had double doors, with large tapestries hanging on each side; another had billowing curtains.

After a brief pause to take in the lavish surroundings, Marra made her way towards the curtains, noting how cool the tiled floor was under her bare feet, and finding floor-to-ceiling glass doors, opened to allow the breeze. Beyond a paved terrace was an expansive, well-maintained garden. She inhaled deeply the scent of the roses and daphne.

"Escaping won't be that easy unless you can fly," Shayr said, shaking her head. The girls had followed and now stood behind her. "We might be on the ground floor, but the garden walls are high and there's no exit."

Marra turned and, having regained her confidence in walking, trudged across the large room to the double entrance doors. They were locked. "Shit!"

"Why would you even want to leave?" Florin grabbed for a handful of grapes as she followed and popped one into her mouth.

"Are you deaf?" Marra turned to glare at her. "Because I'm a prisoner and my uncle has kidnapped me. I have my own house to take care of."

"I'm...sorry to hear that." The young girl stepped back, looking contrite at the outburst. "We are well cared for here. As far as being a prisoner goes, it could be far worse."

"Far worse than being a whore for a fat, drunk and his cutthroats?"

Shayr and Leesa went red with anger.

"How dare you. We are not *whores*!" Shayr snapped. Her nostrils flared when angry.

"Oh, so you can say no to who fucks you and when?" Marra retorted.

"I've had enough of this deranged brat." Shayr turned and stormed off. "We'll need an animal trainer to beat some sense into her before she's of use to anyone. I'll not be training her."

"I'll take that as a 'no'." Marra hated this place already and had abused the first people to show her the slightest hint of friendship. She swore under her breath and plonked herself on the nearest lounge, grateful the cool breeze still reached her. Her head still ached, so she brought her hands up and massaged her temples.

"What is this training Shayr is on about?" she asked eventually, seeing Florin was still lingering.

"I shouldn't spread gossip." Florin paused ever so briefly. "Grape?" She held out some grapes for Marra, who accepted and nibbled them. Smiling, Florin continued, "But if truth be told, there are great plans for you. I hear you're now betrothed to a very important man and must be taught the wiles of men so as to please him."

"Betrothed? I'm not marrying anyone! And what great man? There are none left in all Jaranabi." *Surely, they don't expect me to marry my own uncle!*

"An important foreigner, from what I hear."

"If he's so great, let him have Shayr—"

"He was going to, but since you arrived, the High Lord changed it."

"Overnight? Why so quickly?"

"I cannot say, Marra." Florin looked lost, now that all the gossip had been told. "This foreigner is arriving in a few weeks. Perhaps I'll overhear more later."

Pillow talk, more like it. "Thank you...Florin, is it? I—I did not mean what I said before, or to snap. I was angry and confused." *Still am.* Marra took the time to look at her properly.

The young girl was gorgeous. Maybe a year younger, about seventeen, and shorter, with shining green eyes, fair hair, and a sprinkling of freckles across her slightly upturned nose.

"You mean when you called us whores?" Florin put a shy smile on her face at the scrutiny. "I know I'm not the smartest girl here, but you are right. It is sort of what we are. Some of the others have airs—hoping for a life out of their reach. For me, this is what it is. What I do know is, I'm far better off in here than out there. If my body is the only skill I have, then I will use it for as long as I can. But it's also a school, and they teach us new things—other than whoring—every day."

Marra looked at the girl for a moment, thinking she had mistaken her youthful appearance. "Who said you weren't smart? If we have a place in the world, knowing it is half the battle. I've only been here a very short time, but your wisdom might be greater than many of those already here, from what I've seen. Far more than some of the other nobles I've met."

Florin blushed at the compliment. "I should go back to the lessons. This one is history...but we can chat more later if you like?"

"Yes. Of course."

Florin smiled and darted off.

It's not like I'm going anywhere soon. Marra rested more and ate sparingly from the sumptuous array of food on the table, but her mind was in turmoil. Kidnapped by her uncle and now apparently destined to marry a complete stranger.

Perhaps my uncle is securing treaties with bordering countries to keep the peace? She wondered. *If he has a war to the north, he doesn't need threats on other flanks. Unless I'm to marry some noble from Klarget?*

Going back to one of Froshingha's lessons, Klarget's ruler was Logar Glerin. He had a son—an heir—but...Logar the Second was twelve. *Far too young.* Dran'ali was a desert land of nomadic tribes. She shuddered at the thought of being dragged around and living in a tent with their brutal ruler, Urgad Jorakif.

Overwhelmed by the sudden turn of events, Marra teared up for her loss; the loss of her life and her house, losing her friends and her family. She was not as close to her father as she should have been, but since her mother passed in a difficult labour—and losing the baby, a son—he was a changed man. Not neglectful or anything, just...different. They grew apart; she kept to herself, read, and rode Sleena more often. Pertram —High Lord Olber—buried himself in running the country or hunting.

And I haven't even mourned for him yet.

EIGHT

THE HOUSE OF SECRETS

Marra woke. Disoriented by her new surroundings, it took her a few moments for the recent events to return.

It was early. She grabbed some grapes from a silver bowl and went to the garden. There was a clear sky above, and it promised to be a warm day. Walking to the far end of the garden, she turned to study the mansion and its roofline, wondering if she could work out from what she knew how to get to the other parts of the large house.

Their dormitory, dining hall and baths were all situated in the west wing, which was one floor, but the other sections were multi-level. Then there was the meal hall. She rarely saw the cooks, but there must be access to the kitchens. *And from there...who knew?*

This garden provided free access to the outside. The only other way out was when some of the other senior girls were escorted to meet a client or carry out duties for the seneschal. Not likely something they would be allowing her to do any time soon.

Her contemplation was interrupted when she heard heavy breathing from behind a hedge of camellias. She ventured nearer to investigate. Marra was surprised to see Florin lying on the ground, panting, seemingly in pain.

"What *are* you doing?" she asked, stepping around the foliage. Then her thoughts grew darker. "Did someone hurt you? Are you injured?"

Florin squinted in the morning sun, her grimace turning into a smile. "Morning. It's called *exercise,* to keep fit and strong. Haven't you ever seen soldiers and guards doing it?"

Marra breathed in relief. She was beginning to like the young girl, though she did some strange things. "Well, of course, but why you? Here and now?"

"The grass is soft, it's quiet here; later it will be too hot. And, I'm doing it so I don't get soft and flabby, like you."

Marra looked down at herself, suddenly self-conscious. "I am not!"

"No, you're fine." The young girl giggled. "But what do we do all day? Sit around, study, eat, and gossip. Pretty soon, that tummy won't be flat, and you'll lose the energy to do anything. And if there's one thing I've heard about whoring, we need lots of energy. And flexibility. Men love energetic and flexible women."

"And you are so well-versed in that aspect?" Marra sat down on the soft lawn.

"Be nice." Florin pouted. "I could say the same for you."

"Sorry." Marra offered some grapes. "You know I hate what this place is."

"A whorehouse." Florin nodded and continued with her sit-ups.

Marra watched for a while. "Wouldn't it be easier without the nightie?"

"You trying...to get...me naked?" the young girl asked during each sit-up.

Marra choked on her fruit, laughing. "Sorry to disappoint. Not at all, it just looks awkward."

"Yes, but the lawn is very itchy. And the grass blades get into areas grass shouldn't ever go." Florin rolled over to stretch and lowered her voice. "You should do it too. If you're going to escape from here, you'll need to be fit and strong. Sure, we don't know how long it'll be, but you should start. The sooner the better. I'll show you. We can push each other to do more."

Marra swallowed the last grape. "Why not?" And lay down beside her.

Florin showed her the way she had been taught to position herself.

"Hands can go on your thighs at first. When it gets easier, move them to your chest or stretch them above your head for more of a challenge. Bend your knees...so. Try not to lift your feet when you rise."

After a few minutes getting tangled in her light gown, Marra got up, frustrated. "I'll be back in a minute." When she returned, she had a wide, rolled rug.

She shook it out and laid it flat, nodding with satisfaction.

"Now there was no chance of the grass getting where it's not wanted." Marra stripped down to her smalls, as did Florin. The exercises were much easier without the tangles, and their clothes weren't wrinkled or sweaty afterwards.

As the days progressed, Marra got into a routine, exercising before breakfast—Florin introduced her to meditating too— sitting in on a few lessons ranging from geography, history, and the subtle differences of each country. She already knew much of what was being taught—these classes were geared for the commoners off the street without a formal education, but there were the occasional snippets she had either simply forgotten, or Froshingha hadn't included in her lessons. There was nothing about the ancient histories her father had mentioned.

During class, she counted about twenty women, most of whom she hadn't met previously, ranging from her age to the mid-thirties—the age her mother was when she passed away. Florin was the youngest. The many students were also housed in other dormitories, based on their age and experience, but all came together for meals, served in a large hall.

Reluctant as she was to admit it, her uncle certainly did not scrimp on the food or the amenities for his...*harem*. As she met more of the other women, she discovered most of them had similar backgrounds: they'd been passed on from lower-class, poorer families who couldn't afford the burden of an extra mouth. Some had been widowed. With no other prospects for anything more than a meagre living, this was a better life for them. There were no other nobles among them.

Why would there be? "I can't believe he has this huge domain," Marra asked, making an attempt to converse with the other girls sitting around the table for lunch.

"You know he has another house?" Florin slipped into the chair beside her, her hair still damp. Sweat beaded off her brow as she reached for the bread rolls.

"He what?" The food fell from Marra's fork before it reached her mouth.

"He has large tracts of land. There's a smaller house closer to the main road."

"Didn't any of you *nobles* ever visit him?" Shayr interjected. Like Florin, she had just arrived and pushed in, opposite to where Marra was sitting. "I thought noble houses stuck together in all things."

"Ah, well, you see, your boss isn't noble born. He married into it and is a…"

"A *commoner*." Shayr sniggered and shook her head. "The highborn aren't much better, it seems," she muttered.

Marra was at a loss for words. *Surely, Father must have visited him.*

"Maybe the High Lord's out so often, reporting to the main Houses, no one needed to come here as they'd have only recently met or been updated," Florin suggested.

"If these noble houses were so interested in matters of state, maybe they should get off their fat arses and do their own snooping," Shayr retorted.

Shayr's snide tone wasn't lost on Marra or the other girls from the way they suddenly studied their bowls, but she chose to ignore it. *No sense in causing more friction.*

"Perhaps he met them at this other house," Marra answered Florin. The girl was the most amiable and likable of all the girls she'd met so far. She changed the subject. "Why does he have a harem in the first place?"

Shayr scoffed. "Obviously, so he can play with us *whores.*"

Again, Marra refused to take the bait. After the first encounter, there had been nothing but animosity between them, and Shayr seemed to be itching for a fight, spreading dissent among the other girls.

"We do get a lot of foreign visitors," Florin said, filling the growing silence. "And lots of the girls go away for weeks, even months, until they graduate. Then they get a permanent posting."

"They do? To where?"

"Everywhere. Anywhere. While it's a harem, it's also a training school for information gathering."

"You're the *spy network*?" Considering one of the last conversations with her father, the irony of where she was now wasn't lost on her.

"Some of us. I heard there's a training school for males nearby. We learn about the details of other countries and important people. When we go out to work, we listen. People say things during *pillow talk*. Knowing a bit about what they talk about helps put pieces together."

"Like a puzzle game?" Marra considered.

"I guess. We were poor, so I'm not sure what you mean. We didn't have games."

Shayr caught Marra's eye. "Playing games is all nobles are good for. And we *commoners* are its pieces."

Marra ignored the comment. As she finished her meal and was about to excuse herself, the double doors opened.

A horn was blown in a subdued fanfare for the seneschal's imminent arrival.

"Quickly, everyone, line up," Shayr ordered. "Leave your plates and move!"

Those girls who'd experienced this before were already on their feet, but a few others, Marra and Florin included, were caught unawares.

"Do I have to come around there and drag you myself?" Shayr was already on the move towards them.

Marra was on her feet as it was, so she was beside Florin as the younger girl pushed her chair back.

"I'm coming. No need to get your nethers in a knot," Florin replied.

"You little—" Shayr's arm swung, but Marra intervened, blocking her slap.

"Good leadership doesn't resort to violence for the most trivial of matters. It's the refuge of bullies and those with insecurities. It might be prudent to know that for future reference."

"Your seneschal visiting is not a trivial matter."

Marra shrugged. "It is to me. And he's not my seneschal."

From one of the doorways came the sound of sandals scuffing the tiles.

"We'll discuss this later." Shayr raced away to take her position by the door.

"Whenever you feel you need to vent, I'll be here," Marra called after her.

Florin was flustered. "Th-thank you for that."

"I abhor bullies. If there's one thing that irks me, it's them. We'd better go, though." She followed the last of the girls to the line. Whispering over her shoulder, she continued, "Don't tell anyone this, but while I have my point of view, if I'm a guest here—even if under duress—I should show some respect. This seneschal didn't kidnap me."

Just as she positioned herself next to Florin at the end of the line-up, the seneschal entered with his small retinue. All were eunuchs, and she recognised Ont'eba immediately. Each one was chubby and bald, but the master had a dark tan, and his juniors were both fair-skinned. It was when he got closer, she noticed the seneschal had many tattoos—hard to see against his dark skin.

She assumed different coloured tunics denoted rank. The master's was a dark blue, and his two underlings wore blue pastel robes.

"Ladies, ladies. So very lovely to see you all again. Many thanks for your service, and well done so far on the progress of your training. Applause all round." He started clapping at them, his many wristbands jangling.

Everyone took the hint and applauded with him. When he stopped, they stopped.

"I'm here this day for a couple of reasons. First and foremost is to congratulate our star pupil." He beamed at Shayr. "Please, Shayr Reguk from Slamand, come forward."

Shayr beamed at the adulation. She stepped forward proudly to the applause of the other students—some were more enthusiastic than others.

Marra clapped and said to Florin through the side of her mouth, "Make a mental note of her followers. I have little doubt that, as her friends and confidants, anything you say or do will get to Shayr's ears as quickly as a rash goes through a brothel."

Florin struggled not to laugh, but her smiling face could readily be assumed as support for Shayr. "I've already worked that out," she whispered back.

"Now, now, ladies, there have been some recent and drastic developments. Because of this, Shayr will soon head north, and with proper guidance, I'm confident she'll learn all she needs to become a House Mistress in a short time."

A small number of cheers arose at this news. Shayr nodded in acknowledgement, but she sent dagger glances towards Marra.

"So, moving on to our new girl... For those that haven't met her, allow me the privilege of introducing Lady Marra Olber from House Olber, who has joined us under tragic circumstances for a very special assignment. She's to remain pure—untouched—and therefore excused from several lessons—physical lessons specifically—though she is to attend as many theory lessons as possible in the short time she remains with us," the seneschal extolled. "Marra dear, I am Ont'eba Quillin and the administrator of this institution, and I'm sorry to hear of your recent loss. I met High Lord Olber only once, but it is an occasion I'll never forget. He treated me with dignity. Please do not hesitate to reach out to me. I'm busy and away a lot, but will endeavour to look after you the best I can."

He has absolutely no idea… "It is my pleasure to finally meet you, Master Quillin." Marra bowed as to an equal. She felt the brimming of tears, but blinked rapidly and continued. "I can't thank you enough for the respect you have shown. Rest assured, as the new head of House Olber, you will be remembered for your consideration." *Pure? That's what they call "keep her a virgin"?*

Some of the girls chatted softly when she said this, but the senior girls shushed them.

Ont'eba beamed at her words, then addressed the ladies. "High Lord Blarik will be visiting us in the near future to enlighten us closer to the date of her special assignment. I understand it's an extremely honourable role as befitting the head of an esteemed noble house, and I, for one, am so proud this institution has a role to play in her future.

"Now, to other matters." Pleasantries aside, the seneschal became more officious. "A list of the postings for the next graduates will be placed on the noticeboard shortly. This is, of course, assuming those soon to graduate continue with their impressive results."

He moved along the line and spoke briefly to each girl before departing. Door locks snapped loudly as the last of the group of eunuchs left.

Shayr extricated herself from some of the women and came over to Florin. Marra watched her every move, ready to intervene again.

"Since you're the junior girl here, I'm passing on the task of guiding our 'very important noble' in all matters of the school. Her actions and behaviour are now your responsibility. Do you think you're ready?"

"I'll do my best."

"You better." Shayr flounced off with several girls in her wake.

Florin looked cheekily at Marra. "If you're not doing anything, Lady Olber of House Olber, I'd best start showing you around. This place is full of secrets."

"Oh, I'd better check my agenda and see what my staff has arranged for my day."

Florin stuck out her tongue. "Let's go then, before your staff finds you." The younger girl grabbed her hand and pulled her towards another door.

"Ont'eba Quillin... what's his story?" Marra asked as they walked down a tiled hall.

"What do you mean? I thought you knew him."

"Well, only from sneaking in on meetings. I know little of him personally, like being a eunuch for starters, his dark skin, and all those tattoos."

"I hear he's from the Farquo Islands. The eunuch part is obvious. Can you imagine having a hot-blooded male in charge of a harem? The women in here are all so gorgeous, as are you, of course. It would be very tempting for a man to take advantage, or even the girls to take some advantage. It is what we're training for..."

"Why not a woman?"

"Jealousy, perhaps? Some women can be bitchy, and also just as guilty of taking advantage of a situation." The young girl lowered her voice. "Can you imagine what this place would be like if someone like Shayr was in charge?"

"Excellent points. And I guess, depending on what age he was before the castration, a eunuch might have the tastes of a male, but the inability to act on it. So, he could be a fair adjudicator in all respects."

"I don't know that word, but I think I know what you mean."

The pair stopped by a large indoor palm, which obscured a corner of a wall where a large tapestry of a mountain range ended. The young girl reached behind and pressed a section in the corner. There was a soft clunk as an unseen mechanism was released, and part of the wood panelling sprang in slightly. Pushing on it revealed a dark, narrow cavity.

"I hope you're not scared of the dark or tight spaces." Florin stepped in and motioned Marra to follow and to pull the door shut. Once closed, they were in total darkness. It was warm and musty.

Marra felt something brush against her briefly before a smooth, soft, warm hand clasped hers.

"This can be one of the more interesting lessons," Florin whispered close to her ear.

Marra was gently pulled along the narrow fissure. Her clothing snagged on the rough construction. After several minutes, her eyes adjusted to the dark interior. It was then she noticed the spots of light in the walls. The place was riddled with peepholes. There was barely a room that didn't have some access, whether it was only a peephole or an entire secret door. Every now and then, Florin shushed her to silence and pointed to a spot of light in the wall.

"Remember why you're here?" Florin leant forward, close enough for Marra to feel her breath on her neck and whispered softly.

Her breath was refreshing, with a subtle minty aroma. The closeness of her companion wasn't lost on her either, but considering the cramped conditions, it wasn't surprising.

"If you're to learn the wiles of men and how to please them without actually doing them," Florin continued, "this is the only way. *Doing* it is one thing, but seeing how others do it is surely the best idea."

"A voyeur's wet dream." Marra put her eye to the hole. In the next room was a dark man and a woman she'd not met in the throes of their passion. "And what have *you* done?" she whispered to her companion.

"Oh, these are things one shouldn't ask a lady," Florin softly breathed.

"That's why I'm asking *you*." Marra squeezed her hand, indicating it was in jest.

Florin's voice sounded husky in the dark. "Maybe I'll show you."

AFTER THE HOUR-LONG excursion through the walls, the pair emerged covered in dust and webs. With little airflow, the crawl spaces were warm and musty. Their nightgowns were dirty and damp with sweat, making them uncomfortable to wear.

"Time for a mineral spa." Florin led her along a passage to a larger washroom adjacent to the main hall.

This bathing area was warm and humid, despite the large openings in the roof letting the fresh air in and hot air out. Along the far wall was a terraced indoor garden and fernery. The opposite wall had another exit. A few other bathers were using the facility, some relaxing and others swimming.

"Where does that lead?" Marra indicated the other door.

"It's one of the accesses to other dormitories. This bath-house connects to them all."

"Does it now?"

"There's no escaping that way either. All the dormitories are basically the same."

"I wasn't really expecting it to be that easy." Marra shrugged, turning back to examine the large room. While there were floor tiles around the perimeter, the bath itself was really a natural rock pool.

"There's a hot spring underneath us," Florin explained.

"You should have shown me this earlier. All I've had is a basin in the room."

"Blame Shayr, but now I'm your guide, what I say goes."

"Yes, ma'am." Marra curtsied. "Maybe this is why Blarik has this house here. Hot water at your beck and call would be very handy."

"Perhaps. I'm not arguing." Florin peeled off her grimy nightgown and tossed the dirty garment into the corner, then stepped lightly across the tiles and, with a satisfied growl, lowered herself into the steaming pool.

Marra hesitated a moment.

"Not going all shy on me, are you?" Florin grinned cheekily from the water.

Marra shook her head. "No. That's not it." With a sigh, she shrugged out of her silk nightgown, leaving it in a heap with Florin's, and stepped cautiously into the pool, feeling the uneven floor with her feet. She stayed close to the side.

"I can see why they chose you over Shayr." Florin admired Marra as she stepped into the water and joined her. "Shayr's attractive, at least on the outside—all the curves in the right places—but you're stunning."

"As are you." Now she had found level ground, Marra ducked underwater to cover her embarrassment. "But I'll not be anyone's wh—concubine," she continued when she surfaced.

"But you're betroth—"

"Florin, you want this, you chose it, and I respect the fact that you know where you want to be, but it's not for me. I need to get out."

"I–I can—"

"Help? You can't! I won't let you. You'll get into trouble, and I don't want that to happen. Not because of me."

"If you say so." With her hair flowing behind, Florin swam breaststroke slowly along the pool's edge and stopped by a tray of sponges and washcloths.

"I do say so. And stop thinking about it," Marra chastised, following slowly. "I have a few weeks. You continue showing me around the domain, and I will take it from there. With all these secret passages, there *must* be a way out."

"Deal. I mean, I'd rather your company—everyone else is too serious." Florin offered her a sponge. "But if you do have to leave, I'd prefer you to go where you want. It's much safer south, and I hear women on the run go to The Crags."

"The Crags?"

"Yes. You can't be considering going back to your domain?"

"I'm not." Marra waded around, relishing the flow of water across her body. She began washing herself with the sponge. "I've heard of The Crags. Full of witches, and where women go to kill themselves. Must be a sad place."

"They do no such thing! At least, not according to Zaran, our cartographer. He says there's a small female community there, with pirates. Of course, you could ask our seneschal. I hear he was a pirate."

"Really? A pirate without testicles? Is that a thing?"

"Perhaps the Red Sails caught him."

"Red Sails?" *Why does that sound familiar?*

"They come from The Crags, too. If they cross any male pirates, they castrate them."

"Ouch. You're serious?" Marra couldn't keep the incredulity from her voice.

"It's true," Florin said, splashing her. "I've seen them."

"Pirate testicles?" Marra asked with a cheeky grin.

Florin laughed out loud. Her laugh echoed around the room, causing the other girls to turn and look. "No, the Red Sails," she said when she was able to speak.

"I remember now. It was several years ago. I snuck into my father's study when he was conducting trade talks. One of the topics was pirates and how they were becoming more of a nuisance. Our fleet is small, lacking resources to cover both the north and southern shores."

"It's mostly barren cliffs down south anyway."

"Did you remember that from geography? I thought you'd be too busy ogling the teacher..."

"Well, there *is* that." Florin blushed. "Plus, I came from a southern coastal village. Fishing boats tend to get damaged a lot along rugged cliffs, so we use nets or dive for various shellfish along the shore. Sometimes, depending on the weather, I've seen red-sailed ships going along the coast. That must be them."

"Well," Marra continued, "there was an idea to seek volunteers to police the southern area. It was laughed at, until they received an offer from a new community, supposedly a women's refuge, requesting funding—"

"Must be from The Crags."

"Seems likely. It was decided a small allowance would be paid just to support the refuge, but there would be more if they could do something about the pirates. They could also keep fifty per cent of the haul. But it wasn't expected they'd amount to anything. Women pirate-hunters? Unheard of."

"So, we do have pirates without testicles." Florin giggled at her joke.

Marra laughed with her. "Privateers are what we call those with valid authorisation."

"How about Sea Witches? Sea *Bitches* is better."

"Somehow, I don't think they'd take too kindly to hear either of those terms." Marra threw a wet sponge at her, laughed, and pushed back, heading to the other end of the pool.

"It gets hotter that way," Florin warned, and began swimming after her. "And deeper."

Marra stopped and started to turn. *What was I thinking?* The water here was up to her neck already.

"Come on," Florin encouraged. "It's not really too hot."

"No. I-I don't know how to swim."

"You can't?" Florin was beside her again.

"I've never needed to."

"Ever?" Florin looked surprised. "What about rivers and lakes?"

"If I'm crossing, it's either on a ferry or horseback."

"I learnt to swim before I could run. I was good at diving, too."

"Really? I didn't really think a 'bath' would be too deep. If *only* I knew someone with all these worldly skills to teach me. Woe is me. I should just end myself now and be done with this cruel world." *Some days, she'd thought about it.*

"I think you're toying with me."

"Do you?"

"I don't mind. It's better than the alternative."

"Which is what, treating you like a decent person?"

"That would be nice. No, I meant being ignored. Until you arrived, I was ignored by nearly everyone."

"I suspect Shayr is using her influence—no one's tried to get to know me, except for you."

"Are you with me because there's no one else? Perhaps you think I'm a burden."

It was only for a second, but she almost pouted. Marra had to give it to her; Florin could come across as a mature young woman. Bubbly, confident and perhaps overly forward in many respects, but in times like this, when she felt betrayed or used, she could easily revert to the sad, lonely child she once was.

"Not at all." Marra reached out and placed her hands on her shoulders. "You're lovely, easy to talk with, intelligent and helpful...and you've been assigned by that she-devil to teach me all you know. From the sounds of it, I'm here for only a short time, while you'll be here until you graduate. Shayr could make things difficult for you once I manage to get out of here."

"She does that anyway."

"Not while I'm here, she won't."

Florin moved closer and lowered her voice. "You could help me in my lessons, then perhaps I can leave sooner."

"Sure. But I'm the new girl, remember?"

"Yes, but you're a noble and much older. That has to account for something."

"Oh, *much* older, am I?" Marra chuckled and pushed her underwater.

Florin resurfaced, laughing and spluttering. "Okay, okay. Maybe not *so* old." She kicked away towards the deeper end. "Now I'm going to teach you to swim."

NINE

A NEW PORT

Even towing the *Tormentor*, with favourable winds, they would arrive in the port of Savarik by mid-afternoon the next day. Captain Sienna was cautious not to tire her elementalists and had only used them sparingly.

Fortunately, there had been no further encounters with pirates, and only fishing vessels were seen in the distance. Savarik, the main harbour for the Titonu Islands, was far to the north, and this area of the Herdoln Archipelago was devoid of large trading ships.

The island group rose from the waves on the eastern horizon. According to their charts, there were spurs on this section of the reef, making it fine for fishing boats with shallow drafts, but treacherous for larger vessels.

As the two ships finally approached Savarik, dockside workers stopped, and a crowd began to gather along the piers, all gawking at the sight of the *Revenge* entering the harbour. Wharves followed the curved shoreline, with piers of various lengths jutting out.

Dozens of fishing boats and twice as many small coastal traders were already docked.

"I didn't think it would be such a busy little place," Corra remarked to Tully.

"I've 'eard of it. Since it be the only 'arbour of any good size, most, if not all, the trade comes through 'ere. Quite a few stories goin' about too."

"Looks like I need to hang around taverns more often."

"Yah." Tully nodded. "You learn a lot in bars."

"You must be very wise indeed, then," Corra joked.

Two-thirds of the way around the shoreline was the mouth of a river. The wharf continued non-stop; therefore, only rowboats and barges could go further. A couple of bridges could be seen further inland before the buildings obscured the curve in the river. Typical of waterfronts, warehouses of varying sizes were built facing the docks, making it hard to see much more of the township. The bulk of the town was nestled in the valley. Further inland, some of the statelier homes were visible on the escarpment. There were many fishing boats moored along the southern end of the shorefront, and with the reek of stinking fish, the further the better.

On the north hillside, a long wall protected the palace. As they watched, a group carrying a sedan chair emerged from the gatehouse to make their way along the road leading to town.

"Who's the boss?" Corra asked, looking at the procession with the spyglass.

"A 'rotund' fellow from all accounts. Likes jewellery and beheadings."

"No doubt information gleaned in a bar?" Corra shook her head, smiling. "I can tell already this is going to be fun."

"You have a weird sense of fun, Cap'n."

"All these years and you just realised?" Corra chuckled as she moved to check on the prisoners huddled at the bow. A canvas sheet had been stretched across the bow, both for protection from the cold of the night and for discretion; her crew on watch didn't want to see pirates relieving themselves.

Understandably, there was concern at the sight of the pirate vessel, and several local armed men appeared on the wharf and started to clear the immediate area of spectators. By the time the two vessels had tied up alongside, another squad of armed men wearing the colours of the royal house blocked access to the pier, but also to the town.

Due to the limited room, the *Tormentor* was secured to the pier, with the *Revenge* tied on the outboard side of the pirate vessel. This allowed for their rapid departure if necessary, but also served as a means of security: they had not visited Savarik before, and no one had any first-hand experience of the locals, nor the reception they'd receive. Few ports were amenable to a pirate ship sailing into their harbour. If there was any trouble, the *Revenge* could readily be released and moved a safe distance.

To allay any fears and panic, an unarmed Captain Sienna met the entourage while the bulk of her crew waited on the ship. Only Tully and Saiba, one of the more powerful aeyrons, stood on the pier by the gangway.

The local leader and his entourage arrived in good time and stopped near the blockade. The bare-chested servants lowered the sedan chair. A carpeted step was immediately placed by the opening to enable the occupant to alight easily.

Two guards marched forward to bar Sienna's approach, but an order was called out to allow her passage. The guards followed closely as she passed.

"You have the privilege of being in the presence of the Ruler of Savarik, his Excellency Olpu-tu Savarik-an," an official called as he pulled aside silk curtains.

From the covering, a heavy-set man stepped down to the

pier. He was dressed in a full-length robe of a fine, shiny material. Several earrings glittered as he turned to survey the ships.

The gathered crowd, already excited with the new vessels in the harbour, started cheering and waving at the appearance of their leader.

"Greetings, Your Excellency," Corra said loudly as she introduced herself when the tumult died down.

Olpu-tu raised a hand for silence. The large rings on his fingers were of a darker metal than his other jewellery and did not glisten as much.

"What is the meaning of this?" Olpu-tu demanded, waving an arm in the direction of the two ships. His wrist jangled with his many gold and silver bands. "Why have you come here with that vessel?"

"We recently captured it, Your Excellency. You may not be aware that we are part of the Red Sails fleet. We have a commission from Lord Olber, High Lord of Jaranabi, to intercept and capture any and all pirate vessels we come across in the waters around southern Harando."

"We here in Savarik do not recognise this High Lord. He carries no influence here."

"As it should be, you are your own sovereign nation. You asked why we're here. Under our charter, I am to take the captured vessel to the nearest harbour. Savarik was the closest port to where this ship was captured. The *Tormentor* was operating within the Herdoln Archipelago. Captain Erdun Walsch of the *Dimantin* notified us of the recent attacks on the *Gon Falmo*."

"The *Falmo*? That's a ship from this very port!" one of the officials stated, turning to Olpu-tu. "It left here for Lashalk last week."

Corra nodded, pleased to hear her information was correct. "We heard she took heavy damage, but was able to continue."

Olpu-tu looked to the *Tormentor*, his face hardening when he saw the pirates being assembled. "And *you*...managed to capture them?" His tone, more than his words, indicated his disbelief that women could do such a thing.

Having heard it all before, Sienna merely answered with a nod. "We brought them here for you and your people to see justice done."

As they spoke, Tully cleared her throat. She had moved up behind Corra with young Jag by her side.

"Also, your Excellency, this young fellow was a captive. Held against his will." Sienna put a reassuring hand on Jag's shoulder. "If he could be reunited with his family or friends? He tells me they're in a small fishing town south of here."

"I'm sure we can work something out," Olpu-tu said without enthusiasm, looking somewhat disdainfully at the young urchin. He put a perfumed cloth to his nose. "Tell me, what of the pirate captain?"

"Dead and tossed overboard."

The ruler smiled and nodded when she explained the Red Sails' actions with any pirates they come across, obviously not irked by the bloodshed.

"If what you say is true, then these miscreants will be beheaded."

The citizens close enough to hear this cheered and raised their clenched fists.

"Your Excellency is a just ruler. May I humbly suggest that the branding for the first-timers and the castration of the others to be taken into consideration? Perhaps hard labour? Make them repay with their sweat and help out with your glorious city. If any lives were lost on the *Gon Falmo*, then a reciprocal number of the pirates should also lose their lives."

The majority of the crowd went silent. Some low mutterings were heard.

"One is not accustomed to having One's judgment questioned. You are strangers here. And as I am a just ruler, I will overlook this transgression. You are forgiven."

Again, the gathered people applauded the gesture from their liege.

"You have my gratitude and apologies." Captain Sienna bowed her head briefly.

"Accepted." Olpu-tu waved for silence. "My men will deal with these prisoners." He gestured for his men to take charge of the pirates who had been herded down to the pier. As an afterthought, he motioned Jag to go with them.

Jag hesitated, looking back at the ships, then up at Corra.

She knelt and spoke quietly. "Jag, we spoke about this. You'll be far better with your family back in your village than on a ship full of angry women." She watched sadly as the young boy was taken gently away by a kind guard.

"My Lord, there are too many for our dungeons," a senior soldier said as the last of the pirates were hustled off the ship. "We'll need to set up a holding pen."

"Do what is needed." Olpu-tu dismissively waved his man-at-arms away, then turned back to Corra. "Tonight, we will hold a banquet to thank you for this service. You and your crew are to attend the palace at sunset."

Without waiting for a response, he turned and climbed back into his sedan chair. The handful of guards escorted him back to his palace.

Tully, never far from her captain, especially when ashore, stepped closer and spoke quietly. "Reckon we keep a handful of our best mancers back tonight."

"You suspect something?" She watched the men-at-arms march up the hill. The bulk of the crowds dispersed, but a few moved closer to the water's edge to look at the ships.

"Pfft. Always. But I've heard scupper yarn. Old jingle-wrist is wily. As treacherous as the reefs that surround this rock, they say. And there's that..." Tully subtly inclined her head towards the end of the pier. Several men were taking a keen interest in their vessel, pointing and discussing animatedly.

"They're wearing pretty good clothing, not the get-up of the average villagers or fisher-folk," Tully added. "Merchants, I reckon. They wandered over from that tavern."

Sienna followed her gaze. "I suspect it's time for another lesson?"

"You're buyin'." Tully turned and made a signal. It took only a moment for their weapons to be brought from the ship and donned.

The interior of the Tangled Net was well-lit and full of dockworkers, fishermen, and sailors from some of the other vessels in port.

"Popular place, it seems," Corra noted.

"Must mean good ale then." Tully made her way to the bar and ordered two mugs of the house ale. "Normally this busy?" she asked as the young lass poured their drinks.

"A bit more 'n usual coz of that ship. Our lookouts spotted it before it come through the heads."

"Ah. And a fine ship she be." Tully winked at her.

"Flirting with the locals already?" Corra joined her first mate, dropping some coins on the aged bar top.

"Been at sea awhile, Cap'n."

The penny dropped when the lass realised who she was serving. She blushed.

"We'll take our drinks over there. Thanks." Corra pointed with her head and made her way through the crowd to the window overlooking the plaza and port, Tully in her wake. A patron who was bumped turned to complain about their spilt drink, then decided against it when they saw the twin blades across the tall woman's departing back.

"Smart man," Tully sniggered in passing.

Placing their drinks on the wide windowsill, they looked out and leant on the scarred and stained wood. Over the hubbub, they caught snatches of conversations about the visiting ships and the occasional criticism of women at sea. There were a few glances their way.

"It's bad luck, I'z reckons," one bearded fisherman said. "Womin on ships at sea'n'all."

"Could work out good for some. I mean, where are they gettin' laid? Got to come ashore sometime to 'ave some fun in the sack. Even *you* might get lucky," his short friend joked.

The bearded sailor didn't look convinced and continued drinking. He casually looked around.

Tully caught his eye and winked, raising her mug.

The man coughed, spilling his ale. When he looked back, Tully had turned away with a grin.

The fellows who had taken a keen interest in the ship were walking quickly towards the tavern. Two remained outside while the other pair stepped inside. After a moment, they began pushing towards the window where Corra and Tully were chatting.

"'Ere we go." Tully swallowed her ale and waited.

"Ladies." The taller of the two men bowed his head. "Nice vessel you got there."

"Nice for you to say so." Captain Sienna nodded. "She certainly is."

"I've never seen its like before."

"Considerin' who we are 'n' what we do, that's prolly a good thing," Tully replied with a smile. There were no scars or tattoos on his otherwise clean, tanned face.

"Ah. Yes. Privateers, I hear."

Corra nodded. "It's not for sale."

"Quick and to the point. You haven't heard our offer."

"That's fine. We don't need to, because it's not fer sale," Tully answered.

The man nodded, annoyed. "I believe I was talking to the captain?"

"You believe correct, but the ship is still not fer sale."

"Why not let the lovely captain say so?"

Tully placed her mug down. "Maybe you've 'eard what we do to men that cross us?" From one of her vest pockets, she pulled out a rusty pair of serrated-edged scissors and placed them beside her mug on the sill. The long blades were stained to dullness, even though it was bright outside.

His companion whispered in his ear.

The man slowly looked down and blanched when he saw the dried blood. "Ah. How witless of me." His voice lost a bit of volume and confidence.

"If you're in need of a ship, the *Tormentor* is available." Corra pulled another sip from her mug. "We'll let her go for a good price."

"What's a good price for you?"

"More than likely one not so good for you, but I'll leave that to your imagination and the weight of your purse."

"Come now. It's not as if you paid anything for it."

"Is that so? Everything has its price. Weeks at sea? My girls risking injury...and death? You think taking her was easy?"

"Well, according to your reputation—"

"So, you *'ave* 'eard of us?" Tully spun the dull scissors.

"Rumours, to be sure," he covered.

"Hmm. You don't seem that good at negotiations. Do strong women frighten you?"

"Ladies. How about I buy another round, while my

colleague continues this discussion?" The companion stepped closer, nudging the taller man. "Allow me to introduce myself, I'm Nethan D'Longe."

Muttering, the taller man turned and headed towards the bar.

Corra introduced Tully and herself. "We have a royal banquet to attend, so we can't parley long."

THE PAIR STROLLED BACK to the ship, nodding at the folk who smiled or waved. Some ducked their heads and moved off quickly.

"Can't believe they'll pay another five hundred pieces for it," Tully remarked, hefting the bag of gold coins.

"I can't believe those scissors worked." Sienna laughed. "They probably won't pay the other half, though."

"Reckon they'll renege?"

"Or something. It's not as if we're going to be hanging around for long."

"And they prolly know we don't want to take it with us."

"Correct. But we'll finish emptying her of all cargo first."

Distrusting the sly merchants and the ease of the *Tormentor* negotiations, she kept ten of her most powerful elementalists back. She also arranged for the newlings to help move the remainder of the cargo from the *Tormentor* under their guidance.

"Banquet, it might be, but we don't know these people. It may be nothing—and if so, I'll owe you all a feast—but just in case... I'd like a ship to come back to."

At DUSK, an escort of armed soldiers in the colours of Olpu-tu arrived to take them to the palace.

"By day it may seem peaceful, but the streets become a dark place at night."

"Most places do," Tully murmured.

Sienna nudged her. "And I dare say His Excellency requires us to leave our weapons behind?"

"It is as you say, my lady. We both have differing customs; it would be a shame for this first meeting to have an abrupt and tragic end."

"It wouldn't be good if your men were injured by women."

"Indeed." He smiled and led them towards the palace silhouetted on the hill.

CHAPTER

TEN

HAIRPINS AND HOW TO
USE THEM EFFECTIVELY

"These are some very important tools of the trade," Shayr was speaking to the girls. Dozens of jars, vials, and tubes were laid out on a long trestle covered in an embroidered cloth. "Some are plain and simple; some are more exotic and potent. What you use depends on the client, the situation, and potential gain. Remember, your body is also a tool. Sex is the work—*some* of you might need to work harder—but the goal is to get all the information we can with the client oblivious to it."

"This one here is particularly effective." Shayr picked up a yellow vial and walked down the line, allowing the trainees to sniff it. "We call it *Beast*, as it really gets a man wild." She winked. "And very talkative."

"Where does it come from?" Leesa was next to Marra. She sniffed it and quickly pulled away, screwing up her nose.

Shayr bypassed Marra. "You won't be needing it," she muttered, and moved on down the line.

The pungent musk and nutmeg odours were still potent enough for her to smell it from a distance.

126

"It comes from female rockions," Shayr informed them.

"Are rockions even real?" someone further down the line asked.

"They most definitely are. This comes from the glands of the bitches. You've seen Col? All gangly legs and unruly hair—"

"And groping hands," Amba stated.

"The silly git loves trying to kiss me every—"

"Yes, yes. So, we *all* know Col, our rockion keeper. With the help of our mancers, he can collect some, but only a couple of times a year."

"What mancers?" a girl at the other end of the line asked.

"We have rockions here?"

"Yes, I just said so, didn't I!" Shayr retorted testily at all the questions.

Not trusting Shayr to give a straight answer, Marra turned to Florin. "Where are these mancers and rockions?"

"You know about them?"

"I know of the mancers. Three elementalists came into the last High Council meeting, and Blarik ordered them to murder my advisor and guards." Marra went quiet as the scene unfolded in her mind. She shook her head. "And Blarik has a rockion keeper too?"

"Because High Lord Blarik has three rockions—" Florin answered quietly.

"He what?"

"He has only three *now*. I heard one of the males escaped last week, but he still has one male for mating."

That's very interesting.

"Are you two paying attention?" Shayr snapped. "We'll be discussing poisons next, and there will be a test. If you make a mistake, Marra, it could be the end of you, or your little friend."

You wish. "I think she's jealous," Marra whispered to Florin as she assumed a chastised look.

FLORIN CAME IN, covered in dust. "I can understand why Shayr is so vexed at you."

Marra looked her over, noting the dust and sweat. "Passage peeping again?"

"A girl's got to learn somehow." She nodded, flushed. "A Dran'ali merchant is visiting, staying over with the boys."

"That's right, there's a male school equivalent, isn't there?"

"Yes, and since we are all trainees, part of the study program is to work together. Boy seduces girl, and vice versa. They're tested, putting their wits against each other."

"And this news?"

"Apparently, this Dran'ali horse trader visited the High Lord recently."

"Visiting the other residence? And?"

"Dran'ali laws forbid certain activities, so the High Lord offered the trader use of the male facilities with a senior student."

"Oh. Right. They do that too, don't they?"

Florin grinned and rolled her eyes. "You think it's only the girls that get together?"

"I've not had as much exposure as others to this side of life. I didn't really think on it at all until now. So, this visiting trader. How do you know...?"

"Jofine was scheduled to work with Polt, a male student. Polt was nervous, or maybe that was the act. Anyway, he needed a lot of work, so Jofine used that rockion lotion. He was babbling in a few minutes. The trader was here in preparation for a betrothal ceremony next month."

"I'm betrothed to a horse trader?" Though Marra wanted no part of it, she was still put out at how low her importance had become.

"No. Not the trader, silly. The man from the east you're betrothed to is none other than Urgad Jorakif—"

"The ruler of Dran'ali?"

"Of course you'd know about him." Florin looked crestfallen that her news wasn't as much of a surprise as she'd expected.

"A bit, mostly by eavesdropping when my father had visitors. But please, tell me what your snooping uncovered."

"That's it. If he's an Overlord, does that make you a queen—assuming that's what the wife of an Overlord is called? *Overlady*?"

"Assuming those barbarians know what a queen is," Marra said.

"I hear he can be quite forceful. Shayr prefers it that way."

"Yes, but it won't be Shayr, will it!"

"And that's why she's vexed. She was going to be the bride—his queen."

FLORIN WAS MEANDERING through the lounge when she happened upon Marra, who was reading through some notes by the fountain. The young woman looked tense, as though she'd just received bad news, and Florin leaned in close.

"Marra, can I have a quiet chat...outside?" Florin asked.

"Of course, Florin. It's a lovely day, may as well enjoy it." Marra rose and walked casually outside to enjoy the fresh air and sunshine with the bubbly girl. They wandered in a relaxed manner around the edge of the long, shallow water garden full of lily pads. Now and then, there came a flash of orange from a goldfish. They passed a small group of ladies, also out enjoying the sun and air. After a brief exchange of pleasantries, they continued.

"Do you think we're friends?" Florin asked abruptly when they were at the far end of the pond.

"I thought we were." Marra searched the younger girl's face, her eyes tracing over her smooth skin, trying to fathom what was wrong. "I know it's been less than two weeks; you've been nothing but helpful and approachable since I arrived."

Florin blushed. "I know some people better than others; you, I hardly know, but I've spent more time over the last few days with you than I have with anyone else. You're easy to talk to. Thank you."

"No one should have to thank anyone for friendship. There are no set conditions."

Florin nodded, looking relieved. She spoke softly. "Shayr's up to something."

"I reckon Shayr is *always* up to something." Marra shrugged.

"A scorpion has claws and a tail. If she is openly offering you help, watch out for her sting."

"It isn't hard to see the animosity there." Marra slowly nodded.

"She was selected to be this Overlord's queen until you came along. She wants you gone so she can take that place again."

"Shayr can have it."

Florin looked around, then kept moving. "She's all talk and won't do anything herself, but there are plenty of guards who would readily do her bidding for a few hours of play. Men always underestimate women. Since they're stronger than us, they think they are in control, but in the heat of sex, they are the weaker ones. Two heads, but only enough blood for one."

Marra sniggered at this description, which set Florin to giggling.

By the wall, they reached an alcove with more daphne and shrubs surrounding a bench.

Florin gathered her silk nightgown and sat, inviting Marra to join her. She did, breathing in the subtle fragrance of daphne. From her coiffed hair, Florin extracted a hairpin. "If you ever need to, when a man is busy with you, push this into his ear." She handed Marra the pin. "Do it quickly, do it hard, and push it all the way."

Marra held the hairpin, not dissimilar to the ones she already had. "I do know what a hairpin is." She handed it back.

"They need to be distracted." Florin replaced the pin in her hair, then reached out and gently stroked Marra's brow, brushing strands of her black hair away from her blue eyes, slowly running her fingers to the back of her head, drawing her nearer. "It might be during a kiss." Florin's whisper was sultry; her scent rivalled that of the daphne. "Or anything, really, as long as you can reach the side of his head, then slide it into his ear while his mind is on other things."

Their lips touched, and Marra's heart thumped in her breast when she felt the warm moisture of the other girl's tongue gently probing. A moment later, she flinched sideways when she felt a wet finger in her ear.

"Just like that." Florin giggled, her green eyes shining with mirth.

Marra laughed with her, feeling her face reddening. "What are you up to, young lady?"

"Apart from giving you pointers on how to kill a man? I'm practising flirting. There's no man about at the moment, and I'll need to be able to do both."

"I see." Marra smiled. "Homework? Extra-curricular activities?"

"Others do it. I thought..." She suddenly looked worried. "You don't mind, do you?"

"The flirting?" Marra laughed lightly. "Florin, if I did, I would have stopped you the first time."

"First time?"

"Brushing against me in the secret passages? Always leaning close to whisper? Taking every chance to hold hands or touching when you can. It all adds up."

"How embarrassing." Florin's shoulders slumped in disappointment. "Am I that obvious? I'll be hopeless as a spy."

"Not at all. And I'm flattered. I've always assumed I'd find some fine man somewhere. I've not given this situation much consideration...until now. Besides, you're helping me study, so how can I not reciprocate?"

"I think I know what you mean." She blushed again, her eyes searching Marra's face. "Well, how was it, then?"

"That was..."

"Fun?" Florin reached for her hand. "Nice?"

"Yes, and wet."

"The kiss?"

Marra playfully slapped her, laughing. "No. Your finger."

"Oh. Good. I thought I was losing my touch."

Marra knew her cheeks were glowing. "No, not at all."

Florin took a breath and moved closer, about to say something, but the dinner bell tolled. "Shall we?" she said instead.

Marra stood, releasing her hand. "I think it best, yes. Lesson postponed."

ONE OF THE eunuch underlings rapped gently on Marra's door. "High Lord Blarik has sent me to escort you to his dining hall," he said when she answered.

Marra went white, and her breath caught. "Do I need to bring anything?" *A knife, or a chastity belt?*

"No. Just yourself. Shall we?"

"Just a moment." She turned back into the room. She was no prude; if you were, you wouldn't ever leave the room with the skimpy, body-hugging, see-through nightgowns the girls had to wear. But this was her uncle, and a lecherous pervert. She reached into her closet and pulled on her two other gowns. The triple layers were sufficient to prevent light penetration, but they were still lightweight enough to hug her curves. The only other option was the drapes.

Marra was looking at the getup in a cheval mirror. "Looks horrible," she muttered. "Just what he deserves." She also adjusted a hairpin to pull her hair into a semblance of order.

"Shall we proceed?" the eunuch prompted.

With trepidation, Marra nodded and followed.

The girls lounging in the main room watched, whispering to each other as she passed. Florin was nowhere to be seen. *Passage peeping again, no doubt.*

The normally locked double doors were opened. Two guards stood by to prevent any of the girls from leaving. Their hungry eyes soaked in as much as they could of all the nubile flesh in the dormitory before the eunuch passed—their cue to close and lock the doors once more.

Marra looked around the new area, trying to place particular features with what she had heard or seen from her garden studies.

A long, wide corridor went in both directions, marble columns every ten paces or so, and large tapestries in between. At the centre of the mansion, a set of stairs with stone balustrades on either side led to the upper levels. As they climbed the stairs, they approached a balcony.

There were more double doors directly in front of the top of the stairs, but the eunuch turned to another door two columns to the right. In her estimation, this should overlook the garden. She would have seen these windows from ground level. *Which meant anyone in here could watch over them.*

It suddenly dawned on her she had a eunuch underling all to herself, with no one around, and only a very short time to chat. "Have you been here long, Gamir?" she asked.

"Several years, when I answered the call from Master Quillin."

"Are you from the south? Master Quillin is from the Farquo Islands, but surely not you?"

"South-west, actually."

"Were you a pirate, like Ont'eba was?"

"I was, but as for Master Quillin, I am not at liberty to discuss his background or that of any other person here."

She shrugged. "A girl has to ask."

"Indeed."

"And..." she paused, considering the delicate question. "Did you come across the Red Sails?"

"The question answers itself. We have arrived." He knocked, then opened the door. "My Lord, the Lady Marra Olber is here."

They stepped in, and the eunuch showed her to the table. There was no chair for her, just the one for her uncle on the far side.

Marra turned to her escort. "Nice to chat, Gamir. Thank you."

He bowed slightly as he backed out, closing the doors.

Blarik had risen from his chair, with all the pretence of meeting an equal, all smiles and graciousness. The moment Gamir closed the door, her uncle sat, helped himself to a flask of wine and continued eating.

"I see the nose is fixed." She looked around the room, taking in the four guards several paces away and watching her every move. "I should've gouged your eyes when I had the chance."

"That's the difference between you and me, girl. If I see an opportunity to better myself or remove an enemy, I do it." While he chewed noisily, he cast his eyes over her, clearly disappointed she'd chosen to wear multiple layers.

"You? You'd have difficulty tossing a salad." She was amused that she could so easily bring him down, and had to try hard to keep her amusement at his easy defeat out of her tone.

"You've learnt nothing here. Still an impudent little shrew."

"Rape and kidnapping tend to have that effect on people. And I've learnt some things; I know now you had my father assassinated with your rabid pets. I will kill you for that."

Blarik's belly laugh was spontaneous and loud. Once he stopped chuckling, he poured more wine and continued feeding his face, talking between mouthfuls. "The official story is your father was killed by rockions. Nothing to do with me."

Bastard. "It was *your* rockion. Probably the one that *oh so conveniently* escaped..."

She studied the table as she spoke to see what she could reach in the off chance an opportunity presented itself. It would take the guards only a moment, maybe a few seconds, to intervene. Any success would be extremely remote, but she had to try and had nothing to lose.

There was always her hairpin. But the thought of getting that close to him disgusted her.

"I can assure you, there's nothing convenient about rockions roaming free."

At least he didn't deny it.

"Would you care to know my great plans for you?" He grinned evilly. "I've managed to extract a deal from Urgad

Jorakif, the Overlord of Dran'ali," he said between mouthfuls of food. "He'll be here in a couple of weeks and bring with him one hundred of his fine horses, for you, his new bride."

"Like that's ever going to happen!" she scoffed. Already aware of the fate he'd planned for her, she glared back at him. His dismay at failing to shock her showed in the scowl on his face.

"It is your destiny, and it will happen!" Blarik slammed his fist on the table. "Stop acting like you have any say in this. You're lucky I've made this deal; otherwise, you'd be thrown to the men for their entertainment. With his down payment of fine breeding stock, the two hundred more after the wedding, and a promise to continue this every year as long as you produce him sons, I won't be letting you squirm out of this arrangement."

"Keep having these fantasies if it makes you feel better," she muttered. "Procreating another generation of barbarian horse-herders is not on my agenda. Seeing you rot in your grave is, though."

Her uncle spoke over her, ignoring her words. "With this arrangement, I'll soon have the beginnings of a magnificent cavalry. This will secure the borders for generations."

"Which wouldn't be needed if small men with delusions of grandeur stopped having pissing contests."

"My dear girl, all of Jaranabi will benefit from your sacrifice."

"Sacrifice? And you? I don't see you making any sacrifices." She waved her arms to encompass the domain. "This opulence doesn't come from the allowances the ruling houses provide. You're just a corrupt, obese parasite, milking the country for yourself. If you make me do this, I can guarantee you he'll be dead in a month."

"And Jaranabi will rejoice at your heroism. But then you'll

be a dead hero." Blarik beamed. "I win either way, but I'll throw a memorial service in your memory to appease them."

"So, you need me? Why not Shayr?"

"I'm disappointed in you. I took you for someone with a semblance of intelligence. Have you not realised you're pivotal in this? Shayr is tall, cunning, and deliciously voluptuous, but other than that, she's nothing. You were a High Lord's daughter. Your oh-so-precious noble blood is what separates you from the rest of the trash. And, of course, your precious virginity. It means so much to these backward horse clans."

So, he dare not kill me, and my virtue needs to remain intact. "Good. I just wanted to be sure." Marra leapt across the table, displacing the food and wine in all directions. She was going for a knife, but a broken wine glass presented itself. She snatched it and thrust it at his neck.

Caught off guard, Blarik pushed away clumsily to avoid her wild swing. His chair overbalanced, and he fell back with a cry, cracking his head on the tiles. He didn't move.

Marra's progress was hampered by the spilled food; her hand slipped on the puddle of bechamel sauce, and she found little purchase on the smooth tablecloth. But her uncle was on the floor, motionless. Marra wasn't sure if the shard had cut him since his beard covered his neck. Eager to take advantage of the situation, she tried again.

As she slid off the table, the guards pounced on her and dragged her away from where their lord lay. The glass shard was knocked out of her hands, so she lashed out with her feet and fists, scoring hits but only bruising herself on their armour. The head guard pulled her head back by her hair and punched her with his gauntleted fist, bloodying and bruising her face immediately.

"Get the healer for the High Lord," he ordered. "Take this

wench to her quarters," he told another, pushing her roughly to him.

Marra shrieked both in pain and fury at having missed her opportunity. Her eyes teared up, and she felt the tang of blood in her mouth. She could feel a couple of loose teeth with her tongue.

An older guard grabbed her by the upper arm and forcibly removed her from the dining hall. She stumbled, trying to keep up. They were halfway along the corridor heading towards the stairs when the nausea hit. Marra tried to warn him, but he ignored her. She reached for the balustrade for balance. He jerked her back, his other hand ready to slap her. She deliberately vomited over him.

"Bitch." He swore and slammed her into the railing, twisting her arm cruelly behind her. "Such a pretty little vixen. Think you're so high 'n' mighty that nothin' can happen to you?"

"I know it," she croaked. When the threat of darkness diminished, she laughed, feeling his hands lifting the back of her nightgown, his boots pushing her feet apart. Her anger and frustration at her failure drove her out of her mind. To consider desperate acts...

The balustrade cracked and trembled. Small fragments of mortar dropped from the ceiling.

Pretty weak masonry.

Unused to having to find his way through several layers of clothing, the guard was having difficulties. She laughed at him. More blood dripped from her nose and mouth.

The windows along the hall lit up; thunder crashed outside.

Marra spat to clear the blood. "Do what you want. Show me how much of a big, brave man you are. I dare you," she invited with a passion borne from despair. Her head throbbed;

her nose was definitely broken and was getting clogged. She had difficulty breathing, so she blew it as best she could but nearly blacked out with the pain. She would have fallen if the guard wasn't holding her, pushing his body against her. Her blood had sprayed across the balustrade and tiled floor below, but she could breathe better now.

"You'll be doing me a favour," she continued her insane bluff. "But know this: as your fat boss just said, this pretty little *virgin* vixen is promised to Urgad Jorakif, brutal Overlord of Dran'ali. I can guarantee your captain is already a dead man walking for punching my face, and if you do me harm, I'll ensure Urgad, *my betrothed*, will have your head as well as Blarik's. Seeing your ugly head on a pike will bring much joy to my heart. So please, do your worst. I look forward to it. I'm trained to help you if you need it. It looks like you do. Been a while, has it?"

His groping stopped, and he swore, stepping back. "You'll get what's comin' to you, crazy trull."

"I'm sure I will, but not from the likes of you. Now, get your small mind out of my pants and get me back to my quarters," she ordered.

ELEVEN

AN OPPORTUNITY

With the rattling of the keys in the door, everyone who was in the opulent lounge looked up expectantly. There were cries of shock and astonishment when Marra walked in. The front of her nightgown was slathered with her blood, making the damp material cling even more.

Even Shayr blanched at what she saw. She jumped up and raced across the room, as did the others, taking Marra from the guard and helping her to a sofa. A couple of girls fetched damp cloths to swab gently at the blood covering her face and neck. They crowded around, all asking questions and swearing at the guard.

"Thank you. We can manage." Criss and Rhian, two of the slightly older women, were very gentle and attentive.

The younger girls still fussed, mostly out of shock.

"Be still. We've done this before," Criss said with confidence.

"Who did this?" Rhian checked Marra for any other wounds. She frowned at the multiple layers of clothing.

Many pairs of eyes turned accusingly at the guard, who was hurriedly backing away.

"It wasn't—" he stammered.

"Not so fast, Kips," Shayr called to him. "Go and fetch Corum the healer, immediately!"

"I don't answer to the likes of you!" Kips spat.

"You will, or I'll personally inform Master Quillin what *you* did to this wretched girl."

"Me?" he yelped. "I didn'—"

"I don't give a damn. It's what I'll be telling him. Who do you think he's going to believe?" Shayr glared at him, eyes blazing. "You're wasting time. I've a mind to get Vern to visit you later."

At the mention of Vern's name, he stiffened. "You're nothin' but a bitch, just like all of them."

Shayr stormed towards him. "Yes, but this bitch's going to have your tiny balls in a jar by her bed tonight if I have to tell you again."

Some of the girls giggled at the heated conversation and the look on his face.

Kips backed away, turning once he was through to the hall, slamming the doors in his wake. His boots could be heard quickly receding.

With the doors closed and entertainment finished, they turned back to Marra, looking serious that one of their own— even if she was a noble-born brat—should be treated in this manner.

"Thank you for that, Shayr." Marra couldn't believe she was saying those words to her.

Shayr looked with distaste at the girl's bloodied features. "Think nothing of it. I'm sure you'd do the same for me."

I probably would. Marra nodded. The words were said, but she heard no empathy behind them. She wriggled back against the cushions when one of the girls put a blanket down to prevent any blood spilling onto the expensive fabric.

"Besides," Shayr continued, "the eunuch would have my tits if anything happened to you in here."

"He'd need a very big jar, though," Amba joked, laughing nervously with the others.

Criss and Rhian rinsed the bloodied cloths in a bowl, then continued their treatment. "Could you fetch another fresh bowl, please, Amba?" Criss asked.

The dark girl nodded and dashed away.

Corum the healer arrived shortly after. She looked aghast at Marra's brutal injury and quickly examined her. With curt instructions, Marra was then helped to her room by Criss and Rhian, where the healer spent hours administering to the wounds. Balms and poultices were concocted quickly and efficiently from the ingredients in her bags. If anything was needed, a quick summons was all it took.

"How is Blarik?" Marra asked, hoping for the worst.

"He'll recover, but will have a bad headache for a few days. You, however, need more attention."

"Is it that serious?"

"The injury, yes. You're lucky the nasal bone didn't get pushed back into your brain. But also, Master Quillin will no doubt hear of this and will want to check for himself. The better you look when that happens, the better the outcome will be for all, including me." She laid a cool, aromatic poultice across the girl's face. "It's very lucky you have strong bones and good skin."

"Do you know what happened to Blarik?" It hurt to talk, but it hurt just as much being quiet, and she wanted to know the outcome of her futile attempt at ending him. "What did they say happened?"

"The guards were reluctant to say anything, but I can only assume he got too drunk again and fell."

No doubt, too embarrassed to admit I did that under their watch!

"Dare I ask how your injuries occurred? " The healer examined Marra's knuckles, gently dabbing at them, then smudging a pale green cream over the injuries.

"The guard captain punched my face."

"Did he now?" Corum raised her eyebrows in surprise. "Considering who you are, and your imminent future, he should have known better. What a fool."

"You'd think," Marra agreed. "But guards aren't known for their overabundance of intelligence." Her mind fleetingly recalled her personal guard. *My Trinol was an exception.*

"This is true." Corum busied herself with her bag for a few minutes.

"Mind you, I was just as stupid trying to kill Blarik, and attacking armour barehanded and in sandals."

"Also true." Corum glanced down at the girl's bruised feet. "I want you to drink this. It's horribly foul, but will help in your recovery, I can assure you."

Even with her clogged senses, Marra knew immediately the foulness was understated. She took a ragged breath, upending the fluid quickly and swallowing before she gagged. Even the effort of drinking caused pain.

"Good girl. Now rest. I'll be back in a couple of hours to change the poultice. Try to keep as still as you can." Corum gathered her materials and left.

Florin came rushing in, bursting into tears the moment she saw Marra's bandaged face.

"It's okay, Florin." Combined with the bandage, the damage to her nose gave her voice a muffled, nasal quality. "You should see the other guy."

Florin dropped to her knees and gave her a gentle hug. After she'd wiped her tears, she looked at the large poultice covering Marra's face, at a loss for words, tears brimming again.

"Yes, it's painful. I probably deserved it, but I was this close to slicing Blarik's neck." She held two fingers close together. "The fat bastard fell back and concussed himself instead."

"Why did he want to see you?" Florin wasn't reassured by her words. "Has anything changed?"

"No. He wanted to gloat about his glorious plans for the pending arranged marriage. If you hadn't told me the gossip already, it may have worked, and he would have seen the look of horror on my face. But he was sorely put out when I didn't flinch. That look of disappointment was worth it all. His concussion was a bonus."

Florin's tears gradually dried up. "Glad I could help."

Marra reached out for her hand and held it in both of hers. "Girl, you've been nothing but a help since the day I arrived at this cursed place. In fact, if not for our exercising, I doubt I could have jumped onto the table to stab him. So, I have you to thank for that as well."

Florin got up and moved a small chair over to sit more comfortably.

"There's a drawback to this poultice, though." Marra tried to grin, but the effort caused tears. "No more exercise for a while, and looks like I'll be having soup for a few days."

"At least you can still meditate." Florin smiled wanly. "I thought you were going to say no more kissing."

"Ah, well, you may kiss my hand. I *am* noble born, don't you know?"

"Oh yes, my lady. You know by now I'd be happy to kiss any—"

A knock at the door stopped the chatter. They looked up to see Shayr looming in the entrance.

"Master Quillin is here," she said in annoyance. "Begone, Florin."

With a nervous smile, the young girl got up and ducked through the door.

Moments later, the seneschal came in, his sandals slapping the tiles. He paused at the threshold, his eyes widening when he saw Marra's face. He opened his mouth, but Marra beat him to it, surprised at seeing the genuine concern in his eyes.

"Master Quillin. It looks worse than what it is, truly. With Shayr's insistence, Corum came to see me almost immediately. I apologise for bringing this problem to your door."

The master turned. "Scoot." He shooed Shayr and the gathering of prying eyes and ears away and pushed the door closed before coming to the bedside.

Marra saw the dark look in Shayr's eyes as the door shut in her face. It brought a grin—as well as pain and tears—to her own face. Dismissed in much the same way as she had dismissed Florin.

The teacher's pet sent away like a stray dog.

"What? Nonsense, child." Quillin sat on the chair Florin had used minutes earlier. "I have been remiss in my duties. I should have seen this coming. It pleases me, Corum saw to you; she's a fine healer indeed. Tell me everything."

Marra wriggled to a half-sitting position. The seneschal even got up to adjust her pillows for her. "Thank you, Master Quillin—"

"Please, call me Onty when no one is around."

"Thank you, Onty. Do you know the real circumstances leading to my arrival?"

"To marry—"

"Forgive me, but before that. How I came to be here in the first place, that night after the meeting of the council?"

He shook his head. "Only what High Lord Blarik told me. I did think it unusual, but as you are related, I let it go."

Marra nodded, not surprised in the slightest that he'd make some story up. "I guess since you're loyal to your boss, you'd have to believe everything he said."

"Within reason. I am aware of his...reputation." Ont'eba looked apologetic.

"Aren't you the spymaster?"

"Technically speaking, it's a joint effort. My predecessor was the real spymaster. She had an untimely departure, and as my role is in recruiting, I'm away a lot for various reasons, and I don't always get the latest information from our birds."

"I think I understand. He's the face—regrettably—and you're the brains."

"Well..." He shrugged. "That's a nice way to put it. More of a trainer in the art of deception. Hence why I'm now administering the schools.»

"And all these trips away?" Marra asked. "Sorry to pry."

"I roam the land to judge the calibre of potential trainees. It's both an exhilarating and depressing role: finding brilliant potential in some, and having to turn away others because they won't make the grade. I have to be firm, however. This isn't simply a refuge or foster home. Everyone here has their skills. But enough of that. You're saying you are here as a prisoner?"

"What did Blarik tell you?"

"That, with the death of your father, your life was in peril. You were sent here for safety until the arranged marriage."

"You think it's something my father wanted? Or I wanted?"

"My dear, I have dealt with many people, both noble and

gutter trash. I have seen and heard it all, and I don't make judgments on their likes and wants."

Sitting up and taking a slow, deep breath, Marra told him, "A rockion killed Father, highly unusual this far away from the Black Hills. And then I hear Blarik has a skulk of rockions—of which one escaped—a convenient story, don't you think?"

"That would be typical of him." Ont'eba nodded. "And yes, he has rockions."

Marra nodded, then relayed all she knew or suspected of the tragic events leading up to her arrival here.

"And you say being here, and this marriage is against your will?" the seneschal asked.

"Definitely, but I don't see any way out of it. And now, having spoken to you, if I escape, it will look very bad for you and the school. Blarik will be furious. As High Lord, he has control of the military. You wouldn't be safe. Or..." she considered fleetingly, "perhaps it's best I do go. I could escape from Urgad. That way, there is no shame or embarrassment to the school."

"My dear Lady, you have been treated so poorly. I'm touched you would even consider us over your own well-being. No, this will not do. I will have to come up with an alternative plan."

"You will be putting yourself in danger."

"I'm used to living in danger. This is no worse a threat."

Marra considered what he was saying. Her head was aching, and the concoction Corum fed her was making her lethargic, but she had to know.

"Onty, forgive any impropriety, but..."

"How did I become a eunuch?"

She nodded. "I've heard rumours."

"Which, as any spy can tell you, has around ten per cent of truth in them. Let me guess, you think I was a pirate—because of the tattoos—and therefore a eunuch because of what happens to those who cross the Red Sails twice."

"Sounds like more than ten per cent of the rumours I've heard."

"So, as you can see, the dangers of being here in this school are nothing compared to the dangers on the high seas as a pirate."

"And The Crags? What can you tell me about it?"

"Only a bit, to be honest. So little information comes out of there."

"You've not been there?"

"No, but I can understand your confusion. It's the actual Red Sail crews that do the de-balling, not those at The Crags." The seneschal opened up—probably the first time in years—about his previous life. Hearing him relate his story, Marra had a semblance of a plan.

I just need to get out.

"Onty, this injury was a result of what I tried to do. In fact, I probably got away lightly, considering most people attempting to kill a High Lord—even a pretender—are executed on the spot. I'm safe here. You do not need to put yourself out in any way to help me. In fact, I'd suggest you take a longer absence than normal. That way, if anything should happen while you're away, you can't be held responsible for it."

"Are you sure? I'd like to help."

"Can you make Blarik disappear and make me High Lady?"

To his credit, and much to Marra's surprise, Ont'eba actually paused, giving it thought. "Not before this arranged marriage. And after would be pointless. I can promise you this, though: I know how to tweak his ego and will subtly turn my efforts into weakening his base."

"What about Urgad?" she asked. "I understand he's quite keen and can be violent."

"He may be powerful in Dran'ali, but over here, I'm not going to lose sleep over a disgruntled horse-herder. Blarik made the overture to him. I'll let him deal with the fallout."

"I'm also concerned for Florin. She—we—have developed a close relationship. She was alone when I arrived. She's young and impetuous. I feel she might do something foolish."

"We've all been there. I'm not that old to forget my young and impetuous youth. Let me think on it. I'll come up with a plan for her, too. And, yes, I'm not ignorant of the animosity Shayr has for Florin because of her association with you."

"I cannot thank you enough for that, and for coming to see me." Marra reached for his delicate hands. *Far too smooth for a pirate.* "Even though it was a fleeting visit, my father thought highly of you. If it means anything to you, so do I."

"My Lady, you are your father's blood, without a doubt." He put a hand on her shoulder. "A truly noble woman with a truly noble heart."

"You'd better go before I cry, and crying hurts. I'm honoured to have met you. I hope we can speak again under better circumstances."

"The honour is mine. Until that fine day, I wish you calm seas and strong winds, my lady." Ont'eba stood and bowed low.

He turned and opened the door. He waved briefly, sending his bangles ringing, then left.

CHAPTER

TWELVE

THE BANQUET

The banquet was laid out in a large semi-circle with a clear area of slate tiles in the centre. The royal table was situated on the opposite side, on a raised section that overlooked the hall. A half-dozen columns supported the vaulted ceiling. A pair of flaming torches, one on each side of the earthy-coloured pillars, shone ample light across the tables.

The crew were escorted to their seats by young, liveried children. As guests of honour, Corra and Tully were placed directly opposite the royal table, while the rest of the crew were seated on either side. They marvelled at the silver goblets, plates, and cutlery. Platters of fruit and jugs of various beverages filled all available space. The row of tables behind them, forming another semi-circle, began filling up with beautifully dressed people.

As Corra took her seat next to Tully, she spied a familiar head moving behind the other guests. She quickly got up and intercepted the young boy.

"Jag? Why are you here? Is everything okay?"

"They said until I go home, I should help out. I had to have a bath!" He didn't sound happy about it.

"Well, you did smell." Corra ruffled his newly cut hair. "No doubt, like all of us. But they're treating you well?"

"I guess." Jag shrugged. "They eat funny stuff."

The ornate doors opened, and the minstrels opened up a fanfare announcing the arrival of His Excellency.

Corra stood as the royal procession entered and made their way to the seats.

Olpu-tu at the head, two young women sat to his immediate left, and a third to his right.

Corra tensed. She noticed her crew going grim-faced. No doubt they were thinking the same thing as herself: the girls on the left were no older than the newlings. She shook her head subtly. This wasn't the time or place for any trouble. When she looked down, Jag had been taken away to carry out his duties. She was also politely encouraged to return to her seat.

By the time she was back next to her First Mate, standing like all the other guests, the royal party had arrived and taken their seats without preamble. The guests then took their seats, and the hot food was carried in on laden trays.

Olpu-tu stood, and everyone stopped what they were doing immediately.

"My friends, welcome. You will all know how I dislike making speeches." He chuckled.

The locals tittered at his humour, as expected.

"But we do have special guests, so this is one of those rare times," Olpu-tu continued. "Even so, I'll be brief. Here this evening, we have the pleasure of Captain Corra Sienna, her first mate, Tully, and the valiant crew of the unusual vessel currently in our harbour. I hear they are part of the Jaranabi Red Sails fleet. I'm told they are a force to be reckoned with on the high seas as they track down and capture the vile scum that infest our waters and attack our ships. There's a captured pirate ship that reportedly attacked one of our very own traders. As evidence of their prowess, these fine ladies captured them and the vessel and sought to bring them to Savarik for justice. A few unfortunates will be part of this evening's entertainment. Be welcome, ladies. Please partake of our delicacies and festivities as an acknowledgement of our gratitude."

There was polite applause as many eyes glanced their way. Dignitaries, both local and from surrounding villages, had also been invited. Many had not had the opportunity to see the new ship, and they were curious to see women privateers.

During the evening, through the many courses of prepared meats and other exotic dishes, the dignitaries took turns to meet with Captain Sienna and crew. During the conversations, the need arose to explain the difference between pirates and privateers.

"So, you legally board ships and attack the crew and confiscate their cargo? Nice. I'm sure our merchants would be pleased if we adopted and approved that methodology." Some of the dignitaries' lackeys chuckled, nodding at this prospect.

While various acrobatic acts were performed in the centre of the tables, music played softly in the background. The instruments were more or less similar to those in Jaranabi, but now and then the music reached an uncomfortable pitch, making the newcomers wince. Looking around, though, it seemed to Corra and Tully that most of the guests were familiar with this music.

After an hour or so of eating, Corra and Tully were invited to join His Excellency.

His wives had left—or had been sent away—to make room for the guests.

They chatted about the food and wine for a while before Olpu-tu lowered his voice.

"We have heard on occasion of a ship of females out there. We thought it was simply a story told by traders to impress us islanders and to try to charge us more for services we were not aware of." Olpu-tu looked at the women seated around him. "Tell me about your vessel. I have not seen its like before."

Corra spoke in general terms about the Red Sails Fleet and their mission to patrol the seas to the south of Harando, the continent. "You're right, though. The *Revenge* is an unusual ship, and one of three. We also have the *Vengeance* and the *Emancipator*."

"Interesting. And how much would one require to pay for such a vessel?"

"While I'm certain Your Excellency could amply afford such a fine vessel. I'm afraid that it's not for sale; nor am I in a position to make any arrangement to sell any ship while under my government's decree. While I'm lucky to command it, High Lord Olber of Jaranabi is the rightful title-holder of all the fleet. Perhaps I could arrange for negotiations to start on my return? Our Lord is quite approachable to matters of trade."

"Perhaps." Olpu-tu sipped his wine. "This is displeasing news...but in the quest for possible trade and alliances, I will not pursue the matter. However, I will take the pirate vessel off your hands."

"Your Excellency, with regret, a Master Nethan D'Longe has already approached us to purchase the *Tormentor*."

"This is also indeed disturbing news." He slowly put his gold goblet down. "How much did this miscreant offer to pay for it? I will double it!"

Corra shifted uncomfortably. She had no doubt D'Longe was a shady character, but it wasn't in her nature to double-cross anyone. Even if it meant disappointing a powerful and somewhat ruthless ruler.

At her hesitation, Olpu-tu leant forward, his earrings

dangling. "You're a guest here, and new to our ways. I could take the vessel from you and not pay at all. I could even imprison you all without impunity and take your *Revenge*. But I won't, of course." He raised a placating hand at the rising tension. "We're a small island nation, and I'm used to getting my way, but again...the potential for alliances dissuades me from any heavy-handedness, so I will say this to you.

"I'll purchase this pirate vessel and pay three times what D'Longe offered. I've dealt with him before, so leave him to me. D'Longe will not be pleased, but he'll understand the situation. In fact, he did you a disservice by putting you in this predicament, knowing full well my interest in establishing a larger fleet. I wouldn't put it past him to have considered this very conversation. He's sly and probably scheming at this moment. I'm suspicious by nature. We shall see."

"Your Excellency, what you say is true. Small nations always do well with strong trade arrangements with allies. I don't in any way speak for High Lord Olber, but I'll send word to him on my return and inform him of our discussions. As for the *Tormentor*, I'll put my faith in your words. While I'm loath to renege on a done deal, to decline would be awkward for any future relationships between our countries. The vessel is yours."

Olpu-tu put his bejewelled hand out and they shook on it. "Now, while I send for the payment, we can enjoy the culmination of tonight's entertainment."

The entertainment, a dozen lithe and oiled dancers, had already started. A troupe of almost naked men and women flowed across the tiled floors in an undulating rhythm. The drumbeat started slowly, then grew in intensity. Each dancer held a heavy-bladed weapon of exotic design. They writhed and spun with precision, the blades glinting with the light from the flaming torches.

The diners all gasped in concern at one point when it looked as though each dancer was about to impale another, but at the last second, they ducked and weaved with unbelievable grace. The movements looked very much like some of the various sword forms used by elite militaries. This went on for some time, and Corra had to admit their stamina was impressive.

Going by the growing beat of the drumming, the dancing was coming to a climactic end. The gyrations of the dancers were mesmerising as they continued to spin and twist, defying gravity.

As the sconces dimmed, a large orb above the dance floor began to glow brightly. It was the first time the *Revenge* crew had witnessed any form of elemental magyk from these people. On the edge of the dance floor, now cast into gloom, a dozen trolleys appeared, each one with a semi-naked figure laid out on it.

As the figures came within the glow of the orb, they could all see a dozen pirates.

The drumming built up. The dancers writhed and spun in a blur. A horn started softly but grew in volume.

Tully gripped Corra's arm as the realisation hit.

The horn grew louder as the beat of the drums changed subtly, seemingly more sinister now that the intent was obvious. The dancers moved out in a wider circle, their bodies gliding past the captives who were alert, though unable to move.

Suddenly, the drums reached a crescendo. The horn blast stopped. The hall was silent. The dancers stopped in perfect placement. And a dozen blades swiftly descended.

Heads rolled. Blood gushed onto the slate-tiled floor. And the people gasped.

The torches flared brightly. The locals erupted, standing up and clapping.

The *Revenge* crew were stunned and left speechless at the blatant carnage.

It took several moments for Sienna to get over the shock and to feel a tugging at her waistcoat. She looked down, surprised to see young Jag was there, looking frightened.

"The other pirates are loose," he whispered.

THIRTEEN

HEALING

As expected, Florin came in shortly after the seneschal left.

"So, what did he say? Are you in trouble? His face remains so bland, you never know his thoughts or moods." Her worry made her chattier than usual.

"All is well." Marra considered briefly how much to tell her. "No, I'm not in trouble at all, which is quite remarkable."

"Ont'eba is stern but kind; nothing like the High Lord."

"True. And I don't think Shayr's going to be a problem for you...later on."

"You mean...after you leave? I understand." She looked sullen for a moment. "But we had great times, didn't we?"

"We had and still will. Me leaving isn't going to happen overnight, and when it does, it won't be the end of the world."

Florin nodded, eyes moist. "It pleases me to hear that."

"Silly. You think I haven't enjoyed your company? You think I could forget you?"

"Times change. People move on."

"This is also true. Other than heading south, I have no idea when or where I'll go when I manage to get out of here."

"You should go to The Crags."

"Isn't that too obvious?"

"Perhaps, but what can they do? No man sets foot in The Crags without their permission. It's also true that it's guarded by a powerful witch."

Marra never could tell when she was joking. Her young friend had come up with crazy-sounding rumours before, and those turned out to be true. "Why would a man want to go there if they castrate them?"

"Now look who's silly. Not *all* men, it's the Red Sails that do that, and only against pirates. I've heard the community allows some men there: sons, nephews, some trusted traders."

"More pillow talk and passage peeping?"

"I heard these stories in my village. I wasn't born here, you know."

"I know. I'm teasing."

There was a knock at the door, and the healer entered.

"Time to change that poultice and see how things are going. Florin, dear, if you don't mind?" Corum held the door open.

"Certainly, Cor." Florin gave a short wave to Marra, then swanned out of the room.

The healer closed the door and sat. "Lie back, dear, and I'll put a fresh poultice on."

Marra settled down onto the bed as asked, so Corum could tend to her injury.

"How are you feeling?" the healer asked as she was preparing another poultice. "Have you had a chance to rest?"

"Not with Master Ont'eba visiting. He stayed quite a while, which was very kind of him."

"It's the way he is. Busy, absentminded occasionally, but

kind when he can be," Corum spoke of him fondly. She gently peeled the old poultice off. And gasped.

Marra went cold at her reaction. While always complimented on her supposed attractiveness, she didn't give it much thought. But when she saw the look on Corum's face, she fervently hoped she wasn't disfigured. "Wh-what is it?"

"My dear...Have you been Tested?"

"Tested?" *I'm still a virgin, can't be that!* "For what?" *Surely it can't be for magyk.*

Marra started to think of any recent diseases or ailments going around the local villages. "A healer came around for leeching, and several months ago, there was a sickness in—"

"No, dear." Corum chuckled. "For any Talent."

"Talent?"

"Perhaps your brain has been rattled?" Corum deftly lifted back Marra's eyelid and studied her eyes. "Hmm... Magyk, my dear. Have you been properly assessed for magyk?"

"Oh." Marra had to think back. "Several years or so ago, I believe. Why? What is it? How is my nose? My face?"

"You tell me." Corum held up a mirror for her.

Holding her breath, Marra took a quick look. Her face, while still slightly bruised, was mostly healed. "I... It certainly felt a lot better. I thought it was that vile potion, or your poultice numbing the pain."

Curom shook her head. "I know I make an excellent poultice, but not to heal this fast."

"Was my injury not as bad as we thought?"

Corum looked doubtful. "You did have very bad swelling. I could tell by the bruising around your eyes that your nose was broken, but it was pushed in, not to the side as a normal punch. I was going to give you a sedative and set it once the swelling reduced...but this is nothing short of amazing."

"I can't be a magyker. They go crazy."

"The men do, yes."

"Don't the women? I know I've attempted some crazy things—like trying to kill Blarik. Am I going mad?"

Again, the healer looked unsure. "Not that I've heard of. No. But I have only a little knowledge of it. My talent is so minuscule, but I could never do this." She examined Marra's face again, then the other healed injuries. "Remarkable. Perhaps you should be Tested again."

"Can talent simply appear overnight?"

"Not overnight, no. How old were you when you were tested?"

"About thirteen." Marra shrugged.

"Had you reached puberty?" Corum continued at her hesitation, "Was it before or after your first bleeding?"

"Oh." Marra blushed. 'Before...I think."

"Then you should be Tested again," the healer advised.

Like that's going to happen soon. "Put the poultice on anyway," Marra suggested. "We can't let anyone know."

"But this is absolutely wonderful news!"

"Corum, if Blarik hears about this, he'll use me for his own ends, the same way he uses those crazy elementalists he drags around with him. Please swear you will not tell anyone."

The healer sighed. "You're a patient. Of course, I won't tell. You should get training, though. It can be dangerous to wield magyk without it." She placed the new poultice on, gently lifting Marra's head to wrap the bandage.

"This school—"

"Is not for training elementalists."

"Is there one?"

"For men, yes. Women...I have no idea."

Marra briefly considered how she could possibly get training in a male school. Now that *was* completely insane. She moved away from those thoughts. "What do I do then?"

"Without proper training?" Corum shrugged, considering. "Avoid stressful situations. Relax and keep calm. Anger, fear... are generally the worst states of mind which, so I understand, weakens control, making it easier for whatever it is that allows the magyk to flow to take over."

"Avoid stressful situations?" *Right.*

"Yes. This's what I've heard over the years, not from any personal experience. Women elementalists are rare."

"But you said you had some magyk..."

"Barely. I should say *strong* elementalists. In my case, it seems to give me a slightly better ability in healing, but that's it. I don't even know how I do it. I dare say anyone mastering a skill like healing, sword fighting, blacksmithing...they probably all have a touch of magyk, but not enough to be elementalists, and not enough to even consider testing."

"So, perhaps you did in fact do this healing? You said you don't know how it's done."

"Not like this. Besides, the poultice alone couldn't have done it, and I wasn't here."

"Onty was."

Corum was packing her materials away. "He is the most sane and mild-mannered person I've met. It is not him."

"Florin was here for a while..." *And she does do some weird things.* Marra couldn't bring herself to say that out loud; she had too deep an affection for her. "I will speak with her."

"Marra." Corum stood with her bag, a cheeky grin creasing her face. "If you don't know her by now, I dare say you never will." She smiled. "I can do no more for you, but if you need me for anything else, send for me immediately."

"You will need to make regular visits to keep up the pretence."

"Of course. In that case, I'll call in tomorrow, after breakfast and before dinner."

"Lovely. Thank you so much."

"A pleasure," the healer said as she was walking out the door.

AFTER THE MEETING with Blarik and the guards, Marra had slowly been included in some of the activities of the other girls. The rapid healing was explained as a combination of Corum's healing abilities and that the wound looked far worse than they first thought.

Tiffan sat chatting with Amba, Jofine, and Leesa. When Marra returned from her bath, she waved her over, offering to try different styles with her hair.

"Corum's simply an excellent healer. It was mostly bruising," Marra explained to those who asked. "We know the guards are stupid and clumsy, but not so dumb they'd seriously injure any of us. If not Blarik, I'm sure the seneschal would readily deal out punishment otherwise."

Amba poured her a glass of red wine.

"Sure, why not?" Marra agreed, simply relieved to finally have some acceptance. Not wanting to spoil this new development, she knelt on the rug near the lounge and accepted the wine. "Thank you."

"You've never been to Herith?" Tiffan asked. "It's in the north. This is the favourite style there."

"I've not travelled all that much."

The three girls, all from the northern regions, started telling her about their towns and what to look for when travelling there.

Shayr sauntered into the loungeroom, saw Marra with the girls, and wandered over.

What is she conniving now? Jealous, I'm now being included?

"May I borrow Marra for a moment?" It may have been put as a request, but not going by her I'll-take-no-nonsense tone, it was anything but. "I need to speak with her."

Tiffan and the others moved away, and Shayr sat where Tiffan had been. "Herith style?" Shayr noted. "It's not quite right. May I?"

Unsure of her motives, Marra nodded, not completely trusting her, but equally not wanting to cause any more animosity between them. As with the other women, they'd spoken more ever since that day, but not with what could be regarded as anything like warmth.

"I'm glad to hear and see you've recovered so well." Shayr started with small talk. "Corum is such a fine healer."

Other girls wandered in and sat nearby, poured some wine for themselves and started to chat quietly.

After several stern looks from Shayr, the girls took the hint and moved to the far side of the fountain where Tiffan and her friends had congregated.

"I've arranged to help you get away." Shayr moved her lips closer to Marra's, as if sharing a secret. "My man, Vern, will come and see you tomorrow night," she whispered. "We've arranged a pony in the woods near the back of the compound."

"You did? That's...a surprise."

Shayr sat back and kept toying with her hair. "Not at all. Some girls were made to be here, others not. To be honest, you're causing too much trouble. I only want the best for my girls. With you gone, it will be quieter." When satisfied with the chosen hairstyle, Shayr fleetingly kissed Marra lightly on the cheek. "I wish you well," she said in parting.

Marra stood and moved to a mirror to check this northern style. Perhaps it would take some getting used to, but it was not to her liking. Too high and coiled. *Looks like a hive for bees.*

Seeing the other girls still chatting, she went over to thank them for their choice. They admired her hair and overall look, telling her how her long, slim neck was accentuated by this particular style.

"And men just love it." Tiffan ran her eyes over her. "You look adorable."

The others nodded, smiling.

Even though she suspected most of it was tripe, Marra blushed and wished them all a good night. She went to stand by the tall glass doors leading onto the terrace for some fresh air and to let her hair dry as it was still damp from her dip in the pool.

It wasn't long before she saw Florin walk in. The girl headed straight for the table, grabbed a tray, and loaded it with food and wine. Seeing Marra by the window, she strode over and stood beside her, resting the tray on a sideboard.

Marra marvelled at how gracefully the young girl moved. "You look radiant," she approved. "Busy night?"

"Not overly, no. But it was surprisingly...fulfilling." Florin filled her glass from a bottle and drained it.

Marra raised her eyebrows. "Fulfilling? No offence, but that's not a word I would think to hear from you."

Florin tossed a grape at her, then popped one into her own mouth. "No offence taken. I only heard it this afternoon, myself." She giggled.

They laughed a bit longer before Marra shared the news of the planned departure.

At first, there was silence. Florin chewed some hard cheese and swallowed it down with more of the red wine. "I don't believe for one minute Vern will have a horse in the backwoods," she said eventually. "I don't know what they have planned, but you must be prepared for the worst." She reached for the wine and poured one for each of them.

"I've got some food and clothing." Marra accepted the glass

of wine from her friend. "I'll get more food later. See what else I can scrounge. Men's clothing, perhaps, so I can get rid of these stupid silk nightgowns."

"If I get more *fulfilment* beforehand, I might be able to help there." Florin winked. "And your hairpins? Have you got them?"

Marra nodded, reaching for the coiled hair. "No. It's gone! Shayr did my hair when she told me the news."

"That sly cow took it. She knows all too well its usefulness." Florin looked around. A couple of girls were chatting here and there, but Shayr was nowhere in sight.

"Here, take mine. I have several and can get more." Florin led Marra to a lounge and sat, placing her glass carefully on the tiles. "Better kneel here so I can reach properly."

Marra tossed a cushion on the floor and knelt between the young girl's shapely legs. Florin deftly rearranged the hair and slid the hairpin home. "Please tell me this hairstyle wasn't your idea."

"Hardly. It reminds me of a beehive, but Tiffan offered—perhaps a gesture of goodwill—which I could hardly refuse. Then Shayr took over. Why? Don't you like it?"

"It's nice...I guess...but only because of that lovely long neck of yours." On the spur of the moment, she undid the locket from around her neck and leant forward to show it to Marra. "Remember that aphrodisiac called *Beast* that'll make any male do a woman's bidding?"

"I do. Is that what this is?" Marra held the silver locket in her fingers. "Why have you got it?"

"You forgot my *fulfilling* moment already? I took some just in case, but I didn't need it after all." Florin clasped the chain around her friend's neck.

"I'd not think any man would need it with you administering to them." *Or woman, for that matter.*

"Oh! Now look who's flirting. But you say the nicest things." Florin's fingers ran lightly across her back and shoulders. "I hope you haven't forgotten how to use your hairpin as a lockpick."

"How could I? We went over it and over it." Marra rolled her eyes.

"You sound like you're whinging." Florin retrieved her wine glass from the floor.

"I'm not whinging."

"That's what all guilty whingers say. You know, there's severe punishment for whinging."

"There is no such thing. And I am not whinging."

"Well..." Florin downed the last of her wine. "I'm well-versed in the art of whinging, so I should know, and I can safely say, you are most definitely whinging."

"Okay, okay, I would *so* hate to argue with a subject-matter expert." Marra sighed, emptying her glass. There was no table in reach, so she put it on the floor to the side of the lounge. "Pray tell, what's the dire punishment for *over*-whinging?"

"The punishment," Florin said in an overly pompous voice, "handed down from generations upon generations of whinger-experts is...a tickle-attack." Quickly tossing the empty glass onto the lounge, Florin grabbed Marra's waist from behind and drilled her fingers into her ribs.

Marra recoiled, chortling like a child. Between gasps and giggles, she said, "I've...not been tickled...in years." She rolled onto the rug, twisting out of reach.

"Then you should get double." Florin slipped to the floor and straddled her before she could get up. Grabbing her wrists, Florin held them to the floor above Marra's head.

Marra struggled to breathe, writhing on the floor, her ribs aching from the laughter. Tears of mirth trickled from her eyes. "No matter what happens, I'm going to miss you," she said, when it seemed the attack was over. She looked up in wonderment at Florin's eyes. *So green.*

"And I you." Florin bent down and kissed her warmly.

When their lips parted, Marra breathed deeply, watching her. "Are you flirting again as well?"

"Can't you tell?"

"I wanted to make sure it wasn't just the wine."

"I don't need wine for this."

They kissed again. This time, there was no pulling away. They paused to catch their breath. Florin lightly kissed Marra's cheeks, then nuzzled her neck.

CHAPTER

FOURTEEN

A BLOODY ESCAPE

Marra jolted awake, fighting a moment of confusion before she vividly recalled the last few hours.

This was not her bed, and her arm was draped across Florin's flat belly. She gently lifted her arm and wriggled back. Strands of Florin's blonde hair had stuck to her lips, which she had to free or risk waking her. Marra then stealthily climbed off the bed and quickly searched the floor before finding her nightgown. She shrugged into it quickly, checking to see that Florin wasn't disturbed.

As Marra was about to reach down to pull the sheet up to cover the young woman, her eyes paused to drink in the sight of the elegant form bathed in moonlight. If there was only one appealing aspect of the barred windows that represented their captivity, it was how the shadows accentuated her curves.

A glance out the window showed dawn would soon approach. Even as she stepped towards the door, Marra took one long last look, burning the scene into her mind.

She wondered if this meant she was no longer a virgin? *Maybe there's no need to flee?* The thought was brief. *No, if word of their nocturnal activities got out, Florin would be in peril.* Blarik would be fuming if his plans were thwarted.

Meeting Florin had been the best part of this horrid, despicable place, the only memory she wanted to keep. She had half a mind to ask Florin to join her, but...the girl was happy here—wanted to be here—and Marra had no idea where she would be in a few hours.

She sighed at how unfair life could be. There were also the plans the seneschal had for her. Anything Onty came up with would far surpass what she could manage while on the run.

We both knew this was going to happen, and no promises were made...or expected.

Quickly and silently on bare feet, she moved through the main hall towards her room. She reached the door just as Shayr opened it.

"What are you doing in there?" Marra asked.

"Looking for you! Where the hell have you been?!" Shayr whispered fiercely.

"You said tomorrow night!"

"It's changed. I've had to keep Vern amused for the last few hours."

"No good deed goes unpunished. I hope the entertainment wasn't in my bed." Marra muttered.

"What?" the tall girl hissed. "I'm trying to help you here."

"And I appreciate it. I'm here now. Where's Vern?" Marra looked beyond, into the empty room. Her bed hadn't been slept in.

"Get your stuff—not much, mind—and I'll fetch him." Shayr pushed past her, cursing under her breath.

As soon as her back was turned, Marra went into her room to collect her pack by the door. Wrapped inside was a blade, cheese, cured meat, bread, and a small flask of water.

Earlier, Marra had suggested wearing something more

practical to sneak out, but Florin had warned it would raise suspicions.

"Won't sneaking around the grounds in the dark raise suspicions?" Marra had asked in return.

"And here I was, thinking I was the slow one. Consider where you are and what we do." Florin covered her mouth to stifle a laugh. "In your nightgown, no. In men's clothes, definitely."

"Ah." Marra rolled her eyes. "Whores sneaking around at night from one room to another is what we do. So, no suspicions raised."

Smiling at the past conversation, Marra checked that she still had her hairpins. The beehive hairstyle was gone, replaced by a far more practical braid. The pins were slipped into the braid. *And the skimpy nightgown left nowhere to conceal a blade.*

"Past time ta go, lovely," came a soft voice in the dark. "I'm Vern."

Marra turned, seeing the tall shadow looming behind her. "I remember you." *And your reek.*

Despite his size and studded leather armour, Vern stealthily moved out the door. She noticed his short sword was strapped so as not to jangle as he walked across the floor and out into the garden. He was careful to walk on the grass and not the gravel pathway, but seemed to be oblivious to his visibility in the bright, moonlit night.

Sneaking is one thing; being discreet about it is another. Marra had heard he wasn't gifted with the ability to think, and decided, if given the opportunity, she'd use that to her advantage.

At the far end of the garden, now in the shadows near the wall, he slowed. "We 'ave a back gate here. Somewhere..." He examined the area. "It's sort of 'idden, mainly used by the gardeners so they don't go carryin' stuff through the 'ouse."

"There it is." Marra pointed to a clump of vines.

"Good eyes as well." Vern moved briskly to the obscured gate while extracting a large key. The lock made surprisingly little noise when turned, indicating regular use or maintenance.

He pushed it open, waited for her to step through, then pulled it closed behind her and turned the key.

"Off we trot." Vern took the lead, pointing down a cobbled lane paralleling the high garden wall. On the opposite side was the back wall of a large building.

"Those are the stables," said Vern, confirming her thoughts of the smell's origins. "Guards' quarters are way down there." He hooked his thumb over his shoulder. "Pretty 'andy, when yer think 'bout it."

Marra smirked at his back. *As if you ever thought about anything other than food and sex.*

She was very familiar with the harem, the adjoining rooms for dinner, bathing, and the work cubicles. In her short time here after being acquainted with the secret passages, she'd also learnt the general layout of the house, and where the other staff's chambers were. This part of the domain, beyond the tapestried walls and billowing lace curtains, had remained a mystery. Until now.

The smell of the stables lessened as an overriding pungent odour dominated the air.

"Is there a tannery or abattoir here? Or did something die?"

"Sorta," Vern answered cryptically.

"Which one?"

"Well, things die 'ere regularly, so I guess yer could call it an *abatwa*."

"And this is the way to the horse? The one you have in the woods?"

The surly creep continued walking, ignoring her.

May as well talk to the stone walls. She huffed at his non-answer and continued to follow. She was trying to reason why they were walking away from the stables.

Surely that would be the place to get the horse.

The lane they were on opened up into a larger, fenced area, like a corral, with the silhouettes of other buildings surrounding the small plaza. She stopped dead in her tracks, hearing a soft rumbling growl somewhere in the darkness to her right. Her hackles rose, and goosebumps ran up her back and arms.

Vern turned to look, chuckling at her hesitation. "Thought that might surprise yer."

Marra nodded, not trusting her voice. After a moment, she cleared her throat. "Rockions?"

"You bet. Lovely beasts; I 'ear they can be brutal, too. Like I were sayin', thing's die 'ere regular-like. Nothin' left ta skin."

"First time. Shayr sez yer talk a lot. Must be yer nerves. Yer scared?"

Before Marra replied, another figure emerged from one of the stone buildings. From the description Shayr had given during the perfume and poison lesson, Marra supposed this gangly man with the long hair to be the rockion keeper.

"Dat you, Vern?" he asked.

"'Course 'tis, Col. Who else yer reckon?"

"No one. Just checkin'. Who dat? Brung me another play toy?"

"A toy, yeah, but not for yer to play with."

"Aww." Col looked over to the enclosure. "Me girls ain't 'ungry yet."

Marra went cold. *Death by rockion. First my father, now me?*

"No rush, Col. Reckon they can play for a while...but, so can we."

Ready for her to take flight, Vern's arm whipped out and

seized her cruelly with his right hand, his strong fingers digging into her shoulder.

She wanted to scream, but having heard the occasional woman scream in the night, she knew nobody would respond. *And it would probably just amuse these creeps more. Only you can save you.*

He ripped her pack out of her hand and tossed it over the bars with a grin. "You won't be needin' that." Vern dragged her closer to the enclosure, which was built of iron bars rising more than twenty feet. He held her up against the bars roughly and pushed himself against her to prevent any chance of escape.

Her head struck one of the bars. She winced at the pain. "You don't need to do this!" she whispered intently. "Let me go. I won't tell Shayr!"

"You ain't tellin' no one nuthin'." The guard laughed. "Col, get o'er 'ere and grab 'er other arm 'n' lift it up." Vern brought her right hand up and held it.

When the keeper came into view and followed the order, the guard tightly grasped both her wrists with his one hand.

"I 'eard she tried ta scratch the boss's eyes out," Vern explained.

"Rockions will eat bones 'n' all," Col said beside him, eyes running up and down her figure. "But not clothes."

Vern looked down. "What a pity. I guess this 'as to come off." He grabbed her nightgown by the neckline with his free hand and ripped it off. "Can't leave anythin' behind, can we? No trace of you passin'." Leering now at her nakedness, he ran his rough hand over her and found the locket hanging between her breasts. "What 'ave we here?"

"They're called breasts. Shayr did say you were slow," Marra hissed.

"What else did my lovely say?"

"That was the highlight," Marra retorted. *Did Shayr really put him up to this? Was she so vindictive as to want her dead?*

Only half listening, Vern flicked open the locket and took a whiff of the contents.

"I know it. Called an *afro disac*," Col said proudly. "Dat comes from me girls, it do."

"So, t'is. Reckon this'll brin' 'em to ya." He upended the locket and dribbled it all over her, then took a moment to rub it over her breasts. "You enjoyin' this, are ya?"

"Bathing with leeches would be less distasteful."

"You..." The insult slowly dawned on him.

She tried to knee him in the groin.

Vern laughed at the attempt and slapped her, then dragged her to the enclosure opening. "Let's 'ope these beasties take their time with you."

"This must be Shayr's idea. I doubt much happens in your filthy little mind."

I must be going mad, irritating this cretin, but if he gets angry enough to make a mistake...It's a slim chance...but I'll have zero with those beasts.

"Can I 'ave a turn?" Col asked, licking his lips with anticipation.

If Vern was about to do anything, Col's request stopped him.

The guard chuckled, looking at his companion. "Why not? I won't tell yer bitch, Clare."

"Aw. She ain't me wife or nuthin'," Col mumbled as he approached Marra.

"You ain't got time for both Clare and these beasties anyhow. 'Ere, I'll 'old 'er still. Be quick." Vern pulled her arms up again.

Col hesitated, looking at her and wiping his hands on his shirt. "Look away," he said to Vern. "Don't want you watchin'."

Despite the dire situation, Marra let out a snort.

"Idiot—" Vern vented.

"Close yer eyes," Col insisted.

"Blow me!" Vern gripped her tightly and turned away. "Get to it. Sun's arisin' soon' n' we need ta be gone."

Col, according to Florin and the gossip among the girls, had his 'difficulties'. He couldn't get it up, so he only used his hands. The scent of *Beast* also affected his reactions.

Marra groaned in pain as he forced his calloused hand between her thighs. The sound encouraged the simple man, but it was his rough fingers that caused her reaction. Judging by his rising enthusiasm, he liked it rough, or he thought she was somehow enjoying his attention. Col then tried to kiss her.

You are *an idiot.* Her mind flittered back to what Florin had said: 'Men think we're weak, but when it comes to sex, it's the men who are weak.' *And some are also particularly stupid.*

Distasteful as it was, Marra made sounds to encourage his kissing. He was lost in the moment, kissing her deeply. *Perfect.*

She clamped her teeth down firmly. The welling of his hot blood filled her mouth as she bit down on his tongue hard.

Col's gurgled scream cut through the night. He clutched his face and fell back, hitting the ground and whimpering like a child.

If circumstances were different, she might have felt sorry for him, but not tonight.

Vern glanced down in surprise at the sight.

"Bitch!" The guard let go of her wrists and punched her hard in the stomach.

Air exploded from her with the impact. The tongue and a mouthful of blood gushed over him as she buckled over, gasping. She collapsed to her knees in a daze. It seemed like an eternity before she could breathe again. Her gut hurt, but it was worth it to see Col rolling in pain on the ground, mouth dripping blood down his shirt and neck. Vern stood between them, wiping the blood off his chest, but merely smearing it more.

She tried to move away, but the guard's boot lashed out and knocked her down.

By the growling in the dark, the smell of gore and the noise must have reached the rockions in their lair.

"Quick, throw me the key." Vern motioned to the keeper with his bloodied hand.

Col shook his head, wiping blood from his chin. "-atch," he mumbled, pointing.

"What?"

The keeper shook his head. "Om-y a -atch. 'O key." Pointing with a bloodied hand.

Vern looked to the gate, realising it was a simple spring latch mechanism. He then nervously studied the darkness, seeing only shadows. He grabbed her braids and dragged her closer.

Marra reached up and grasped his hand to lessen the trauma to her scalp.

He paused, checking that the immediate area was clear. With a shaking hand smeared with blood, he unlatched the gate, pushed it open, and unceremoniously shoved her in before pulling it closed. He stepped back with a white face, hands shaking.

Marra was covered in scratches now, after being dragged across the cobbles and dirt. In the dark, she stumbled forward onto the rough ground. She fell to the dirt, adding scraped palms to her cuts and bruises. Breathing hard, she looked around with wide eyes into the gloom. She knew they were there. She could sense them. The air vibrated with their low, rumbling growls.

She also noticed the slight tremor in the ground. *They can't be that heavy...*

The soft padding of large paws reached her ears as the shadows separated from the darkness. Two large, six-legged beasts prowled towards her from different sides, sniffing the air.

One moved closer. The mouth, sharp teeth clearly visible, was only inches away. Its breath was worse than Vern's. She could feel the beast's whiskers on her skin. At any other time, it would have tickled, but now she held back her shriek of utter fear. The rockion's nose sniffed along her arm to her hands.

A massive tongue, feeling like wet sand, ran across her palm, licking the blood off. The other beast shouldered its way closer, sniffing her. It nuzzled under her, rolling her onto her side. The rasping sensation of its tongue ran over her scraped knees, then moved up her body.

Numb with fear, Marra forgot her pain. It was nothing compared to the terror of these massive jaws, inches away. The sniffing continued up her body until it reached her breasts. Some of Col's blood had dripped down her neck as well, but the beast hesitated when taking in the scent of the locket. After several more sniffs and snorts, it backed away to join its partner, mewling in confusion at the mixture of scents.

Marra didn't know how long she held her breath, but she needed air. With immense control, she released her bursting lungs slowly, then inhaled deeply while her panic-stricken mind considered her options. The cheese knife was wrapped in her pack and out of reach, leaving her with a hairpin. In any other situation, she'd laugh at the ludicrous idea of fending off a bloody and gory death by sticking a hairpin in a rockion's ear.

The beasts now circled her, large noses constantly sampling the air. She couldn't stop her body shaking with the fear of her imminent mauling.

A boot scraped on the cobbles in the lane. Marra turned to the noise, as did the rockions with a growl. With utmost care and suddenly glad of the recent exercise regime back in the harem, she strained her muscles and managed to sit up to look around. *Nowhere to crawl to.* She saw a gate leading to their lair. *Maybe in there?*

Col was now standing next to Vern. The two men stared, transfixed by the sight. In the fading moonlight, a naked woman sat on the ground, two rockions looming over her, tails lashing from side to side.

The keeper said something incoherent. Wincing, Col wiped his mouth, which was still dripping; his arms were covered in blood.

Another plan, just as crazy, formed in Marra's foggy mind.

They may not be hungry now, but cats do love to play. And chase.

A long shot, but the potential outcome was better than taking on these beasts with cutlery and hair accessories. Grimly, carefully, she stood and made a step towards the gate, cringing at the imminent, clawing death from behind. When nothing happened, she stepped again. Still nothing.

"Yer ain't gettin' out that easy." Vern belatedly staggered forward towards the entrance.

"You're right. *I'm* not." She beat him to the gate, put her small hand through the bars and lifted the latch. Marra glared into his bloodshot eyes. "You'd better run," she whispered to him, then stepped back, pulling the gate wide open.

Shocked with the realisation that four dinner-plate eyes were now focussed on him, Vern instinctively reached for his sword, forgetting it was tied down. He turned and fled with a scream.

Go play, ladies. Marra held her breath as the two shadows of death loped by silently.

Covered in his own blood, Col was an immediate target for the first rockion, which pounced the distance between them in one leap, crushing his chest beneath its claws before dragging the corpse around the lane. Col hadn't stood a chance. He was dead before he could scream.

Vern managed to get a bit of a distance, but he was swept up in large, toothy jaws. The rockion tossed his body into the air. He hit the cobbles with a splat. The beast did it several times, each time punctuated by a high-pitched growl.

Marra knew she was lucky to still be breathing. She had to move before either of the rockions decided she wasn't really what she smelt like, and there was also the inevitable fact that the compound would soon be swarming with guards as the noise they made cut through the otherwise quiet night.

Her nightgown was ruined, but it would still serve a purpose. She picked it up and wiped up Col's congealing blood, then threw the rags into the enclosure. "Let them think I'm also dead."

She had no idea where the locket was now. Gathering her dropped pack, she raced away from the gory scene to where Col had come from, as it was the nearest building. It was dim, but still enough moonlight entered through the broken window to allow her to see.

A quick search found some other clothes and boots. She didn't let her mind consider when they were last washed, if ever. Running around in silk nightgowns was one thing, but she could not run around completely naked. Not even from a whorehouse.

That would most definitely invite more unwanted attention.

She donned the clothing, snatched a satchel from a chair and stuffed her pack inside, then slung the satchel over her shoulder.

"Now, how to get the hell out of here..." Moving carefully, she found a back door that led through a lean-to, then a lane. The sounds of men yelling and screaming, punctuated by the occasional roar and growl, came from her left. Fortunately, judging by the position of the descending moon, she needed to turn to her right to head back to the stables.

Though it was less risky, she could have simply run to the nearest woods, but trying to escape on foot would be foolhardy, especially in boots that were far too big. They'd track her down before dawn. The riskier, but far more practical escape, would be mounted. She only had to head towards the rousing guardhouse, saddle a horse, and race off before anyone spotted her.

Marra heard several horses snort as she entered the stables. One sounded familiar.

"You're going crazy, girl. One horse snorting is much like any other," she mumbled, going from one stall to the next until she reached the last one.

"Sleena?" With a cry of joy, Marra ducked under the railing to hug the horse she thought she'd never see again.

Sleena reared in the stall, pawing the air and whinnying in fear, setting off some of the other horses.

"Shit." After a torturous moment, she realised she was wearing a scent that would terrify any animal. And no doubt the clothes reeked of rockion, too.

Backing away, she scanned her surroundings. Nearby was a water trough. It was a far cry from the hot mineral spring she had grown accustomed to, but with no other option, she climbed in and quickly doused herself, rubbing fiercely at the clothes for as long as she dared, mindful that any moment, guards would be coming in.

While talking calmly to soothe her horse, her second approach to Sleena was far more successful, but the attempted hug was still too much. The horse whinnied, lifting and turning away. Marra had to settle for giving a neck rub.

Once the horse was saddled, Marra walked Sleena towards

the doors. There was an old cloak and a straw hat on a hook. She reached out and grabbed them before mounting, hoping her manly clothes, along with the cloak to cover her curves, would prevent anything more than a glance. The hat didn't fit. She pulled the now-bent hairpins from the tangled and blood-spattered mess of her hair and tried again. The hat now obscured her long hair.

The sun was cresting the horizon as she moved onto the road, where she nudged Sleena into a slow trot.

More cries and screams came to her ears. Sleena's ears twitched nervously.

When Marra had decided on the ludicrous plan to avoid being slaughtered, her thoughts hadn't gone further than avoiding the immediate threat. Now she hoped fervently that Ont'eba, Florin and the girls remained safe in their gilded cage.

Marra leaned forward to whisper in her horse's ear and scratch her neck until they rounded a bend where she felt it was safe enough to increase their speed without raising undue attention.

"Let's get out of this cesspool." Letting Sleena pick the pace, Marra revelled in the wind rushing through her quickly drying hair.

FIFTEEN

TO THE DOCKS

Olpu-tu overheard the young boy warn of the pirates escaping. He jumped up and banged his goblet on the table over the celebrations of the recent beheadings to get everyone's attention.

"Guards! To me!" he yelled.

From out of the shadows, a dozen armed house guards raced to him. In moments, he was surrounded. Several went to confront Corra and Tully, thinking the foreign women were the threat.

"Not them, fools. D'jurr, take nine men and scour the palace. The pirates have escaped. You!" he barked at the remaining guards, "to the barracks. Get everyone to the harbour." He then turned to Corra and pointed. "Follow that path. A back gate leads to the docks."

Corra nodded her thanks, slipping past the guards and shouldering her way through the panicked crowd to her crew. The decapitated bodies of the pirates were now forgotten.

"With me," she ordered.

The women jogged out of the pavilion and into the night.

The gardens were swathed in darkness. The first moon was still low on the horizon, making the path hard to see. They had to slow down or risk losing their footing or rolling an ankle. Behind them, the banquet broke up in turmoil, and there were distant sounds of clashing steel in the palace.

One of her crew channelled a small amount of spirit to enhance her night vision and led the way. In a matter of minutes, they found the gates. Unknown to them, a runner—a young boy, no doubt with better knowledge of the terrain—had beaten them there. Two guards had already opened the gates. "I'm Garan," the boy introduced himself, then promptly ran off again, leading them through the gates and beyond.

Corra and her crew followed as best they could. The path turned into a rough, paved road with a gradual descent. Garan knew the streets well and was waiting at the corner. They could hear the ring of steel and yells echoing off the rough-hewn walls, and they were only male voices.

When they caught up to him, he pointed.

"Docks, down there, m'lady."

"We can smell it," Corra called as she passed. "Stay safe."

"Thanks, lad," Tully added on her captain's heels.

Down an alley and rounding a corner, they burst out into the plaza in front of the Tangled Net. In the plaza, dark shapes lay unmoving on the flagstones, and other figures were seen running or fighting. The *Tormentor* was alight with pockets of fire.

"*Revenge* has separated," Corra called in relief.

Tully ran to the nearest body—a guard—and relieved him of his sword. She tossed it to Corra, then searched for another weapon. The other members of the crew broke up and followed suit. It wasn't only guards and a couple of pirates bleeding on the cobblestones. Townsfolk, including a few women, had also fallen victim.

Once armed with whatever weapons they could find, the crew made their way to the *Tormentor*. As they approached, all those involved in the fighting became clearer, lit by the flames. Many of the pirates who had been branded had made it onto their ship and were now fighting a few of the town guards.

Sienna ran past them, only getting involved if they threatened her or her crew. Her main goal was to see how the *Revenge* fared. It was now further out into the harbour, so she had to get further along the pier to see it clearly.

"Who the rifts started those fires?" Tully asked as she caught up with her captain.

"That sly bastard, D'Longe. Jingle-wrists said as much. It's a distraction to keep the guards busy. He's after our ship."

Now, beyond the glare of the other vessel, they could see what was happening with the *Revenge*. Three other smaller boats were close, but rough waves and gusting winds hampered their approach, forcing them back, while archers in the rigging and crow's nest were peppering them with arrows.

Affected by the rough water, any return fire from D'Longe's men on the pitching and rolling vessels went off into the night.

"M'be sly, but not too bright, then." Tully chuckled.

The attack was in its infancy. As they watched, the waves crashing into the small boats were gaining in strength and force. One boat was being pushed up against the *Tormentor* while the other two were nearing the pylons supporting the pier.

"If they had any doubts about how we ladies capture pirates, now they know." Tully chuckled again.

Corra shrugged. "Looks like they don't need our help...not that we could do much from here." Even as they watched, a boat was rammed into a large pylon by the force of a crashing wave. The sound of splintering wood and screams reached them as the boat rolled and cracked. The men on board were thrown into the maelstrom. The few that made it to the barnacle-encrusted pylons were hammered by their own heaving boats and slipped unconscious into the dark, churning waters.

"Still some fun to be had." Tully turned to the small skirmishes on the *Tormentor*.

By the time the pair raced up the gangway, the last of the pirates had been cut down. The local guards were breathing heavily, and all had wounds of varying degrees of severity.

Jag suddenly scampered up the gangway, his pint-size figure ducked and weaved past them all, quickly disappearing into the captain's cabin.

"Flippin' anchors and chains!" Tully swore.

Panting, Yana came running up the gangway.

"Sorry, boss. I couldn't leave 'im behind, not after what's goin' on. Soon as we got near, he run off. Kept sayin' 'got to find 'er'."

Following their captain, the three of them found the young boy frantically searching Granna Forjin's cabin.

"What the rifts, lad?" Tully fumed, perplexed.

He ignored her as he tapped the deck. "Fion?" Jag called out repeatedly, then added, "Moon shadow. Moon shadow."

A moment later, they heard muffled calls and faint kicking coming from under the captain's table.

Yana and Tully dragged it across the scratched floorboards, then Corra rolled back the threadbare matting.

Jag darted in, sobbing with relief as he pried open a trapdoor to reveal a young girl not much older than himself. She was tied and gagged, laying on a rough bed in an area no bigger than a coffin.

"What the rifts?" Tully repeated, seeing the girl, then looking to the young lad.

"She's me sister," he said as he pulled her gag down.

"Took you long enough," she said calmly, her voice sounding a bit rough.

They lifted her out gently in case she had been injured, and untied her.

"Are you hurt?" Corra asked. Without waiting for a reply, she called for a spiron.

"Off you go." Tully nodded to Yana. The woman left immediately, but returned with a healer in moments.

When they were sure Fion was uninjured, they began to help her to the *Revenge,* which had berthed alongside again.

Jag shadowed his sister.

A commotion on the pier caught their attention as a group of guards escorted their ruler across the plaza.

"You go ahead. I'll join you shortly."

"Righto, Cap'n." Tully nodded.

Corra made her way down the gangway to the pier and walked to where Olpu-tu had dismounted from his horse.

"Saved your ship, but it got a bit singed," she said to him. "Looks like D'Longe made a play for the *Revenge.*"

"I see they failed. Where are they now?"

"Can't be sure. Their boats either capsized or ran into the pylons."

A quizzical look crossed his plump face as he surveyed the now calm waters and clear sky. Olpu-tu turned to her. "I seem to have misjudged you all. A crew of women...capturing pirates. If I hadn't seen it, I'd not believe it."

Corra nodded. "We get it all the time."

Olpu-tu ordered his guards to search the area for D'Longe and his men. Tossing his reins to one of the two remaining guards, he made his way onto the deck of the *Tormentor.*

"And the fire... A distraction?" he asked as he surveyed the superficial damage.

"Reckon so. To keep people busy dousing the flames while they made a go at taking my ship unhindered."

The Savarik ruler nodded. "I cannot see any reason why—or how—they would have released the pirates. They'd have simply made a run for their ship."

"It would have only hampered their plans," Corra agreed. Another suspect formed in her mind. "Your Excellency, you'll understand my girls would want to depart sooner rather than later."

"As in *now*? What about the tide and all that nautical stuff?"

"You might not be too surprised to hear we don't need it."

Again, Olpu-tu nodded. He clapped his hands, making his wrist bands jingle.

A guard ran up with a pouch.

"I had actually considered it a possibility. Here's the agreed sum for the *Tormentor*."

Sienna looked surprised. "Seems I underestimated you, too, Your Excellency."

"Do not fret. I've had years of mentoring to relay that very image of flippant opulence to others."

"Glad I'm not an enemy, then."

"Likewise." He reached out to shake her hand. "It is our hope that we can open up trade. Maybe your High Lord will deign to visit us?"

"I'm simply a go-between." Corra shook his hand. "But, I'll send him word."

"Until then, I bid you and your crew fair winds and farewell." Gathering his robes, he strolled down the gangway to his horse without a backward glance.

Corra watched him for a moment, then grinned at the bag of gold in her hands. She turned back to the *Revenge*. She had a question for Jag. In fact, she had quite a few questions for both siblings.

She found the children in the crew's mess eating cheese and bread. Tully and Yana were watching over them. Corra motioned the healer over to speak.

"How is she?"

"Suprisin' good, Cap'n. Not eaten or drunk for a day or so. Right as rain with a good feed."

"Thanks." Corra strolled over to join them, swivelling a chair around and straddling it while they ate. She caught Tully's eye and nodded slightly towards Yana.

"Hey, Yana. Looks like we can 'andle it from 'ere. Might as well see to what can be done on the uppers."

"Righto, Tulls."

Captain Sienna watched as the two children tucked into the food.

"Fion, is it? Welcome aboard the *Revenge*," she said.

"It's smaller than I thought." The girl looked around.

Corra looked to Tully, then back.

"Maybe you'd like to tell us about what you thought, and why?" Corra suggested.

"She has visi—"

"I 'ave dreams," Fion cut Jag off. "A lot, and not only when I'm sleepin'."

"Dreams. Like what?

"Well, I seen a fire mountain surrounded by... I dunno. It's all white for as far as I could see."

"White...like ice? Or snow? "

Fion bit her lower lip and shrugged without comment.

Young girl probably doesn't know what snow or ice is. "And you saw a ship in your dreams? This ship?" Sienna prompted.

"Don't know if this's the one...'cept the red sails, and the funny look of it."

"This is really no place for either of you. We should take you both home." She held up a hand to stop their protests. "But I wager you don't want to stay with your da, and would soon be looking to get on yet another ship, which could put you in more trouble." *And risk more lives.*

Both nodded their heads vigorously.

"Too right," Jag said through a mouthful of food.

"We're overdue for our return as it is, and further than our normal patrol." The captain nodded and sighed. "So, we'll take you back to The Crags. There are those there much wiser, especially those with Seeing."

While the two children were about to share their story, Tully reluctantly excused herself and went up to ensure all was well.

"Don't want ta 'it the damn 'eadland." She sauntered up the stairs.

They soon heard her yelling and swearing at the crew and felt the rise and fall of the ship as it entered the deeper water of the archipelago.

The original story from Jag was only partly true, and Corra was hearing a lot more than she expected.

Their da, Hargen, had worked on the *Gon Falmo* for years until an accident took his arm, rendering him useless on any ship. For months after, he had trouble getting work and putting food on the table. With their mother passing last summer, life took a turn for the worse.

The *Gon Falmo* was back in port, and the captain, sad to see how Hargen's life had fared for the worse, offered to help. Their father asked if Hargen could take his daughter to Por'sit, where his sister lived. She could look after Fion better than he could. Then he and Jag could fend for themselves better.

"Your da knew of these dreams?" Corra asked.

"Aunt Resur's a witch," Jag said.

"Is not!" Fion turned to punch his arm. "She's gifted, like me."

"We know lots of witches." Corra smiled at them.

"You do?" Jag's eyes went wide.

Corra nodded. "They're good folk. Handy to have around. Now, let your sister continue."

"Just after we left Savarik, I dreamt me and Jag on a ship with red sails."

"Do you know what we do?"

"Only what I saw in me dreams."

"Please continue," Corra prompted.

"Can I 'ave more cheese?"

Corra got up and went to the galley, returning with a tray and two bowls of stew.

"Got something better." She set it down, and they started eating.

Through mouthfuls of food, the story was eventually told. Fion knew both of them would end up here.

It could only be guessed that the *Gon Falmo* was going to be raided, and the *Revenge* was going to eventually find them.

"Did you tell Krusam any of this?"

"Were that the cap'n?" Fion shook her head at Corra's nod. She continued eating.

Avoiding eye contact. Corra surmised that whether or not Fion advised Krusam of the pirates, it made little difference.

"Why were you there, Jag?"

"I stowed away," Jag said after slurping the last of the stew from the bowl. "To stay with Fi."

"Is that why you released the pirates in the palace?"

The wooden bowl clattered to the floor, and the boy looked about to flee,

"You're not in trouble," Corra reassured him. "I just want to know your reasons. It was very dangerous, and their holding pen was nowhere near the banquet hall, yet you were the one telling me."

The young lad looked like he was about to cry. He turned to his sister before turning back to Corra. "I...I had to get back to the ship to help Fi."

Corra nodded, guessing the rest. The boy couldn't get there alone, whereas the escapees would head to the ship, and therefore, so would everyone else, and he'd be able to get out in the chaos. *Smart.* She saw no reason to traumatise the lad with the deaths his actions had caused, but she kept it in mind. *They may be young, but there was a cunning survival instinct at play.*

"Why were you tied up in a box?" she asked Fion.

"The cap'n was miffed coz I said we was safe."

"You lied to him?"

"It were safe for me and Jag." She shrugged. "It felt right to be 'ere and I knew you'd find 'em. And us."

"It was risky."

"No. Coz I saw me and Jag on 'ere."

"And you didn't call out after the ship was taken? My crew could have had you safe much sooner."

"Didn't know." Fion shrugged. "I was meditin'."

"Mediting? You mean *meditating*?"

The girl nodded.

"And how do you know about that?"

"A year back, me aunt 'elped before she left. She said it'd stop the dreams...to shut 'em out."

"And did it?"

Again, Fion nodded. "But then I 'ear voices."

"Voices?" Corra was disturbed to find herself repeating whatever the girl was saying. "What do they say?"

"Dunno. They're very soft...and they use weird words, except..."

"Except...?" she encouraged.

"I reckon I 'eard flyin' ships, black void...and somethin' like *gentics*...but just silly carpin', I reckon." She yawned, which set Jag off.

"Looks like you're ready for bed. Last question: Why did Jag call out 'moon shadow'?" Corra asked.

"Me aunt said I needed a word—somethin' not us'lly said —to wake me from me medit-a-t-ing."

"Okay, then. You've had a busy time." Corra looked around.

The crew's sleeping quarters were at the end of the crew mess, but with the changing shifts, she didn't want the kids to be disturbed by their noises and mutterings.

"Follow me." She led them to the back end of the ship and entered her cabin.

Her bunk was big enough for the two small children to share. They'd get a good rest here, and she preferred to keep them from the crew. Fully clothed, they climbed onto the blanket and snuggled. It didn't take long for them to drop off to sleep, and Corra left them wrapped in her blankets while she went back on deck, her mind turning over the story she'd just heard.

They had a seer onboard—albeit a young one—and many would be interested to know the future. Fion, as sweet as you'd expect a young lass to be, had proven without a doubt that she had an agenda. Already, the *Gon Falmo* and the *Tormentor* had fallen victim to her manipulations.

Corra was determined to not let the *Revenge* also fall afoul of these 'visions'.

"How are we faring, Tulls?" she asked when she reached the helm.

This far north in the archipelago, they no longer needed to risk Keel Haul Strait; several substantial channels in this section of the reef allowed safe navigation, one of the main reasons why Savarik was positioned where it was.

"All's good, Cap'n. 'Ow's our two passengers?"

"Sleeping." She breathed deeply of the fresh salt air. "I'll need a bird to send a message home."

"I'll get Flerr on it. She'll call one in." Tully waved one of the crew over. "Fetch Flerr, will ya?"

With a curt nod, the woman was gone.

"I reckon it'll take about twenty minutes afore a bird comes," the first mate informed Sienna.

"Thanks, Tulls." Corra's gaze swept the open water. "I'll pen a note shortly."

Tully turned the wheel slightly. "Some strange shite 'appin'," she said after a few moments of silence.

"Aye. Truer words were never spoken. Strange shite indeed."

Lost in their thoughts, the only sounds were the wind in the sails, the thrumming of the lines, and the soft chatting of the crew.

"Channel ahead," a voice called out.

Lit up by the waxing moons, white water could be discerned a few hundred feet ahead.

"All slow!" Tully barked as the captain strolled forward.

The experienced crew looked lively as they started taking in sail. Deep channel or not, drifting to port or starboard could still find a spur. Tough as the ship was, there was no need to risk holing their hull. The carts they had by Farand Shis were the most accurate in the southern hemisphere.

After a tense quarter of an hour, the rough water was behind them.

"All clear," the lookout called.

"Tulls, let's get her home."

"Aye, aye, Cap'n, 'Ome it be."

The deck of the *Revenge* skewed as she steered south-west.

SIXTEEN

REVELATIONS

Ont'eba was out and about, investigating the disturbance moments after the first scream. His years as a pirate served him well in the sense that he was a light sleeper. As he grabbed his scimitar, his nimble movements belied his size. Another benefit of years on a heaving deck was that he was good on his feet, though maybe not as agile now.

He was judging whether the screams and snarls were getting closer when he spied movement to his far right. Down the lane behind the dormitory garden wall, he spotted a lone figure slinking towards the stables. Not relishing a confrontation with any rockions, the spymaster went after the secretive shadow, wondering if the culprit had released the beasts, and if so, why the stealth, rather than run full-tilt from certain death.

Whoever it was, they were swift and agile and had already saddled a horse by the time he snuck in through the rear of the stables. Ont'eba hefted his weapon, considering how best to confront the stranger, then he caught a glimpse of tresses of black hair before it was tucked under a hat.

Marra? He couldn't be certain, but the slim figure definitely fit her build.

Before he could speak with her, he heard the creaking of the floorboards of the loft above him. It was only then that he recalled that the gardener's assistant usually slept there in preference to the staff quarters.

If Dursy saw him speaking to the person on the horse, it could be awkward. The poor lad wasn't gifted with the normal number of wits, so trying to entice him could be problematic, and threatening the poor lad was out of the question. The lad had had enough trauma in his life.

Instead, Ont'eba backed out and jogged to the end of the guardhouse, which abutted the stables, endeavouring to spot which way Marra left. He hoped and assumed she'd head south. Sure enough, and much to his relief, the horse and rider turned right.

By this time, the guards were beginning to stir in the adjacent building. Time for him to be scarce.

THE RUNNER FOUND him in the empty rockion enclosure examining a bloodied nightdress.

"Sir Ont'eba, High Lord Blarik requests your presence." The young runner had stopped several feet away, eyeing the bloodied corpse that had been Col.

"Of course he does. Very good. I'll be along as fast as my chubbiness allows. Don't wait for me."

The runner hesitated, watching the spymaster check the gate and the area nearby.

"It's okay, lad. I know where his office is," the spymaster said. "Korin, isn't it?"

The young man nodded, surprise showing on his face that such an important man would know his name.

"I dare say you're not in such a hurry to race back," Ont'eba continued. "Beck is up and fixing food for the rabble that's currently out chasing the rockions. She might need a hand."

Korin touched his forehead with his hand. "Right you are, Sir Ont'eba. I should spend a few minutes helping her."

"I'm sure she'd be grateful for your assistance. Off you go."

"Oh, Sir, High Lord Blarik is at the boys' school," Korin added as an afterthought.

"Is he? Good lad. Thank you."

When Korin had moved around the corner of the building, Ont'eba bent down to retrieve the necklace he had covered with his foot when he heard the young runner arrive. He sniffed the locket, recognising the content's odour. *Interesting*.

True to his word, Ont'eba trudged along the lane that would eventually take him to the male dormitories. On his way, he came up with a story to fit everything he had discovered, without letting on to everything he had seen.

"WHERE THE BLAZES have you been, man?" On horseback to make a quick escape, Blarik was surrounded by twenty nervous and wary guards. Several mancers were also nearby; a couple were still caged in their wagon, but some—the less violent elementalists—were milling about, waiting for orders.

"My Lord, I'm not as agile as some. I was in the rockion enclosure, examining the area."

"You were? Why the hell did you do that?"

"Why, to work out what had happened, of course. You

recall we already had a rockion escape not too long ago. I'm sure you'll recall the tragedy that caused." He watched Blarik as he said this and discerned a change in his demeanour. "Two escapes in quick succession...I was ascertaining if it was an accident this evening, or on purpose."

Blarik took a deep breath. "And pray tell, what did your inquisitive mind discover?"

"It was on purpose, but I suspect the plan backfired. Col, the keeper, is dead—poor lad—as is one of the harem guards; Vern."

"What? Why? How?"

"*Why* is unknown at this point. *How* is obvious: the gate was unlatched, and the beasts got loose. Did I not already make a suggestion that the gate should be lockable, not a simple latch? Anyway, I digress. I also have some tragic news." He paused for effect and looked down at the floor.

"What? More tragic news? My precious beasts escaped, and my men killed? Pull yourself together, man. Out with it." A distant snarling made his already spooked horse skitter sideways. Blarik yanked the reins viciously.

The guards raised the few torches and became deathly quiet, silencing their nervous mutterings as they peered into the darkness.

Ont'eba licked his lips, not oblivious to the fact that out of everyone present, he was not the best physically equipped for this situation. "My Lord, I also found a silk nightdress inside the enclosure. I believe one of our girls has been..."

"Eaten? Who?" Even Blarik blanched at this news.

"Unknown at this point, as there are no remains to be found. I had heard rockions consumed everything, I just didn't believe it." The spymaster fell silent, waiting to see if Blarik would come up with the next obvious step.

While his men warily watched the darkness, Blarik remained on his horse, considering the news.

"We should conduct a search of each of the dormitories to see who's missing," he said eventually.

Ont'eba nodded sullenly. "I'll see to it. I feel responsible, though, how one of them managed to get out of the dormitory area is a mystery...unless she was assisted..."

"No. I'll check on the girls. You can stay here and get the men to recapture my beasties." Without waiting for a response, Blarik trotted off down the road.

EVERYONE in the harem woke early with the yells and screams from beyond the high walls. The kitchen staff were also woken. With little else to do, the head chef harried her staff to prepare breakfast. It kept them occupied and stopped them from gossiping and worrying.

"Our lasses are awake too, and fretting. Food's good for the soul. And with this ruckus, we all need it to keep our spirits up."

Rumour quickly spread that the keeper, several of the guards, and a mancer had been slaughtered before the beasts were quelled by half a dozen elementalists.

Florin was worried sick. Marra had gone missing during the night. *And what plan did Shayr have to get Marra out? Surely it wouldn't include rockions.*

Shayr was in a foul mood and stayed in her room, refusing to speak to anyone, much to everyone's relief. She was sour enough when in a good mood.

"That's because her man was mauled," Leesa said quietly.

"Vern? He was an arse," Florin said.

The other girls looked shocked.

"But I guess he didn't deserve to be mauled to death. How beastly," she added to mollify their horror at her callousness. "Has anyone heard anything about Marra?" Florin asked, unable to hide her worried look. "She's not in her room, and her bed's not been slept in." *Because she spent the night with me...*

Everyone around the breakfast table shook their heads.

"Maybe Ont'eba or High Lord Blarik sent for her?"

Amba looked around, then said to her in a soft voice. "I heard one of the gardeners talking about a hidden gate being opened last night."

Florin promptly slid off her chair, leaving her breakfast unfinished, and walked along the garden wall until she found the area in question. She came upon a pair of gardeners working in front of the old gate where some of the plants had been trampled.

"Morning, Filo, what happened here?" she asked innocently.

"G'day, lass," the old gardener said, dipping his cap. "Damn big-booted, 'alf-witted guards, is what

"I didn't know that gate worked."

Filo looked around warily. "We *used* to use it. Can't go traipsin' our muddy boots inside. But nows we lost one of tha keys. Reckon one 'em dim-witted guards that's always 'angin' about 'ere 'ad it."

"You mean Vern?"

"That be 'im. Vern. The mean, smelly one tha' got 'imself deaded."

"Truly? What happened? Was it the rockions that deaded him?"

"Did you not 'ear 'em?"

"Oh yes, of course. It sounded terrible." Florin put her hand to her mouth, feigning her horror. "I just didn't know who got deaded."

"Yep, guards, tha beast keeper an' a maid, I 'ears."

A maid? Florin's face paled. "Are you sure?"

"Is what they say, lass."

She reached for the wall for support at this news. While she took slow, deep breaths, she noticed the younger gardener glancing her way. He leant sideways and whispered, pointing at her.

Filo gently slapped his hand down and indicated he should keep working.

"What did he say?"

"Don't mind Dursy none, lass." Filo lowered his voice and whispered to her, "'E's a bit daft."

"Does he like my clothes? He was pointing to them."

Filo nodded, looking briefly at her slim figure, then down at his dirty hands. "Clothes like that were also found out there —" The gardener pointed to somewhere beyond the walls.

The young girl went cold. "These...clothes?"

Filo nodded. He was about to say something, then stopped.

"Please tell me. You won't get into trouble. We're all friends this side of the wall."

"It were found in the beastie's cage. All— ripped an' bloody—"

Florin dropped to her knees in grief, her breathing laboured as she cried. Her horror wasn't feigned this time.

"Ah, lass." Filo awkwardly patted her shoulder. "Someone you knew?"

Dursy stopped working and was staring at her, now. He looked like he was about to cry, too. "She not deaded. Gone," the boy said.

Florin was too grief-stricken to take notice of the simpleton, but Filo heard him.

"What's that, lad? Tell ol' Filo what ya saws."

"I saws 'er. Took a 'orse, she did." Dursy nodded.

"Wha…" Florin turned to him, mid-sob.

"Dursy sleeps in the loft of the stables," Filo explained. "'E likes animals, an' no one in the barracks likes 'im. They pick on 'im. Bastards."

"What did she look like? This girl." Florin wiped her tears.

"Perdy…like yous. But not yar 'air."

"Darker hair? Was she injured? Where did she go?" The girl stood up in her excitement. Dursy backed away at her sudden movement, cowering behind the wheelbarrow.

"Easy lad, and lass." The gardener moved slowly to Dursy with placating gestures. "No ones 'urtin' no one. She be glad to 'ear your news, is all."

Dursy nodded meekly, but remained behind the barrow.

"Not 'urt. Rode off…tha' way." He pointed.

Florin followed the direction. *South.*

"Does anyone else know this?" she asked, filled with relief.

"Ain't tol no one. No one asks us anythin'. Think they be better, they do." Filo spat.

"Then let's keep it our secret, shall we? I won't tell if you won't."

"I jus keep me 'ead down, I does. So does Dursy."

"Wonderful. And such a fine garden you have made here, too. It's so lovely."

"Ya. She be a goodun." Filo looked around proudly. "Speakin' o' which, we best be gettin' this done, lass."

Florin nodded. "Thank you so much." She turned and wandered back to the main house, where she heard loud orders and, through the large windows, saw guards lining up all her friends.

~

Once Ont'eba had successfully organised the half-dozen mancers to quell the rockions and recage them, he went back to his office and began penning some missives to his various contacts.

Getting the cypher right wasn't an issue, but he was careful to word each note in the off-chance it was intercepted by someone allied to Blarik. He was deeply disturbed by his own lack of knowledge of what had really happened at the last High Council meeting. In a way, the lack of recent birds from the various noble domains in itself should have created some suspicion.

His neglect angered him—as much as a eunuch could be angered—and though, while the violent urges he'd once known had been curtailed, it didn't make him any less dangerous or conniving, and he was now determined to get to the bottom of it all.

After almost an hour of writing, he ventured up to the aviary with his folio of rolled messages. The enclosure was built onto the terrace of the main building, but was generally safe from Blarik's prying eyes. Something about his demeanour often set the birds off, and he had almost lost an eye once, hence his reluctance to return. If it wasn't for Ont'eba's predecessor clarifying the utmost importance of keeping them, Blarik would have had them wiped out.

Probably would have fed them to his precious pets.

The aviary was quite an elaborate construction, and there were several sections to it. The noble houses had their own ravens, and each had a coloured band on its leg to represent their house. Lesser houses had pigeons. The determination of bird type wasn't a matter of funding, but of rank. Birds were fickle things, and it generally needed a mancer with the right spirit talent to embed in the bird's mind the locations it needed to know.

In that regard, courier pigeons were cheap as they had an innate ability for homing in on the required location. More intelligent birds needed a bit of incentive to coerce their active minds, and that was accomplished with well-travelled elementalists.

Ont'eba, of course, had his own range of birds specifically for his contacts: falcons. While naturally swift and capable of self-defence, the mancers had somehow managed to improve on this, making his birds far more formidable than the average raptor.

He sent off his messages as normal, but he did have one special note to deliver, so he selected the most successful of all the falcons at his disposal.

SEVENTEEN

SOUTHBOUND

Marra wasn't just fleeing in any random direction: the only realistic option for her was south. This was where the bulk of House Olber's allies were situated. It wasn't lost on her that if anyone sent out a search party, this would be the most likely direction to start looking.

Assuming my ruse didn't work, and they think I'm alive. She hoped fervently the bloodied nightgown in the rockion lair—along with the knowledge that rockions ate everything—would be sufficient evidence for them to conclude she was dead.

Even so, she wasn't about to run to the nearest noble house and beg sanctuary; that would only increase the risk of getting caught and ruin another fine noble house, ending any chance of maintaining alliances with the other houses.

There are traitors among the nobles.

No, the best thing about heading south was simply that there were far fewer potential spies. She wasn't kidding herself: there *would* be spies, but fewer than to the north. And if there was troubling brewing that way, there'd be many more travellers.

Marra then had another consideration. Ont'eba would be the one collecting the information, as well as Blarik. She'd need to be wary. For all his faults and depravity, her uncle wasn't stupid. She doubted he'd rely on only one source of information and could have contacts anywhere.

She hadn't been so far from home before, and had always kept her ventures closer to the domain and Carascan, the capital. She took in the features of the landscape in the hope that something would gel from any descriptions she may have heard from her father and his meetings, or from Froshingha's lessons.

Tears brimmed as her mind played back that horrid night and the deaths of many of her staff. She shook her head.

This is not the time to mourn the dead.

Considering her situation, she recalled the information from the few lessons she had sat in on at the harem. Jaranabi was mostly landlocked, which was why the port on the north coast—the only easily accessible harbour—was vital, and why Blarik was so keen to quash any infiltration from Klarget, even if it was an extremely remote possibility. With no harbour access, it would cut off any chance of continuing maritime trade.

Jaranabi's east and west borders were made up of rugged mountain ranges. The geographer, Zaran, who had travelled far and wide, had given one of the more interesting lessons. He was nice to look at, too, hence why his classes were always full. He was about ten years older, but the wealth of knowledge he had was surprising.

While Jaranabi had a large southern coastline, he'd explained, it was all jagged cliffs from border to border. Her country had no east or west coast. Klarget basically had the whole eastern shore, and Dran'ali stretched down the west coast.

Several attempts in the past had been made to establish a southern port, but the remote harshness of the region made nothing more than tiny fishing villages hugging the cliffs viable. *She had Florin to vouch for that.*

With the knowledge that she wouldn't be safe in any noble house—even if they did take her in—the choices of a safe refuge to go to were exceedingly small. In fact, there was only the one place she felt she could be safe, assuming the stories were anywhere near accurate. And the recent development of magyk reinforced the idea of her destination.

The Crags. Even though it sounded like an unpleasant place, she hoped to find sanctuary in the women's refuge. If there was a witch living there—as in a real witch and not just some nasty cow everyone despised—then perhaps there was a chance, even a remote one, that she might receive some form of guidance.

Assuming that I have any Talent at all.

Despite Corum's assurance, she had an irrational fear of losing her mind. Some of the things she had done or attempted to do had created doubts about her sanity. Marra didn't want to go insane—only crazy people wanted that.

You're getting delirious, girl. You need rest and food.

She had been on the road now for almost two weeks, and the meagre amount of food she had saved had gone within two days. Then, when she couldn't forage, she resorted to stealing from the remote farmhouses she came across. She hated having to do that, believing that a farmer would help a woman in her predicament. But if a proper search began, her trail might be found, thereby putting any farmers or helpers at risk.

She avoided all towns, and when she spotted someone approaching on the road, she hid. It would have been better to avoid the roads altogether, but a lone rider was one thing, and since this was mostly agricultural land, a rider traipsing through a field would create more trouble than it was worth.

Several times now, she had been surprised by other travellers. Not being able to get away quickly enough without raising suspicion, she kept her head down and made non-committal grunting noises at any query in the hope they either thought 'he' was a simpleton, or with a sickness.

Whichever the case, it worked, and the strangers moved on quickly, some with a wave, some with a shrug, and one with curses and threats when she feigned ignorance. She put her trust in Sleena's ability to easily outrun any farmer's nag if the threats became reality. Luckily, the threats were nothing but bravado.

Sleena had not failed her yet, but her condition was slowly deteriorating. Several times now, Marra had to clear her hooves of rocks and mud, but a shoe was coming loose, and she had no way to fix that.

Face it, you will need to get help from a town sooner rather than later.

The road she was on, more of a track now, wended up another rise. As always before cresting a hill, she stopped and listened carefully to hear any approaching horses or wagons. When all she got was the soft susurration of the wind, she slowly moved ahead.

At the top of this rise, she saw a small hamlet at a junction where the track joined a road heading more or less east and west. One side of the road was a field with a crop of sunflowers, drooping and brown, ready to harvest. The other was fallow. In the distance, beyond the many fields, was the dark blur of the renowned Great Southern Woods.

Over the last days, she had put together some of the landmarks based on the various descriptions she'd heard from home. She didn't know the name of this village, but if she was accurate with her bearings, the road to the east would lead to the Trallko Domains, House Olber's strongest allies.

"And therefore, a place guaranteed to be watched," she muttered. Sleena whickered, and Marra automatically reached down to scratch behind her ears.

That being the case, she considered, the Nurnup Domain—more neutral than an ally—was somewhere to the east, and the Charoffs were south and west. She recalled the presence of their guards and mancers back at her house after the council meeting, not to mention that Charoff voted for Blarik.

I definitely need to be wary of them!

No patrols had been seen or heard in her weeks of travel, but there were better and faster roads leading south. She hoped her decision to use the less-travelled roads was the right one.

It was slower, but the chances of any unwanted encounters had been greatly reduced.

Let them continue thinking I'm rockion fodder. The main sadness with that is the trauma Florin will be going through. Poor girl. So lovely, so sweet...maybe not *so innocent.* She smiled at that. Perhaps, one day—

Sleena snorted again.

There were hoofbeats on the wind. Marra glanced over her shoulder to see a horse and cart a few hundred yards away. Standing like a dolt on the hilltop, she would be easily seen. Leaving the road now wasn't an option without creating unwanted attention.

"Okay, girl, maybe you'll have a bed tonight and decent food." She clucked Sleena forward and slowly trotted down the hill, turning at the bottom towards the village.

She kept her head down and avoided eye contact with anyone on the street while searching for a stable or a blacksmith. Halfway in, there was a barn attached to the side of a two-level tavern, and after dismounting, she walked over to it. Tying Sleena to a post, she went to the doorway and looked inside, letting her eyes adjust to the dimness. There was one other horse in the far stall, a farmer's nag, not a courier or long-distance traveller's horse. There was no stableman.

Thinking the taverner should be able to help point her to a blacksmith, she reluctantly headed for the tavern door and pushed it open. Her first impression was of a cool and homely interior; not too bright, but comfortable to view without stumbling into gloom or a glaring lantern. There was a wide central aisle, with several tables on either side directing new patrons to the long wooden bar. A large hearth—cold now because of the warm season—took up a third of the wall to her right, and there was a door in the wall adjoining the stable.

The half dozen patrons looked her way, but kept chatting, drinking, and eating; totally relaxed. One serving girl worked the bar, but the taverner wasn't in sight.

Here goes nothing.

Lingering in the doorway would attract attention. Marra stepped across the threshold as the door swung slowly closed and casually made her way to the bar. It wasn't lost on her that she probably reeked, but there was little to do about it, and surely others would be equally odorous after several days of travel.

"Evenin', miss. Any chance of a smithy seein' to me 'orse," Marra asked in a quiet voice when she reached the bar.

She felt ridiculous speaking like this, but part of her ad-hoc spy training had been the importance of fitting in with the local community, whether they be country yokels or city well-to-doers. As the instructor had said, "Only the experienced and well-travelled spy can master this, but ladies, may I suggest you practice with each other as homework. Until you go out in the wide world, it's all you can do."

Imitating a male was only for those with vast experience and practice. She just wanted to sound like a travel-weary woman. Her appearance was certainly that: she was obviously in desperate need of a wash, with her dishevelled hair, dirty fingernails, and smelly clothes.

The pretty barmaid smiled her greeting politely. She was about the same height as Marra, with a marginally fuller figure, and though a decade older, moved with a lithe spring in her step.

"Welcome to Culming. The smithy's out on errands, but he'll be back in the mornin'. Looks like you'll be needin' a drink or three. What'll it be?"

"What've ya got that'll hit the spot?"

"We be low on ale,"—she glanced around the room, indicating with her eyes several groups of quiet drinkers—"but we've got some red wine from the best vineyards in all Jaranabi. The Trallko Domain is jus' up the roads a bit."

"Trallko? I've 'eard of 'em. Sounds like the ticket. And food?" Marra was famished.

"Righto. Let me fix yer drink, and then I'll rustle up some grub." Her dexterous hands uncorked a bottle, and she poured some of the blood-red liquid into a mug. "No wine glass 'ere," she apologised, placing the chipped mug on the counter. "We leave that finery to the rich folk in the cities."

"Not a bother, I'm thirsty enough ta drink outta me boot if I 'ave ta."

"Righto then. Want to sit at the bar or a table?" She moved around the far end of the bar and wiped down an empty table by the cold hearth. "Table 'ere's betta. Plonk that perty arse down there," she said with a twinkle in her eye.

Beautiful green eyes, just like Florin's. Marra sat in the chair backing the wall. It was a simple, sturdy chair, but after a week in the saddle and sitting on the ground, it was bliss.

"Thankya kindly," she said.

The barmaid flicked her long locks of red hair back over her shoulder. "Me name's Nioma. Grub comin' up." Nioma left through a back door into what Marra assumed was the kitchen area.

From under her hat, she cast her eyes around the room while she sipped the wine. No one looked her way with anything more than casual glances. Their voices were not over-loud. It was a nice atmosphere.

Her head was itchy and sweaty. She'd repurposed her bent hairpin to keep her headwear from blowing away on the road, and she pulled it out now so she could remove the hat and hook it over the back of the chair beside her. It was a relief to run her fingers through the long strands, removing what tangles she could. She knew it must look dreadful, but shaking her locks free almost made her laugh.

Nioma returned shortly with a bowl of stew and a small bread roll, which she placed in front of her with a spoon.

"I hope the meal is to your liking," Nioma said softly. "And dare I say, your hair's quite magnificent."

"Why thankya. Jus' needs—" Marra went red-faced, seeing Nioma's grin. The barmaid's yokel brogue was completely gone, replaced by an eloquent accent that would put a high-born to shame. "Are you—"

"Let me introduce myself properly." Nioma held out her hand. Even for a barmaid, the hands were elegant and well-cared for.

Unsure, Marra reached for the proffered hand. When she did, the grip was firm, but she felt the telltale tap-and-scratch sign of the spy school. Marra hesitated, more out of shock, before she reciprocated.

"Welcome to Culming. I'm Nioma Blakthorg, very pleased to meet you."

"And you. You know who I am? Was I that obvious?"

"To a trained eye, yes, but considering the minimal training you've had, it is completely understandable."

Marra's embarrassment turned to worry. *Who was Nioma really working for?* Tired and weary as she was, Marra slowly moved her feet under the table to a position that would allow her to spring up and make a run for the door if need be.

"I know what you're thinking. Please relax," Nioma said in a calming tone. "I should've given you this the moment you opened your mouth to brutalise and torment your first syllable." From the breast pocket of her blouse, Nioma extracted a small roll of vellum. It was expensive, and not what you'd expect to see anywhere in the boondocks. When she unrolled it, Marra saw two lines of scribble.

"Dare I ask..." Marra started, unsure.

Nioma sat down opposite her and lowered her voice. "You are Marra Olber, and you are safe. Onty sent word a raven-haired beauty would be heading south, and here you are; raven-haired and beautiful, though obviously a bit saddle sore and tired."

Marra nodded slowly. *This could also be a ploy.*

"Not convinced? Understandable. If Blarik wanted you captured, it would've happened. In fact, there was also a falcon a couple of days ago, basically saying the same thing as Onty, though 'raven-haired and beautiful' were nowhere in his message."

"What did Blarik have to say then?"

"To notify him immediately if the traitorous wench, Marra Olber, showed her face."

"I see..."

"My sources tell me he's sent the same message everywhere. He has no idea where you are. Lucky for you, though, I work for Onty and not some fat old pervert."

"So, you know my uncle well, then?" Marra grinned.

"I've had the displeasure of his unwanted attentions, if that's what you mean."

"Did he..." Marra let the sentence go and shook her head. "Forget it." It wasn't her business to ask, and she felt horrible.

"I've not seen the fool for several years. Does he have a beard?"

"He does." Marra nodded.

"That's because he has a large scar just below his lip. He tried to get it on with me—men always underestimate women. If he had tried before my training, he might have succeeded, but I'd learnt some self-defence. I broke a wine glass and sliced his chin. Blarik was furious, but Onty stepped in at the last minute and whisked me away. Can't get much further south than here, so here I am."

"I guess my ploy of being devoured by rockions didn't work."

"Guess not, but since the falcon only arrived recently—and you've been on the road for what, two weeks?" Nioma continued at her nod. "Then it worked for a time. How'd you —" Nioma stopped, looking up as a couple more locals sauntered in. The tavern was starting to get busy. "Okay. I have to apologise. This's not the time nor the place." She picked up the untouched bowl and spoon. "Grab your wine and follow me."

Without looking back, Nioma went into the kitchen, Marra following. The realisation that this could be an elaborate trap only dawned on her when she'd left the tavern lounge. But it wasn't. Nioma had another table, slightly better quality and not so worn out, to the side of the kitchen.

"This is your place, then? No taverner?"

"You're looking at her." Nioma bowed slightly. "Have a

seat, and please eat up. Help yourself to more if you like." She pointed to the pot. "I'm going to run you a bath. Nothing like the school's spa, but I'm sure you aren't going to object."

AFTER TWO BOWLS of stew and several glasses of the strong local wine, she followed the directions of her hostess and went to bathe with a sponge and soap. There was even a lotion that stopped the scalp itch! She wanted to cry with relief, and did.

Nioma came in and helped wash her back, then brushed her hair, humming softly.

Any awkwardness about nudity around another woman was long gone.

"I'm going to burn those clothes," Nioma told her as she started braiding. "I have spare clothes which should be alright, though you're slimmer. I could take them in if need be."

"Oh, no. You've done so much. I can sew. Before this nightmare, sewing and embroidery were about the only skills I had."

"I doubt that's true, but it's okay. Let's see how they fit first."

Marra dressed in the clothes laid out for her, a loose blouse with a low neckline. The leggings were thigh-hugging leather, which were practical for horse riding.

"Looks like they fit fine."

"Looking fine indeed." Nioma winked.

The rest of the evening passed like a dream. They chatted, their reminiscences punctuated by pauses when Nioma had to tend to the bar.

"Most of the locals help themselves anyway," the barmaid said. "They're an honest bunch down here."

"Are you a local?"

"Local enough,» Nioma told her a brief family history, but

it was not much different from most of the girls. "It helps with the dialect, though. I blend in."

"I must have sounded atrocious." Marra looked aghast.

"Honestly, I reckon I suffered internal damage trying not to laugh."

Marra laughed. "Cow."

"Can't get much more local than a domesticated animal, I say." Nioma laughed too, refilling the wine.

"Shit, Sleena—"

"Your horse is fine. I got one of the lads to take care of her. She looks like a nice mare."

"She is, thank you. Can you ride?"

"Born in the saddle. Dran'ali stock?"

"From my father's estate..." Marra stopped as a wave of sadness came over her. *Damn, this wine is strong.* "You must think badly of me for her condition."

"Nonsense. I've an idea what you've been through, though everyone's trauma is personal. But...enough of that maudlin crap. You must be exhausted, and I dare say if I'm feeling it, the wine will have gone to your head too. I've made up a bed in the attic. It's—"

"Let me guess, noth like the feather-down mattresses ath school." Feeling the effects of the wine hitting her, she put her wine glass down.

"Exactly. Nothing like them. I'll show you. Need a hand?"

"I'll manage." Using the walls as support, Marra followed Nioma along the narrow hall and up the back stairs. *Oh. Nice.* She was eye level with her backside and couldn't help but notice the hypnotising sway of her hips...the way her butt—

Nioma stopped to open the door.

Marra bumped into her. She nearly slipped down the stairs, but managed to regain her balance with the help of the railing.

"Oops. Got distracted there." She giggled, feeling her face getting warm.

"It happens. As you say, the room's nothing like you'd be used to," Nioma said by way of apology.

"If it's more comfortable than a pile of leaves or a barn, I'll be happy." Partly because of the wine and exhaustion, tears of relief ran unbidden down her cheeks. "I honestly can't thank you enough." She swayed for a moment before ascending the last few steps.

Nioma put a steadying hand out to help.

"I'm fine." Marra shook her head, but not too much or she'd get dizzy. The stairs and doorway were narrow. Sliding past her hostess, Marra paused, breathing in. *Even her sweat smells divine.* Looking down, she couldn't help comparing cleavages. *Her breasts are the same as mine...* "Achtlly, I think I'm drunk," she declared.

"You're in a tavern. That happens on occasions, too." Nioma chuckled, helping her through to the room, which was small but comfortable and clean. "Need a hand getting undressed?"

"Aha, I see your cunnin'...plan. Takin' advantage of me..." She pulled the blouse up, which tangled in her long hair. After a brief wrestle, hair and blouse finally parted.

Nioma plumped up her pillow. "I could've taken advantage of you when you bathed."

"Ahh...but I wasn't tipsy then." She stuck her tongue out.

"Do you need to be?" Nioma asked softly, but Marra was battling with the leggings. And losing.

"I've grown fat..." With the leggings down to her knees, she lost balance and fell onto the bed. She knocked her head, but laughed it off. "'Kay... You can help."

Laughing with her, Nioma knelt and peeled off the boots, then eased the trousers down the remainder of her slim legs before lifting Mara's feet onto the bed. "Cunning plan, indeed," she muttered.

"Did you say somethin'?" Marra asked through a yawn, lying back.

"Girl, from the way Onty talks about you, I'm surprised he let a treasure like you go." Nioma moved up, leant on the pillow and stroked her hair.

"He had no choice," Marra mumbled.

"Is it true you were going to be married?"

Marra smiled at her, though her eyes were slightly unfocused. "You could say that. Blarik palmed me off to the Overlord of Dran'ali. I'm not a...*broodmare* to spawn a foreigner's bloodline."

"Dran'ali?" Nioma made a circle with her lips. "Their horses are legendary."

Lying back, Marra closed her eyes. "I'd put in a good word for you," she burped. "But my belov'd horse-herderer overlord would skin me."

"I can't blame him. Your skin is exquisite," Nioma admired, running her eyes down her lithe body.

Marra yawned again, snuggling into the soft pillow. "So's yours." She rolled over onto her side, drifting to sleep.

"Liar." Nioma chuckled.

"Night...dear...Florin," Marra whispered.

Nioma had to stifle her laugh as Marra was already asleep, snoring slightly.

"Rest easy, beautiful lady." She pulled the sheet over her and watched her for a few moments before getting up and softly closing the door.

EIGHTEEN

THE RETURN

"Okay, bitches. Jus 'cos these 'ere waters be safe now doesn't mean we slacken off." Tully looked around the deck. It was, like always, spotless. "Rina, the damn jib sail's flappin'. There're lines need takin' in. Get back to your part-o-ship and check it. I'll be doin' the rounds later, an' if I find somethin' amiss, you'll know it quick smart. We'll be back in The Crags soon enough. You can gaggle all yous want then. Step lively now." The First Mate hustled her crew to work before heading down to the crew quarters. "And where be 'em damn newlin's?" she muttered.

Corra looked up from her charts as Tully passed. "No rest for the wicked?"

"Pfft. Can't let 'em think I'm gettin' soft. They can rest a'plenty when we're docked. Now I'm chasin' damn street urchins. Like a damn nurs'ry." Her tirade faded as she disappeared down the hatch.

A week of relatively smooth sailing got them back to The Crags with only one day of little wind, where the aeyrons took turns for a few hours to maintain their speed. Now they were nearer to The Crags, the waters in this region had become safer due to their presence. They spotted a few traders and the small groups of fishing boats working the rough southern coastline. It was good to see merchants using the southern waters again, a testament to the work of the Red Sails.

Ever reluctant to see idle hands, Tully had tasks for everyone; the crew not directly involved with sailing were taking care of the retrieved cargo, and the newlings were continuing with their ship-borne training. Even Jag and Fion were being taught basic sea-going knowledge.

"Everyone pulls their weight on me ship," she told them. "Else they be a liability."

IT WAS MID-AFTERNOON, and The Churn had started, so the *Revenge* circled for several hours until the waters were calm enough to enter safely. Only at this time did Tully relent and give time off to the bulk of the crew.

The newlings, with Jag and Fion in tow, leant on the railings to watch The Churn and explain it all to the two youngsters.

"Our place is inside that." Olinda pointed. "There's only a narrow gap to let the water in and out. When the tide rises... You know about tides?"

Fion and Jag nodded, so Olly continued.

"When the tide comes in, there's lots of water getting pushed through that narrow gap. It's very noisy and rough. That's The Churn. When all that water leaves, it's called The Swirl."

"Can't our mancers get us inside?" Milyn, one of the newlings, asked Dara, who was watching over them.

"Risky, and there's no need. We just wait a couple of hours.

Time to relax." Dara said, then went on to explain in greater detail. "In theory, our mancers could do it—like we done in Keel Haul Strait—but only in an emergency would our cap'n risk it. We only got three ships, an' need to make sure they're workin' good all the time."

"Where'd they come from, the ships?" Olly asked.

"Were always here. There's a book in our library that has all the details," Dara told them.

"Can't read," the boy replied.

"You'll learn," Olinda said.

Between what the newlings told them and the interjections from passing crew, Fion and Jag learnt a bit about the origins of The Crags while they waited for the tide to ease.

The first group of bedraggled women had made their treacherous way south over a century ago. Holandia Burgett, one of the more powerful seers at the time, had visions of a rough coastline where women like herself, often abused and mistreated in a male-dominated society, could find sanctuary.

After her last ordeal at the hands of her drunk and abusive husband, she took the few possessions she had and snuck away in the dead of night, stumbling southward. Part of her visions hinted that there were other women and girls in a similar plight living rough in the great southern forests.

She found them after almost a month of travelling. With her wisdom, visions, and persuading words, they joined her in the arduous trek south. Among the group of over two-dozen women—some barely out of their teens—half had the ability to channel elemental magyk.

Mancing was quite common among the menfolk but forbidden for women in any way or form, punishable by incarceration and severe beating. Their powers were similar, though the outcome of female mancing resulted in far less violent or destructive outcomes. But women with the ability to use elemental magyk were simply not permitted to use it, facing severe consequences if they did; they were like birds prevented from using their wings, or fish not allowed to swim freely.

In secret, small groups of women got together and experimented. Like the men, they did this away from prying eyes, but being less destructive, such experiments didn't require them to travel any great distance from their homes and villages to do it secretly.

FINALLY, as the white water of The Churn calmed, the *Revenge* made its way gracefully to its dock. Much of the community was waiting for them. The sound of the cheering and rejoicing of friends and lovers alike reverberated off the rough stone walls. The newlings were greeted warmly, then whisked away to their quarters.

"We'll see you again soon." Olly waved as they were led up the stairs.

The two children were wide-eyed at the sight of the high cliffs inside the hollow volcano.

Even with the celebrations going on, several eyes watched with interest as Corra took the two children up the path to meet Ildara, who was waiting for them at the base of the stairs. Being the most senior member of the community, it was her duty to welcome returning ships.

"Welcome home, Corra. It's been overlong. I gather it was a fruitful venture?" She eyed the pair of young children with interest.

"Ildara, thank you. It's yes to both, and so wonderful to be home." Corra quietly told her about the loss of Jinan and her burial at sea.

The elder took a shuddering breath at the news.

"And who have we here?" she asked calmly, full of smiles.

"Fion and Jag," Corra introduced them. "They were found on the *Tormentor*, one of the pirate vessels we encountered."

"I know of it." The elder appraised the children. "And I dare say you two have a story to tell. Welcome to The Crags. Are you hungry? We can get some delicious food."

"We already et," Jag stated.

"Is that right? Excellent." Ildara nodded with a smile. "I still think I can find something you'd like."

"If I may suggest, Ildara, perhaps you should get to know them a bit more first. They *do* have an interesting tale to tell."

If Ildara was surprised by the suggestion, she didn't show it. "Certainly, we can get some plates brought in, of course. She reached out to hold their little hands. "Please come this way."

Fion held her hand immediately. Jag was a bit dubious about such an old woman, but when she turned and started walking, he caught up with his sister and held her hand instead.

Corra excused herself once they reached Ildara's chamber. "Got a few things to check on the *Revenge*, but I'll see you at dinner," she said to the elder. "And you two, behave. Or I'll send Tully to come looking for you."

"That's fine, dear. I'm sure I can manage. Besides, the other elders will no doubt be calling in shortly. May as well order more food and wine for us all."

"Let me do that—"

"Nonsense. Go tend to your ship and crew. I've plenty of helpers to call on. Be off with you." She gave Corra a brief, one-armed hug. "It is good to have all of you back."

With a smile and a nod, Corra closed the door.

When Ildara turned back, she found the children had already made themselves comfortable on a lounge and were looking around at the strange 'room' carved into the rock.

After the story was told and the children questioned, they were sent off to have a bath and then dinner. The other elders remained to discuss what they had just heard.

"She's young to be a seer," Yarin the healer noted. "Have you had a chance to test her. Or the boy?"

Ildara shook her head. "Not yet, no. They just got here. Let the lass rest for a day or two first."

"Yarin, is it true those spirons that can't heal and don't appear to have any obvious strength with that element can sometimes speak with the dead?" Kio'on asked.

"Yes, I encountered a couple in my travels before I came here. There are fewer of them now, it seems," the healer said.

"These voices she hears, this *soft talking*... Could that be whispers? And the visions of a fire mountain surrounded by white... Could that be the Isle of Whispers?" Elann wondered.

"Little is known about it. " Tiswan shrugged, then continued: "It's a myth, surely. Men and women have sailed the oceans for centuries, encountered dozens of nations over the three continents and thousands of islands. No one has ever found it. Few have even heard of it."

"And yet," Elann replied, "we have a child from a remote fishing village talking about it."

"Visions can be misinterpreted, especially if the one perceiving the visions doesn't have the knowledge to make a sound determination," Drina commented.

"A 'fire mountain' and large tracts of 'white'? Surely that's a volcano and snow...or ice. It's probably the way I'd describe them." Tiswan looked around the others. "Well, I'm only guessing. What else could a fire mountain be? Or the white as far as the eye can see?"

"There's only one region I know of that could fit that

description. There are still many areas of our oceans we haven't fully explored," Radson suggested.

"Because it's suicide to go there. You're talking about the Ice Plateau?" Xan asked. "Anyone venturing to the Southern Ocean disappears, probably taken by kraken. Even those getting close are confronted by storms, icebergs, and mountainous seas."

"I'll scour the library for any information on the Ice Plateau and also mention of the Isle of Whispers," Drina ventured.

"Is there any benefit in what the dead have to say?" Hiorlo asked.

"Depending on the age of the voice, it could shed more light on our history, for starters," Drina said.

The head of security shrugged. "Even so, no one's heard spirit voices from more than a few decades back. It's a waste of time if you ask me."

"Lucky no one's asking, and it's *her* time to waste. Haven't you a bridge to watch or something?" Kio'on retorted.

"Ladies, I think we all need rest and to sleep on it," Ildara intervened before the discussion got heated. "What I do know about visions is they're open to interpretation, and cannot be rushed. I'll test the girl when she's rested to gauge her potential strength and any other abilities she may possess. Otherwise, we go about our duties until something more positive develops."

"Morning, Ildara." Sienna nodded, striding into her chambers. "How are our two new younglings faring?"

The *Revenge* had been back for a week. Any maintenance or repairs had been carried out efficiently, and the retrieved cargo removed and sorted. Some of the crew were already itching to return to the sea.

Ildara gestured to Sienna to take a seat by the small table. "Jag's a mischievous devil and full of life. There are those—like me—who are confident young Fion will become a powerful seer one day, and a few think she's crazy."

"Though I'm not an elementalist, I can vouch for the sanity of this lass. I spent the last week on our return from Savarik talking to her. In some areas, she's quite naive—as expected from a street urchin from a remote fishing village, but she has her wits about her. She managed to manipulate two ship captains so her visions would come to fruition. Three, if you include me bringing her here."

"I agree. And she has very interesting visions, and information even we scholars barely know, which brings me to your presence here." Ildara poured two cups of tea. "I dare say you have already guessed your next assignment?"

Corra considered her answer as she blew on the hot beverage. "Fire and ice? You'll want us to do a reconnaissance of the Southern Ocean and the Ice Plateau, but," Corra continued as Ildara was about to speak, "it would be foolhardy to do that without an experienced navigator. My next assignment is to get hold of Farand Shis."

"Exactly. I shouldn't be surprised you worked it out."

"Thank you for your confidence, but having been at The Crags for so long under your guidance, it wasn't difficult. We have a potentially powerful seer—albeit very young—talking about things she should have little knowledge of, considering her limited background; you wouldn't send the ship and crew into the uncharted waters without some sort of plan; and you certainly know I wouldn't do it blindly."

Ildara placed her cup down. "Well, if you put it that way..."

"The only thing going for us at the moment is knowing where Farand lives, assuming she's home."

"How long will it take?"

"To get to Herantia? Assuming favourable weather and no encounters, around two weeks there, so a round trip of around a month. But, there's a lot of ocean out there, and we've not done many patrols that far north."

"Expecting trouble?"

"Expecting, no; preparing for, yes."

"Do you think Farand would be interested in our planned expedition?"

"I'm surprised she hasn't gone there already, though by all accounts, she's not witless. No, we won't have any trouble convincing her for at least two reasons: she'll get to ride on the *Revenge*, and she can be part of history."

"When can you sail?"

"After the next Churn, if you like."

IT WAS FAR TOO dangerous for a child to go on such a voyage. Corra felt the girl was sly enough to try to wriggle her way onto the ship by announcing another 'vision', and insisting she was needed. Before she sailed, though, the captain of the *Revenge* called in the newling dormitory to check on both children.

It was no surprise to her to find young Olinda keeping them company. As they had created a rapport during the return trip, she had been given the task of showing them around The Crags.

"Are we going to see the fire and ice?" Fion asked when Corra walked in. "Where is there ice?"

"Far to the south," Corra told them. "The Southern Ocean has lots of it, stretching as far as the eye can see."

"Then we should go there," the young seer affirmed.

"Oceans are large. This one is particularly dangerous. Many ships have been lost. A few rare survivors speak about very large creatures. From their descriptions, we call them kraken."

"What's a kraken?" Fion asked.

"Ever seen an octopus, or a squid?" Olinda asked.

Fion nodded.

"We et one once," Jag offered. "Lots get caught in the nets."

"Well, picture one twice as large as a ship."

CHAPTER

NINETEEN

IMPORTANT VISITORS

"Hey there, sleepyhead. How was your sleep?" Nioma greeted Marra halfway along the hall. She gave her a warm hug and a quick kiss on the cheek.

Marra tingled at the intimate contact, noting the scent of her perfume. "Hmm. That's lovely. Lavender mist?"

"Well done. You have a good nose, too."

"Mist is one of my favourites. And yes, it was truly the best sleep I've ever had."

"I'm sure it felt that way." Nioma turned. "Come and have a seat in the kitchen. I'll put breakfast on."

"Please, let me help. You cook and care for people all day."

"Because I enjoy doing it. If I'm not out with the horses, then this is where I'd rather be. Now stop fretting and sit." Nioma changed her accent and pronunciation to one that would have fit in seamlessly with the High Council meeting. "You are in *House* Blakthorg now, and you will follow the instructions of the head of house to the letter. Do you understand?"

"Yes, ma'am." Marra curtsied, smiling. "And that was very good."

"Why's thankee m'lady. I jus 'av this knack, dun'ya know. Now git yerself sat."

Marra's smile stretched from ear to ear as she sat where the plates had already been laid out. It wasn't long before her cheeks and jaw needed massaging to relieve the ache from smiling. It was such a change of circumstance from the last couple of weeks. She watched Nioma getting the food prepared. She looked different, and it took several minutes to see why. Her hostess had fixed her hair up and was wearing nicer clothes.

"That's a charming blouse," Marra complimented. "It suits you completely."

When Nioma brought a pot of tea and two cups, Marra swore she saw a rosy look to her cheeks, which hinted to her that she herself was the reason for the extra care. No point dressing up for sheepherders. Marra realised it might be wishful thinking, but it warmed her heart. She felt like she belonged here—for a short time at least.

"Breakfast won't be long." Nioma smiled, then went back to the stove.

Marra watched her busying herself. Even in the kitchen, she moved with grace.

"Forgive me if I'm out of line, but I think you're wasted here." Marra poured the tea for both. "You have so much untapped talent."

Nioma turned and winked cheekily. "Oh, believe me, my talents have been *tapped*."

Marra grinned and blushed when she realised Nioma's meaning.

"These clothes are a good fit, too, thank you. A far cry from those silky and clingy nightgowns we had to wear. Surely only a man would think of see-through clothing for girls." Her mind went dark thinking of Blarik's debauchery.

"Would you be surprised to know it was a woman? She started the school about forty years ago."

"A woman started this?"

Nioma nodded. "Madam Dolors Phian. She despised men and loved the female form so much, she only employed young, beautiful girls and wanted to look at them all day."

"Plain girls can't spy?"

"Sure, they can. The spying is relatively new, at least for the school, started by Ont'eba. Perhaps it was because of his past, but he saw an opportunity to better the country. While Madam Phian only ran brothels for females, Ont'eba created one to cater for males as well."

Marra mulled this information over while she watched Nioma work. "When does the tavern open?" she asked as a pan of eggs and bacon was brought over.

"Why? You want something to do?" she teased, then answered. "Lunchtime until late. If I had paying guests, I'd be here for them, otherwise the time's my own." She dished out equal portions of food for Marra, then herself.

"Oh, about that..."

"Don't you dare offer payment! Other than being insulting, as far as I'm concerned, this is spy work. You're just in deep, deep cover."

Marra opened her mouth.

"And no thanks are necessary, either. I've had nothing but farmers and sheepherders for months, and while they are a nice bunch, your arrival is like a breath of fresh air. I should be thanking *you*."

Having placed the pan back on the bench, she returned to the table and sat. Nioma sipped her tea, then started eating.

"Now, down to business," she said after she swallowed. "What plans have you got? Do you have a final destination?"

Marra chewed thoughtfully. "It sounds crazy."

"Should be a good cover, then. No one will think of it. Tell me."

"I was heading for The Crags," Marra said tentatively.

"The Crags? That is crazy. Brilliant."

"You think so?" To her, it was an idea borne of desperation, but if Nioma, with all her experience, agreed with it... She felt a release in tension.

"For you, sure. Not for me, though."

"Sometimes I think it's ludicrous, other times it would seem obvious for a woman in my situation. What do you know about it? I mean, I've heard stuff, but if you're so local..."

Nioma related all she knew about The Crags, which wasn't too much different from what Marra had already heard.

"Corum said there was a witch."

"Oh yes. She's old and very powerful, but there are many of them there. How do you think the community has survived so long? You think the men that run this place want a women's refuge becoming a bona fide community?"

Marra hesitated. Her father had been 'one of those men', though he'd never struck her as being a misogynist.

"Oh. Sorry," Nioma looked contrite, realising what she'd just said. "I didn't mean your father, not personally. Like any ruler, unless he is constantly travelling the realm, what he knows is relayed to him by others. No doubt some men have their own agendas and probably feel your father didn't need to know every bit of the goings-on in the boondocks."

"Like Blarik?"

"Exactly. He tells your father one thing, then does something completely different. Undermining him when it suits to further his own ends. I hate politics," she said after sipping more tea. "Have you thought about an identity, a name? Background? What did they teach you at spy school?"

"The specifics of spying weren't top of the agenda. Seemed my studies concentrated on the mysteries of manly wiles."

"Oh, a short course then." Nioma laughed. "It isn't like it's a long list—tits, arse, and open legs will get his attention every time."

Marra blushed again at the ribald description, hiding her face in her cup.

"It's true!" Nioma nudged her.

"I don't doubt you." She put her cup down. "I've not... When— The only attention I've had from men was brief, brutal, and clumsy."

"You never...?"

Marra shook her head. Not with a man.

"What about any friends at...Never mind. None of my business." Nioma gave her a long, soft look. She changed the subject, moving away from the awkward moment. "But a Dran'ali queen would have been such a magnificent posting."

Marra sighed, relieved. She didn't know why being a virgin was such a taboo subject, or why it caused so much awkwardness. "Sure, if you overlooked the constant fucking and beating. Can't do a great deal of spying on your back in bed."

"Actually, you can. That's where pillow talk comes into it. Why do you reckon they have spies in a brothel?"

"Oh. Of course." Marra rolled her eyes at her silly comment. "I was excluded from all the actual training. Blarik just wanted the bride deal with the Dran'ali. I don't believe he had any plans for me to be a foreign agent. He wanted a cavalry." Marra told her of the horse dowry.

Nioma's eyes widened, and she nearly choked on her tea. "A couple of hundred Dran'ali breed stock? Might just be worth it." She laughed at herself and wiped her chin. "Okay, seriously though, I've thought of the perfect identity for you: Taerryn Kronyer. While not noble, she has a slightly similar history— only child, deceased mother, father not around, and abused. Should be easy to fill her boots, considering the similarities."

Nioma gave her all the background while they finished their breakfast. "She was a cover I used briefly in the north. I very much doubt any residents of The Crags will know of her, and if you've no other persona, she's already developed down to the fine detail."

"You've been north?" Marra poured the last of the tea.

"As far as Whelron. I had a short stint there, yes, but Onty managed to get me back here."

"Was that Blarik overstepping again? Someone should deal with that arsehole. I made some feeble attempts, but would roundly applaud anyone who managed success."

"You never know. The opportunity to complete it may present itself."

"I can't imagine it happening. Not if I'm ensconced in The Crags."

"Perhaps, but did you ever think you'd be at a spy school? Or be a Dran'ali Queen, or heading to The Crags?"

Marra shook her head.

"Never say never," Nioma said sagely, then started clearing the table.

After helping wash the dishes, Marra wanted to see Sleena. Nioma directed her to the back door, then began preparation for another day in the tavern. When Marra entered the barn, she saw a barrel-chested man tending to Sleena's hooves.

"Mornin'," he said, looking up.

"Hello to you. Chaz, isn't it? How is she?" Marra stepped in and gave her horse a neck rub and some apple pieces.

"Not overly bad, but any longer on the road, it coulda been worse. I'll redo the lot, miss."

"You're too kind."

"Pleasure." Chaz inclined his head. "Besides, Ny would 'av me balls if I didn't. She knows 'er 'orses, she does. This mare is lovely, too."

The day passed slowly. After noon, the usual crowd arrived either singly or in pairs. They ordered their drinks and food and sat to discuss the state of the weather, the flock, or the crops.

Chaz had done a fine job on Sleena. Marra spent an hour or so giving her a good brush and getting the tangles out of her mane and tail. She also found a very well-stocked saddle kit and decided to give the saddle and all the gear a thorough cleaning. She started pulling everything apart, straps and all, then wiped the encrusted dust off all the surfaces before rubbing them down with the saddle soap.

Nioma approved later when Marra told her of her afternoon.

"Do they have horses at The Crags?" she asked later when there was a quiet moment. The wine was out, so they sat side by side, chatted, and sipped quietly.

"I don't know. I can't see it happening. The community is on cliffs. Mountain goats might be better."

"Sure, I'll ride off into the sunset on my trusty mountain goat."

"You'd be going the wrong direction to get to The Crags." Nioma laughed. "You'd be in Lutwan in a couple of hours."

"Other than the Trallko Domain, I know little about this region," Marra admitted. "A fellow student and a good friend of mine—in fact, my only friend—said she came from a town like that. Are there many down here?"

"At last, I found my calling, a trip adviser to wayward spies." Nioma went on to give a general rundown of the area. "There's Dobigh, and Lutwan, fishing villages hugging the cliffs, and both are south and west of here. Huttern is the only other village on the coast and is way over to the east. What was your friend's name?"

"Florin Allcin. She said she came from a village where the fishing was difficult, but they harvested lots of shellfish. She was a diver."

"Ah, Florin." Nioma smiled knowingly.

"You know her?" Marra asked in disbelief.

"No, but you said her name last night."

"I did?" She blushed.

"Marra. Seriously, it's alright." Nioma put an arm across her shoulders for a brief hug and continued. "I don't know the family name, but I'll keep an ear out now. Never know. They might appreciate knowing their girl is doing well." Nioma paused. "Is she?"

"Doing well? Oh, yes. She's the youngest there, but she's got spunk and doesn't stop."

"Sounds promising. And now, the list of bitches, if you please."

"List?"

"You said you had one friend, and she was the youngest? Remember, I've been there. I can see it now. The youngest student—always picked on and treated like trash—then a new girl comes along. Before you know it, she reaches out, desperate to make a friend before the others get their claws into you and turn you against her."

"I...I never thought of it like that!"

"But it's true though, isn't it?"

"Sadly, it's very accurate in hindsight." Marra finished the last drops of wine.

Nioma poured two more glasses and had a swig from hers. "Okay. New subject. Name the head bitch."

Marra sniffed and wiped her nose. "Shayr Reguk. I think

she comes from Slamand, also in the north. Not sure if the pronunciation is right."

"I'm not surprised. She was a young student when I was there. She was vindictive even then."

"Hasn't changed," Marra told her the horror of the rockion trap. "Do you think she intended that? To have me killed?"

"That environment can change a person, especially one set amongst a horde of women from everywhere. Men, they just go and bash each other, then it's done. Women nurture and feed grudges until an opportunity arises. And you stopped her from becoming a queen!"

"Not that I wanted any of it."

"She wouldn't have cared. With no chance of getting at Blarik for dropping her, she aimed her wrath at you. It's cruel how some men go out of their way to make our lives a misery. But, when they're not horrid, some can be magnificent. Some women, on the other hand, can be far worse."

"May I ask how old you were when you joined?"

"Twenty-six. I was working near Horkin. I was surprised to see a eunuch in town. A couple of unruly patrons were giving this bald, chubby guy a hard time. I hard-timed them back instead. Then Onty introduced himself and asked if I'd join up. And that's me. Well-travelled, well-tapped, and well-versed in all things deceptive."

"And still so young and vibrant."

"Flattery works too." She reached out and touched Marra's fingers for a moment. "So..." Grinning, Nioma brought out a slip of parchment and a pen. "I'd better send Onty an update. Let him know you're here and safe."

"What if Blarik gets it? Don't these messages sometimes get intercepted?"

"Falcons are very fast birds, which is why we use them,

plus the fact that they are also hunters. Rarely is a falcon taken."

"Well, maybe not in the air, but what about on the ground after delivery?"

"Welcome to the conundrum of spying—getting information across accurately without others getting it. That's why we have a cypher."

"Cypher?"

"Another subject you didn't need, apparently. Coded messages. It won't make any sense to anyone unless they have the key." Nioma looked at her thoughtfully for a few moments, then put pen to parchment, scribbling in code, and gave it to her.

"What language is that?" Marra stared at the text with little comprehension. She even turned the slip of parchment upside down.

"Spyspeak, silly."

"And they're actual words?"

"Coded. Yes." Nioma shrugged, smiling.

"What's it say?"

"Not telling. And it's yours to keep."

"Isn't this for Onty?" She held it to her.

"Oh, he wouldn't want that one." Nioma chuckled. "That one's for your eyes only. Maybe you'll decipher it one day."

"I'd never be able to do that." Marra stared at the scribble, perplexed.

"Then my secret's safe." Nioma winked and pulled out another thin slip of paper. "I'll write another to tell him you've arrived and are safe, heading to The Crags. Even in code, though, I won't mention your name, or even 'raven-haired beauty', or The Crags, but he'll work it out."

"And you have a falcon?"

"Several, but they belong to Chaz."

"Is he…"

"A spy? No. But he helps me out in many ways."

"Lucky him." Marra smiled cheekily.

Nioma chuckled. "Funnily enough, not that way. He has a family."

"Oh, sorry. I just assumed."

"Easily done, especially after considering what you know of my background."

"Which is hardly anything, apart from spy training."

"Chaz is the only spiron in the area. That's why he deals so well with horses."

"A male spiron?"

"Rare, but he's not very powerful in the way you probably mean. Some spirit mancers have very subtle abilities."

There was a knock at the door. Chaz's large frame filled it a second later. "Ny. A raven from 'is lordship. He's comin' through tonight. Needs all the beds."

"Oh crap. Now he tells me!" She jumped up. "Marra—"

"Point me to where I can help."

"Good girl. Knew you were smart."

ONT'EBA'S OFFICE and quarters were on the top floor of a wing of the male dormitories.

He tried to devote as much time to both schools, but the young males were more high-maintenance and prone to infighting regularly.

In his earlier days, he jokingly thought they could all do with castration—it would certainly remove the violent impulses—but detrimental to all that was being accomplished here. And while it would make his day less stressful, there was absolutely no call for eunuchs in a male brothel. So, his rooms were located here simply because it was more efficient to deal with the frequent interruptions to his already busy routine. Looking out the large windows to the manicured lawns stretching to the woods, the spymaster contemplated all he had gleaned over the last week.

Marra had managed to get away, that was certain. But it wasn't just his luck to witness a girl of her description leaving on the Olber mare—one that threatened to bite anyone—he also based it on keen observation of the rockions. Gruesome and bloody as that night was, the only 'missing' body was the wearer of the nightdress. The rockion keeper, several guards, one mancer, and an unlucky member of the house staff had been cut to ribbons and mauled but not consumed.

The bulk of the human body would be evident even with predators as large as these rockions. When the beasts were eventually returned to their enclosure, there was no telltale bulge in their bellies. Nothing had been eaten—certainly not something as large as a human. A check of the dormitories showed Marra was missing, and he did nothing to quell the belief that the poor girl had been taken. He also did not bring the absence of Sleena to anyone's attention. He would rather let them think he had overlooked some aspects of the investigation than reveal to them the truth.

Ont'eba was also interested in the matter of the assassination of High Lord Olber, but the length of time with his current tasks precluded him from carrying out any in-depth investigation.

Several weeks after Marra's presumed death, he was given instructions to send birds to all the noble domains, both major and minor houses, with the summons—he worded it as an invitation—to attend the "wedding of the decade", where two nations could finally put their animosity and differences aside with the joining of the Dran'ali Overlord and the daughter of a major noble domain.

Since the spymaster's allegiance was with the legitimate ruler, it was understandable that Blarik would keep several key decisions from him. He was only made aware from his conversations with Marra that *she* was to be the Dran'ali Overlord's bride, and now realised why the noble houses had to bring their daughters. Unfortunately, because he was sending the invitations to all houses, and not his normal network, it would be pointless to code a warning in the messages—it could indicate to some of Blarik's allies that the spymaster was undermining the new High Lord.

So, the invitations went out to all and sundry, depleting his stock of birds for several days. Not being idle, he penned cypher-coded missives to his normal contacts in bordellos scattered across the lands, to get warnings to the various houses aligned with the Olbers. As the birds returned, he sent them off again after their rest.

Chastising himself for his neglect of late with the ongoing bickering and intrigue of the noble houses, he was going to have to remedy that. His continued presence here at the school would be unusual and might cause Blarik to become suspicious of his motives.

When all his messages had been sent, he prepared for his usual recruiting foray, but this was a ruse. He intended to relocate to his office in Port Algers, the main trade hub of Jaranabi. It was close to the disputed territory bordering Klarget, and the major route for all international trade, and that meant information. From there, he could rely on his network to keep him posted on Blarik's activities while having better access to information on this brewing war.

CHAPTER

TWENTY

FULL HOUSE

Preparing as many beds as they could in a short time was sweaty work. Chaz was too bulky to get to the loft, so Marra went in and dragged out some extra bedding, disturbing several mice in the process. Once the extra bedding was dropped through the hole, she climbed back down.

"You're a treasure." Nioma stood below as Chaz helped her down the ladder with a steady hand.

Once down, they grabbed the bedding and the pair headed to the rooms to start making the beds. There were five in this room, though it was a squeeze. Even four bunks was cosy.

"They'll simply have to leave any of their kit outside." Nioma dabbed at her brow and face with a damp towel and passed it to Marra. "Damn lucky I've got no boarders."

"Where would Lord Trallko sleep if you had no spare beds?" she asked, dabbing her own face and neck.

"Shit, if it came to that, Harrod would have my bed, and I'd hit the barn."

"You'd do that? Give him your own bed?" Marra tossed the towel near the door and continued making the bed.

"Sure. Can't have the local noble bedding the local taverner."

Marra threw a pillow at her. "Not that—though I've no doubts it's been done."

"Many times over the years, I'm sure, but not with me, and not in my tavern."

"How many can you fit in?"

"I only do one at a time. I have my principles. There are those howev—"

"Nioma!" Marra looked shocked. "That's not what I meant at all."

"I know. I just love stirring you and seeing you riled. And blushing."

"I am not blushing."

"No?"

"No. I'm just hot and sweaty."

"Bath time later."

"You're incorrigible and have a one-track mind!" Marra laughed.

"All in the training, and I topped that class," Nioma joked. "Okay. No bath."

Having finished with the bunks here, they moved to the next room and continued.

"And how many have we coming?"

"No idea, but he's never had more than twenty, so we should be alright. If pushed, and the men are short and slim, I can house about fifteen inside, another fifteen in the barn."

"Does he do this often? Harrod always seemed so logical and orderly."

"Only once before—"

"Let me guess: that was an impromptu High Council summons at my place?"

"When that summons was put out, he rolled straight on through. No, it was a couple of years ago—one of those rare Dran'ali incursions over the mountains."

"I didn't know they'd tried to invade. Must have been a meeting I didn't sneak into."

"Not an invasion, more of a local southern clan flexing its muscle. They lived in the highlands and found a narrow rift to get through. It was over in a few days, and House Trallko and House Hommin gained several Dran'ali horses for breeding. Would just love to get my legs over one of those."

"Nioma!" Marra did go bright red this time. "That's...that's..."

"Now look who has a one-track mind." The taverner laughed again. "It's okay, I've no Dran'ali blood, so I'm not interested in mating with any horses."

They both burst out laughing.

"Oh, stop it." Marra held her sides. "My jaw and ribs are hurting."

"Sounds like you're needing another massage..." Nioma winked.

Marra paused. "You think we have time?"

"Regrettably, no." Her friend sighed and stretched. "Fair enough. Back to it, then."

Before long, the last bed was made. Approaching hoofbeats could be heard from the window. Both girls glanced out.

"Advance guard," Nioma guessed.

"Oh...he's here! Trin's here!" Marra almost jumped like a child and spun towards the door.

Nioma was there before her, blocking the exit. "Marra, you can't go. Your presence has to remain a secret!"

"But it's Trinol! My head guard. He's absolutely wonderful

and trustworthy." Marra tried to push past, but Nioma had a surprisingly strong grip.

"Believe me, I know it's hard, but hear me first." She let go. "I can't force you not to go. Well, I could, but I won't. You need to understand, Blarik has eyes and ears in most noble house-holds. Trallko's no exception, and being a strong ally of House Olber, you can be certain Blarik will be keeping tabs."

"Can't something be done about them?"

"We can get rid of them, yes—and we know of at least two —but then new ones are eventually sent, and it would take time to determine who they are. At least this way, we know who to feed bad information—or keep at arms' length."

"I can hear him laughing." Marra stared longingly back at the window. "It's good he's well and happy, and I'm glad he managed to get away with his family. I've spent weeks worry-ing." She turned back to her friend. "I understand. Thank you for being so strong. And I'm sorry."

"Oh, girl." Nioma held her again, but in consolation, not annoyance. "It's me who's sorry. You need and deserve some happiness, and I seem to be the one standing in your way. This is a burden I wouldn't wish on anyone."

Marra hugged her back, taking the time to get her emotions under control. It was a prolonged hug, one that neither seemed to be in a hurry to break.

Nioma nuzzled her neck, then pulled back to look at her, her green eyes, moist and longing, searching those deep blue eyes. She cupped the back of her head, threading her fingers through her dark locks. "Marra, I know there has been heartache and trauma leading to you being here, and if I could, I would take it all away, but for all the wrong reasons. I'm glad you are he—"

Marra interrupted with a kiss that was pure and passion-ate, and Nioma reciprocated in kind.

The whinny of horses and raucous laughter of several men broke through the haze of their longing.

They parted, eyes sparkling, and laughed with newfound joy.

"I guess you'd better see to the men."

"Work, work, work." Nioma kissed her quickly, then turned and flounced away, a new spring in her step.

Weak-kneed all of a sudden, Marra slumped back onto a freshly made bunk for a moment to catch her breath, thinking, not for the first time, how lucky she had been to stumble into Culming.

With a deep breath, she got up and washed her face before heading downstairs to start the food preparation. She seemed to move in a daze.

Nioma was soon back in the kitchen and looked over with a coy smile. "You okay?"

"Better than I can remember."

"Wonderful. Me too. Want to do the vegetables?"

"Sure. I'm a woman with skills other than sewing, remember." Marra took a moment to absorb the feeling of contentment before getting to work. Soon, several piles of vegetables covered the large table, and she began cutting and peeling.

"I dare say that'll be Lord Trallko this time," Nioma said at the sound of more horses approaching. "Stay here, don't go into the bar, and keep away from the windows."

"Yes, ma'am." Marra curtsied. Practicality and security aside, she was still disappointed at not being able to speak with Trinol to let him know she was alright.

"And don't pout. You know the reason." Nioma blew her a kiss and went to greet the new guests, making sure the door was closed.

"Ner ner ner." Marra tossed vegetables into a pot. "Shit!" she cursed, annoyed that her little tantrum made the hot water splash and hiss over the stove top. She stopped it up and put the lid on, slightly askew so it wouldn't boil over, then started preparing the meat.

A few minutes later, Nioma stormed back inside, almost slamming the door. "Shit. Shit and double shit! " She put several more lengths of wood in the stove and started to angrily stir the pot.

"What is it?" Marra looked up from the bench where she was now cutting the meat.

"Mimia is with him."

"Harrod's daughter? I haven't seen her in years."

"Damn it. Damn her!"

"Why's that a problem? She's not too bad, a bit of a stick-in-the-mud, but she's okay."

"Because she can't very well sleep in the rooms with the men, and definitely not in the barn. That means she'll have to have my bed. And her maid will have to sleep on the floor."

"Your room? *I'll* sleep in the barn, and she can have my bed," Marra offered.

"No can do, my pretty one. Firstly, I can't very well send our noble-born lass to the smallest room in the tavern—"

"You did it to me."

"*And*"—Nioma tossed a cloth at her—"You can't be seen, remember? These chaps will be tending their own horses and tack. They'll be in the barn for ages. And I reckon one or two will probably sleep there. Plus, there'll be patrols, and if they find some buxom beauty in the hayloft... You see where I'm going with this?"

Marra nodded.

"Harrod even apologised for the short notice," Nioma said. "He'll be sharing a room with his captain of the guard; the rest of the men will bunk where we can fit them. Chaz is rear-ranging a couple of bunks as I speak."

As if on cue, the sound of furniture scraping on floorboards sounded from above.

There was a sharp knock at the door, and Lord Trallko walked in.

"Nioma, as a token of good—Marra!" The bottle of wine Harrod had been carrying fell to the floor and smashed on the flagstones. Glass shards scattered in all directions, and red wine splashed across the tiles and ran along the joints.

Within a heartbeat, booted feet came running, and three guards barged into the kitchen.

Trinol was one of them. He stopped and stared. "Marra!"

"Well...fuck!" Marra and Nioma swore.

"Marra...What are you doing here?" Harrod stepped over the broken glass and hugged her. "We thought Blarik had some dark plans for you. For weeks, we beseeched him for news. Every time, he ignored us."

Marra hugged Harrod back. While he was also a lord, he had been a very close friend of her father and her mother before. She wept tears of joy to see him, sad for the memories he stirred within.

When she backed away, Trinol was watching with wide eyes. Tears streaked his face.

He dropped to his knee. "My lady..."

"Get up, Trin."

In a single motion, her previous head guard stood. She reached out, and they hugged like brother and sister. More tears were shed, and she realised everyone in the kitchen was staring at her, dumbfounded.

Nioma, after a moment of hesitation, went to the tavern door and closed it.

"Lord Trallko, no one can know of her presence," she stated.

"What? This is cause for celebration." The nobleman looked from face to face in confusion.

Marra explained quickly about her kidnapping and subsequent escape. "I'm truly glad to see you again, too, but this—me being here—must remain a secret, as Nioma said. I was hoping he would think I was dead, but if that ruse didn't work, Blarik would be searching high and low." Marra went on to explain her predicament.

"Yes, yes, of course. It will be as you say. You are still High Lady to me and to those loyal to House Olber."

Marra wept. Nioma looked surprised at hearing this and looked to Marra with questions in her eyes. *High Lady?* she mouthed.

Marra wiped her eyes and gave a brief nod. "Where are you all off to at such short notice?" she asked, changing the subject.

"We had another summons from that fat fool. This time, with dire threats if we don't bring Mimia with us."

"Your daughter? Why?"

"All the Houses are invited, their daughters especially, for a wedding ceremony."

"Wedding? Whose?"

"Urgad Jorakif."

"Is he still coming?"

"You knew?"

"It was supposed to be me that he was to marry. Blarik planned for me to be the Overlord's strumpet. That was part of the reason I escaped."

"The message stated Urgad is marrying one of the daughters of a noble House. It's a surprise—which is to say we don't know who yet. It's promised to be the biggest event of the year. Of the decade. All nobles are invited. There'll be an equally large ceremony in Dran'ali."

"Surely someone knows who this replacement bride-to-be

is?” Marra wondered fleetingly if Shayr had got what she wanted. But Shayr wasn't a noble, so...

“If they do, they're not saying. Probably the daughter of one of his friends up north.”

“You can't say no to this? The wedding is a farce, and he's not the High Lord—it was a coup.”

“True, but he has the power and the men to enforce it, and taxing us to the hilt in the process.”

“Your guards—”

“Most have been conscripted. See many young men around here? Mostly all old farmers or the infirm. What you see here is half of what I have left, and I'm lucky to have these as it is. I even had to hide Trinol for a few days.”

“But, there's no war...”

“Not yet. Reports say it's hotting up, though.”

“Reports from who? Blarik's sources? If he's the one saying it, I wouldn't believe those reports.” Marra looked at their faces. “Sorry. You're not here for political discourse. And I'm out of the picture, so I have no say.”

Harrod opened his mouth, but Mimia strolled in, pushing past Nioma, and looked the place over with dissatisfaction.

“Mim, look who it is!” Harrod said.

Mimia was slightly shorter than Marra and slightly on the plumper side. Her brown hair looked as listless as her hazel eyes. She wore a plain beige dress—nothing too spectacular, and practical for hours spent in a carriage.

“Oh, Marra. I'm pleased to see you again. It's been too long.”

Marra smiled. It didn't take any spy school training to see the lack of authenticity of her words. “Mimia. Likewise.” Marra embraced her quickly. “And how is Trisch?”

“Oh, Mother's having one of her moods. She won't be able to make it to the ceremony. Her loss.” From the look on her face, Mimia wasn't overly impressed by the kitchen. "Is there somewhere I can wash this disgusting dust off?"

"M'lady, if'n it pleases you. I'll show yer to yer bunk," Nioma curtsied, catching Marra's eye and winking. "Tha' frock becomes yer, m'lady. Pick it yerself?"

Marra had to fight hard not to burst out laughing, especially at Mimia's horror when she heard 'bunk'.

"Very well, lead on." Mimia walked a few steps after the taverner. "Oh, Marra. We must chat later. Lots of gossip to catch up on and all."

"Of course, Mim. I'll be he—"

"Pru?" Mimia called out, cutting Marra off. "Goodness, where is that woman? Pru!"

"M'lady." Another woman came in, loaded with several bags. Pru may have been pretty, but right now she was so haggard and dusty, it was hard to tell. "Comin' right up."

Marra opened her mouth and stepped towards her.

Trin quickly intervened. "Please, Pru. Allow me."

"Oh, Master Trinol. It be okay."

"Good. No arguments then." He grabbed the bags and carried them easily. The relief on Pru's face was palpable. "Let's be off, then. Can't leave dear Mim waitin'. The poor flower will wilt at any moment." He winked at Marra as he passed.

With Nioma and Trin gone, Marra was left with Harrod and two guards. "I...I'd better clean this up," she said, looking to the spilt wine and broken glass.

"Oh. Yes. Um. I will see to the men. Marra, it is truly good to see you again."

"And you, Harrod. We will talk later," she promised.

"Of course. As you wish." He bowed. "My lady." He turned and left, motioning his men to follow.

Marra slumped in a chair to breathe. She could hear Mim pointing out the deficiencies as she progressed to her room.

"... and dusty, these stairs are too steep...and too narrow."

She was glad Trin was there to prevent Ny from doing something stupid.

Several minutes later, Nioma came down the stairs, followed by a grinning Trinol. Ny went to the bar and returned a moment later with three mugs of ale and set them on the table. She filled all three mugs and immediately started drinking hers.

Leaving his mug untouched, Trinol looked to Marra. "My lady—"

"Trin, we've moved on from that." She reached for his hand.

He smiled shyly. "Marra... I should see to the men. We will chat later?"

"Assuming you're not guarding Mim's door from assault." She looked at Nioma's fuming visage.

"I'm sure Lady Nioma will not be a concern." He grinned at them both, then left.

"That's him, isn't it?" Nioma smacked her lips and started on the mug she had set out for Trinol.

"Him who?"

"Your fantasy man. When you grew up, and the only man in your little noble girl's life was your guard. He's nice."

"Married, older."

"They're the best kind." She winked.

"He is not, nor will ever be, my lover."

"Fair enough. I can't talk. It's not like I followed through on *every* fantasy." She sat and drained the mug.

There was a shriek from upstairs, followed by foot stamping and Mim's screeching. "Pru, get that mouse! I hate this hovel."

Marra pushed her mug towards Nioma. "I think you need this more than me."

Nioma grabbed the mug she had poured for Trinol instead and took a swig. "I must say, your judge of character is sorely misplaced if you think that cow is only a stick-in-the-mud. I swear, I'll tan that brat's hide if she wipes her finger across something again looking for dust."

"She has changed. Not for the better, it seems," Marra conceded. She put a calming hand on Nioma's. "She'll be gone tomorrow, and life will be as it should be."

Nioma softened her tone. "The highlight is, Harrod has supplied his own stores, so mine won't be too depleted." She lifted another bottle of wine. "And he brought this as well."

"A nice vintage?"

"Nice? Surely you jest. The cost of this bottle is more than my entire bar selection."

Marra examined the label and the cork. "Then we might have to save it for a special occasion."

TWENTY-ONE

TRAGIC NEWS

To minimise any knowledge of Marra's presence, Lord Trallko and Trinol decided to dine in the kitchen so they could converse with Marra during their brief stay out of eyesight and earshot from Trallko's contingent of house guards.

So as not to disturb her regular patrons, and in a subtle effort to further reduce any casual sightings of Marra, Nioma arranged for a trestle table to be erected under the awning covering the front of the building. This way, the soldiers would remain outside, and her regular patrons wouldn't be too put out with any of the rowdiness one expects from the military.

Mimia remained in her "cupboard" of a room, and sent Pru down regularly to fetch this and that.

"Forgive, Mim," Pru said to Nioma. "This up and leavin' on short notice—"

"It's character building. And she needs it. A lot," Nioma answered, without mincing her words.

Pru looked askance at such a statement, worried.

"Pru. It's just you and me here. Most nobles don't care what the staff think or say, so no need to worry."

The maid smiled in relief. "Truth be told, the young lass *is* quite needy."

Nioma nodded knowingly. "There's a deep, dried-up well out back past the henhouse. Give me the word, and Mim will be at the bottom of it." Nioma winked.

That was all too much for Pru. "I best be goin'." She grabbed the tray and quickly escaped upstairs, nearly bumping into Marra. "M'lady," she apologised on the run.

"You scaring the staff now?" Marra asked Nioma as she walked into the kitchen.

"I was suggesting to Pru that Mim could easily disappear if she just gave the word."

"Some of these older staff, so entrenched in the proper decorum of a noble house, they can't take a joke anymore..."

"Who said I was joking?"

"You're wicked."

"Thank you. It's a natural talent. The school simply perfected it."

Dinner was a quiet, casual affair. Nioma was kept busy serving the normal patrons as well as the guards.

Marra wanted to help, but for obvious reasons, couldn't. She busied herself looking after Harrod and Trinol, though her ex-guard looked abashed at being served by his high lady.

"If you call me 'my lady' again, Trin, you'll be wearing this stew."

Not trusting himself to respond without the risk of assault, he simply nodded and smiled.

"Maybe, after all this fracas settles, you can emerge," Lord

Trallko said. "You are always welcome at our place, especially if you can keep Trinol and the men in line."

"Harrod," Marra said to him softly, "my uncle's obsessed. The only way this will end is with one of us dead."

"Surely not—"

"Please. Enough. If you want me to dine with you, I'd rather not spend the precious hours with you two talking about that poor excuse for a man."

"Who?"

"Exactly. Now, tell me all that's going on at home. I hear Trisch isn't well? How's the Hommin Domain, and the Kindair's? Start from...after that night."

It was late by the time they finished their meals. Other than the small contingent of patrolling guards, everyone went to bed soon after. As Nioma had said, the bulk of the guards went upstairs via the bar access, and a few preferred the hayloft and the horses as the rooms were cramped.

Nioma entered the kitchen after dousing the lanterns in the bar. Marra greeted her with a glass of wine.

"You're a treasure." Nioma sat wearily at the table, joining her friend.

"Least I could do. You worked so hard."

Nioma shrugged. "Part of the business." She sipped and yawned, almost spilling her wine down her front.

"You're exhausted. I'll finish up here. I'm almost done anyway. You get yourself up to the loft. I'll be up there soon."

"Right. I'd better wash first." Leaving her wine, she headed up the stairs.

Marra smiled, then drank the wine, watching Nioma's retreating figure. She cleared the table and washed the remaining mugs and plates, then banked the stove. With one last wipe of the counters, she took the lantern off the hook and made her way up the stairs to her room.

Nioma had collapsed on the edge of the bed and was already in a deep sleep. Marra undressed and slipped in behind her. It was cramped, but Nioma had been so tired Marra doubted she'd wake her. Draping her arm across the other woman's warm body, she closed her eyes and was soon snoring with her friend.

THE SOUND of horses and men stirring woke her. From the low angle of light through the small window, Marra realised it was just after dawn. Nioma was nowhere in sight. Quickly throwing on her clothes, she went downstairs.

"You should have woken me!" she grumped when she arrived in the kitchen, seeing Ny busy over pots of porridge.

"I tried."

"Liar. Want me to do the eggs?"

"No. You keep stirring this. I have to go to the henhouse to fetch them."

Soon, the breakfast was taken out for the guards, and the two women could sit back and have their own meal.

"It's a sad realisation that, with these things going on constantly at home, I never even considered how it was for the staff until now."

"Welcome to the real world. They'll be out of here soon enough."

"Then we can relax—"

"Then there's stripping all the beds, washing the linen, storing that bedding back up in the loft, sorting the remaining stores, feeding the hens, then preparing for the usual crowd."

"Yes, but what am *I* going to do?" Marra grinned, then laughed with her, more out of relief that they would be left to themselves for a few hours.

THE DAYS PASSED for Marra as if in a dream. She was very happy; happier than she could ever remember. She had plenty to keep her busy, which took her mind off things. After waking up with the most beautiful woman in her life, they'd both have breakfast, do a few chores, then take Sleena and Bragante, Nioma's own horse, for a ride before it got too warm. Nioma was able to join her because, with the extra hand, she had more time to do the things she loved.

Nioma proved she was indeed born in the saddle. Marra thought her horse was just as magnificent as Duyma and Sleena, and said as much, then she found out Bragante was the offspring of the captured Dran'ali stock from several years back.

The tavern was a comfortable place to be. Food and drink were in abundance, and the company was better than she'd ever imagined it could be. Admittedly, she considered, her life experiences had been fairly minimal, if you took out the recent traumas.

Marra had never been in a serious relationship—though the memories of her brief time spent with Florin always put a smile on her face—and now here she was sharing her life with the most wonderful woman she could ever hope to meet.

And that in itself was a total surprise. The school had been an alien environment, neither good nor bad. For anyone, being part of a harem of beautiful, scantily clad women would inevitably lead to exploration of new desires and interests. It had felt as natural as breathing. She idly wondered if it was the same at the school for males. Did they, too, explore new horizons? Did it feel as natural to them as to women? *Or is it just me? Am I in a minority?*

Nioma came into the kitchen and busied herself. She smiled, came over and gave Marra a nice, long kiss, then went back to work.

Marra watched Nioma whenever she could. She was such a high-spirited and vital powerhouse of energy. Her new partner could laugh with the old folk, help shoe a horse, even assist Chaz in fixing a wagon wheel, and drink anyone under the table. The ideal lover, in her estimation. *Are we lovers? How are they different from partners?* She considered this. Being in a relationship was all so new to her. "Maybe it's the sex..." she guessed, smiling.

TWO WEEKS LATER, word came from a trader that Lord Trallko's party was a day behind him. There was little more information forthcoming since the reticent man left as soon as he'd had a meal.

Having had ample notice this time, preparation was far less frenetic. Even the stables were cleaned out with fresh straw. The trestle table again was set up on the balcony with barrels of ale and a tray of mugs at the ready.

While Nioma was busy, Marra went up to her—*their*—room and cleaned it from floorboards to rafters. "See if Mim finds dust this time!" She stopped before she called her a brat. *That was probably me up until a few months ago.* She also made up her old bed in the attic.

The arrival of Lord Trallko and his entourage wasn't the happy occasion expected. The horses ambled in, almost at a casual stroll, not the normal pace to travel cross-country. The guards were sullen. They barely raised a hand in greeting and went directly to the stables to take care of their horses.

Trinol dismounted and came over. His armour looked the worse for wear, far more than what would normally be expected from mere time spent on the road would do.

"Let's talk inside," he said simply. No sign of any of his usual formality.

They followed, and Marra looked over her shoulder for Lord Trallko, but he was nowhere to be seen. Neither was Mim.

"The wedding was an utter disaster," Trinol started. "A tragedy."

Nioma sat him down, poured him an ale, and both women sat across from him to listen attentively. Marra had never seen him so down. She reached out a hand to touch his fingers.

Slowly, the story unfolded of how the wedding went and the chaos that ensued afterwards.

"Much of this was behind closed doors, but word gets around. Urgad was displeased that the promised bride wasn't there. Blarik begged him to reconsider, offering Urgad his selection of the young noblewomen present in an effort to hold to his promise."

"I reckon that was why Blarik insisted the nobles bring their daughters." Nioma nodded, sadly. "He knew this was going to happen."

Trinol nodded. He sipped the ale. "During the arrival banquet to celebrate and welcome the Dran'ali entourage, all the nobles were introduced, along with their daughters. It would seem from that, Urgad made a selection."

"Like a bloody flesh market," Nioma spat.

"Who was the...chosen bride?" Marra asked.

"It was announced that the betrothed was Prisila Phillit."

"Lord Phillit's granddaughter? He is no ally to Blarik."

Trinol shrugged. "There was another day of feasting and

preparation for the big day. Many visitors congratulated young Lady Phillit."

"Any idea how Prisila felt about it?"

"Officially, she was delighted and honoured, though nervous."

"Officially," Nioma scoffed. "And in reality?"

"We will never know," he said, and kept talking before they could interrupt. "The wedding itself was magnificent..." he looked into his mug.

"Trin, what are you reluctant to tell us?" Marra asked.

"Lady Phillit...is dead. We won't know the truth about whatever happened during their night together. What we do know is she was screaming and crying when she fled the bed chamber, she tripped when running down the stairs and...and was fatally injured."

Marra and Nioma gasped in horror.

"The whole thing was a disaster. It would seem the brutality of the Dran'ali Overlord was not exaggerated. Lord Phillit's heart failed at the news. He is also dead."

"Prisila was his only heir... so House Phillit is no more?"

Trinol nodded. "They were the last of their line."

"I wouldn't be surprised if Blarik didn't somehow suspect this would happen. He's a conniving and despicable arsehole."

"I haven't received a falcon for a while now..." Nioma considered as she turned to Marra. "I wonder how Onty is? He wouldn't allow this."

"I did not see the dark-skinned eunuch at the wedding." Trinol had no knowledge of his whereabouts.

"Trin..." Marra hesitated to ask. "Where...where is Harrod? Is he......"

"He's alive." Trinol's voice broke. "Lady Mimia also passed away, from injuries received during a horse stampede. Her father's mourning in the carriage with her body."

"No! It can't be!" The two women cried out and burst into tears, not hearing his last words. They reached for each other and sobbed. They didn't have to like the girl to feel the loss of the flesh and blood that had walked these floors just weeks earlier.

The two women got to their feet, but before they could move away, Trin reached for their wrists.

"Don't. Lord Trallko insisted he's not to be disturbed."

Sobbing, they resumed their seats. Other than the sound of weeping, it was quiet in the kitchen. Trinol left after briefly laying a consoling hand on their shoulders.

THE REST of the day was a numbing blur. The regular farmers and locals arrived in dribs and drabs, but within a very short time, having picked up on the morose atmosphere, soon left them to their mourning.

The guards, while still feeling dejected, ate and drank. They were fighting men and used to death and loss. Lord Trallko barely ate. Pru, no longer caring for Mimia, had shifted her attention to looking after him, and though she came and went, she too had red and swollen eyes.

Marra's identity was unknown to many of the guards, and since they were now returning to the domain, she did what she could to ease the workload for Nioma. Between doing the rounds to provide meals and drinks to the group, she gleaned sufficient information from the overheard conversations to piece together the tragic events.

Of all the lessons she had spy school, this ability to listen undetected and to pull information had been the most beneficial.

In the aftermath of Prisila's death, all the nobles were

demanding an explanation of the tragic loss of her life on the night she should have cherished. Even Blarik's closest allies were outraged.

It was clear from the outset that Urgad took no responsibility for the death. He was displeased with Blarik's betrayal. The Dran'ali Overlord made an ultimatum to Blarik: provide the promised High Lady Marra Olber, or face the combined wrath of the Dran'ali clans. If there was any blame for the circumstance, then it was his, for he had broken their agreement!

"Like all Dran'ali," Urgad had said, "we honour our oaths. This union of the two greatest clans was to cement the borders of the two greatest nations, and provide many sons and daughters for future marriages."

Urgad had turned to the red-faced Blarik. "Does your word mean nothing to you? You promised, and it was agreed, that my bride would be the first and finest noble lady of all Jaran-abi, the High Lady Marra Olber of House Olber.

"I come here in good faith, trusting you on your word, and what do I find? Not the promised High Lady, but some wilting and snivelling brat who can barely endure her first bedding. Bring me the Olber woman, or expect my wrath. My clans will descend upon your loathsome lives. Our magnificent horses will trample your crops, your lands, and anyone who stands in our way. My riders will rape every able-bodied woman, kill every male, and enslave your children." He had drawn a dagger, sliced his palm, and raised his fist so all could see his blood drip down his forearm. "This is my blood oath! "

Violence had erupted in the streets after this threat. Several people died in the melee, but just as many died when the Dran'ali steeds stampeded through the crowded streets. Mimia was one of them. Several of the other nobles and their children also sustained injuries.

The Dran'ali were last seen heading home, though fewer in number. They, too, had suffered injury and a few deaths from retaliation, but the fighting in the streets was short-lived when Jaranabi soldiers moved in.

Marra dropped the tray in dismay as the shock took hold. These deaths, this tragedy, was all because she ran away.

The nearest guard helped her, then patted her on the rump as she made her way to the kitchen. Leaving the tray on the sideboard, she slumped by the table, ashen-faced until Nioma found her.

"They want me. This is all my fault!" Marra wept.

"That is utter nonsense!" For the very first time, Nioma's anger was directed at her. "I'll not hear that from you again. The blame of this tragedy lies squarely on Blarik's shoulders." Then Nioma hugged and rocked her for what seemed like hours before she slipped away to do her own work.

Once the guards had their meals and drinks, those not on patrol took themselves to bed.

Nioma locked up. The kitchen was empty. She spent several minutes cleaning and rinsing plates and mugs, wiped down the tables and bar before heading to bed, physically and emotionally exhausted.

At dawn the next morning, when the two women went outside, the street and stables were empty; the guards had already departed to the Trallko Domain where Mimia was to be buried.

TWENTY-TWO

STRANGE CUSTOMS

Gromal Harbour was so wide it could be called a bay.

"This be too open for a decent port." Tully shook her head. "Rifts! Any decent swell could easily push a ship against tha wharf and ruin it."

Corra was standing beside her at the helm using her long-eye. "Not everything appears like you think." She nudged the first mate and gave her the scope while holding the wheel. "Take a look."

"Careful yer don't drift to starboard," the first mate warned.

"Which way's that again?" the captain retorted with a laugh.

"'There be ne'er any port *left* in the bottle'," Tully quoted the ancient mnemonic. "Port is left."

"Oh, so starboard is the other side?"

"You catch on quick."

"I try."

While their banter continued, Tully followed the distant landline. The main port was situated between two headlands.

She pointed out several ships scattered around the area; two stood out as warships as they were running the Herantia flag.

"What tha rifts be *that*?" Tully exclaimed after spending several minutes squinting at the port area and trying to decipher what she was looking at.

"Beats me, but we'll be finding out soon enough."

"Aye." She handed the scope back to her captain and resumed her duties at the helm.

As they sailed closer, the rest of the crew could also see what had confused the first mate and the captain. A pair of low walls, spaced about two ship's length apart, stretched across the width of the bay. Each wall stood several feet above the current waterline. They could now see the buoys that indicated the gaps through each wall. They were offset, so any vessel would need to go in slowly, then turn to navigate through the next exit. The arrangement also negated any waves or swell from penetrating all the way into the port.

"All ahead slow," Captain Sienna ordered her aeyrons. "Helm, between those buoys, if you please.

"Aye, Cap'n."

Most of the sails had already been reduced. The *Revenge*'s speed slowed to walking speed as they approached the sea wall.

"Kinam," Tulls called to one of the crew standing nearby. "Take 'old."

The tall, athletic woman held the wheel firmly while the first mate went to the nearby table and examined the charts she had rolled out.

Looking up at the sun and judging its angle, she then made a small note to the side.

"Tide markings?" Sienna queried.

"Aye. Not been 'ere afore. We be near 'igh tide, judgin' by

tha waterline on tha wall. Interstin' to know 'ow far it drops t'night."

Corra nodded. "No doubt Farand can give us greater insight."

"Ta, muchly." Tully resumed her place by the wheel, and Kinam went about her other duties.

A sharp spin on the wheel to turn the ship hard to starboard, followed by a sharp turn to port a minute later, took them safely through and into the protected section of the port.

"Interesting." Corra had the long-eye out again.

"Aye." Tully nodded. "It be that. I reckon we be 'eadin' over there."

As they steered towards a large contingent of ships, a skiff came out at speed to intercept them. A small pennant fluttered from the flagstaff on the bow.

"Looks like they have their own mancers too," Corra noted. "Reckon it's the pilot to come aboard."

"Pfft," was Tully's only comment. Then, at the captain's look, she relented. "Lower a ladder over tha side."

The skiff did a loop around the *Revenge* before expertly swinging about and matching speed perfectly as it came alongside. A line was tossed up to the ship, and the skiff was secured. A short man was about to climb from the smaller boat, but the ladder was hauled up quickly at an order from the first mate.

"What be your business?" Tully came over as soon as Kinam took the wheel.

"Port Authority," he stated. "No vessel enters without a pilot and approval."

Tully looked to the captain with a frown. "We lettin' 'im aboard?"

The nearby crew grew silent as Corra considered it. "I'm sure every nation has different customs to ours." She walked over and looked down at the pilot, watching him, and then saw a woman sitting in the small cabin. *The mancer?*

"And if we don't allow you to board?" Corra asked finally.

"Then you can turn around and leave our fine port," he said, testily.

"Do you board every vessel docking here?"

"Only the first few times for those vessels not registered here. Once they get the gist of the layout, I am no longer required." He looked up, squinting into the sun. "What seems to be the problem?"

"Most of us have this thing about allowing a man aboard."

"Mere superstition?" He looked like he was about to laugh, but seeing how many armed women were glaring down at him, he managed to keep a straight face.

"No. It's a matter of safety," Corra informed him.

"I assure you, I'm no threat—"

The crew laughed at this comment.

"We be talkin' 'bout yer safety," Tully said. "Not good for negotiations when the pilot loses 'is balls."

"Lower the ladder," Corra ordered as the pilot went pale. "Let's not scare our pilot too much. We're after Farand, and if we need to comply with this custom to accomplish it, so be it."

Tully's uncertain frown turned into a shrug. "Aye, cap'n."

As the pilot climbed up, the first mate turned to the crew. "Best behaviour, ladies. Dara, cover the wing-wheel."

Grabbing a length of sail that was neatly positioned in case of emergencies, Dara and Barb quickly dragged it over the unusual mechanism, away from prying eyes.

"Welcome aboard the *Revenge*. I'm Captain Corra Sienna. That there's my First Mate, Tully." The pilot nodded his greeting as he fished out a notebook and began a new entry.

"They call me Bant. And what port do you hail from?"

"Port? We call it The Crags."

The pilot frowned. "I've not heard of it." He tapped his pencil several times. "Nationality?"

"We're from Jaranabi."

"Ah. You mean Port Algers, then? That's the only port Jaranabi has."

"We know of Algers...but we don't come from there."

With a huff, the pilot wrote 'Port Crag'—Jaranabi, next to the ship's and captain's names. "And your business here in Gromal Harbour?"

"How about opening trade negotiations for starters, and we're looking for a decent chart maker and navigator."

"We've got some of the best here." Again, the pencil wriggled in the notebook. Bant looked up. "Very good. If you'd be so good as to steer to the port side, Pier 6, Berth 9 is available." The pilot gave directions to the helmsman. "Keep your starboard side to the left of those floats."

"What can you tell us about that sea wall?" Corra asked. She stayed close to him, partly for his safety and partly so he wouldn't stray. But it seemed he was intent on doing his job only and not overly interested in the ship.

"Ah, yes. Things were quite a different story before that was built, quite chaotic, so I'm told. After our illustrious ruler, King Hunthal III, enticed several terrons to create the wall. Ever since, the trade has prospered, and Port Gromal is now a haven for all ships."

Tully was standing near the side, keeping tabs on the skiff. As the mancer shifted in her seat, she noticed a collar around the woman's neck. The first mate's knuckles whitened with her grip on the gunwale. The collar was chained to the back of the chair.

"Captain," Tully called out.

Corra looked over. While she was annoyed at the interruption, she knew Tulls well enough to know she wouldn't butt-in without good reason.

"Excuse me a moment, Bant." Corra wandered the few steps to the side and looked at her with a question on her lips, then followed the first mate's subtle pointing. "I see..." Corra went stony-faced and turned back to the pilot.

"You have a remarkable vessel," he said when she was again by his side.

"We do."

"All metal? Very expensive," he continued at her nod.

"Bant, as you'd be aware, we've not been here before, so your customs might vary greatly from ours. I see the woman on your boat has a collar. Since I'd rather not have my girls doing the wrong thing unintentionally, what do the laws here say with regard to mancing?"

The pilot nodded, still watching the approaching pier. "Ah, yes. You mentioned the possibility of opening trade negotia-tions. We pay a premium price for good mancers. They'd need to be Tested, of course, before any price is set, though."

"Ah. A premium...You see, where we come from, slavery is abhorrent."

"Oh, goodness me, no. These aren't slaves. They're well-cared for, even doted on by some of the more generous benefactors. King Hunthal III is magnanimous in his care for His subjects. There's an obscure bylaw from ages past: every female elementalist must be chaperoned. It's for their own protection, of course."

"Protection? From what?"

"Not what, whom. Male elementalists, of course."

"Why?"

"Because of the duelling rights."

Corra breathed deeply and slowly. "Bant, again, you'll have to excuse my ignorance of this custom. Could you explain?"

"Umm…" Bant judged the distance to the berth. "Half speed there, young lady."

Corra nodded to Tully, who repeated the order. The aeyrons reduced the wind to a mere breath.

Bant noticed this and looked concerned. "Your mancers… They're not chained or collared?"

"We also have different customs. On this ship, our mancers are free women, there's no need for protection, and they are part of my crew." She didn't feel it necessary to mention that female mancers were persecuted in her country.

His mouth opened and closed several times.

"Please, tell me about these duelling rights," Corra continued.

"Any mancer can challenge a female mancer to a duel to the death. And, obviously, because the males are much stronger, the woman generally dies. This was regarded as horrific, so for their own safety, female mancers are now chaperoned and thus, protected. It's quite civilised."

"Yes. Quite." Corra had to tell herself to relax. "Why not just abolish these duels outright? Or maybe register the male mancers, since they seem to be the ones instigating the trouble?"

"Oh, no, we couldn't do that! We need our male mancers for such things as building and maintaining the sea wall. And it wasn't politically prudent to go against any previous royal decree. Now, if you'll excuse me, I must complete the mooring." He stepped away and ensured the waiting dock handlers were ready and efficient.

Tully joined Corra. "Did I hear correctly?"

"If you mean the duelling, yes."

"What a backward bunch," the first mate muttered darkly.

Corra nodded. She knew she should push the "different customs" line, but she felt it was hollow. "Yes, but we're not in a position to change it. Our task is to get Farand down here and then get back home."

"Will our girls be safe as long as they don't do anything?" she asked Bant as he was about to leave.

"They will need to be registered, of course." The pilot was looking over the side and didn't see the looks on any of the crew's faces at these words.

"Registered?" the captain queried.

"Oh, of course, you would not know this." Bant faced her again. He had to look up; she being much taller, and he had to squint against the high sun. "Yes, indeed, all male and female mancers must be registered. It's a royal decree and cannot be revoked or ignored by anyone." Bant apparently mistook their looks of umbrage for concern about breaking the royal law. "But, please, don't fret. I'll tell you what, I'll inform the Elemental Administrators, and they'll be over as soon as they can for the Testing."

"And I assume there's a cost?"

"Absolutely not!" The pilot looked most affronted. "Charging for a royal decree would be preposterous and grossly uncivilised. However, I should warn you there's a hefty fine for *not* registering. Possibly imprisonment."

Tully swore under her breath. Corra was glad she was professional enough to not need restraining. "And, apart from public degradation, what purpose does the registration serve?"

Bant rolled his eyes. "To keep our King and the royal family safe, of course. We can confiscate weapons, but a mancer in disguise could be an assassin. I really must go. And welcome to Gromal."

The gangway was put in place, and Bant stepped down to the wharf and walked off.

Corra leant over the rail. Some of the crew were already on

the pier, double-checking the lines. "Belay that. Release all lines," she ordered.

The girls hesitated.

"You 'eard the cap'n," Tully barked. "We be leavin'"

Confused but disciplined, the crew did as ordered, tossing the lines free and running back onto the vessel. The gangway was then pulled in immediately.

"Let's be gone," Corra ordered.

Tully whipped out her whistle and gave it a few blows.

Most of the crew were still on deck to see the new harbour, so it was only a matter of moments for the mancers to form up.

Captain Sienna climbed onto a crate to address them. "Sorry, ladies. We didn't escape one yoke just to find another: Gromal requires all mancers to be Tested, registered and collared. It's mandatory here, but we're having none of that. Hefty fines and prison to follow, so let's not get caught." She hopped off and went to speak to the aeyrons specifically, while Tully called the orders to turn the ship about and raise maximum canvas.

"No doubt they'll be after us shortly, so let's put on speed to avoid capture. We'll need to be flexible to navigate the two entrances, but once we're in open water, we can wave goodbye."

"We'll do it, Cap'n."

"I've no doubts. You've never let me down before."

"Let's do this, bitches!" Tully called out. "This ain't like afore. Sure, they be goin' to give chase. They've mancers too, but we got 'alf a league to get to flyin' speed."

The aeyrons started their chanting, the sails were soon full, and the *Revenge* picked up the pace, heading for the first gap.

"They can't do what the *Revenge* can do, though," Corra pointed out.

"And we be leavin' 'em in our wake, Cap'n."

"Cap'n," the spotter called down again. "Look ta the 'arbour."

Glancing back to the docks, Corra could see a red plume of smoke billowing up at an unnatural speed.

"We be far enough ahead ta get away," Kinam said from the helm. "Dey not be catchin' us now."

Tulls and Corra swung their gaze from the wharf back to the two seawalls and beyond.

"Ships f'wd!" came the cry from the crow's nest. "Port 'n' starboard"

Corra had been watching them with her long-eye. The two vessels seen earlier, lurking near the entrance, were still in position, but they were raising anchors and sail.

"Reckon we can get to the entrance before them?"

Tulls gauged the distance each vessel had to cover. "They ain't got favor'ble wind...but they 'ave mancers...and closer." She shrugged. "We can make it ta the first gap, not both."

"What I thought." Corra scanned the wall ahead and swore.

The first mate took a moment to take a look as well. "Bugger." She moved over to the helm. "I got this." Tully adjusted the wheel slightly, aiming for the gap between the inner wall.

Captain Sienna ran through the limited options available. There were two seawalls, each with its own opening to allow vessels to pass.

The *Revenge* had the advantage of the waterwing, making her faster, but the warship could block them easily. She could get her girls to harass the warship, much like they harassed pirates, but that would then violate several maritime laws.

And I didn't come here to start a war!

The only other avenue was going over the wall.

It was unfortunate that the tide had been high when they entered Gromal Harbour. After the time to get to Pier 6, the tide had turned. While the aeyrons were able to achieve sufficient speed so the waterwing could do its work, there may not be enough water beneath them to clear the walls completely.

Time to get our hydrons working.

Tulls was concentrating on the helm, so Corra summoned her water elementalists. As an afterthought, she called every other mancer not directly involved with the running of the ship.

"Ladies, we'll need as much draft as we can to get over that wall without ripping the wing, just like Keel Haul Strait. I hate to ask this of you, but not as much as I know you'll hate being collared."

"How can we assist?" one of the other mancers asked.

"I want you to share your strength with the hydrons. I know some of you aren't the strongest, but that'll be irrelevant if we get caught."

"Leave it with me, Cap'n." Lida, one of the stronger healers, took charge and positioned the remaining mancers so the hydrons could draw on their strength if required.

The chanting started, and the bow started to rise.

Feeling useless, Corra moved back to the helm, standing beside her first mate.

"Ya got the best bitches, Cap'n. We got this."

"I know." Corra kept her head on a swivel. The sails were full. Their speed was so great, she could see the spray of the waterwing rise higher than the gunwales. Looking back, the two warships, realising that blocking the gap was pointless, powered on parallel to the wall.

And slowly falling behind!

The draft of the *Revenge* at flying speed was roughly three feet in ideal conditions, and while the hydrons had managed to achieve some of their best work in such a short distance, the reduced swell in conjunction with the ebbing tide meant they had little avenue for error.

The second wall was approaching fast.

Two mancers collapsed, drained.

When the waterwing scraped across the top of the wall, the ship slowed slightly, dipping forward, causing several of the crew and mancers to stumble and lose concentration. Luckily, no one fell overboard, but they still lost valuable speed. Some of the sails cracked as they flapped.

"Dara, Barb, get that trimmed, quick smart!" Tully yelled.

Corra raced forward with some of the other crew to help her people up.

"Get the injured below decks and seen to," she ordered. "I know you're tired, but do what you can."

When she stood, she saw her hydrons had moved to lend their strength to the aeyrons.

The flapping sails were trimmed, and once again the canvas bulged.

The *Revenge* was clear of the wall and now in open waters.

"The chase be on!" Kinam cried.

Corra, along with most of the crew, had to reach out and grab hold of whatever they could as the *Revenge* unexpectedly veered to port.

"Rifts, Tulls! What are you up to?" she called back.

The first mate was pulling hard on the wheel. "Reck'n the wing be bent, sendin' us askew!"

Corra moved to lean precariously over the side. Sure enough, the waterwing didn't look straight.

"Oi, Dara 'n' Barb. Give a 'and," Tully called the waterwing girls over. The first mate was a robust woman, but Dara and Barb made her look petite.

Since Tully was directing them to "keep the ship in a straight line", Corra moved forward to the sweating mancers.

"You're doing a damn fine job, the lot of you," she said proudly. She could see the strain on some of their faces.

They all nodded their thanks and affirmed their readiness, despite their weariness. Two were leaning against the mast while another sat nursing a bruised and swollen knee.

"Sorry, Cap—" one started.

"Stow it. Get spirons here when you can!" she called over her shoulder, then turned back to them. "You heard the water-wing's bent and pulling us to port? We can't afford to slow down, but as long as we can maintain flying speed, we'll be fine. They might have aeyrons themselves, but they're nothing like you, nor are their ships anything like the *Revenge*. So"—she pointed to the jib—"if you can take turns to push on that a bit to starboard, it should offset our pull to port. This will be a prolonged pursuit. Can you do it?"

"If it's avoidin' a collar, it'll get done." All the other mancers nodded their agreement.

"That's what I wanted to hear. Well done." Corra looked around the deck to see where she was needed, but she was proud that her crew had made the best of the situation. Seeing Tully working hard at the helm with the other two burly women, she looked for Flerr. She found her aft helping stow some loose crates.

The woman came over when she saw her captain approaching.

"Flerr, reckon you can manage to call a bird?"

"Sure thing, Cap."

"Good. Don't suppose you can get a bird to Farand?"

"Sorry Cap, no can do. Never been there?"

"Thought so. Then we'll need to get a message home. I'll pen a note and bring it up shortly." She turned her gaze further astern, watching the pursuing ships.

TWENTY-THREE

THE TEST

Shortly after the tragic news, an invitation to the funeral of Lady Mimia Trallko was received.

"I'm worried about Blarik's snoops. With this invitation, word will quickly spread around the Trallko Domain, you're here."

"Maybe they won't know where 'here' is," Marra reasoned.

"Perhaps." Nioma considered. "But they'll be wary, extra vigilant."

"Then...cut and colour my hair. They're expecting a long-haired beauty—"

"And only a short-haired beauty will be there instead," Nioma agreed to the disguise.

"Chances are, no one but a couple of the guards, Trin, and the Trallkos will know me from a horse's arse."

"I still don't like it."

"Nioma." Marra stepped closer and clasped her hands behind Nioma's neck, looking into her eyes. "I love you dearly, but I cannot remain completely enclosed in your tavern forever."

"Okay, okay. I'll cut and dye your hair, but...only...on...one...condition. Would you stop kissing? I'm trying to be serious!"

"Oh, rejection." Marra moved back slightly, but left her fingers clasped. "Pray tell what these onerous conditions will be."

"One, not plural, and nothing onerous about it. Remember that fake persona I talked about?"

"Taerryn...something."

"Taerryn Kronyer. We have a week before we need to be there. I'm going to drill into you—"

"Promises, promises."

"Drill into you her pertinent details," Nioma insisted. "So, if anyone asks, you'll be able to answer any question without fail. If we succeed, you'll be able to take on her persona without thinking."

"Yes, ma'am."

"Listen to me," Nioma insisted. "These people could be highly trained—"

"Or simply yokel busybodies."

"Highly trained to pretend to be yokel busybodies. Don't you understand? I do not want anything to happen to you."

"Yes, I know." She held her tight. "I feel the same way. I never expected it, but here we are."

"Now, down to business," Nioma said once they'd released each other.

"Straight away?"

"We need to deal with your hair. Cutting it short isn't enough."

"How do you lighten black hair?" Marra glanced at her reflection in a mirror on the side table.

"In stages, which is why we need to start that first, and now. I'm going to empty out the stove, and you can empty the fireplace. Bring all the charcoal and ash out the back."

"Umm...what? Why?"

"Trust me?"

"To the Farquo Islands and back."

"Good. Then do as I say—not that you have any idea where those islands are." Nioma sniggered.

Once all the charcoal and ash were collected, Nioma emptied the buckets into an empty ale barrel on a table in the kitchen. Marra watched with doubt as Nioma then poured water into the top.

"Fetch one of those empty buckets and stick it under that tap."

Marra did so as Nioma explained.

"By the time the water drips out the bottom, it isn't water anymore. I heard an apothecarist call it lye. It's a strong alkali that will bleach your hair. This is why it'll have to be done in stages. We can only do so much in the time available, but I hope to get a light brown out of it when finished."

"Will the black return?"

"Yes, as your hair normally grows, your natural black will come through. I'm going to cut your hair now. Short hair will take less time to dye." She finished with the water and put the pails together under the table. "And now, the lesson begins."

With surprisingly skilled hands, Nioma began to remove the long, black tresses.

Marra grew quiet, almost teary, when the first locks were cut.

"Yes, it's gorgeous, but it'll grow back in a few months. Then you'll be as ravishing as ever."

When Nioma finished, she brought out the mirror.

"I look like a boy!" Marra turned her head from side to side to see. Her hair was so short, clipped around her ears and neck.

"A devilishly handsome boy, and one with breasts, too." Her words didn't cheer her friend up. "The less you look like

'Marra, the raven-haired beauty', the better. Looking like a boy is a success in my books."

"Now what?" she asked as Nioma collected the bucket of lye.

"Lightening your hair. It's easy, but time-consuming if we don't want to injure you."

"Injure?" Marra asked, unsure.

Nioma got her to lie down face-up on a trestle table out the back with her head hanging over the edge. "Lye can burn the skin if it is too strong. Hence why I have more water and old wine—"

"You're going to douse my hair with old wine?"

"Relax, it's basically vinegar. It weakens the sting of the lye. Several rinses will stop it completely. We'll let it dry, see how it looks, then do it again."

"How many times?"

"As many as you can stand, or until the colour is light enough to then dye."

"Can I have red hair like you? It's wonderful." Marra reached for Nioma's hair, but Nioma playfully slapped at her hand.

"Reds aren't all that common—a travesty, I know—but two red-heads together will draw more attention than not."

"Especially two beauties—"

"Exactly. Keep still, here we go."

Three times over the same number of days, Marra underwent the lye treatment. When it became uncomfortable, Nioma gently poured water over it, then gave it several douses with the wine vinegar, then a wash. Once her hair was a much lighter shade, Nioma brought out the last of the henna and applied it. The result was short, pale auburn hair.

～

EVERY MOMENT of the day during their chores, Nioma asked questions—grilling her on Taerryn's life. Some were the same but worded differently to make sure Marra was concentrating, even during their lovemaking.

In the middle of the night, she'd wake her to test her.

Marra didn't object. "It simply means more time spent awake in your arms."

"You're incorrigible."

"And it's all...your...fault." Her rebuke was punctuated with kisses.

DURING BREAKFAST, Nioma refused to reply to anything Taerryn asked or said unless it was in the proper accent, including a subtle inflection on certain syllables.

"Are we taking this too far?" Marra asked.

Nioma continued stacking the firewood.

"Are we takin' this too far?" Marra asked again in Taerryn's northern accent.

"Perhaps, but better to be safe than dead. You need to take on her persona without even thinking about it. But we'll find out tomorrow. I dare say many nobles from far and wide will be there. Some of them may know Marra, but they won't know you or me. Point them out, and we'll steer well clear of them. I can guarantee they were all at the wedding. Now, everyone across the lands knows the name and will be on the hunt."

Marra was quiet for a while. "How'm I doin' so far with bein' Taerryn?" she asked.

"Quite well, actually."

"I was trained by one of the best." Marra threw a towel at her. "Don't sound so surprised."

Upon their arrival at the Trallko Domain, they had a quick word with Trinol, who was manning the gates. Her old head guard recognised Sleena and was about to say something before he slowly recognised Marra. He nodded and smiled before sending them on their way. A quick audience with Harrod and Trisch was arranged to share their condolences; after that, it was agreed to keep apart.

Trisch was listless and barely said a word, so deep was she in grief. Harrod hated the idea that the true High Lady of Jaranabi should be rendered to such efforts to disguise herself, hiding like a criminal.

"As a wise woman tol' me, 'Better safe than dead'." She had to remember to sound like Taerryn, even when talking to Harrod.

Then the real test began.

As expected, many dignitaries were present. Marra knew quite a few of them, and the pair did their best to avoid them, which wasn't too hard considering they were "nobodies of consequence", as one peacock muttered loudly enough to be heard.

Marra fumed, but Nioma's calming presence distracted her sufficiently to ward off any confrontation.

"The nerve!" Marra seethed. "That fool actually tried to kiss me a few years back."

"Did you break his nose too?"

"No, I pushed him, and he fell into the fountain."

"You know what this means, don't you?"

"Second-chance revenge? I can—"

"It means the disguise and the Taerryn persona are working."

Marra opened her mouth.

"But it doesn't mean we can flaunt it." Nioma sidestepped a servant and grabbed two wines from a tray. "And stop pouting."

The service was carried out in the House chapel. It was a sombre affair with many tears and long faces. After a private farewell with Harrod and Trinol, the women mounted Sleena and Bragante and returned to the tavern.

EACH DAY RESOLVED into a routine of chores, ride, chores, and relax. Even resting in the bath, with Marra's back to her, Nioma kept up the testing of the Taerryn persona.

She was looking at Marra's hair. "So, my not-so-raven-haired beauty, what do you say to keeping it short and coloured now that we know the disguise works? You'd be a great help to me running the tavern and engaging more with the patrons and travellers, since you don't want to stay in the back and out of sight doing nothing."

"I'm actually beginning to like the new look. Much cooler and practical." Marra turned her head this way and that, seeing her reflection in the mirror. "You know, I think I should cut and dye your red locks."

Nioma caught her eyes in the mirror. "Marra, fuck off." Then she laughed and quickly tickled her before kissing the back of her neck.

Marra leaned back into her, and all was right in the world. "I'm glad I found this place, and you," she sighed. "Seems so long ago, but it's less than two months."

"Any more thoughts about going to The Crags?" Nioma spoke languidly into her ear.

Marra reacted like she'd been punched, sloshing water over the rim of the tub when she jolted upright. "I thought… Can't we stay together?" She looked away for a moment, blinking back the threatening tears. "Do you want me to go?"

"What? No. Not ever!" Nioma leant forward, wrapped her arms around her and pulled her close. "No, no my love. That wasn't my meaning, but it was your big plan before—"

"That was before I met *you*. Now, I haven't given it a second thought."

"Good. I'm sorry I mentioned the place. It will never pass my lips again." Nioma started caressing her long, sinuous neck with the sponge, and the water trickled down her spine. "You wander into my life and abuse my ears with that drawl, and the first time I looked into your beautiful blue eyes—"

"You fell for me?"

"I thought: *here's someone who has no bloody idea what she's doing.*"

"You did not!" Marra splashed water at her.

"And *then* I fell for you."

THEY QUICKLY DEVELOPED a new routine working in the tavern, getting to meet the locals, and learning all their idiosyncrasies. With Chaz's help, they even started a garden plot for herbs and vegetables.

Returning from their daily ride, which they'd been doing now for a couple of weeks, they were rubbing the horses down in the stable when Marra stopped and doubled over. A feeling of cold dread overcame her. She dropped the brush and staggered, falling sideways against Sleena before regaining her balance.

"Marra, what is it?" Nioma was at her side in seconds. "Chaz," she called out.

The large man lumbered over quickly to help.

Marra saw them through a haze of pain. The only times she had felt this way was when she was under dire threat. But the day was beautiful and sunny, with a nice southern breeze. The ride was sensational. Nioma had taught her a few tricks. "I...I don't know," she eventually answered. "Something I ate, perhaps?"

"I ate the same. Are you sick?"

Marra shook her head. "Not sick. I do feel bad...like a terrible thing has happened. Or is going to happen." Her mind went to her previous experiences, but none felt this bad.

"We'll take you inside and get you to bed." Nioma wrapped her arms around her and assisted her to her feet.

"Bed? Yes. Good idea. They say sex is good therapy."

Chaz chuckled and winked at Nioma.

"No." Nioma elbowed him. "Not sex."

"Well, I don't know about you, but I feel good afterwards."

Nioma had to chuckle at her. "No sex," she repeated.

"No sex if I improve, or no sex if I don't?"

Nioma shook her head. "Girl, you've changed from the sweet and innocent lass you once were."

"And you love it." Marra winced again.

"True. And you, but I'm worried. You look so pale. Has this ever happened before?"

Marra nodded. "First time was when I was nearly raped, then when beaten, and that time when I was almost rockion fodder."

Nioma shared a look of concern with Chaz. "Now you have me worried."

"You?" Marra chuckled. "You're a rock."

"Am not."

"My rock," she insisted as they moved to go inside the tavern.

At the sound of an approaching wagon, Nioma and Chaz looked up to watch. Some crazy fool was racing down the road, far too fast.

"If he don't slow..." Chaz was saying.

They watched as the wagon turned at the junction to head west. It leant over onto its left wheels, but miraculously didn't topple. It righted itself with a bounce and continued, leaving a trail of dust.

Chaz watched in disbelief. "What the blazes got into 'em?"

Minutes later, several figures topped the rise: six horsemen and a wagon. They paused, as if surveying the terrain, then continued their descent on this side.

Marra groaned. "They're here."

"They—Who?" Nioma looked again, but it was still too far to see most details, and she couldn't discern that the wagon was caged.

"There are mancers in that wagon. Nioma. Chaz. You both have to go! They only want me."

"Then they're dead men. I want you more." She turned to the smith. "Chaz, fetch whoever you can. Bring whatever weapons you can find."

"Right yer are, Ny." Chaz bolted.

Nioma found the strength to carry Marra inside and through the tavern into the kitchen. She sat her at the table, bringing towels and water to cool her, wiping her brow.

From outside, they could hear a bell clanging. It was generally used to sound an alarm for fire or some other catastrophe. It wasn't used often, and when anyone heard it, they'd all come running.

"You stay put or so help me; I'll tan your hide when I get back."

"No, you won't."

"Okay. No sex for a week."

"That's just mean."

"Girl, I'm serious! Stay here."

Marra smiled, wanly. "Deal. I ain't movin'."

TWENTY-FOUR

A COWARD AND A BASTARD

Nioma was through the kitchen door in moments and reached for the sword under the counter. She rarely brought it out. There was no need here.

She now regretted not training Marra in the basics. Her previous life wasn't one she was proud of, and not the life she wanted for Marra.

Wrapping her hand in the leather hilt brought back vivid memories. *Still too vivid. Too dark. Too bloody.* A past she had tried to forget. It seemed like hiding in the furthest reaches of Jaranabi wasn't enough.

"Idiot," she muttered. "You can't run away from memories. Where you go, they go with you."

But not this day. This day, with the way Marra was reacting and the ominous arrival of several strangers, she relied on those vivid and bloody memories to revive her rusty skills.

She was damned good with a blade—extremely good, but that had been another time. Another life. If it meant keeping Marra safe, she had no regrets in wishing that life back now. Pulling the gleaming cutlass from its scabbard, she admired once more the ornate pattern. Of all things, this was a gift worth a High Lord's ransom, but at what cost to her and her friends? It worried her that, having no family, she had no idea who would eventually pry this exquisite blade—one of a pair, she'd discovered—from her dead fingers?

Nioma flourished the blade in a complex pattern before turning to the door with a look of deadly determination. Any opposing individual would think twice about attacking.

THROUGH HER ROARING HEADACHE, Marra heard the noise of fighting: the shouts of challenge, the clash of steel, the screams and groans of men in pain. There was distant thunder as well. She pressed herself to not get involved; she'd be useless out there anyway, especially with the way she was feeling. Then she heard a woman cry out.

Nioma?

Marra pushed herself upright. After drinking water from the bowl, she doused it over her head. The chill revived her a bit, enough at least to ward off the pangs of nausea.

"Looks like no sex for me this week." Her dazed mind reeled at the thought. How could sex be a priority when her lover might have just been injured? Marra moved out to the tavern, then staggered table to table until she reached the front door.

She stepped outside. *Funny, the way those dark clouds are forming.* An arrow thudded into the wall beside her.

She ducked back, looking for the archer. Her gaze took in the street in front of her.

Several men, strangers from the looks of them, definitely not local, lay unmoving in the street. Further along, there were a few locals among them, equally unmoving. On the side of the hill was a caged wagon. Several men stood nearby; two men stood shoulder to shoulder behind a third. She couldn't see them clearly at this distance, but recognised the formation: mancers.

There was a clash of swords close, but out of her view, and a woman swearing.

Nioma? Moving unsteadily to the side, Marra approached the wall of the adjacent building and looked around the corner.

Chaz was across the road, dealing with one of the sword-wielding outsiders. After a flurry of swings, the man fell when the farrier crushed his skull with one of his hammers. From his appearance, Chaz had been nicked a few times, but nothing fatal or disabling. He turned to check on Nioma, but then noticed Marra standing there. He waved her back inside.

In amazement, Marra stared at Nioma. Her red-headed lover was a stranger. She moved like a cat, reminding Marra briefly of the rockions. The memory only turned her thoughts darker.

Two men were fighting against Nioma. And they were losing. Marra had never seen such swordplay—not even among her best house guards—and never expected her friend to be able to do such things. Whenever one swung to slice her, her sword was there, fending off the edge, then she was bringing the hilt up to the face of the man to her left. Her leg lashed out, kicking his partner in the groin as she spun to meet the next attack.

Nioma must have seen Chaz in the corner of her eye. She flicked a glance back to where he was looking. "Get ba—" but the fighting resumed.

The mancers were waiting, watching from a safe, cowardly distance. There was a figure on a horse—not fat enough to be Blarik, but there was something about him that tugged at her memory. The elementalists stood nearby, close to one another.

Unlike the ones she had encountered at home, these weren't acting like fools.

Maybe the madness hasn't quite taken hold yet, she pondered. Then, one of the mancers pointed down the hill. *At me?*

Their leader must have said something as Marra suddenly felt her limbs constrict. She was being bound!

Not that again!

The ground began to shake.

Nioma pulled her cutlass free and shoved the last man to the side with her boot. Breathing heavily, with blood and sweat making her blouse cling to her, she turned and quickly crossed the road to Marra, looking unimpressed.

She even moves like a rockion.

"What did I tell you, young lady?" Nioma said in a stern, weary voice.

Marra could barely breathe. She tried to say something to her, but was unable to utter a sound. She felt a tug, weaker, but it was like the time she'd been lifted over the balcony. She tried to resist, but she had no idea how, like she'd had no idea how she healed back at the school.

The tugging faded. *Am I doing this?*

Suddenly, Nioma was in front of her. Her green eyes blazed. "How the hell can I keep you safe if you simply waltz into danger?"

Was that anger, or love, or concern? Marra couldn't speak. Could barely breathe.

Nioma opened her mouth and froze. Her sword dropped to the ground, and a look of pain crossed her face. Then, a look of shock and confusion. Blood trickled from her breast as she fell forward. She flung her arms up to wrap over Marra's shoulders. She clung for a moment.

Nioma! Not you. Not this!

"I...love...you...girl." Nioma coughed. Blood dribbled from her mouth.

I know I know I know. Marra wanted to wipe the blood from her lover's lips. *And I love you too.* Marra sobbed, but the words didn't reach her lover's ears. She wanted to cradle and rock the only true love she'd ever known. A love so pure and freely given with no expectations of reciprocation.

But the love *was* reciprocated. Equally and freely, with abandon.

Marra dragged her gaze from her lover and looked up at the hill.

The man on the horse was lowering a bow.

Coward! Once again, another loved one had been taken from her. *Bastard!*

This ends now!

The elementalists, now with arms on each other to provide more power, were concentrating. But they were now struggling. She could feel their binding weaken.

As she struggled against her invisible bonds, the ground shook violently; it was no minor vibration this time. The fields were already empty, as the livestock had scattered earlier, but tiles rattled and slid off the tavern roof, and windows shattered. The forming clouds billowed and grew darker before they let loose a torrent of rain, hail, and thunder.

A tide of blackness rose inside her. The ache and desolation of her loss overwhelmed her nausea. Her world had collapsed around her, leaving her alone. In a matter of moments, she was saturated, as was everything in sight. Puddles formed, and rivulets of muddied water ran along the empty street.

Marra screamed. It was the cry of lost love. Fuelled by her rage, her anguish breached the elemental planes, the fabric that held the balance in the real world. It was the cry of an abandoned soul. It was the cry of devastation and of pain. It was the cry of despair, and it now had no bounds.

Marra opened her eyes. Her sparkling blue irises, the white of the sclera, were gone, replaced by black orbs. She was revenge. She was retribution!

And now I have a target.

Even with the ground buckling around her, Marra stood firm. The tavern walls cracked, and the roof caved in. Within minutes, flames licked up from the fallen timbers in the kitchen. The townsfolk must have left when the fighting started; the streets were deserted. Their small houses toppled one after the other.

Yet Marra stood steady and raised a slender arm—an arm that would never feel the caress of her lover again—and she pointed at the men on the hill, the three elementalists protecting their lord who was mounted on his agitated horse.

Gone was the impotent child merely scratching at her attacker. Gone was the girl brandishing a broken wine glass. Her scream was all she had, and she filled it with all her pent-up pain, anger, and rage, directing all her fury at them.

A shimmering haze formed, a dome of protection over the remaining men, but any binding or restriction on her had dwindled to nothing. Through the haze, she saw one elementalist crumple to the ground, then another. The one still remaining, now on his knees, was exhausted. The shield dome he had raised for protection shimmered, faltered, then faded completely. The last mancer fell sideways over his colleagues, unmoving. Dead or exhausted, she didn't care.

Bucked from his frightened horse, the leader was now on the ground. The horse reared, whinnying in terror and ran, disappearing over the edge of a precipice that had formed as the ground crumbled away.

Marra's slender arm lowered, and the tremors stopped.

When the dust settled, the man on the hill struggled to his feet and looked around him. He was now on a perfectly circular outcropping several paces wide. A pit spanning twenty feet, and equally as deep, now surrounded him. The broken ground on this side of the pit was ruination, looking like a blasted desert, whereas he was still on lush grass.

Die!

Marra collapsed beside her dead lover.

WHEN THE YOUNG WOMAN WOKE, she stood, swaying slightly, and stared blankly around her. She saw a lone man on a strange, rocky knoll. Her blue eyes moved on. A village, collapsed and smouldering, surrounded her. There was no other soul in sight, and no animals, only a stiff breeze blowing the dark rain clouds away.

That explains why I'm soaked.

A woman lay face down at her feet, an arrow protruding from her back. Kneeling, the young woman waved a hand over the corpse, and the shaft disintegrated to dust. She rolled the body over and cradled the dead woman's head in her lap. Using the hem of her blouse, she wiped the blood from the woman's beautiful face.

She stroked the woman's damp red locks, the silky strands flowing through her fingers. She then gently caressed the dead woman's brow as her eyes ran down the length of the body, drinking it all in, from the blood-encrusted blouse to the black leggings and riding boots.

"Such a beautiful thing." She studied the look in her eyes. "Eyes so green. If there was ever a look of love, that is what it would be like. Who was it you loved so dearly, beautiful lady? If only someone loved me like that..."

Distracted by a distant voice, she raised her eyes at the man who was now calling to her. He seemed angry and upset, then pleading. She ignored him. *What a strange individual.*

Gazing once more at the woman in her lap, she ran her fingers over the eyes to close the lids. "Who were you, dear lady?" Her whisper disappeared on the wind. "It would've been nice to meet you. I'm Taerryn."

PART TWO

CHAPTER

TWENTY-FIVE

TOWARDS THE SOUTH

Stumbling along the weather-worn goat track of a road, Taerryn rested against a boulder. For several days, she had trudged south. Her boots were damaged but still functional, and her clothes were torn from her foraging for food through the thickets and brambles of the Southern Woods. She hoped the lady fighter she'd buried didn't turn in her grave when her very expensive-looking sword was put to use hacking through the thorny vines.

The wild berries she had found yesterday weren't fully ripe, and they didn't sit well in her stomach. She was desperate for water.

Taerryn looked around for the umpteenth time at the barren steppes that made up the bulk of the southern coast. It had been almost two days since she had seen any vegetation other than occasional thicket and the long grasses rippling in the wind. And for the umpteenth time, she tried to recall why she was here in the first place.

She knew she was making her way to The Crags. An unappealing name for an unappealing shanty town situated along

299

the rugged cliffs of the southern coast. Whenever she'd over-heard travellers speak of it, their words always conveyed the same sentiment: it was a nothing place, full of hags and the constant smell of stinking fish. To Taerryn, it sounded ideal, and a place she doubted anyone would bother searching for her. Only the desperate would ever venture there.

But was she desperate? Why?

She couldn't remember, and that bothered her more.

A week ago, she'd woken up in the main street of a destroyed rural village with no recollection of where, why, or how she'd got there. The town was deserted, not counting the several dead men around her. And there had been a beautiful, red-haired woman lying at her feet. It saddened her to realise she was also dead. She was so close to her. Was she a travelling companion? *We're wearing similar clothes...Why can't I remember?*

She had no concern for the men, but the woman... She was unable to leave her lying there in the street. It had seemed so wrong. She felt a need to bury her.

When she got up to search for a shovel, she heard yelling. There was a man on an island of rock. *That's really weird.* How did he get there in the first place? There was no bridge or anything, and there were three other bodies. Taerryn had gone over to see if she could somehow assist, but the man called her names and was very rude and unruly. He must have struck his head, or was crazy, because he was confusing her with someone named Lady Mary Older—or was it *Olber*? It was hard to hear, and he babbled a bit. She had heard of a noble family named Olber, and there might have been a daughter, but this man was deranged if he thought she was her. The man kept waving at her and pointing.

Nobles weren't part of her life by any stretch of the imagi-nation. *Or were they?* He had been very insistent.

At the edge of the broken land, she'd looked down and seen several dead horses and a broken wagon at the base of the strange fissure. She looked back at the crazy man and was wondering what to say, but he picked up a bow and began to look for an arrow.

The dead woman had an arrow in her back.

"Jump, you crazy idiot!" Taerryn yelled abuse back at him, then ran, but when she looked back, she realised he had no arrows to shoot. After that, she'd ignored him even though he continued to call out to her. But he was no threat, so she'd continued with her unenviable task.

She hoped digging in the soil wouldn't be too bad, this being an agricultural area. A burnt-out tavern was the closest building, so she checked around the back first. There was a plot —the beginnings of someone's vegetable garden—so she dug a grave. Returning to the body, Taerryn had been struck once again by her beauty. Even in death. The woman wore a scabbard, and beside the body was a sword—a cutlass, if she remembered correctly. She'd picked it up and admired it, though she had no idea how to use one. The nice leather hilt and pretty filigree down the length of the blade made her think it was a woman's sword. She did know they were unusual, and this one was probably custom-made. The filigree pattern also matched the pattern on the scabbard.

Were you friend or foe? A robber, or a defender?

Since it appeared she was the only other woman around, and they were dressed similarly, Taerryn assumed she must have been a friend. *Why can't I remember any of this?* The question repeated over and over in her head. Her lack of memory irked her.

Sliding the blade into the scabbard, she'd been about to wrap it up with the body in a blanket for burial, but then, as an afterthought, decided a sword might be of use—though she would probably cut herself.

"Why am I doing this for a complete stranger?" she'd asked herself as she filled in the hole. "Goodbye, beautiful stranger. I hoped you were loved as you truly deserved. Thank you for the sword. I will try to take care of it for you."

By the time she'd finished, it was almost dark. The collapsed houses didn't look safe in the slightest, and, not relishing the idea of sleeping in someone else's bed, Taerryn had found a spot in the remains of the hay loft, though it was now on the ground.

She'd had a nasty thought, but after a quick search, she was relieved to find no horses or other livestock trapped under the fallen timbers. She'd sat and ate what food she could find and drank the water in a barrel by the tavern back door before spying a bottle of wine, miraculously unbroken, under the table. After spending far too much time groping for it, she was happy she had because the taste was exquisite. *Trallko Domain* was inscribed on the label.

Another one of those uppity noble houses.

She'd toasted the woman and had another swig. Followed by several more, as it was so divine. Eventually, with her mind in turmoil and confusion, she'd returned to the ruins of the hayloft and fallen into a deep slumber, though it was full of weird dreams of people and places she'd never met or seen.

In the morning, feeling seedy and with little appetite, she'd started another search of the tavern for some gear, perhaps a change of clothes. It was hard to get to many areas safely as a lot of the collapsed beams were unstable, but she did score another shirt, leggings, and boots. Since the clothes she was wearing were covered in dust and blood, she changed into the new ones, surprised that the fit was so good—almost like they were her own. She did wonder why her clothes were covered in gore. She had no wounds, so the only person whose blood it could have been was the lady she'd buried. After hitching the scabbard, Taerryn stepped into the late morning sun.

The man was still there, marooned on his rocky knoll. He was sitting, listless, barely moving. She felt sorry for him, but only for a moment; then she recalled his abuse and the arrow in the woman's back.

"I don't know who you are or what you did, crazy man, but you deserve whatever is comin' to you." She'd watched him for a moment, then she heard horses approaching from the east. Luckily for her, she was out of their sight. She peeked through the fallen timbers to see. There were about a dozen men; they looked like soldiers or guards.

The thought of being found here had made her feel uncomfortable. With no idea where she was, how she'd come to be here, or why, the possibility of being mistaken as a looter didn't sit well with her. There was no chance she'd be able to grab any of her food unseen, so she'd turned and fled south through the crop fields before anyone spotted her.

"Mopin' here isn't goin' to get you there any sooner," Taerryn muttered through her cracked lips. She pushed herself off the boulder and kept walking. It wasn't much longer before she heard an unfamiliar sound. There was also a new smell in the air.

The track ahead disappeared, indicating there was a subtle rise and a crest.

With renewed vigour, Taerryn plodded up the winding track. She topped the crest and struggled to keep her balance against the sudden onslaught of the harsh wind. Her knees threatened to give way, and she promptly squatted on the grass, utterly amazed at what she saw. Never having seen the ocean before, she gasped at the magnificence of the vista spread out before her. She paused to appreciate the view of the vast blue horizon, the fluffy clouds fast approaching from the east, and the rugged coastline stretching as far as the eye could see.

To her immediate right, a rock ledge jutted out. Nothing unusual about that, except for the large, almost circular shell on a solid wooden pedestal. She took a quick detour to examine it, walking around it. The shell was almost as big as her, and at one point in her examinations, she thought she heard voices. Taerryn looked around, but there was no one within sight, let alone earshot. She even looked into the water, but couldn't imagine any ship or boat lasting more than a minute in the crashing waves before getting smashed to pieces.

Taerryn moved back to the trail and studied what was going to essentially be her new home. All the descriptions of The Crags were true, and the onshore breeze definitely reeked of fish and seaweed.

Dilapidated wooden huts clung precariously to the rugged surfaces of the volcanic rock spires jutting out of the water almost a hundred paces away from where she stood. It amazed her that the wooden huts didn't get blown into the churning waters below.

The trail now became a series of zig-zagging steps leading down to a gate tower about twenty feet below the crest. It was built of rough-cut stone, evidently quarried from these same cliffs, as they were identical in texture and colour. Beyond the gate, a narrow bridge arced from the mainland to the nearest spire. The design of the bridge was like nothing she had seen before; long, slender, with no other visible means of support. As she descended the uneven steps, she saw that the gates were wide open. With nothing to stop her, she walked through.

As she stepped onto the walkway, a gong echoed from deep within the distant, rocky spire. Taerryn pressed on, cautious of the dangerous drop into the maelstrom on both sides of the narrow path. She observed small holes, drilled every five paces in the middle of the slightly convex walkway. The smooth surface made each step risky. With a sigh of relief, she passed through the gateway at the end of the path.

Four women armed with spears, dressed in sturdy leather armour, appeared from an alcove in front of her, and, upon hearing a noise behind her, she turned to see a couple more similarly garbed guards emerge from a hidden door to block her exit. They looked at her briefly, then back along the empty bridge.

"You are alone?" one woman asked eventually, eyeing the scabbard.

One of her companions walked around her, looking at her and even waving their spears side to side.

Surprised at the question and at their unprompted actions, Taerryn glanced briefly back to the empty bridge.

"As you can clearly see." She tried to sound confident, but realised she probably sounded testy, as the arduous days had taken their toll. This was not the way she had envisaged her arrival would go. She took a deep breath and adjusted her tone. "Thank you for the welcome."

The lead guard nodded, and after another cursory glance to the path beyond the gate, moved aside, beckoning her to follow while her two companions remained by the entrance.

She was surprised they didn't take her weapon. *I guess I don't pose a threat.*

Without another word, she was escorted through a marshalling yard and along a narrow path to one of the larger and slightly less dilapidated buildings hard up against the escarpment. Inside, built into an overhang, was larger than expected. A series of trestle tables, some occupied by other women and girls chatting and eating. They looked up, curious at the newcomer, before continuing their banter.

A young boy brought a large bowl of water, rough woven cloth and soap, and she was encouraged to wash. Afterwards, the escort pointed to the food laid out at a separate table. Some of it was familiar to her, but she was unsure about a few of the dishes.

Fish was prominent, as well as a variety of molluscs and shellfish. The salad looked...different.

"I was also doubtful at first. The salad is mostly seaweed," the guard said. "It's an acquired taste, but worth it."

"Thank you." Taerryn nodded, still hesitant.

"Once you've finished, a healer will attend to any injuries you have. 'Tis a hard and perilous road that brings one to The Crags'."

"But only a clear path will take one away," the other girls nearby intoned automatically.

"When she's finished eating, one of you take her to see Yarin." The guard then turned and left without waiting for a response.

From the various bowls on the table, Taerryn decided on a simple meal of field mushrooms and a fish stew with a bit of dark bread to soak up the juices. She began eating in earnest, having consumed nothing more in the past few days than berries and whatever she could scrounge along the way.

The few girls snuck glances at the newcomer. One ventured over and introduced herself.

"Welcome to The Crags. I'm Vyolett." She propped herself on the side of the table.

"Taerryn." She wiped soup from her chin as she studied the

tall girl, judging her to be about the same age, with fair hair and skin, though there was the faintest hue of old bruises on her left cheek. "You sound like you come from the north."

"Everywhere from here is north." Vyolett noticed her bedraggled state. "Besides, we don't discuss our past here."

Good, because I know shite about mine.

"On the road for long?" Vyolett asked her.

"Almost a week, though I can't be sure exactly; my memory is a bit vague. How long have you been here?"

"Several weeks now."

"What's it like here?" Taerryn continued eating as she listened.

"I reckon it's different for everyone. Better here for me than where I came from, for sure. Others, you'd have to ask them, but it won't be long before you know who hates it here." Vyolett winked, gesturing slightly with her head towards three girls sitting in the far corner. All had darker hair, but it was too dim to see any other details clearly.

The boy who had brought her the washing bowl was at a table with another girl.

"Why is there a boy here?"

"That's Jag and his sister Fion," Vyolett whispered. "She's supposed to be a seer...or at least she has visions and dreams."

"And the boy is her brother?"

Vyolett nodded. "I don't think they'll be here long. They were rescued from a pirate ship."

"Truly?" Taerryn watched them for a moment. She swallowed the last spoonful and mopped up the remaining smears of soup with a crust, then pushed the bowl away. "Where do we wash these?"

"Oh, we each have our tasks here. Someone will take it away shortly." Vyolett slipped away from the table. "Time to go see the healer."

The tall girl led her across the room to a door that opened onto a carved path. They followed its meandering way around the rough cliff face and under an overhang, and again the path plunged into the open where, at every turn, the wind buffeted them. Where it became a narrow ledge, thick rope was strung along so the unwary wouldn't topple over the side. Below, the roiling waves foamed up and down the rocky walls, relentless, hungry, but unable to reach the people above.

An overhang turned into a cave with several tunnels leading deeper into the rock. Choosing the left tunnel, Vyolett stopped after a few paces in front of a large, woven curtain and rang a small bell that hung from a length of twine.

"Enter," a cheerful voice called from inside.

Vyolett parted the curtain, but Taerryn stopped to examine the strange texture. She guessed it too was also a form of dried seaweed. It certainly smelled like it.

"We weave those here." Vyolett urged her through.

They entered a small alcove, but Taerryn could see yet another cave through another woven curtain. *This place is like a honeycomb*, she thought.

"Ah, a new patient," the lady said.

"Yarin, this is Taerryn."

"Welcome, Taerryn. Vyolett, come closer to the lantern and let me look at you." The healer glanced at the girl's cheek. "I see it's healing nicely. Good. You can go through and run a bath for Taerryn, if you'd like."

Vyolett nodded and moved further inside.

"Now, your turn, dear," the healer said to Taerryn.

The woman looked to be in her late forties, with long braided brown hair, hazel eyes, and tanned skin. Tattoos adorned her arms from her wrist to her short sleeves.

"I'm from the Slorgasha Islands," explained Yarin, who had

noticed her looking at all the tattoos. "Are you familiar with them?"

"Um. No? I've never been to sea." Taerryn had heard of some islander communities where people had their skin decorated with illustrations, which led her to wonder why an islander would be in this place.

"Perhaps we'll remedy that failing soon. Now, sip this slowly and let me look at you."

A cup of a hot herbal concoction was placed in her hands. While Taerryn tested the brew, Yarin knelt and peeled off her boots. It was in this quiet, secluded place that Taerryn realised how badly she smelt.

"Tsk." Yarin inspected the various blisters on the girl's feet. "These are not good, but I've healed worse." The healer then started asking about internal injuries; where did it hurt, and her diet during her travels. She nodded knowingly at the answers. "As expected, but you never know. So, nothing too serious: a bit of malnutrition and dehydration, a few scratches, blisters, and bruises. Now, be honest: were you sexually assaulted?"

Taerryn coughed her drink. "Nothin' like that." *Surely, I'd remember that?*

Yarin nodded. "There's no disgrace or dishonour in it, of course, but I had to ask. It can be very difficult if these things go on for too long, unrevealed. Finish your drink, dear."

Later, after Yarin attended to her minor injuries, she was directed to an alcove where a bath had been prepared. Taerryn looked at the water, which was murky and pale green.

"Full of herbs and minerals that will make you feel better quickly. It will revitalise your skin from the harsh weather on the road," the older woman told her. "Just don't drink it."

Taerryn had to fight back a laugh as she sounded like one

of those viper-potion salesmen on the back of their carts in the markets. *Where did that memory come from?*

"Thank you, Yarin. I must stink."

"Dear child, you're not the first, nor the last, to endure the long trek. We've had years of experience—decades—to refine our techniques. In a few years, it may be something entirely different, as I've no doubts it was very different in the past, but for now, this is what we have."

While Taerryn undressed to bathe, Vyolett brought in a change of clothes. She was about to remove the old clothes when she saw the scabbard. "This is lovely." She picked it up.

"Um, yes. It's a gift...from a dear friend."

"Are you any good?"

"I can wave it around without losin' my fingers, but I'll need some trainin'."

"I can't imagine a sword like this given to someone unable to use it." Vyolett was looking at it closely and appeared to be about to draw it.

"Well, they did. So... Please put it down. It's very sharp."

Vyolett huffed and returned the weapon to the chair where she found it. "Sorry."

"It's okay. Me too. Just a bit tetchy from the long walk."

"You think they'll ever build a proper road?"

"To here? Why would men encourage women to seek out a refuge from them? It would only make it easier for us. A better idea would be for men to be decent, keep their hands to themselves, and their cocks in their own pants." *Where did that come from?*

Vyolett stepped back at the vehemence. "I...I best go."

Taerryn nodded. "My turn to apologise, again."

When Vyolett left, Taerryn sank into the bath and relaxed for the first time in... She didn't know how long. When the water cooled, she reluctantly climbed out. She dried herself and put on the fresh clothes.

She picked up her old clothes and sought out the healer.

"Ah, Vyolett forgot? She does that at times. Sweet girl, but not altogether there, if you get my drift. Slip these sandals on, and let your blisters heal."

Taerryn slipped into the sandals, finding them a bit big. "Will you burn those clothes, or—"

"Oh no, dear. We haven't got the resources to waste good material." Yarin inspected the clothes. "These are of very good quality. A wash and some darning, they'll be as good as new. You will get them back in a day or so. I'll take care of these. You must be exhausted, but just one more visit, then you can sleep as long as you need. I will see you tomorrow to check on your injuries."

Two different escorts were waiting to guide her down a winding tunnel. Two doors blocked the end of one of the many branches.

"Ildara would like to see you alone. It's something we all do the first time, so you can relax." The guards then stood silently by each side of the door.

With apprehension and wondering who Ildara was, she pushed open the rough timber door and stepped beyond the threshold into the gloom. The scent of fish and seaweed diminished, taken over by the smell of aromatic herbs and incense. As Taerryn's eyes adjusted, she could discern a figure hunched over a cluttered table. This cave was quite large and had some old, heavy furniture which wouldn't look out of place in a mansion, but it was strikingly unusual for a cave on a coastal cliff.

"Come closer, young one. Let me see you clearly." A candle suddenly lit up as Taerryn moved closer. "Interesting. Bathed and refreshed? Good. All our new arrivals are Tested for any talents they may possess. Are you willing to do this?"

"Will I be sent away if I fail?"

"Not at all. You're safe here and may remain with us for as long as you wish. We simply test whether you have Talent, and measure the aptitude and capabilities. There is no failing. We might be a small community, but we have many trades and crafts that need women with various abilities."

Taerryn sniggered ruefully. "The only talent I possess is pissin' off my friends."

"Some here make that an art," Ildara chuckled. "But we shall see. And you came with a male friend? Perhaps an escort?"

Taerryn wondered at this. It was the second time she was questioned about being accompanied. "No. I came alone."

"But the gong sounded."

"Yes?" Taerryn shrugged. "The gong at the gate, you mean? It was to notify your guards of my arrival, wasn't it?"

"Your appearance was noted before you crested the cliff. The gong is an indicator when a male mancer arrives."

"Mancer? You need a new gong. I've been alone on the road for almost a week."

"And no male was with you?"

"No one. Until I arrived here, I'd not seen a soul." *Not living.*

"Could it be...?" Ildara looked at her closely.

"Is everythin' alright?" Taerryn looked worried.

"Yes, yes. Have you been tested before?"

"Tested?" Taerryn looked away, unsure.

"Yes, dear. For magyk." She sounded a bit irritated now. "Everyone should undergo The Test. An untrained mancer can be dangerous to both themselves and those nearby. This is why it is prudent to do it early, to be sure, one way or the other. Any traumatic or turbulent event could trigger an episode. In some cases, it has been a minor tremor or cutlery flying across the room. You should've had it when you were much younger."

"Perhaps I did... When I was a child. I don't remember." Taerryn shrugged. *What harm could it do to allow the...this test?* She was in no position to argue with the old woman. *Do I have a choice?*

"Ah, well. At least The Test is straightforward and quick. We should do it now, under the circumstances."

What circumstances? "As you wish...Ildara?"

"Ildara Soshys." The old crone nodded. "Perhaps you've heard of the Hag on the Crags?"

Taerryn blushed. "I would never—"

"Tut tut, child. It's all true. Also known as the Sea Wytch." The woman poured some tea. "Drink this, then we'll start."

Taerryn drank, then replaced the cup and nodded. She was ready for whatever this test was.

Ildara's cold, thin fingers gripped her hands as she stared into her eyes for an uncomfortably long time. On completion of this odd examination, Ildara carefully unwrapped a long crystal shard and placed it in her left hand while holding her right. This went on for several minutes while the crystal vibrated and pulsed through a rainbow of colours. Suddenly, it cracked.

Ildara's eyes widened at this, and she jolted back in shock. If she hadn't been holding Taerryn's hand, she would have fallen off her chair.

"Are you okay?" Taerryn jumped up, worried for the old crone.

"Yes... Yes, dear." Her face looked flushed and sweaty. "A wobbly chair leg is all."

"And the crystal? Was it supposed to do that?"

"An aberration to be sure, but they are delicate. Give me a moment, I need to rest."

"An aberration? Like the gong?" Taerryn poured more of the tea for the woman, though it was tepid.

"It happens."

After several minutes, Ildara resumed her seat, motioning Taerryn to do the same, and The Test was repeated. She brought out another length of crystal. The crystal still pulsed and vibrated, but remained clear.

"Ah, see? An aberration. It does seem you have a strong latent ability that is yet to manifest into anything of use." Ildara let go of her hands and took a deep breath.

"So, everyone is safe?" Taerryn found it hard to refrain from sounding snide.

"Safe? For now. Rest, and we'll meet again in the morning."

The pair of guards was still outside. They nodded when Taerryn closed Ildara's door.

"Now to the dormitory and to find you a bunk. No doubt you're tired," one said.

Taerryn was led inside to yet another building. Like the food hut, the structure was a façade, and it opened into the cliff face itself. The dormitory was essentially a large cave, like many of the living spaces she'd seen so far. She recognised some of the girls from the dining hall sitting by a long table. Some gave her a casual glance, then returned to their own tasks and conversations, while others didn't look up at all, engrossed in their thoughts—their own traumas.

It's to be expected, I guess.

LATER IN THE EVENING, Ildara sought out Radson. She found her on her balcony watching the sunset, an ale in her hands.

"You heard the gong earlier?"

"I did, but the guards tell me it was an anomaly as no elementalists were present."

"No *male* elementalists, correct."

"Your meaning?"

"I'm unsure yet."

"That in itself is troubling. Tell me about this new girl."

Ildara explained what had happened during The Test, and then the second test showing nothing.

"Is she able to hide it, you think?"

"I don't believe she knows she has it. This could be subconscious self-defence. Even now, we still know so little about it."

"We have many women elementalists of varying power. Admittedly, we would like to learn more, but—"

"But I'm talking about male elementalism."

Radson scratched her thick curls and took a long pull on her ale. "We are talking cross-currents here. Are you talking about the girl, or a male?"

"Yes."

"Be clear, you old wytch. It has been a long day with some very recalcitrant students. I have a mind to cast them back. Jordia in particular."

"You know we don't do that."

"Not yet, but these ones are making me reconsider our century-old policy."

"The gong sounds with the presence of a male elementalist," she explained, like speaking to a new student. "The testing also picked up strong male elementalism."

"You mean to say—"

"Yes, this new girl may have both."

Radson put her mug down. "We had a merchant just three days ago. He was saying he heard that Culming had been razed."

"That village towards the Trallko Domain? I'd only heard a

rumour about a fierce storm…" Ildara sat, looking pale. "I might have some of that ale now."

"By all means. I'll fetch another mug." Radson stood and stretched her robust frame before ducking inside. She returned shortly. "There ya go." Radson resumed her seat and continued. "As I said, it was word of mouth from another trader. He said nothing was left standing in the town itself, and there's a section on the north road that's no longer there. There's a deep hole about twenty or thirty feet deep in its place. There was a large rocky spire in the middle, perfectly flat at the top; the grass untouched."

"Says he was told Lord Charoff was stranded there for days. Can you believe that?"

"And this was a week ago?"

"Yep." Radson took another swig, but stopped halfway to her mouth when she saw the look on Ildara's face. "What is it?"

"I felt it. A disturbance."

"Over all that distance, and no one else did?"

"No. Not in the physical sense. It's hard to explain, but…like that feeling when you think someone is watching you. To be honest, I've felt it several times recently."

"No idea who or where?"

"Not specifically, but there were subtle differences. The first was much further to the north, and then there were a few very minor ones. I thought nothing of them—just some novice experimenting—but there were more last week, much closer and much stronger. Apart from the strength, it felt similar."

"Can you explain these subtle differences?"

"Not really."

"Educated guess? You are, after all, the most powerful female elementalist we know of. If anyone can work this out, it's you."

"If I had to guess, I'd say they were the differences between masculine and feminine elementalism."

"You can't tell if a woman elementalist is channelling?"

"Oh, doing water and air and all, sure. But if I'm right, this was a woman doing *male* elementalism...and that feeling I do not know."

"How do we proceed?"

"Quietly, and with the utmost caution. We don't want to be seen to treat Taerryn differently from all the others, but we also don't want to put her in a stressful or traumatic situation."

"She's here. Doesn't that mean, like all our unfortunates, she has been abused? That would surely have resulted in stress and trauma."

"Perhaps it did, and if I am right, what I sensed was her reaction to that... but it is too early to tell. I think I'll get Drina to send a bird or two, see what news we get back."

They brooded and drank, watching the horizon and the clouds scudding from the east.

Ildara continued, "If Taerryn is this dualist, then we need to tread very carefully. She needs nurturing. Bringing her around slowly is the best and safest course. Until we know exactly what happened at Culming. I don't want that to happen here. We're on a dormant volcano!" Ildara took a generous swig from her ale.

"I do know this, and yes, it would be very bad."

Ildara nodded and sighed. "Now then, tell me you sent out a rider to Culming."

"You bet I did. Same day. We should have a better idea soon."

TWENTY-SIX

EXPLORING THE CRAGS

"You'll be late for breakfast." These were the first words she heard when she was shaken in the morning.

Taerryn had slept soundly, being exhausted from her time on the road, so she was quickly alert. She was also hungry. Climbing out of her bed, she pulled on her clothes, hitching her scabbard as she trailed after the last girl in line, hoping it was the direction to the food hall. Sure enough, within a few minutes, she had a bowl of gruel and a hard biscuit in hand.

Fish was also on the menu, but the taste of seafood to her palate at this hour didn't appeal to her. The other girls were still mingling in pairs or small groups, but no one seemed to want to venture close to her. She didn't see Vyolett anywhere, so she moved closer to a couple of girls.

"Mind if I join you?" Taerryn asked one pair.

One nodded, while the other barely managed a shrug.

"Thank you very much." *Very encouraging, not.* "I'm Taer-ryn," she introduced herself as she carefully stepped over the bench seat and sat opposite them.

"I'm Myrta, and this is Sabon," the girl who'd nodded said.

They both seemed of similar ages, several years or so older than herself.

"Nice to finally chat with others. Is everyone here normally this quiet?"

"Some of us have our problems and choose to avoid others," Sabon said, without looking up from her bowl.

"This is true, and I understand. Everyone's grief is their own, but a burden shared is a burden lessened."

Sabon scowled, then resumed eating.

Myrta looked at her friend, then at Taerryn. "Some find even talking is too hard."

"Perhaps. What affects a person one way will be different to another person."

"Are you a sage or somethin'?" Sabon asked.

Taerryn nearly choked on her gruel. "Not 't all."

"Then just shut up." Sabon got up and stormed off, leaving her unfinished bowl.

Myrta watched her go, then looked back at Taerryn. "She's in a dark place."

"Should someone go after her?" Taerryn queried.

"I will, but in a minute, to give her time. She does have these moods."

"I'm sorry if I said anythin' wrong."

"It happens a lot with her. Don't feel bad. Yarin is doing her best."

Taerryn thought it a good time to change the subject. "Been here long?"

"A month, Sabon, about a week later. I've sort of taken her under my wing...not that it looks like it's any help."

"She's still with us, so there's that. People in very dark places...do extreme things."

"I think that's why we're all here."

Taerryn looked at her empty bowl. "Does everyone stay here forever?"

"Only Ildara." Myrta laughed. "She's been here forever."

The door opened, and everyone in the room became quiet. Taerryn looked over to the entrance.

"Who's that?" she asked.

"Radson. The Disciplinarian and Head Instructor."

"Instructor?" Taerryn queried. The woman was the tallest person she'd ever seen. She had to duck her head coming through the door.

"Apart from a refuge, this is also a school to teach us various crafts so we can be a viable part of the community and maybe crew the ships."

School? Why does that sound familiar?

"She's big and scary on the outside. Big and scary on the inside, too." Myrta chuckled quietly, then went red when Radson looked their way and ventured over.

"Morning, ladies. Myrta, isn't it? How are you faring?"

Myrta gulped. "Well enough, thank you, Radson. This is Taerryn; she arrived yesterday."

"Ah, yes. My apologies for not greeting you earlier." Radson put out a large hand. "Pleased to meet you."

Taerryn accepted the handshake. "Thank you...Radson."

"Has anyone shown you around yet? I find myself with some spare time this morning. Perhaps I could be your guide? Myrta, you're welcome too, if you'd like?"

"Oh, thank you, but I best be off to see how Sabon is." Myrta nodded her goodbyes and left with her empty bowl.

"Nice child, that one," Radson addressed Taerryn. "Flighty, but nice enough. I see you've finished breakfast. Shall we start?"

"Yes. That'll be good." Taerryn stood, looking for a place to take her bowl.

"First part of the tour. There's a scullery over yonder." Radson pointed.

Taerryn saw Myrta reappear from the scullery and leave through the door Sabon had used.

Taerryn wandered over and left the bowl on a bench with many other bowls, plates, and cutlery.

"There's a roster for the scullery and other tasks throughout the community," Radson said. "Everyone helps out one way or another, and their tasks will depend on individual abilities, age and experience."

"Do you help out?"

"When my schedule allows it, yes. Same with Yarin and even Ildara. No one's above the menial tasks."

Taerryn nodded, impressed.

"Mind you, we do keep a very busy schedule." The big woman winked. "I'm assuming you've only seen Yarin and Ildara, and curious how we have continued to be a viable community for all these years on a cliff?" Radson continued at Taerryn's nod. "Not is all as it seems. Hardly anyone hassles us because we look like a hovel. I dare say you've heard the stories that women come here to die?"

They exited the food hall and were going through the maze of tunnels Taerryn had only glimpsed the previous evening.

"I can't remember a lot of things until about a week ago."

"Is that right? Interesting. And sad, of course. But these things happen, and they can take time to heal. Perhaps, in time, your memories will return."

"If they're that bad, would I want them too?"

Radson shrugged. "You may not have a choice."

"I do recall the healer wanted to check on my injuries."

"Well, we are about to pass her door, so good timing."

They turned a corner and, sure enough, Taerryn recognised the curtained entrance to Yarin's alcove.

"I'd never have guessed the size of this place," Taerryn admitted. "These tunnels make it very deceivin'."

"That's the idea. Part of our secret, but if you think this is something, just wait." She rang the bell and walked in. "Yarin, you old bat. Wake up."

Yarin emerged, a pestle and mortar in her hands. "I beat the sun up and have done for the last twenty years, as you well know. Ah. The new girl. Taerryn? Just a moment." The healer disappeared, but returned promptly. "Let's have a look at you then."

Radson stepped to the side and started poking around the shelves of the many different vials.

The healer didn't even look up. "You know if you break anything, you'll be doing bath and washing duties for a week."

"So you keep telling me." Radson sniffed this jar, then that one, and deliberately put them in different places.

Taerryn got the impression these sorts of antics took place regularly. She smiled at it as she slipped off her sandals.

Yarin began the checkup, lifting her tunic to check on the scratches and bruising. "Girl..." She looked and gently rubbed her fingers over Taerryn's skin, confused. Then bent to observe her feet.

"Is everythin' okay?" Taerryn asked.

"You appear to be fully healed already! The bruising and scratches had disappeared, along with the blisters."

"That's lovely. You look surprised. I thought I recognised somethin' in the bath."

Yarin shook her head, puzzled. "Not in all my years have I seen the like."

Radson moved closer to listen. "Don't get your hopes up, youngun. More than likely, Yarin misdiagnosed you yesterday, or she's losing her memory. So, a clean bill of health? No need to linger then, is there?"

"I have never misdiagnosed a patient's injuries." Yarin, normally mild in manner, sounded testy. "You said you recognised something in the bath?"

"If it's a help, I recognised a smell from somewhere," Taerryn offered.

"Well then, this's an improvement." Yarin turned her attention back to the young girl. "The senses of smell, as well as hearing, can trigger many lost memories. Do you know what it was?" She continued at the shake of Taerryn's head. "There was a mix of herbs, but the most potent essence we call *lubin*. We get it from Klarget."

"You trade with them?"

"Dear, we trade with anyone and everyone. *Lubin* is sourced from rockions. Some wealthy Klargetians have them as pets."

"The smell doesn't bring anythin' else back." Disappointment tinged her tone. This not knowing was frustrating. *What happened to me to forget it all? Some accident, and I healed quickly? The other lady was fatally injured... Maybe I had been injured, but was somehow healed...like now?*

"Oh, one other thing." Yarin reached for the side table. "This was found in one of your trouser pockets." The healer handed her a rolled-up piece of parchment.

Frowning, Taerryn took it from the woman's hand. The parchment was stained and scrunched up after being at the bottom of a pocket for the duration of her southward trek. She unrolled it only to frown more.

"I can barely make out what it says."

"Is that right, dear?" Yarin paused. "Oh, of course. Many of the girls here can't read, but we have classes for that too."

"I can read; I just can't read this." She held it out to Yarin.

The healer took it back and cast her eyes over it. "Cypher."

"Cypher? Can you read it?"

"No, but I do recognise it. I know who can." The healer handed it back. "We are a small part of a much larger information network."

Taerryn looked at it again. "Hmmm. It does look familiar… but I still can't make any sense of it."

"Is that right, dear?" Yarin looked briefly at Radson. "I do have a busy morning, but Drina can help you."

"Drina?"

"Another one of our elders here. You've not met her yet," Radson told her.

"Would you prefer I take care of it?"

"Oh, no. You're too busy." Taerryn hopped off the chair and tucked the message into a pocket.

Radson moved towards the exit and held the curtain open for Taerryn, then turned to give her farewell to Yarin. "See you again soon, no doubt, old fish." Radson gave her a few hand signals and left. *Speak with Ildara about this.*

Dropping the curtain behind her, Radson continued her tour. "Okay then, youngun, you're in for a big surprise. We'll get that note to Drina soon enough. This way."

They moved down another passage, now walking against a strong air current with salt and seaweed overtones.

"What's that vibration?" Taerryn asked, feeling the ground tremble.

"That would be The Churn."

"The Churn?"

"Yep." The instructor nodded.

Taerryn was waiting for more, but her guide moved on silently. Shrugging, she had to move faster to keep up with the big woman's strides, but the sandals threatened to slip off. The passage dipped and turned slightly, so there was no clear view of the exit until the last minute.

Radson's promise of a 'surprise' was an understatement.

The rough passage opened up onto a wide path with a stone wall along its entire length. Beyond the wall was something she could never have imagined. On her initial sighting of The Crags, it seemed to be an outcropping of rugged rocky spires formed by the ocean eroding the mainland cliffs. But it was an island, and what she was seeing here was truly amazing. The island was hollow, and she was looking down into a roughly circular harbour.

Her tour guide had a grin from ear to ear. "Gets 'em every time!" she continued, though with the occasional chuckle. "The Crags is really an extinct volcano. Looks nothing like it from the mainland. We've even changed the cliff face a bit to keep it hidden from unwanted prying eyes. It's important to keep it secret."

"It works. I had no idea!" Taerryn nodded. "What about visitors? Traders?"

"They don't see this part at all. If anyone did, their stories would be regarded as imaginary or rumour." She had to raise her voice over the ever-growing noise. "Watch and learn. This is the Churn I mentioned."

A vast amount of water was flowing inland through a narrow fissure to the south. Beside a dock below, a ship was being buffeted mercilessly. It rocked from side to side, though it didn't seem in any danger of capsizing, and the masts swayed back and forth.

The Churn was their terminology for the rising tide. But it suited it. Having never seen the ocean before, Taerryn had the barest concept of tides.

"Our moons have an effect on the water. When the tide comes in, the level beyond the harbour wall is higher," Radson explained, leaning close to Taerryn's ear to be heard. "But it rises faster than the entrance can cope with."

The noise was incredible and clearly explained the

rumbling she felt. The water below was a seething mass of turbulence, eddies breaking out suddenly on the surface and mountainous waves gushing over the wall.

Radson tapped her on the shoulder, and they continued along the path, which zig-zagged down about twenty feet. Other levelled areas and more wooden structures could be seen against the cliff.

Taerryn looked up, her eyes following their path back to their exit, surprised to see there were other levels further up, and also seeing people hanging high above on ropes. She asked about them, but the noise drowned out any answer. When they entered the nearest building, the noise lessened somewhat. At least here they didn't have to yell to be heard.

"It will get quieter soon, but the worst of it is over. When the water level inside matches that of the ocean, it's as calm as a bath. Until the Swirl, which is when the process is reversed."

"How often does this happen?"

"Twice a day. We have a schedule and keep tabs on it so we don't get caught unawares."

Taerryn nodded, unsure why it happened twice a day, but she had other questions. "What's goin' on up there? People climbin'?"

"Rock climbing and abseiling," Radson answered. "You can try that if you like. Have you done it before?"

Taerryn shrugged. The large interior was clearly a classroom, with many tables taking up over half the floor. A big chalkboard covered most of the far wall, and on both of the side walls hung ropes of all lengths and diameters.

"Everyone who volunteers to be a crew member undergoes theory training, followed by practical training later."

"I saw the ship. What do you use it for? It doesn't look like a fishin' ship."

"We have three. You never heard of the Red Sails? We use

them for trading and bringing in cargo. As you would have seen, there's no adequate road, which is fine by us; otherwise, it would simply attract many more people. And that could be trouble."

"I honestly don't know. Why red?"

"There's a kelp here that we use to make the red colour. Discovered by accident, and now it's intentional. It's our trademark. When other ships see it, they know exactly who we are and what we're doing."

"Which is what? What do you do other than run a women's refuge?"

"The refuge is very important, but it's only a part of it. We are privateers." Radson had to explain after seeing Taerryn's blank face. "We have a commission from High Lord Olber to police the southern waters for pirates and smugglers."

Olber? The name that the strange man yelled back at that town. "At least I know that name, Olber."

Radson shook her head. "Well, he's dead now, died in a hunting accident, they say, and Sir Blarik is now High Lord, but I hear something unusual happened. It always does when Blarik is involved. The young Olber girl went missing, too. Betrothed to the Dran'ali Overlord, apparently. She didn't turn up. Smart girl. He's an animal, and I mean no disrespect to animals. But that's mainland stuff, and has little to do with what we do, except for the official papers making us privateers. Without that, we'd struggle and might have had to resort to other means of survival ourselves. But, for now, pirate hunting is what we do, and we do it very well."

"How long have you been here?" Taerryn asked.

"Me? Almost twenty years."

"Is that a long time? I mean, other than Ildara, how long does one stay here?"

"As long as you want, as long as you need. Some stay and

become ingrained within the community, like Yarin and the other elders. She's been here a few years longer than me."

Taerryn wandered over to look at the ropes hanging on the wall. Some were coarse, others were smooth to the touch; some were thick as her arm, others as thin as her finger. "So, I could walk out of here tomorrow?"

"You could, of course, though I suspect the reasons you came here were sufficient cause for you to make the long journey from wherever you came from. But essentially, yes. No one is a prisoner here, though some make it out that way. They're only prisoners within themselves. We are a refuge, yes, for safety, but we do help everyone get over their grief and trauma. A burden shared—"

"Is a burden lessened," Taerryn finished.

"Exactly." Radson's white teeth split her dark face when she smiled.

Back outside now, the noise had abated, and the pair moved to the low wall. Taerryn was stunned to see the ship had risen much higher, as had the dock.

"You said you had three ships?"

"They're out and about." Radson nodded, then changed the subject. "See those three large mooring posts?" she pointed. "We learned a long time ago how to use them properly. As the water level changes, the mooring point slides up and down the posts. If we need to, we can even lock those mooring points and keep the ship up when The Swirl happens —when the tide goes out. We can then do hull maintenance easily."

"Does that mean it's stuck there until the next Churn?"

"Good question. No, we can lower it manually, if need be."

"I thought your mancers could do that?"

"You know about them?"

"Only a bit from what I overheard during meals."

"They could," Radson continued, "but we use the elemental magyk sparingly and only when necessary."

Taerryn nodded and continued looking over the wall. The ship and dock were still lower down, but looked like they had both risen greatly from when she first saw them.

"The average tide is thirty-six feet, but it can vary, depending on a few things."

Taerryn turned, surprised at the answer to the unasked question.

Radson laughed. "I've seen that look before, and when they see the Churn or the Swirl, it's a question I hear a lot. If you decide to become crew, we get serious with it in the second week of Navigation. Too complicated to get into now."

The water turbulence had settled greatly, and the ship-board activity had resumed.

"You say you learnt how to use the moorin' posts…You didn't build them?"

"No. They were here a long time before The Crags became a community, as were the ships."

"Who built them?" Taerryn asked.

"We've no idea." Radson looked at the mooring posts for a few seconds before bringing her attention back to the present. "Shall we move on? Happy to wait, but we have a few other highlights with the tour."

"Sure, let's continue." Taerryn looked away. "It's all fascinatin'."

"That it is. Even after all my years here, I still get a kick out of it now and then, especially seeing the surprise on the new faces. Now then, seeing that you've an exceptional blade by your side, off to weapons training we go."

The incline of the path gradually lessened as it wound around the perimeter of the harbour. The ringing of metal on metal soon reached their ears. Shortly, they came across a wider section of the path leading to a natural alcove in the high cliff face, ideal for weapons training or other physical activities that needed a large, open space.

Taerryn counted over a dozen girls, women, and even two boys going through the motions of sword-fighting drills.

"Ah, you're in luck, Tiswan is here. She's our resident weaponsmith." Radson waved her over when she had looked their way.

While they waited for the trainer to separate from the students, Taerryn asked a question that had been bugging her since her arrival. "If this is a women's refuge, why are there males here? I saw one at the main gate when I arrived, and I've seen a few more now."

"Some women come here pregnant. As you now know, Yarin is our main healer, and there are others who help out, as well as midwives. We raise their children as our own. No one's going to turn a son out of the refuge. We aren't man-haters here by any stretch of the imagination; we only hate those who bully and abuse women. Ah, here's Tiswan."

Introductions were made, and the inevitable question came up.

"May I?" Tiswan asked upon seeing the scabbard.

The weaponsmith examined it while Radson looked over her shoulder.

"This is a fascinating cutlass," Tiswan said. "One of our captains has a similar blade, almost identical, in fact."

"I guess you would like to know where I got it?"

"Not that I wish to pry. We only divulge information about our past that we choose. Sometimes—well, most times—it can be too traumatic for months, maybe years."

"I don't recall where I got the blade. As Radson and Ildara know, I don't remember much past a week or so ago. I know that sounds so wrong, but I didn't steal it... Well, if I did, I don't remember. I know it looks bad—carryin' a rare and expensive sword with no knowledge and no ability to use it."

"Perhaps you've forgotten that, too? Once you start sword-play, it might come back to you."

"You think? I hope so."

"The mind is a very difficult area to understand," Radson spoke up. "Trauma can make us forget, but just as equally remember. You won't know until it happens, not that I wish you to be traumatised again. I was... Never mind."

"Ildara said I might have some talent...but it hasn't manifested into anythin' yet."

"Did she?" Radson feigned any knowledge of it. "Well, there's one way to find out, but we don't need to do it now."

"So then, young Taerryn, weapons training is here if and when you want it." Tiswan gave the blade back.

"Um...Would you mind keepin' it here? I'm not goin' to use it, I don't want to leave it under my mattress, and it looks out-of-place on my hip when I'm wanderin' around."

"Certainly. That'll be no problem. I'll keep it safe in my office."

Taerryn unhitched the scabbard and handed it to the weaponsmith. "Thank you."

"Not at all. Maybe this will mean you'll pop in often?"

"I don't know." Taerryn shrugged. "See what my trainin' regime looks like." She turned to Radson.

"Ah, well, yes. Depending on what you want to learn. We do need a scullery maid. *No?*" She saw Taerryn's look and grinned. "I always find fitness is best. A fit body is the foundation for a fit mind, I say."

"And you'll need to be fit and strong to wield a sword for any length of time," Tiswan added.

"Does that mean I'll need to get hot and sweaty?"

Radson laughed. "Only if you do it right. If there's nothing else to preoccupy you, you could always try rock-climbing and abseiling. It can be fun, builds your strength, keeps you fit, and if you do decide to join the crew, it'll be a benefit climbing the rigging."

Waving to Tiswan, they left. "One more place, then time for lunch." Radson led her to yet another alcove, much smaller. They ducked through a narrow tunnel. It opened up into a grotto, and towards one side, a waterhole took up a third of the floor. Six girls stood on the edge.

"This place is ideal as the water level here barely moves, certainly not too drastically, except in storms."

Suddenly, a waterspout erupted from the pool and splashed those by its edge, resulting in curses and laughter.

"Are they elementalists?" Taerryn queried.

"One hopes they'll be, but yes. Trainees. And if Ildara said you might have a knack for it, perhaps this will be a good place to start your training. No pressure, of course. But in my experience, if you sit around idle for too long, the mind can wander, maybe put you in a dark place."

"Where is Ildara? Isn't she a powerful magyker?»

"She is that, indeed. Xan here is also quite good, but since Ildara is running the Crags, she generally attends to the most advanced students. Having said that, she does occasionally pop down for a couple of hours."

The mancer instructor joined them, and introductions were made.

"How do you do it? Is it hard?" Taerryn asked, watching the girls practice.

"Some find it hard, others almost impossible. Meditation is key," Xan said. "It would help with any problems you feel you have. But also, in elementalism, you need to have a relaxed and focused mind to control the elements. It would be the difference between nothing happening and a decent result," Xan explained. "However, a distraction or stray thought at a crucial time could lead to a catastrophe."

"Is it true male elementalists go mad?" Taerryn asked.

"It is, and they do eventually, but for a variety of reasons: drawing too much power too soon, not having the correct training, or not having a focused mind."

"Do women go mad?"

"Not nearly as much. We think it's because the earth element is a fixed, solid material, whereas water, air, and fire, for instance, are dynamic and very malleable. But men always want more, so they do things with stuff that isn't to be meddled with."

"And women can't work earth?"

"Correct. It's a conundrum elemental scholars have argued over and studied for centuries; *we* can work with water, men can't. Some men may have minimal talent, barely enough to register, but instead of going crazy, they just get angry and violent."

"Why do they use earth if it makes them crazy?" Taerryn quizzed.

"Because it's everywhere, and some men are lazy, some men are impatient, and some men are both. Sure, if they were on a ship and could work water, that would be a completely different story."

"Air and fire are available. Everywhere."

"True, they can manipulate air and fire to some extent, but it takes a lot of air to do anything of merit, and it takes time. The bulk of the men want something powerful, and they want it *now*. Fire can give them that, but it's difficult to control. The slightest mishap can leave one scarred for life or dead. So, many tend to keep away from it. Want to give it a go?"

"I...I don't know." Taerryn looked dubiously at the trainees.

"I can leave you here, if you'd like, or I can take you back,"

Radson offered. "I've just remembered an appointment which I need to attend."

Taerryn watched another waterspout. This time, it was much larger and moved around in a figure eight across the pool's surface. "I'll watch here for a bit longer, if that's okay. It looks very interestin'."

"Fine with me. I'm sure you can find your way back easily enough. Or someone will surely show you."

Taerryn smiled her thanks and kept watching, mesmerised.

Radson nodded and stepped back, but before she left, Xan subtly signed. *I got Ildara's message. I'll watch her carefully.*

"Shall we get closer?" Xan indicated joining the other trainees. "You can meet the girls. All are novices, so if you do have any talent, you won't be too far behind."

Taerryn looked unsure. "I've never..."

Xan winked. "None of us did...until we tried."

The pair wandered over to the group.

"Ladies, we have Taerryn joining us today. Take a few minutes and get to know her." Xan turned to a tall, thin girl. "Better, Madin, but less volume until you have that sequence down pat. Not everyone here can swim."

The group, still damp from her previous attempt, laughed. Madin blushed and stepped to the end of the line, laughing with them.

Taerryn didn't think she'd remember all their names, not straight away. They had a brief chat and seemed far less morose than the girls she'd seen upstairs.

"I'm sure they are all nice, but they're not elementalists. We seem to have a different mindset," Madin said.

"There are a lot of women who are lovely and vibrant without the need or ability to be a magyker," Andula argued.

The discussion became slightly heated before Xan stepped in. "Okay, girls, enough of that. Everyone has their place, and we all help out one way or another. We'll have no more talk about whether elementalists are better people or not.

"So then, back to a few minutes of meditation, I'll have a word with Taerryn, then we can continue." Xan motioned Taerryn to join her. They stepped away from the group and moved closer to the rock wall.

Taerryn looked back to watch the others. They all sat on the sandy floor, crossed their legs, closed their eyes, and did nothing at all.

"As I was saying before, young Taerryn, to control the elements, one must be focused and have a clear mind. When you meditate—and it does become easier the more you do it— your talent is free to do what it needs to do. Now, let's sit, and we'll begin." Xan simply squatted into a cross-legged position.

Taerryn had to bend down, then sit and cross her legs. *Fit bloody body, fit bloody mind.*

"Close your eyes and breathe slowly and deeply. Feel the air coming in, hold it, then slowly release." Xan watched Taerryn do this. "Good. Block out other distractions, just concentrate on breathing and on my voice for the moment."

Taerryn wasn't sure how long they practised, and it took her a moment to get her bearings. "Did that work?"

"Very well for your first time. I'm impressed."

"Beginner's luck, I suspect. I've never tried meditatin' before today." *That I remember.*

"It's a good start, better than some of the girls who've been here trying for weeks. Still, we all have our differences and aptitudes. Let's join the others now."

They moved back to the group, who stood up on their return.

"Not to throw you in the deep end, so to speak, since you excelled at meditation, perhaps you'd like to try now while you are at your most relaxed."

Taerryn baulked.

"It's alright if not," Xan offered, noting the concern.

"I'd like to try." Taerryn took a deep breath. *What am I thinking?*

"Good girl," Xan praised. "Now, take a moment to run your fingers through the water. Feel the flow, the texture... Visualise the water moving around you in a bath, what it looks like, feels like. Focus on one thing, one task. In this case, perhaps see if you can make a ripple. Even the smallest wavelet would be a huge undertaking."

Now it was Taerryn's turn. Nerves tingling with all the others watching, she closed her eyes, returning to the meditative state from earlier and concentrated on only the one thing. Water. She pictured it forming, like the waterspout earlier.

After a few minutes, nothing had happened. No ripple, no wavelet. She exhaled and stood, feeling dejected. Not that she really had any idea what she was supposed to do.

"It takes time, dear. Don't feel bad." Xan directed her back from the water's edge.

As she stepped away, Taerryn swayed on her feet and had to reach for the wall to stop from falling.

Xan moved to her side and helped lower her to a sitting position.

"Relax, dear. This is nothing new for first-timers. But, I *can* say if you had no talent at all, then you wouldn't be feeling this way." Xan patted her shoulder, then turned to speak to the other students. "Now, ladies, from most experienced to newest, line up and see how we go. Madin, you can take a step back since you did quite well with your spout. We don't want to overdo these things."

I've got talent! Taerryn watched the girls form up, but the words Xan had just said echoed within her mind. *I've got talent!*

After Madin, Andula was next, and the line continued. As

Madin moved to the side, she nudged Andula good-naturedly as she moved to the water's edge.

Andula knelt and began immediately. At first, nothing happened, then the water rippled and swirled, slowly spinning, forming a vortex. The girl raised her hand, and the water rose as well. She let it swirl and grow. Taerryn could see the delight on Andula's face, but then her brow furrowed.

The spout became larger, almost touching the uneven roof of the cavern. The water surged, and the pool's water level dropped significantly as more and more water towered over them. Andula cried out and fell forward, unconscious, but the water kept spinning and rising; the sound was like a roar.

There was a scream, followed by several other cries of fear as the group of girls cowered.

The roar of the rising water stopped abruptly. The only sounds were from the whimpering girls. Crouching low, Xan and the girls looked around, disbelief etching their faces. They were inside a bubble while the water surged and swirled around the perfect hemisphere. Other than the dampness from the initial waterspout, the area around them remained clear of water.

Slowly, everyone turned to Taerryn, who stood, white-faced, hands in the air, as if warding off an attack.

Getting over her shock, Xan quickly went to attend to Andula. Her breathing was shallow, but she had simply exhausted herself. The instructor then concentrated, and the water surrounding them slowly dissipated, draining back into the pool. Taking a breath, she cautiously moved to Taerryn, talking to her softly before gently touching her shoulder.

The bubble disappeared with a whisper, and a few drops of water rained on them.

Taerryn flinched and opened her eyes. *Why is everyone staring at me?*

"What just happened?" Xan asked her, a look of surprise and doubt on her face.

"Me?" Taerryn looked from face to face. "There was so much water. I...don't know how to swim." Her eyes rolled into the back of her head as she collapsed.

TWENTY-SEVEN
SERIOUS DISCUSSIONS

"She created an air shield with no training?" Hiorlo scoffed. "I find that hard to believe."

"I'm sure you do, but I know what I saw and experienced," Xan stated to the gathering of elders, discussing the latest stunning developments.

"Was it any good?" Kio'on asked. "This air shield. We can always use another aeyron on the ships."

Xan nodded. "It was a perfect shield, and powerful enough to stop half the grotto from taking us into a watery grave."

"You jest. Can't you swim? And the girls?" Elann asked.

"You know most of us can swim. The water wasn't the worry, but the turbulence. Andula lost control. I doubt even I would have been fast enough to shield all of us as quickly."

"You're saying this waif of a girl is better than you?" Hiorlo asked, incredulous.

"Potentially, when trained." Xan ignored the barb. "At the moment, she's a powerful unknown."

Radson stood to speak. "After a separate but disturbing bit of news, I sent a scout out recently to investigate what happened at Culming." She briefly told them of the rumours of the disturbance in the small town to the northeast. "Late last night, my scout returned. Sad to say, the rumours are true, and the bulk of the town was damaged one way or the other. The scout spoke to some people there. The farrier for the now-ruined stable and tavern was very helpful. He says ten days ago, Lord Charoff arrived with a small contingent of soldiers and three of his mancers."

All those listening knew of Charoff, whose Domain stretched to the west of the Southern Steppes. Some of the girls here were from his Domain, and the stories they told were not flattering.

Radson continued, "You've heard the chatter about the wedding debacle in Carascan?"

"A bird arrived with a message saying the Olber girl went missing, so they found a poor substitute for that Dran'ali brute!" Drina said. "Disgusting—as if our daughters are there to parade for any ruler to pick and choose."

"Apparently, Blarik sent Charoff to Culming because Lady Marra Olber was hiding there, or so he strongly believed," Radson told them.

"Culming? Why in the darkest depths would the heir to the throne go there?" Elann asked, bewildered.

"Our farrier didn't know, or didn't share that information," Radson replied. "However, a woman there *did* fit the description of the Olber girl to the letter, even down to the fine mare she's been known to ride."

"All fascinating, but what's this got to do with this Taerryn girl?" Hiorlo asked.

"I'm getting there. It's all relevant." Radson then went on to detail how the mystery girl stayed at the tavern and was befriended by the taverner, Nioma Blakthorg. It's been said they—whomever this other woman was—had become good friends, possibly lovers. It's also rumoured she changed her looks so she could attend the Trallko funeral."

"Why go through all that bother to attend a stranger's funeral?" Hiorlo asked.

"Unless it *was* the Olber girl," Ildara suggested. "Olber and Trallko Domains are allies."

Radson continued, "When Charoff and his thugs made their appearance, the fighting began. According to the farrier and other villagers who had witnessed the fight, Nioma killed four of Charoff's men single-handedly, until she was shot in the back by the cowardly nobleman. Nioma died in this woman's arms."

"I hate and despise Charoff greatly," Xan stated. She had lived in the region, and he was the reason she'd come here. "But what's this disturbance you mentioned?"

"After Nioma died, the girl screamed like nothing they'd heard before; at the same time, the ground started shaking, and a vicious storm hit. The village houses collapsed, and the few remaining villagers and our farrier fled. When they returned the next day, there was a massive pit around the area where Charoff and his elementalists had been standing.

"My scout saw it with her own eyes: a section of ground untouched by any elemental damage and a perfect circle, much like as if it had been shielded, in the middle of a large pit."

"The mancers shielded Charoff? From...who?" Xan wondered. "Surely there was another male elementalist! Gone rogue, perhaps?" There was a look of shock and disbelief on her face. "And what happened to the girl?"

"No other male mancer was seen, just Charoff's trio, now all dead. No one knows exactly what happened to this girl. But the next day, a contingent of Trallko's men arrived to check on the town. They couldn't find her anywhere, but they did find the taverner in a shallow grave behind the tavern. The farrier also mentioned Nioma's sword—a cutlass—was nowhere to be found."

"So...this other woman is now missing?"

"So it seems, but the interesting thing is, the disguise used by this girl is very similar to the appearance of our Taerryn. Short-cropped fair hair." Radson looked to the other elders as they considered this information.

"This new girl had a cutlass with her when she arrived?" Hiorlo muttered, feeling her suspicions were now well-founded.

"It's not unusual for male magykers to go crazy. Could that have been it?" Elann asked. "Couldn't they have simply gone crazy and attacked each other?"

"There's no sign of any elemental conflict within the shielded area," Radson said. "All the indications are they died protecting Charoff from someone else."

"Protecting him from who, if not from another elementalist?" Elann persisted.

"They say this other woman was the only other person left standing."

"What happened to Charoff?" Kio'on asked Radson. "How did he get off his rocky island?"

"A temporary rope bridge was set up. He took a horse and returned to his Domain."

"Could have just left him there, or better still, let go of the rope," Xan added.

The healer turned to Ildara. "Can it be?" Yarin asked as an impossible realisation was slowly dawning.

Hiorlo stood. "I will send guards—"

"No one is sending guards anywhere." Ildara slumped. "My initial testing was correct; there were no aberrations."

"And what about the gong at the walkway...detecting a male elementalist," Elann asked.

"Technically, it detects earth talent," Ildara explained. "Not *males* specifically. It was always assumed that only males can use earth."

"Isn't that because only males can wield the earth element? Are you suggesting this Taerryn can use the earth element too?" Kio'on asked.

"All indications so far point to it." Radson nodded. "But another significant matter to consider is, if our Taerryn is Marra Olber, we could be housing the most powerful mancer, and Jaranabi's High Lady."

TAERRYN AWOKE. All was quiet; only faint chatter echoed through the tunnels. She looked around her, guessing one cave looked as much as the other, but this wasn't her dormitory. The smell of herbs and incense reminded her of the healer. *Yarin's rooms,* she decided.

She sat up and promptly fell back, dizzy. When the room stopped spinning, she tried again, but more slowly. Taking a few calming breaths, she then twisted to slide her legs off the low bed, delighted to feel a rug instead rather than the cold stone floor.

After a few tentative paces, she was steady enough to walk with more confidence. She slipped into her sandals and exited the chamber. She was in the healer's front room in a few steps. Yarin was rearranging her shelves, making sure the right components were in the right places. The healer must have heard a footfall because when Taerryn entered, she turned and quickly came to her side.

"Hello, dear. How are you? You took a bit of a fall. Can you tell me your name and where you are?" Yarin asked, helping her to a chair.

"Taerryn Kronyer. I'm at The Crags," she replied. "And you are Yarin, the healer. Did you say I fell?"

"Apparently. In the grotto. I wasn't there. What do you remember?" The healer sat and looked closely at her eyes and felt her pulse. "There's a cup of herbal tea when you're ready." She pointed to the side table. "It should still be warm enough."

"One of the girls...Andula?...was makin' a waterspout, then it got much bigger very quickly. She lost control and...that's it. Next thing I know, Xan was helpin' me to my feet."

"And you don't recall anything else?"

"There was a lot of water, and I was scared." Taerryn concentrated. "I must've fainted again."

"Very well, dear. That's okay. Just glad you didn't bump your head."

"Is everyone okay? How is Andula?"

"She's resting." Yarin stood. "As you should too. Tell you what, I'll run a hot bath and pop some of that lubin in. It'll do you wonders, like on your first day." Before Taerryn could ask or say anything else, the healer left the room.

THE ELDERS normally had a meeting once a week. Tonight was the third meeting in as many days.

"How is she faring?" Ildara asked Yarin. "And Andula?"

"Andula's fine. And, our Taerryn is just as she was on the day of her arrival. She can't recall much about the grotto."

"Or says she can't." Hiorlo paced. As head of security, she hated surprise visitors, especially powerful magykers sneaking into her home.

"Either way, we continue the soft approach. If she is Marra Olber, and if she is a powerful and untrained mancer that can work the earth element, I for one do not want to upset her and have this extinct volcano collapse on these weary bones," Elann said.

"Or fire it up," Kio'on added. "Remember what happened in the Larbyiola Archipelago? A once-thought-to-be-extinct volcano took out a whole island and several thousand people. Tsunamis afterwards also damaged ships and other coastal villages hundreds of leagues away."

"How long do we risk this aberration walking among us?" Hiorlo asked.

"For however long it takes," Ildara vented. "This is new territory for all of us! She may be an aberration, but she is also a lost and lonely child. Much like I was at her age."

"I don't like it," Hiorlo grumped.

"You don't like many things," Tiswan muttered.

"We've a shark who doesn't know it's trapped yet. Let's not poke it and see if it bites," Kio'on suggested.

"Okay, no mancer stuff for now." Radson stood and stretched her large frame. "Maybe just some physical work and exercise. She seemed to be interested in that. I'll find some activities to keep her and her mind occupied. By the time I'm finished with her, she'll be too tired to do anything."

"What contingency plans do we have if something happens?" Hiorlo asked.

"None. We've never encountered anything like this. A female terron?"

"And strong with air," Xan added.

"Who knows what else she's capable of?" Kio'on wondered.

"Healing, definitely," Yarin said.

"And those reports of severe storms; is that air or water?" Kio'on asked.

"It's a bit of both," Ildara said. "I will need to keep an eye on her. Xan, you believe she's stronger than yourself?"

"I'm not ashamed to admit that the speed and precision with which she created that shield would have taxed me." Xan shrugged.

The lead elder considered this. "Kio'on, we only have the *Vengeance* docked at the moment. What about *Emancipator* and *Revenge*?"

"*Emancipator* is due any day now. The *Revenge* in several weeks," the harbour mistress replied. "Gromal is quite a distance, and none of us has been there."

"Oh... Speaking of Gromal and the *Revenge*," Drina spoke up. "I received a bird. A tern, of all things. They had trouble in Herantia, turned and left before getting hold of Farand. Corra suggests sending her a bird if we can and arrange a meet."

"Any mention of their troubles?"

"Nope. Guess we'll have to wait longer for that bit of news."

The elders spoke quietly for a few minutes to work out how best to get a message to the cartographer.

"Now, back to the business at hand," Ildara said. "I want at least three mancers to be in a position to quell anything she might do, at all times."

"She professed an interest in sword fighting. We could get her to work out there, too," Tiswan suggested.

"Maybe a few hours every alternate afternoon?" Radson suggested.

Tiswan nodded at the suggestion.

"I'm concerned it's too close to the grotto," Xan commented. "It might trigger a reaction."

"We'll work something out. Leave it with me," Radson said.

"If it came down to it, can we restrain her?" Hiorlo inquired.

"She's too much of an unknown." Ildara slowly shook her

head. "But if three or four of us can't at least quell one girl, then we're in the wrong job."

"I know what I'll do if it has to be done," Hiorlo stated.

"Let's hope it doesn't come to that. While she's a potential danger, imagine what she could do for us, for all women. A female elementalist and—if it is Marra Olber— we'd have an elementalist as High Lady."

"I don't like any of this," Hiorlo repeated. "Too much is happening too soon. The missing Lady Olber is now in disguise? I can understand concealing her identity out there, but why here? And this waif, this noble-born, is now supposedly a powerful elementalist? Does no one else see this as suspicious?"

"Suspicious, no, but as said, too much of this is unknown," Ildara finished. "If this is genuine, we can only benefit—"

"Or it could be our undoing," Hiorlo finished.

Ildara sighed. "I choose to remain positive."

"Morning." Radson addressed the class as she strode in. Her booming voice was enough to stop the chatter. "Some of you know me, some don't. I am the Disciplinarian and head instructor, Radson. I'll be in charge while you are in training. You're all volunteering to be here, so thank you, as we need more crew for our ships. It will be hard, it will be tiring, but in the end, it will be very rewarding for those who crew our vessels. We'll give every one of you as much opportunity to learn what you can to an acceptable level. Out there, you'll see and experience things you couldn't imagine. It will be up to you to make that happen.

"Your two-tier training will begin tomorrow. Tier one: each morning will start with the academic component. You'll learn how to tie knots, the parts of the ship, and basically everything you need to know so you can be a functional part of the crew; otherwise, you'd be a liability to yourself, your shipmates, and the ship.

"Tier two starts after the midday meal, where we'll get into the physical component to build up strength, stamina, and agility. Again, without these, you will be a liability to yourself, the crew, and the ship. Lessons will slowly increase in difficulty until your body adapts to the rigours you may face.

"I stress again, this will be hard—but not as hard, nor anywhere near as traumatic, as the road that brought you here. Take a good look at your sisters around you. Get to know each other, because without them, none of you will get through this. I don't give a damn if you don't like each other, but you *will* work as a team."

"What if we fail?"

"No one fails; they'll simply not be ready for life at sea. We have a growing community here, and there's work for every-one. For the remainder of the day, we'll conduct a walk-through of the mooring points, docks and the *Vengeance*."

THE MOORING POLES and mechanism were a simple but ingenious concept.

A dock was attached to a large hoop around each pole and housed both the wharf and cradle. Any ship could load and unload cargo, but only three ships could remain within the harbour at the turning of the tides.

Before the Churn, each ship was clamped in place within the cradle. The whole structure rose as the water level increased. Once the water level stabilised, the dock was locked in place and could remain there indefinitely. This was ideal for prolonged maintenance. Unlocking the dock before the Swirl allowed the ships to leave once the water level equalised.

"LOOKING GOOD THERE, Taerryn. Since you're proficient with climbing the rigging, how about upping the skill and tying up that loose line?" Egrani pointed. For the last week, she'd shadowed the trainees, somehow managing to be everywhere at the same time, instructing and helping them to learn the various parts of this wondrous vessel. "What's that called?"

Taerryn looked at what Egrani was pointing to. "Lower fore topsail brace."

"What's its purpose?"

"Umm...let's us move the sail to angle with the wind?"

"Close enough. And it's attached to what?"

"The lower fore topsail arm."

"Correct. Now, see how Jordia is straddling the upper arm? Copy that as best you can."

Taerryn looked up and watched the other girl. She'd been here for several months longer and had tried a few things that didn't work out. Now she was trying out for the crew. She was young and ambitious and was excelling at the physical component of the training.

"She's very agile," Taerryn said, impressed.

"And you can be too with training and confidence," Egrani encouraged. "Up you go."

Taerryn was now adept at climbing the rigging and with rope climbing in general. Her few stints at rock climbing and abseiling were a prelude to this. She made it to the upper arm and was sliding out to the brace, which was at the far end. The height didn't faze her, nor the fact that the end of the arm was near the edge of the main deck below.

There was activity in and around the harbour, and from her

vantage point, she could see a great deal of it. There were rock climbing and abseiling lessons along the cliff face to her right; weapons training in front of her, and beyond, the entrance to the grotto.

It seemed nobody wanted to speak about that time in the grotto when she fainted.

What did I do? It's as if they're scared of me...

She looked down as the water level below her receded. Both the Churn and the Swirl were aptly named. When the tide came in, the water was a turbulent, white- foamed monster. When it receded, it was like watching water leak out of a tub: remove the plug, and water poured out, forming a whirlpool. The rough edges of the volcanic crater that formed the harbour created eddies and currents, so a proper whirlpool didn't eventuate, but the water definitely swirled. At first, the water level dropped slowly, then as momentum picked up, the swirling began. And it was doing it now.

Egrani called up to her. Taerryn waved and started doing the task she was supposed to be doing, not gawping. Securing the line was straightforward, and she finished it quickly, then double-checked her work. She was swivelling around on the smooth arm to head back when there was a cry from one of their mooring posts.

A chock holding the ship in place had been knocked by equipment swinging on a line. One of the cradles had slipped several feet. The ship dropped and tilted with a sharp jolt. There were yells and curses as women fell over.

Taerryn had nothing to grab. She was still a distance from the rigging, and the braces were tight, allowing no strong purchase. Her scream resonated with the others as she slipped and fell over the side of the ship, disappearing into the swirling waters far below.

Hitting the water hard knocked the air out of her lungs as

she plunged below the surface. Having never been in water deeper than a bath, she kicked frantically. Her vision was blurred, and the swirling water wasn't clear anyway; all she could make out were long fronds of seaweed. Her movements only served to ensnare her limbs. Writhing against the chaos and willing her lungs not to exhale the stale air in them lest they immediately drew in water to replace it, she clamped her mouth closed.

She tried desperately to keep still, but that made her realise the swelling of movement as the undertow pulled at her. The water grew darker as the rip dragged her deeper into the forest of seaweed. She clutched at the fronds of kelp surrounding her, but her hands slipped, and she was dragged this way and that.

Struggling without air and her lungs burning, the light-headedness hit her, and she lost all sense of direction. Realising she was about to die, Taerryn panicked. She lashed out again with her arms and legs, but the weeds snaked around her, tangling her limbs. Unable to escape from them or to control her bodily instincts any longer, she sucked in a mouthful of seawater before blackness engulfed her.

CHAPTER

TWENTY-EIGHT

NEW DEVELOPMENTS

Egrani picked herself up, shaking her head ruefully at her bruised thigh and the chaos around her. Jordia had been climbing down the rigging and fell the last few feet. The experienced sailor pulled her upright and checked she was okay, then she looked up to see how Taerryn was faring. Shocked to see the arm empty and no one in the rigging, she reached for the rails on the side of the ship and looked down.

Nothing but the twisting and swirling waters.

"Crew overboard!" she yelled. The deck was at a slight angle, and it took a bit of effort to find a float to throw over the side in the hope that when the girl surfaced, she'd have something to hold on to.

"Jordia, tie that line to that cleat, then throw it over the side. Find other floats and toss them in too. Anything you can." Egrani pulled off her boots as she gave orders. "Then get Radson, Kio'on, and anyone you can find."

"What're you doin'?" Jordia asked as she hurried to obey.

"Going for a swim." Egrani grabbed a coil of rope, climbed onto the railing, and jumped.

~

SHE WAS DISORIENTATED AND PERPLEXED. With her lungs burning, she reflexively drew in another mouthful of seawater, wincing at the burning sensation in her throat. It was such a relief when the pain in her chest lessened, but she was still immersed, still tumbling through the churning water.

How am I breathing?

Fumbling with her hands, she gently rubbed the painful area and felt several deep cuts on each side of her neck.

"Gills?" Air bubbles escaped from her mouth with the words.

That's impossible!

Twisting around with eyes wide at the sight before her, it took moments for her addled mind to comprehend. What she saw was a dim but stunning vista of corals of various colours. Rocks and seaweed clumps quickly came within reach before she was dragged away again.

Trying to kick to the surface proved futile and tiring. The darkness grew as Taerryn was dragged deeper by a current. She recalled someone mentioning in a talk about The Crags' harbour, of two exits from the crater: one the ships used and a submersed one a dozen feet lower, where the water came in and out at the lowest of tides.

A sinkhole, they called it.

Confused and stunned at her situation, she forgot her initial panic and worked with the current. This allowed her to move faster with little effort. Moving with the flow brought her to the submerged hole under the main entrance. Beyond, she could discern a slightly darker hue.

The ocean?

Eventually, as the undertow lessened, she managed to kick upwards. Bewildered by the turn of events, she turned to see she was many boat-lengths away from the harbour entrance. Through the narrow fissure, she could see a portion of the *Vengeance* high up in its cradle, though it was sitting askew. There were also a couple of smaller boats in the harbour and near the entrance.

Nervous about being such a long way out to sea, she kicked and floundered toward them. She bobbed in the swell as the ocean rose and fell around her, revealing boats and then hiding them behind receding waves. Each time she rose, she yelled and waved frantically, though her voice was hoarse.

After three or four repeats, someone waved back, and others pointed in her direction. The nearest skiff turned towards her and, strangely, sped up. In a few minutes, it was upon her. It slowed down rapidly, and a strong, dark arm extended toward her.

She reached up, and Radson gripped her arm and hauled her into the craft, where she was smothered in a blanket and held close.

She tensed.

"Relax. You're safe now," a woman said. "You need to keep warm."

"Taerryn, are you alright?" Radson asked.

"We thought you were surely drowned," Andula added.

Covered in blankets and weary, she heard the voices and questions, but they were lost on her. Though her throat was very painful, she smiled and nodded, simply overwhelmed with the relief of being out of the water.

With assistance, she sat up and felt a breeze on her face as the skiff came about and sped back towards the harbour. It slowly dawned on her that there were no sails, and no one was rowing. Racing past the jagged entrance was exhilarating. Now, within the harbour, she saw the wharf full of women, with more coming down the stairs. One woman was pushing through the crowd and weeping for joy with a huge, relieved grin on her face.

Several healers were present on the docks and began administering to her the moment she was carried from the skiff. "Taerryn? How are you, dear?" A healer looked carefully into her eyes. "Are you injured? Any cuts? Breaks?"

"My neck has some cuts." She reached for the area, feeling it gingerly.

Yarin pulled the blanket down to examine her. "Lucky girl, I can't see any cuts, but a redness, like a rash or friction burn. Maybe a rope burn?" the healer suggested. "You were working in the rigging when you fell."

Egrani came over and kneeled beside her. "Such a relief to see you, Taerryn. We were so worried. I thought you couldn't swim?"

"I can't." She looked at Egrani's clinging clothes. "Why are you wet? Did you fall in, too?"

"Something like that." The sailor shrugged.

"Egrani is too modest. She dove in looking for you." Yarin explained as she wrapped the blankets around her again. "Okay, people. Move back, and we'll get Taerryn inside and warmed up."

"Umm...Why's everyone calling me Taerryn?"

Yarin looked at her for a moment. The chatter of the excited women and girls on the wharf dwindled to silence. A worried look crossed the faces of those she could see.

"Who are you, dear?"

"I'm Marra. Marra Olber."

~

Safely ensconced in the healer's rooms, Yarin ushered everyone out except Ildara and Radson.

"Marra, if you can, tell us the last thing you remember?"

"I fell off the lower fore topsail arm. I think there was a problem with the mooring post, or the cradle... The ship dropped, and I fell and... I couldn't breathe...but had to. I... gulped in water and...I must have drowned...or fainted. I woke up underwater...but I was still breathing." She felt for the cuts in her neck, but there were no gills, no lacerations, just a dull ache. "I...I don't know how I survived."

"You say you swallowed seawater?" Radson asked.

Marra nodded. "Before I blacked out."

The women looked at each other after her nod.

"You were underwater for a very long time. Far longer than it would be possible to hold one's breath. Can you recall anything else?"

Marra recounted the tangle in the seaweeds. She explained that she managed to get untangled and allowed the rip to pull her out to sea. "I relaxed, hearing it's better than fighting it. I surfaced far beyond the entrance...and the rest you know."

"Amazing."

The others conferred with each other briefly.

Ildara turned back to her. "And do you have any memory of Taerryn?"

"Taerryn? That name—" She paused mid-sentence as tragic memories came flooding back. "Oh, *Nioma*..." She bent over on the bed; her sobbing was inconsolable.

Radson knelt beside her and put an arm around her, hugging and rocking her like a child. As Marra's weeping slowed and her tears dried, they watched her with great sorrow.

"Nioma was my best friend, but our home was destroyed, and she was killed by Lord Charoff's men."

"You've lost so much," Yarin said. "We have some knowledge of what happened and can barely comprehend the grief you must be feeling. You're no doubt tired, but can you please bring yourself to drink some of this?" The healer held out a warm cup of herbal tea. "You need to have a relaxing sleep without the torment of nightmares and more bad memories."

Ildara was still by her side. "When you wake up and feel yourself, we must have a long talk. Until then, please know you are among friends, safe and loved."

Marra's eyes welled up again and nodded, not trusting herself to speak. She was halfway through her drink when her eyes drooped. Radson was there to catch the cup and placed it on the side table.

Yarin made sure Marra was comfortable, then she moved out with the others.

Marra awoke, still tired, but clearheaded. She looked around, recognising Yarin's quarters.

The door was ajar and she could hear quiet talking in the next room.

Unbidden tears welled up as her dark memories returned. She lay there until she could breathe without shuddering, even attempting a little bit of meditation to control her thoughts and emotions.

She knew the elders were gathered in the other room, and why. Marra climbed out of bed, dressed quietly, then walked to the door.

The Crag's elders were sitting in a tight semicircle. Nine expectant faces turned at her appearance; some with looks of surprise, some with joy, and one with a hint of wariness.

Yarin was by her side in moments, guiding her to a chair.

Ildara stood and waited for her to get comfortable.

"If you are ready, Marra, we need to talk and to ask you a few things. We don't normally question a girl's past, but I'm sure you'll come to understand, if you don't know by now, you're the exception. In your own time, please tell us what has happened to you, and what brought you here." Ildara resumed her seat and waited patiently, though she was tense.

Marra looked around the room at the gathering. She knew some of them already, and others were complete strangers. Radson was smiling, encouraging. Yarin had provided more herbal tea to rejuvenate her.

She took several sips before speaking nervously and recounted everything she could remember of what had transpired over the last several months, everything after the High Council meeting, making friends in the harem-come-spy school, her escaping the two rockions, her travels to Culming... the tragic wedding, funeral, and then Charoff turning up, and the fighting.

Tears threatened to well up at this, but she persevered. *When my love was murdered in front of me. And it's my fault!*

Through her laboured breathing, she continued. "When I woke, I had no idea where I was or why. I buried my friend... Nioma...lying at my feet—the woman I loved—and then I came here, which is where I was heading to until..."

"Culming is a long way from Carascan. Were you planning on coming here, or did you have somewhere else in mind?" Ildara asked.

"Initially. When I heard of The Crags, it was my plan when I escaped from Blarik's harem, which is also his spy school. I rode south for a few weeks, then I met Nioma and I...we..." Her voice cracked. Her breathing was ragged with the loss.

"It's okay, Marra. Falling in love can be so hard for some and easy for others. And seemingly the end of the world when it's lost or taken away. You're blessed to have found someone to share that love under such trying circumstances."

"I met Nioma once," Drina said softly. "She was a beautiful woman. A tragic loss."

Marra nodded and continued. "Nioma was an experienced spy...informer, agent, call it what you will. She despised Blarik and worked directly for Ont'eba. We had been invited to Mimia Trallko's funeral, but I couldn't risk going as myself. Taerryn was a fictitious cover only, one drummed into me so my true identity wouldn't be discovered."

"It was a risk to go to the funeral. Why go at all?" Hiorlo asked.

"The Trallkos are one of House Olbers' strongest allies, and my friends. I could not *not* go." Marra had met the head of security only once before and got the impression she was a very suspicious woman. *No doubt good at her job.*

"I knew Blarik was still looking for me because he still wanted this marriage to Urgad to go ahead. Hence the disguise. If Blarik found out where I was, no one would be safe."

"Blarik doesn't concern us. Believe me when I say this," Hiorlo said matter-of-factly, "no one—no man—crosses the causeway if we don't want them to."

"Back to Culming. Try to remember what happened. You say you fainted?" Ildara asked. "Can you recall why?"

Marra shrugged. "I can only imagine so. I was on the ground when I woke up. I saw the fighting. Nioma was walking towards me...Charoff shot her. In the back!" *Why was it only now that I recognised the man on the horse?*

Some of the elders spoke quietly to one another after this exchange.

"What is it? What am I missing, or what do you think I've done?"

"Charoff was marooned on a strange rock island." Radson described the scene. "We hear he was there for several days until a rope bridge could be established."

"What about his elementalists?"

"Died defending him and themselves."

"Then, another elementalist was there?" Marra asked.

"That's what we're trying to ascertain. There were no other strangers in town?"

"Not that I'm aware of. Nioma would've known otherwise. The rural townsfolk didn't strike me as the type to entertain wandering mancers in secret."

"This fainting you experienced... What other times has it happened?"

Marra sipped more tea, thinking. "I—Taerryn fainted in the grotto."

"What do you remember about that?" Xan asked.

Marra considered, but other than the fear of the water and fainting, she had nothing to add.

"There's absolutely nothing you've conveniently forgott—"

"Hiorlo! That's enough!" Ildara snapped. "I dare say the girl has gone through quite enough this month without being accused—"

"What is it I've done, or you think I've done?" Marra stood, staring at them.

"Marra, in the grotto, you created an air shield," Xan said. "Better than what I could have done."

"Air shield?"

"You created a bubble that protected everyone from serious injury, if not death," Xan explained.

"And in Culming, someone—we believe you—attacked Charoff and his men by manipulating the earth element. His own mancers saved him, but died in the process."

"You think *I* killed them? Three mancers? By myself?"

"Indirectly. Our limited understanding is that they protected themselves, as you did with the air shield; only you outlasted them. They exhausted themselves to death."

"Did you know you have extraordinary healing abilities?" Yarin asked. "When you arrived, you were covered in scratches, bruises, and blisters. The next day, all gone. And, to my regret, it wasn't by my hand."

Marra nodded, but with a look of reluctant acceptance.

"It happened at Blarik's harem spy-school," Marra explained the quick healing there, too.

"Is there anything you can add?" Kio'on asked.

Marra saw all the faces waiting for her answer. "When I am frightened or angry..."

"Yes?"

"It's silly...but I thought I could feel the ground shake, and sometimes there was thunder and storms." *Earth and air? Is it true?*

"Think, dear." Ildara had walked over to place a comforting hand on her shoulder. "Take your time, but it's very important. Try to remember when and where you were, and if you can bring yourself to do so, tell us what was happening at that time."

Yarin poured her another cup of tea while Marra recounted as much detail as she could, with prompting from the elders of all the times she felt the tremors. When she was finished, they huddled together to talk quietly among themselves.

Marra sipped her tea and waited. "What's going to happen to me?" she asked eventually.

The elders resumed their seats, and Ildara came forward. "Exactly as any other girl should expect, dear. We'll love, protect and cherish you like all the other girls, for you are *like* the other girls...with one exception: we firmly believe you are a powerful elementalist."

"Me?" She looked from one to another.

"When I first tested you, the crystal shattered. It should not have done that—not for a female mancer—but a male mancer would do it."

"Like the gong going off? I knew something was different. I didn't want to believe it. Like a nightmare." *Like it was happening to somebody else.* "Why do I remember the last weeks as Taerryn, but only now remember that I'm Marra?"

"The mind is complex," Yarin explained. "We believe the trauma you underwent was sufficient for your mind to wall it off; the grief was too hard to bear. This drowning, we can only guess, was traumatic enough to break down or weaken that wall."

"Isn't that odd? But yes. I know most of you, as I met you over a fortnight ago."

"And now, you might want to rest up. There's a whole community out there that thought you drowned, but you survived half an hour or so underwater; then there are the girls who saw you create an air shield with no training. Needless to say, we'll need to concentrate on your elemental training and announce to all and sundry in The Crags you're a latent mancer," Ildara said proudly.

"And that you are the High Lady Marra Olber." Radson beamed.

Marra looked shocked. "But Blarik—"

"Is a usurper and not our legitimate ruler," Ildara said vehemently. "You are."

~

MARRA ENDURED an intensive month of training. This was new territory for both student and instructor. To keep her separate from the other trainees, partly for safety but also so Marra could concentrate, they used a hardly visited alcove on the far side of The Crag's, facing the ocean.

Ildara was astonished at her progress, though there had been a few drawbacks and one almost cataclysmic accident. What *had* been 'alcove' was now an open-air terrace. If not for Marra's innate ability to erect an air-shield, they'd probably both be dead, crushed under the weight of the roof that collapsed. Indara added her strength, though it had been an afterthought.

"You have a natural talent, girl. It's truly remarkable. What you do now in such a short time took me years to master. Still, there's natural ability, and there's experience. I can guide your ability somewhat, but experience is beyond my knowledge, and something I cannot teach. That you must gain on your own."

"And working the earth element? We haven't touched that yet."

"Not *voluntarily*, no." Ildara nodded slowly, looking at the rubble around them. "But that's something you'll need to do without me. No other woman can use earth. Or fire, for that matter. And I dare say a male mancer wouldn't teach you. He'd probably try to attack you for asking. Or he'd report you."

Marra sighed deeply. "Best keep working on what I do know, then." With Ildara's guidance, Marra spent the afternoon removing the rubble by using air.

HER TRAINING PROGRESSED, and there were times when things became too much. Overtiredness, a day of failure, resulted in loss of sleep, revisited grief and nightmares. The nightmares were a concern to all. During those restless nights, storms raged, and The Crags shook, scaring most of the girls witless. It concerned the elders greatly, too. Enough to consult with Ildara.

With Marra's acquiescence, Ildara requested that Yarin conduct a session or two of hypnotherapy to soften the worst of her fears and memories.

"I don't want to forget...anything!"

"Fear not. You'll still have all the memories, both the pleasant and the not-so pleasant ones, but they will seem... distant. They say time heals all wounds; the trauma and sadness will be far less, but the details will remain."

It was a difficult process, and while Marra's nightmares were reduced and she had far better sleep, the sessions exhausted and taxed Yarin to the extent that she had to rest for several days afterwards.

Marra visited when she heard of the strain she had placed on her, feeling it was her time to look after the healer. She was rummaging through the many vials and jars of the components the healer had in her stores.

"What are you looking for, dear?" Yarin asked. She was in the doorway to the alcove, wrapped in a shawl to fend off a breeze.

"Lubin. There are so many aromas here, I can't pick it."

"The yellow jar, top left corner." The healer pointed.

"Oh. There's so much of it." Marra recalled the amount used at the harem and the difficulties in obtaining it.

"It's from Klarget. A trader brings it when he visits. What do you know of it?"

"My experience is limited, but it's used as a powerful aphrodisiac where I come from."

"Is it now?" Yarin grinned slyly.

Marra blushed. "I—"

"Teasing, dear. If any man—or woman—looked at you and still needed something to get the blood going, he may as well be a eunuch."

"Well, I recall you used it as a pick-me-up on Taerryn—me—which certainly worked. I thought you could do with some in your tea." *I wonder if the girls at the harem considered imbibing it?*

"It's been tried, dear. I've probably consumed or breathed so much of it over the years, it doesn't work. I'd need a lethal dose for it to have any effect." Yarin sauntered back to her bed.

"I have to do something!"

"Keep training and learning; that's the best thing you can do for us."

Marra sat beside her bed and considered how to help the woman who had done so much for her. With a spur-of-the-moment decision, Marra gently laid a hand on the woman's brow.

"What is it, dear?" Yarin asked, then saw the closed eyes and look of concentration on the young girl's face. "Healing the healer, are we?"

Marra sensed the fatigue and distress the healer had been going through, not just for her—though there was a lot of that—but for caring for every girl and woman at The Crags. Marra was grasping at straws and could feel her own anxiousness building. *I might fail.*

She slowed her breathing and tried to relax, falling into a trance similar to when she was meditating. Only when her mind was completely devoid of any extraneous thoughts did an idea form.

∼

Ildara called in to see the healer as she had missed breakfast. She found Marra slumped in the chair next to Yarin, who was sleeping peacefully. After a quick check, she found Marra was in a deep, exhausted sleep.

Fixing herself a cup of tea, she sat in the next room, waiting for someone to stir.

Reading through some of Yarin's notes on herbal remedies, she was halfway through the beverage when the healer emerged, looking spritely.

"You look like a new woman," Ildara remarked.

"I feel like it, and I believe it's all thanks to Marra."

"How so?" The elder placed the herbal notes down and listened.

"We can add spirit to the elements our girl controls. I knew she had some ability when she self-healed, but she somehow removed all my ailments. I don't even have sore knees anymore."

"Utterly astounding." Ildara detailed some of the lessons they had conducted. "I even called on Xan to assist with the air and water, though we'll have to let her do her own thing with earth and fire—that will be both scary and fascinating. Now we can add spirit. That means she's strong in every primary element!"

It wasn't all training, and while she was discouraged from training with the other girls, she wasn't discouraged from socialising with them. Marra took the opportunity and caught up with some of the girls she had met in her first days, Vyolett, Sabon, and Myrta. Their initial encounter hadn't been under the best of circumstances, and now her newfound stature only separated them more. She was treated more like one of the staff or an elder, than a lost girl like them.

She heard them talking quietly when they thought she was out of earshot.

"Nobles aren't like us, no matter what she thinks," Sabon argued.

"Be fair," Vyolett said. "She's been through as much as you or I."

"Maybe *you*," the girl rolled her eyes.

Marra took a breath and walked away. Getting involved would simply aggravate the situation. There were other girls, like Madin and Andula from the grotto, who had more time for her and had a better understanding of what she was going through. All in all, she decided to spend more time training; that way, she would be less of a burden. It was the least she could do for the community that had taken her in and looked after her.

Once again, her life became routine; exercise in the morning, and she included more meditation, then all afternoon she trained with Ildara on her elemental magyk. She worked on manipulating air and discovered that many of the women worked air quite well.

"This is where we are a force to be reckoned with against the pirates. At sea, with our aeyrons working in unison with our hydrons, we can catch anyone."

Mara had heard these terms before, and added terrons and pyrons to the list; those that worked earth and fire.

"And the men? It goes without saying they're generally much stronger than us. Can't they use air too?"

"Not on water. Sure, they can use it to some extent when connected directly to the earth, but at sea, they can barely touch it, and fire is nigh impossible. Yes, they are stronger when relying on their physical skills alone, but we have our own skills plus magyk. We are, essentially, in our element when on water."

ONE MORNING during a strenuous bout of rock climbing, she heard a loud horn blowing. She'd never heard it before and wondered at the significance and why the instructors started to call everyone down from their rock climbing as quickly as they could.

She was free climbing forty feet up and decided this was an apt time to bring some of her new skills into play. Marra concentrated and felt the energy surrounding her, then turned and stepped away from the cliff. She had learnt to manipulate the air-shield concept, so now she was standing on a force of air and smoothly descending to the ground.

"What is it? What's wrong?" she called out as she landed, the air platform dissipated as a breeze, sending up a flurry of sand.

"Not sure," Radson replied. She was helping one of the juniors down. "The alarm generally means we've unwanted visitors approaching. It isn't good, whatever it is. I'll find out soon enough when I go to the gatehouse. In the meantime, can you help get these girls to their dormitories?"

"Sure. Leave it with me."

Now that the young girl was down, Radson turned to leave Marra to help with undoing the harness. The instructor turned back.

"Oh, Marra. I'll see you at the gate when you can." Radson ducked into the tunnel.

Marra was surprised and delighted to be included in this. *She was not just a trainee anymore.*

She decided this incident was too important. *Most treat me as if I'm an elder anyway.* She delegated some of the senior girls to help out, and as soon as they were escorted to the dormitories, she ran to the gate to join Radson, assuming the other elders would also be there.

CHAPTER

TWENTY-NINE

WE WARNED YOU

Many people were milling in the marshalling yard, mostly guards, but the elders were already on the ramparts where a giant clam shell was situated. Marra remembered seeing a similar clamshell on the mainland cliffs when she first arrived.

Radson saw her and waved for her to come up. Several guards were climbing the narrow stairs and blocking access. On a whim, she conjured a strong updraft and rode the current up, bypassing the staring and envious faces.

"Show-off," Radson said when she arrived. Ildara had a slight smile on her face, and the other elders looked surprised at her presence.

"Given the situation, I deemed it practical." Marra winked at Ildara. "What's happening?" She looked across to the mainland, seeing about fifty armed men arrayed along the cliff. There were a couple of wagons she could see, but the crest hid what was on the other side. She refrained from using the air to ascend to a higher vantage point. That *would* be showing off.

She squinted in the bright light. With a bit of concentration, she augmented her eyesight.

"That flag—it's the House Charoff standard," she told them.

"When those buffoons get their act together, we'll have a chat and find out," Hiorlo answered. The head of security had slowly come around to accepting Marra into the fold.

On the cliff, there were a few men on horseback keeping the others in line and yelling orders, but the distance was too far to hear anything clearly. One of them, mounted on a white horse and without any armour, but clothing much too elaborate to be a uniform, started shouting towards them.

Once again, Mara experimented with her newfound skills and augmented her hearing. After a brief trial, it worked, and she could make out the distant conversations like she was standing right there.

When the man on the white horse didn't get a response from anyone on The Crags, he started gesticulating, getting quite annoyed from the looks of things. After a few minutes, a messenger was sent to approach the gates. With a white flag in hand, the man moved very warily along the walkway. The banner whipping about in the wind almost threw him off the walkway.

She clutched her ears when the guards behind her started making bets on whether he'd fall or not. They were painfully loud! She quickly desensitised her ears, relieved that the cacophony abated. *I'll work on that another time.*

"Are you okay?" Radson was beside her, looking down with concern.

Marra placed her hands on the parapet and shrugged. "Just a headache. It's gone now."

The instructor nodded, then turned back to observe the happenings on the bridge.

With one particularly strong gust, the messenger lost his grip on the staff. The truce flag went flying into the turbulent waters below.

The guards behind her laughed and cheered, but Hiorlo told them to either shut up or leave.

The messenger, his footing more secure now that the flag wasn't causing a hindrance, finally got to the gates. He started to talk, but was cut off.

"Tell that clown on his white nag to move closer to the giant clam so we can parley," Hiorlo shouted and pointed. She then indicated the large shell behind her.

The messenger looked unsure, noting where the woman was pointing. He looked up and shrugged.

"Rifts! How dense is this lot?" Hiorlo repeated her words more slowly, as if talking to a child. When the man decided to continue to deliver his message, Hiorlo directed a couple of her guards to drop some rocks to scare him away and pointed to the clamshell on the cliff. It didn't take much to persuade him, and he made his way slowly back to report to his boss.

Again, there was a lot of discussion and hand waving, but finally, the pompous-looking fellow got off his horse and walked to the narrow outcropping of rock where the giant shell had been placed.

"Finally," Hiorlo said. "How fuckin' hard was that?"

The man dressed like a peacock looked around, trying to fathom where the voice was coming from. "To whom am I speaking?" he asked the air.

"Look to The Crags, fool. Yes, over here."

Finally, the fool saw them.

"Whom do you wish to parley with?" the head of security asked, speaking towards the clamshell.

"I believe the witch, Ildara Soshys, is the current leader of your...erm...*community*."

"Correct, but our head witch is very busy." Hiorlo chuckled with her companions.

"Busy?"

"That's what I said. Have you got an appointment?"

"Appointment?" the spokesman squeaked, his outrage increasing.

Hiorlo turned to the woman beside her. "Let Wolon know the shell needs adjustin' when these clowns leave, I'm gettin' an echo here."

"I've had enough of this twaddle. Listen to me and listen well." The man cleared his voice and read from a scroll. "By order of High Lord Blarik, we demand the release and return of one Lady Marra Olber. She is wanted on severe charges relating to the deaths of several of Lord Charoff's personal guards and magykers."

Hiorlo barked a laugh. "One woman did that? I wish she was here to tan your hides and send you lads on your way."

"This is not a laughing matter. She is a criminal of the highest order and must account for her crimes."

"Tell you what. Bring to justice all the men who have assaulted, abused, and raped the women behind me, and I just might give your request some consideration."

Murmurs of agreement followed from behind, but they knew enough not to disturb the parley.

"This is not a request! You will abide by this order or face the consequences."

"And they are what?"

"We will forcibly enter your domain and bring this woman to justice. If this happens, I guarantee anyone hindering my men carrying out their legitimate task will also be arrested to face the full brunt of the law."

"Okay then."

"You will accede to this?" the man asked.

"No. I want to see you try and forcibly enter my domain. You should see what happened to the fools who tried that before. Can you swim?"

"Will you provide—" He stopped upon hearing the laughter of the women. "You test my patience."

"You're testin' mine," Hiorlo called back. "I've got a fish pie goin' cold. The sooner you start, the sooner you'll fail and then scurry home and then, finally, I'll get to have my lunch."

"This is a serious matter!"

"You bet it is. It's *lyunidisia* fish pie, and they only come around once a year. If it's ruined, I'll be greatly vexed."

"*You* will be vexed!" His voice squeaked at his outrage.

"Look. No need to get your panties in a twist. As I said, the woman you want isn't here. Never heard of her."

"We have very reliable sources that prove you to be mistaken."

"Callin' me a liar? Come here and say that, face to face."

The fool turned, red-faced, to his men, forgetting he could be heard. "Captain, you have your orders. If this ghetto burns… let it," he said to the man beside him.

"Very good, sir."

The order was given, and the soldiers came forward, marching to the walkway in pairs. As those on the crest moved down the twisting path, more appeared. Marra estimated at least a hundred men now. She didn't know if she should feel intimidated or flattered.

"Last chance to save your men. You'll be the cause of many widows," Hiorlo warned. She turned to two of her guards. "Those bladders full?"

"They are, boss."

"Let them have it."

A niche along the wall showed a contraption looking

vaguely like the bellows on a blacksmith forge. Hanging onto a support beam, each of the two guards stepped onto a small platform with her right foot. It started going down, but an identical platform rose next to it. They stepped onto that one, and the process was repeated until they were walking on the spot.

"What's happening?" Marra asked Radson. "Shouldn't we be defending the gates?"

"We have a pump and a few barrels of oil. Generally, we use it for the lanterns, but in this sort of situation, we can pump it through small pipes. It oozes onto the walkway...and...well, you'll see the results."

Curious. Marra returned her attention to the bridge. She recalled the smooth, narrow path and buffeting winds, and didn't envy what must be going through these soldiers' minds.

One of the first men slipped and instinctively reached out to his companion. Both men slid off, quickly lost in the turbulent waters below. The next two men stopped, baulking at seeing their comrades fall, but the men a few paces behind, unaware of the accident, kept walking forward. They bumped into the men in front of them. This set off a chain reaction, and four more men slipped and dropped out of sight.

After a horn blast from the cliffs, the men very carefully turned and made their way back.

"I tried to warn you," Hiorlo muttered softly. It was apparent from her demeanour that her tough talk was bravado, and she felt every sad and avoidable death, even if it were men. She turned her steely gaze back to see what the spokesman would do next.

"Bring me the beasts!" they overheard the spokesman order.

Beasts? "Oh no!" Marra went white at the memory.

The gathering of men behind him parted, and two wagons appeared. Even without the shell, they could soon hear the growling, and sometimes a roar.

Nobody on the ramparts was immune to the distress and fear the chilling noise caused.

"Rockions!" Marra gasped in horror, recalling her last experience with them. She also remembered their sense of smell was astounding. They were tracking her. *These are the reliable sources!* She turned to look frantically for the healer. "Yarin. I need some of that lubin, and need it now!"

"Lubin? You want lubin *now*?"

"Yes. You know what it is and where it comes from. Send a runner who knows the shortest way. If those rockions get in here, you're all dead." Marra started to move. "I'll be down by the gate."

Yarin spoke quickly to a guard who left her and sprinted away.

"Marra?" Ildara reached for Marra as she passed, concern in her grey eyes.

"Ildara, believe me, I know what will happen if I don't stop this. If worse comes to worst, I can jump over the side into the water, or fly. Trust me."

Unhappy with the prospect, but not wanting to resort to more serious actions, the senior elder nodded her understanding.

Marra gave her a quick hug and turned. The ramparts were crowded, and the stairway was clearer now. "Excuse me. Thank you," she said to those on the ramparts who gave way and let her through. She quickly made her way down to the marshalling yard. Some of the women who knew who she was backed away uncertainly. Others crowded around to see what was happening. The area was chaotic at best. Marra looked up and caught Hiorlo 's eye and hand-signed to her as best she could, given her minimal training. *Clear the area.*

Hiorlo might be abrasive and uncouth, but not dim-witted. In short order, guards were sent down to clear the gate area.

Radson joined Marra a few minutes later.

Marra turned to the instructor. "I guess it's too late to get everyone onto the ships?"

"Not enough time and far too many of us," was the quick reply. "What are you going to do?"

"Probably something very foolish. Half of these ladies will be glad, others...I don't know."

The runner Yarin had sent raced up, breathing heavily, and handed her a yellow jar. Marra sniffed it, hoping she'd grabbed the correct one. It was. She turned to face the gates.

The noise from the crowd softened, waiting in anticipation.

"Open them," Marra said.

"No way am I lettin' those monsters in," a solid woman said defiantly.

"No. You're letting *me* out."

"What? There are easier ways to end yourself."

"You really think those rockions need an open gate to get in here? Look."

The surefooted beasts were slowly but steadily making their way across the walkway. The oil slick didn't seem to hinder them in the slightest.

"When they get in, they will kill everything in their path. They're hunting for me. And *only* me."

"You're mad."

"Perhaps. It crossed my minds." She winked at their concerned faces. "But I've dealt with these beasts before. Have you?"

The women at the gates didn't know if she was insane or simply had a death wish.

"Someone get her out of here. We've enough to deal with," one called.

Knowing Marra would face opposition, Radson stood behind her for support. "Do it, now! Or I'll make certain Hiorlo puts you on latrine duties for the rest of the year."

Swearing under their breath, the two gatekeepers worked the mechanism. Ponderously, the gates split open, and Marra stepped through. She heard a noise behind her. Radson had stepped through with her.

"What the rifts? Get back inside!" she said.

"I—"

Marra took a breath and grabbed Radson's thick arm, looking at her. "Believe me when I tell you this. I'll come to no harm, but they will kill you. I have seen it before, and it isn't pretty."

Radson wasn't sure if this was true or not, but this woman standing in front of her truly believed it. Radson stepped back towards the gate. "I'll get the archers ready."

"Reckon you'll just piss them off."

"See you soon." Radson nodded.

"You bet." Marra turned back to face the rockions and waited. She hoped her legs didn't fail her, and she took a moment to calm herself, wondering if she should strip. *Nah. These are my favourite clothes, after all.* She walked further out onto the walkway, doused herself with the lotion, and waited. The ratcheting of the gates behind her told her they were being closed quickly.

She glanced over her shoulder. The women and girls of The Crags had utilised every ledge, pathway, or overhang to see the army, but now they saw a lone woman facing off two huge six-legged cats.

Cautiously, the two deadly rockions made their way

further along the path. As the wind blew, they paused, sniffing the air. Their eyes focused on her as they advanced.

Marra closed her eyes, then decided to open them. If she was going to die, she wanted to see it coming. To look death in the face. Nioma must have done this sort of thing dozens of times. *Oh, Nioma, my love. Perhaps I'll be in your loving embrace soon.*

The first rockion nuzzled her. Marra remembered this from her first encounter. The force of the nuzzle knocked her off balance, but the other one sniffing her from the other side countered the imbalance. Her arm clutched its fur instinctively, but it didn't react aggressively. Their snouts ran up and down her body, whiskers tickling any exposed skin. This time, more from sheer relief at not being mauled, she laughed.

There were gasps as the crowd behind her took a collective intake of breath.

One of the rockions turned and growled at them, then continued its sniffing.

Marra sensed something, another tickling, but in her mind this time. She tentatively started patting them and scratching their ears. They were the size of cows, but they were just big cats after all. And kept as pets in Klarget. Were these domesticated? Might they not be normally caged beasts like those at the harem?

Was it her good mood, the laughter? *Or was she truly going mad?*

She knew animals could pick up and respond to moods. Didn't dogs become morose when their masters were ill? Horses certainly did. *Poor Sleena.*

There was a rumble. Marra panicked briefly, thinking it was another tremor that would make the walkway collapse... but no. This was different. It wasn't the ground; it was emanating from the rockions. *They're purring!*

She looked over to the gawping men on the cliffside, disappointed or astounded that they hadn't seen this woman torn limb from limb. These guards, these men, were sent by Charoff on Blarik's behalf to haul her back and to wipe out The Crags. Force her into a marriage not of her choosing.

The rockions growled, then nuzzled her again. She resumed scratching.

But if these girls can pick up my mood...

"Sorry, my beauties. Time for dark thoughts."

It was the day for experimentation. She dredged up all her dark memories: Blarik assassinating her father, Blarik pawing her breasts and trying to rape her, the unnecessary death of Froshingha, being kidnapped and the arrangement of a brutal marriage, the murder of Nioma! Tears brimmed in her eyes at the last memory. She let out a moan as the grief almost undid her, and she tottered forward but bumped into a rockion, which kept her upright.

The rockions growled, hackles up, sensing the mood change.

For a moment, she thought they were going to attack her and prepared to jump. Marra turned her dark thoughts and attention to the men on the hill. The men who kept them captive and away from their own cubs and mates. The men who were causing her and her friends all this grief and misery. She was about to open her mouth to say something, but they sensed that too. They sidled around her, then made their way cautiously back along the path.

"Go play, ladies," she said, though there was no need. *Kill Charoff...*

Behind her, the murmurs coming from the ramparts grew in volume and intensity until there were cheers, whistles, and applause.

As the rockions returned to the start of the causeway, the

handlers came out with their long-collared shafts and whistles. But her girls were having none of that. With a roar and quick swipes, the handlers were knocked sideways like skittles. The guards scattered and fled, screaming. Horses bolted, some dropping their riders, some riders hanging on frantically.

The chase was on. Cats simply loved to play. And play they did.

Turning with the rattling of the gate chains, she saw Radson was there with a towel.

Marra wiped off as much of the *Beast*, or lubin, as she could.

"That was..." Radson started, lost for words.

"Utterly foolish." Marra grinned, elated with the successful outcome.

"I was going to say incredible." Radson looked to the carnage on the cliff. "How did you know they would do that?"

"I didn't. Not for sure, anyway. They were scenting me, and me only. I was hoping since they found me, you'd be safe."

"But they could've ripped you apart!"

"Better that than going back to Blarik, or being married to Urgad!" Marra pushed her way back through the admiring and applauding onlookers.

Hiorlo met her at the gates. "Ildara—"

"Would like a word. Yes. I expected it." Marra suspected there was a different look in the stalwart woman's eyes. A slight upturning of her lips. Marra briefly clasped her calloused hand. "Hiorlo, thank you," she said in passing.

The few trusted men in the gathering—young sons of some of the women—looked after her lustily and started to follow, calling out for her.

"Take a cold shower, creeps," said one of the guards. "You know what happens—"

"No, it's okay." Marra put a restraining hand on the guard.

"With the amount of lubin I'm wearing, I'm surprised none of them has jumped me yet. It's *me* who should be bathing. But that'll have to wait until I speak with Ildara. Better barricade her door, though." She looked at the number of young men. "I didn't know there were so many here."

The female guard shrugged ruefully. "It's a worry."

THIRTY

PLAN AHEAD

"I can't stay here. It's too dangerous for everyone. The point of coming to The Crags was to avoid the situation we just had," Marra said, addressing the elders after she'd had a bath and a change of clothes.

"They know you're here now." Hiorlo sounded resolute.

"Assuming there were any survivors to pass on the information," Elann offered.

Hiorlo shrugged. "If I were them and there was no news coming, I'd be concerned and send more mancers and troops."

"Then quite simply, they'll have to learn I'm no longer here. I need to be seen elsewhere and soon, otherwise they'll be back with more than a couple of rockions."

"Let them," Hiorlo stated proudly. "We could repel any attack."

Marra nodded. "What about a siege, or catapults, that sort of thing?"

"We do train elementalists here," Xan spoke up. "It isn't like we're undefended."

"And I have a very good contingent of soldiers," Hiorlo added.

"Believe me, I've no doubts you can defend yourselves and prevail. My point is, you shouldn't have to. Not on my account."

"This was always going to happen," Kio'on said. "The men who rule don't want a refuge for women. That would lead to a belief that, perhaps, men were aggressive and unruly brutes. You're just the latest excuse for them to act."

"I'm not entirely sure they would mount a serious attack anyway, not with this war he goes on about," Radson suggested.

Marra walked back and forth, listening to their comments. "Let me go north, then. If he sees that's where I am, then he won't have any need to send more soldiers here."

"You can't go by land," Kio'on commented. "You won't get far, not with his people on the lookout for you. We'll have to send you around on a ship."

"I'm happy with that. The sooner we sail, the better," Marra agreed. Other than the recent "drowning" incident, she'd never been to sea. An idea dawned on her. "Have you got any birds?"

"Birds?"

"Messenger birds."

"We generally use frigates. "

"These won't go far inland, though," Ki'ono stated. "They're maritime birds."

"Have you any other birds? Falcons? Ravens?"

"We have a few..." Drina spoke up.

Marra told them of her idea. "If we send messages of sightings of me somewhere else, it will also negate the need for them to come here."

"It would delay them, true, but after that defeat, they'll return, eventually, simply out of spite."

"Then we'll have to make sure they're too preoccupied to do that. By then, I hope to be in the north."

"What then?"

"I've no idea other than stopping Blarik from continuing this war."

"And getting you back on the throne."

"I..." Marra stopped pacing. "One thing at a time. So then... Is it correct that they use spirons to encourage the birds to go to any given location?"

Drina nodded.

"But don't they have to know where that location is?" Elann asked.

"Well, we do have a community of women from all across Jaranabi," Drina pointed out. "I'm sure we can work something out."

"Good. Then all we need to do is write convincing messages of my presence everywhere but here. Oh..." Marra remembered a vital part of the plan; one that could ruin everything. "If it's not in cypher, then no one will believe it."

"Lucky, as your resident spy, I happen to know cypher." Drina smiled.

Marra nodded. "We should send one to Ont'eba as well. Let him know I'm alive."

And about Nioma.

Two days later, all the birds had been sent. Each message was similar in that a woman fitting the description of Marra Olber was seen. Depending on who got the message and when, a pattern would emerge. She was sneaking north with a small but powerful array of mancers.

At the same time, Egrani found her and let her know the *Vengeance* was ready to set sail. Marra grabbed a small duffle bag containing the few possessions she had and quickly followed the experienced sailor who had been assigned to train her.

Marra was nervous, yet excited, and stood out of the way while the crew worked the rigging.

"You've not been to sea before, have you?" Egrani asked her. "And I don't mean your recent underwater experience."

They were both standing at the bow, letting the docking crew prepare the vessel for departure.

"Up until I arrived here, I'd not even seen the ocean. You?"

"Born to it. My da was a fisherman. I could sail and swim before I could crawl."

The Swirl had started. The noise drowned out any conversation, so they simply watched. Still a new experience for Marra, she was fascinated by everything she saw.

The change in the water level of the harbour was astounding. While she watched the foaming waters recede, the dockhands were waiting for the order. There had to be precise timing from both teams, or they risked the ship toppling. There was no chance of capsizing, but the crew could be injured and cargo—while lashed down—had been known to come loose in rough seas.

"Wait!" Tiswan came running down the stairs, grabbing the railing with one hand while holding a scabbard in the other. She ran up the gangway, which was about to be hauled in by a couple of hands.

With a few choice curses, they stepped back as the weapons' instructor boarded the ship.

"What's the delay?" Captain Trewerrin was making her way forward from the helm.

"Ah. Apologies, Bianca. This won't take a moment." Tiswan winked and turned to Marra. "I believe you forgot this." She held the cutlass she'd kept in safe storage.

Feeling terrible at the oversight, Marra took it from her. "Rifts! I can be an utter dolt sometimes." She was aware that many eyes were on her.

"Remind me to tell you about it one day. Or maybe I should let Captain Sienna tell you, she has an identical cutlass," Tiswan called out over her shoulder. As she jumped back onto the dock, the gangway was removed.

"I will. Thank you again." Marra called back. She turned to the captain. "And I also apologise for this delay."

Moments after she felt the ship shudder as the water surged under the hull, the order was given. With mighty blows from two large hammers, the chocks holding the cradle supports swung down.

The *Vengeance* was now floating free but still tied to a mooring point by the dock. As the water level dropped, so did the platform, and along with it, the ship.

Captain Bianca Trewerrin motioned for the crew to continue getting underway and looked Marra up and down, then glanced at the cutlass. She gave a curt nod of acknowledgement after a pause. "Mancer or not, if you're on my ship, you need to learn to fight and defend yourself. Look up there. See those colours? They mean somethin' out there on the blue. When we come across pirates, and they see those colours, they turn and run. The smart ones do, anyways. And when we come across pirates in our travels, I'll not change course, not even for you."

Marra nodded. Two minutes on the ship and she was already getting a warning from the captain. "Captain Trewerrin." Marra gave a slight bow. "My late father went against all his advisors to give the Red Sails a commission to ensure the waters surrounding Harando were kept safe. He believed in you, as do I. I wouldn't expect you to shirk your duties for me or anyone."

"Glad to hear it. Otherwise, happy to have you aboard, High Lady."

~

THE END

continued in Book 2

Isle of Whispers

LOOSE ENDS

Ont'eba looked out across the port from his salt-encrusted lighthouse window. He hadn't been here for several months, so it was a bit musty. The lighthouse keeper was kind enough—for a few gold pieces a month and no questions asked—to allow the use of the 'store-room'. Cleaning it wasn't part of the agreement, and only his local agents had the key to access the room to collect the missives and tend the birds when they arrived.

The office itself wasn't in bad condition, there being little dust out here on the headland, but there was a whistling sound from the wind through a cracked window, and he suspected mice had set up residence behind one of the large wardrobes.

I'll be here for a while, so a good time to get an owl... or maybe a cat.

After Carascan, Port Arger was the next largest city, and arguably the most important since it was the only real access to overseas trade for the entire country. While there were caravan routes to Klarget through difficult mountain paths that were heavily guarded, this ongoing dispute between the two neighbouring nations was local, so trade hadn't really slowed yet. It was only a matter of time.

Ont'eba doubted Blarik had considered the ramifications of any reduction with the current trade. War with Klarget would stop those caravans, and the Klarget fleets could easily blockade the harbour. Sure, despite the drought and Blarik's lies, Jaranabi had ample food but was poor in most other commodities. The country would eventually grind to a halt, and without a large fleet, the blockade could last for an uncomfortable length of time.

And, if Urgad decided to follow through with his threats, a war on two fronts under those circumstances would soon decimate Jaranabi. In Blarik's eyes, only fulfilling the promise of delivering the noble virgin of the previous High Lord would assuage Urgad's wrath. *This has no doubt given Blarik pause to push Klarget to the brink of war.*

Risking treason but ensuring peace, Ont'eba would do his best to delay or thwart the whims of Blarik. To this end, he'd intercept as many reports as possible, modify them before sending them off. This way, the information the usurper received would be false or misleading, thereby making any response impotent. In this way, he hoped Marra would remain safe, and the war effort would continue to fail. That only left the threat of the horse clans. Being nomads, their travels to the south for the summer would delay any attacks for the best part of a year.

Unless they changed their ways...

Ont'eba unlocked the strongbox and pulled out the small pile of messages, and placed them on his desk to sort out. As he was going through them, a familiar name caught his attention. Like all of the notes, the name was of course coded, but he recognised it immediately, as well as the handwriting of one of his assets in the Charoff domain. Reading through the short missive, he fell into his wooden chair, causing it to creak alarmingly.

'Nioma has passed. Charoff injured. Culming damaged. Female mancer missing.'

He sat heavily in his chair and re-read the note with profound sadness. He had recruited Nioma Blakthorg himself and took her death to heart.

Such a young, vibrant and confident woman.

Wiping a tear and controlling his grief, Ont'eba noted the message was almost a month old. There was an icon in the top corner indicating this was one of two messages. He had not received any notification while he was in his office at the school.

Either the bird was taken by predators or hunters, or intercepted by another ...

He knew foreign agents were working in Jaranabi, which was only fair since he also had agents working in other countries.

If they intercepted it, he liked to believe they couldn't decipher it.

But that sort of presumption could get one killed.

Once over his shock, the spymaster yearned for more clarity. How, who, and why were foremost in his mind, as well as glad his southern colleague—aware of Ont'eba's routine—had the foresight to send the message to his two offices.

The Charoffs were several days from Culming and allied to Blarik. Though he had assets in most other domains, the Trallko domain remained not only the closest contact, but also strongly allied with the Olbers.

He scanned the remaining messages in case there were further updates. At the bottom—signifying its earlier arrival—

Ont'eba sighed with relief, seeing Marra had arrived in Culming and was continuing to The Crags.

Another quick search revealed no mention of her arrival in The Crags, which concerned him. *If she hadn't arrived, why? And who was this female mancer?*

Reaching for quill and slivers of parchment, he considered his very wording carefully.

∿

Acknowledgments

Being a writer is a solitary occupation, but nothing gets
done without the assistance of others.
I'd like to thank Catrin Russel for her work on the
excellent cover design https://catrinrussell.com/
And many thanks to Noel Osualdini, for his editing
expertise and suggestions.
I'd also like to give my appreciation to my DnD gaming
friends: Heather Stone, John Geer, Karl Martin and
Stuart Downes for their ongoing interest in my work
over the years, as well as to
Peter J Aldin https://petealdin.com/
for his readthrough and feedback.

Finally, to my lovely wife for her continued
understanding, patience, and support; and the pets,
Gordon - our Jack RussellTerrier,
and Ally - the Spoodle.

About the Author

Andre Jones is a multi-genre author of fantasy and science fiction. Born in Wollongong, NSW, Australia, and now residing in southern France with his Scottish wife and two four-legged companions: Gordon, a Jack Russell Terrier, and Ally, a Spoodle.

As a child, he devoured the works of Enid Blyton, Tolkien, McCaffrey, Asimov, Heinlein and Bradbury, to name a few. As a young adult, he got lost in the many and varied role-playing games, including MERP, GURPS, Harn, Skyrealms of Jorune, good old D&D (and its many variants) and Traveller. He also spent far too much time on video games like Skyrim.

He wore many hats, including: Security Offcer, Police Of!-cer, Park Ranger and achieved the rank of Petty Offcer Electronics Technician in the Royal Australian Navy for almost 20 years (sadly, his role-playing stopped there for too long). As a Navy Veteran, his retirement has provided the opportunity to write, roleplay, draw and potter to his heart's content.

ALSO BY ANDRE JONES

THE SEVEN PORTALS

(also available in audiobook format, narrated by Benjamine Fife)

City of Bridges

Shadow of the Tower

Ripples in Time

THE DEATH WAVE CHRONICLES

RELIC

DRUID

SPHINX

(coming soon)

GNOSTIC

UTOPIA

THE OUTER REACHES

Iconic (AJ Gordon & Peter J Aldin)

Quaestor (Peter J Aldin)

Far Horizons (AJ Gordon)